THE JACOBITE LASS

A stirring and passionate story inspired by Scottish heroine Flora MacDonald

(One of the Highland Romance Collection)

JANET MACLEOD TROTTER

Published by MacLeod Trotter Books

Hardback edition: 2014

ISBN 978-1-908359-42-1

www.janetmacleodtrotter.com

About the Author
Janet MacLeod Trotter was brought up in the North East of England with her four brothers, by Scottish parents. She is a bestselling author of 19 novels, including the hugely popular Jarrow Trilogy, and a childhood memoir, BEATLES & CHIEFS, which was featured on BBC Radio Four. Her novel, THE HUNGRY HILLS, gained her a place on the shortlist of The Sunday Times' Young Writers' Award, and the TEA PLANTER'S DAUGHTER was longlisted for the RNA Romantic Novel Award and was an Amazon Kindle top ten bestseller. A graduate of Edinburgh University, she has been editor of the Clan MacLeod Magazine, a columnist on the Newcastle Journal and has had numerous short stories published in women's magazines. Find out more about Janet and her other popular novels at: www.janetmacleodtrotter.com

By Janet MacLeod Trotter

Historical:
The Jarrow Trilogy
The Jarrow Lass
Child of Jarrow
Return to Jarrow

The Durham Trilogy
The Hungry Hills
The Darkening Skies
Never Stand Alone

***

To my delightful niece, Olivia MacLeod, with much love.

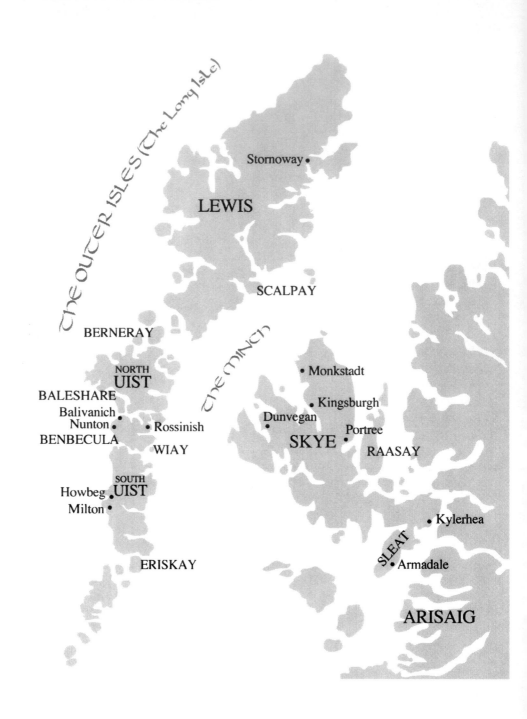

The OUTER ISLES (The Long Isle)

Stornoway •

LEWIS

SCALPAY

BERNERAY

The MINCH

NORTH
UIST

BALESHARE
Balivanich •
Nunton •   • Rossinish
BENBECULA
WIAY

• Monkstadt

• Kingsburgh
Dunvegan •
                Portree
            SKYE •
                 RAASAY

SOUTH
Howbeg • UIST
Milton •

                    • Kylerhea
                SLEAT
                • Armadale

ERISKAY

ARISAIG

Chapter 1

Benbecula, Outer Isles of Scotland, 1722

'Tell me,' Marion urged, watching Mairi's expression like a hawk. 'Is it to be another son?'

The girl's silence was infuriating, unsettling. She sucked on her plump lower lip as she stared at the dregs in the delicate china teacup. But the bard's daughter would not be hurried.

Marion glanced out of the parlour window, anxious that her husband Milton would not catch her dabbling in such superstition; the men were cutting the hay. No doubt her eldest boy Ranald would be running around getting in the way, grabbing at their scythes. His hair was the colour of ripened corn and words flew out of his mouth like swifts; her darling boy. Her younger son Angus followed Ranald about like his small dark shadow.

'No,' Mairi finally said, giving Marion a bold look, 'you are carrying a lass.'

Marion sank back in her chair. Why did she feel sudden disappointment? A girl would be a companion for her in later years and her elderly husband would be overjoyed; a daughter to wipe away his grief at losing his first wife and baby girl so long ago.

'She will be bonny and brave,' Mairi continued in her low mesmerising voice. 'This lass will bring you joy and heartache in equal measure. She will be known for her courage and beauty far beyond the Long Isle – even far beyond the mainland of Scotland.'

'Oh enough!' Marion gave a nervous laugh and stood up. 'You are just trying to flatter me. I can't believe in such nonsense. Tea leaves tell us nothing except the strength of the tea.'

Mairi kept staring at her – the girl had the most extraordinary eyes – one pale blue, one hazel brown.

'I don't need the leaves to see what is to come. It is there in my mind's eye. Sometimes I wish it wasn't.'

Marion was unnerved by the girl's intense look and strange words. She wanted her gone. It was her lively cook Janet who had brought her in for Marion's amusement, distracting her from a dozen housekeeping chores.

'If you go to the kitchen, Janet will give you cheese to take home to your father.'

She crossed the bedroom that doubled as her parlour, already thinking ahead to tomorrow's butter churning and the supplies that needed taking up to the summer pastures. Perhaps the boys could go too; their fizzing energy and the pregnancy were tiring her out.

'You will have other sons,' Mairi said, following her across to the window. 'And daughters too.'

'That's hardly likely–' Marion checked herself. Her husband Milton still came eagerly to her bed, yet he was growing old and already had heirs. But that was none of the girl's business.

2

Abruptly, Mairi reached out and placed a hand firmly around Marion's swelling belly beneath the loose gown. The baby fluttered under her touch. 'But this one you carry now will be the brightest star, outshining them all.'

Startled, Marion flinched away, slapping at the girl's hand. 'You impertinent child; you have no right to touch me.'

Mairi's look turned insolent. 'I'm no child,' she smirked, with a toss of red ringlets. 'And we MacVurichs have just as much royal blood in our veins as you MacDonalds.'

Marion snorted. 'The blood of tinkers more likely.'

Mairi gasped in offence.

The remark was out before Marion could stop herself, but it was the girl's fault for goading her. Marion was proud of her heritage and would not be compared to the family of their lowly tenants. She was descended from the Lord of the Isles through her minister father and from Robert the Bruce, King of Scots, through her mother's family. That was why, eight years ago, a powerful man of the Clanranald clan, Ranald MacDonald of Balivanich and Milton – known by all as Milton – had taken her for his second wife, despite her shameful condition.

Thinking of Milton now made Marion's stomach lurch. Her husband would have no truck with superstitious tea-readings and it did not take much to ignite his temper. He might be as old as her father but he had the energy and impatience of a man half his years.

'I'm sorry if I offended you,' Marion said, 'but you must go now.'

MacVurich's daughter narrowed her eyes. 'You may think you are better than me, Mistress Milton, but for all your boasting of being the kin of the high and mighty MacDonalds, you are as fearful as a mouse.'

'How dare you!'

'I dare,' Mairi hissed, 'because I will be a famous bardess and powerful men will fall under the spell of my words, while you will always be frightened of losing the men you love.' She gave a cold smile. 'Keep a watch on your husband, Mistress Milton.'

'Get out!' Marion gasped. 'My husband will make sure you never set foot in this house again.'

Mairi pulled her homespun plaid over her wavy hair in a gesture of contempt for her hostess. 'No one insults a MacVurich.' She stalked to the door and flung it open. Turning, she jabbed a finger in fury. 'I curse your two boys!' she cried. 'May the salt waters of the Minch be their cold grave!'

Marion stood stunned, gulping for breath. The sound of the girl's bare feet stamping on the wooden staircase died away. She pulled back quickly from the casement window in case Mairi MacVurich should look up with her evil stare as she left Balivanich House. As she hid in the shadows, shaking with fear and anger, Marion felt her unborn stir.

She placed a swift hand over her belly. '*Please* be a boy,' she whispered, 'and prove that witch wrong.'

Back came a defiant kick and Marion let go a sigh of relief.

3

Chapter 2

'You will keep an eye on them, won't you?' Marion fussed.

'Of course, my dearest,' Milton said distractedly as he supervised the loading of pack ponies.

'You'll not let them out of your sight?'

'Not for a minute.'

'Father look!' Ranald appeared round the side of the house dragging a heavy rusty broadsword. 'I'm Donald Gorm, Lord of the Isles!' The seven year old attempted to lift it off the ground but it clanged at his feet.

'Where on earth …?' Marion gasped.

Four year old Angus hopped after him in excitement. 'Let me try.'

'No, Angus,' Ranald pushed him away. 'You're the enemy, remember?'

'Husband,' Marion pleaded, '*please* take that from him.'

Milton chuckled and leaned down to pick up the old weapon. 'You need two hands like this.' In one swift movement, Milton planted his booted feet wide and swung the ancient sword high above his head.

'Heaven's above Milton!' Marion cried, 'put it down.'

The boys whooped in delight and the packmen stopped to watch.

'Stand back,' Milton commanded, wheeling around. With sword still raised he lunged at a nearby peat stack and sliced off the top sods. 'Off with his head!'

Marion screamed and Ranald cried, 'whose head, whose head?'

People darted to the doors of their thatched huts at the commotion.

Milton heaved the sword upwards once more. 'And just to make sure,' he bellowed, 'you split him from the nave to the chaps.' With a loud grunt he brought the sword crashing down onto the pile of peats and sliced them in two. A cheer went up from the tenantry.

'Was it King George?' Ranald shouted in excitement.

Milton stood back laughing and panting. 'Maybe it was. You can help me pull the sword out of his Hanoverian innards.'

'Milton,' Marion gasped, looking round anxiously. It was dangerous to make such treasonable comments, even in jest. Too many of their clan were already dead or forced into exile for supporting the Stuarts in defiance of their new German king. But the cottars just seemed amused as Ranald leapt at the sword, grabbing the hilt, and small stocky Angus tried to muscle in too.

Soon the old broadsword had been carried away and the preparations for the journey to South Uist completed. Marion's insides knotted. Her husband and sons would be gone for at least a month to their southern lands, supervising the movement of cattle to the summer pastures. Then Milton would settle the boys with their maternal grandfather and Uncle Archibald while he travelled on to the Clanranald estates on the mainland. With their chief, MacDonald of Clanranald, in exile in France for his part in the Jacobite Rising half a dozen years ago, much had fallen on her husband's shoulders. There were disputes to settle, business to be transacted and drovers found to take the cattle south at summer's end.

4

'Perhaps I should come with you Milton?' Marion said at the moment of parting, grabbing Ranald to her. The boy flung his arms about her swollen figure and she kissed his head fiercely.

'I need you here wife to run things while I am gone,' Milton replied sternly, 'and the journey would tire you out.' He saw the tears in her eyes and said more tenderly, 'Everything is arranged here at Balivanich for when the bairn comes. You don't want our child born in a bothy at Milton now do you?'

'No,' Marion agreed with a tearful smile.

'So let the boy go; he's growing too big to be mollycoddled.'

Reluctantly she did so. 'You do as your father and Uncle Archibald say. And you must *not* go out in a boat with Angie. Promise me, Ranald?'

Hearing his baby name, Angus chose that moment to grab her skirts and burst into tears, belatedly realising his mother was being left behind. Milton scooped him up in his large hands, wedged the boy under his arm and mounted his horse. Ignoring Angus's wails, he put him firmly on the saddle in front and bound him in his tartan plaid. Ranald scrambled onto his small pony, pushing away Marion's helping hand. 'I can do it Mother.'

With a heavy heart, she waved them away into the bright morning, watching the train of sturdy ponies trotting out of the township of Balivanich and away across the flat moorland studded with sparkling small lochs. But she could not banish the feeling of dread that clawed at her insides as they disappeared into the distance. Ever since the hateful MacVurich girl had uttered her sinister curse, Marion had been a bundle of nerves. Milton had been baffled by her insistence that Ranald be forbidden to go fishing with any of the tenants or with his Benbecula cousins. When she had tried to blame Mairi's witchcraft, Milton had grown angry and said, 'Why would they want to harm us? The MacVurichs have been the loyal bards of Clanranald for centuries; I will not have you insult them.'

Janet, the cook, came to stand beside Marion.

'They'll be back in a blink of an eye, don't you fret Mistress.'

Marion nodded, her throat too full of tears to speak. If only she wasn't carrying this baby, she could have gone with them. It was an age since she had seen her widowed father; he was always so busy with his parish duties, filling every waking hour now that he was without his beloved wife. Her parents match had been one of the heart as well as an alliance of mainland and island MacDonalds. She could not say that about her own. Eight years on, she was still in awe of her imposing husband with his grizzled looks and immense strength. Like all those who knew him, she admired and depended on him; at times when he horse-played with the boys, she even felt a flicker of fondness. But not love. She knew real love was like a burning in the heart, and she had never felt that for her husband. What Milton felt for her, she could not tell. People told her she was beautiful and she came from the prosperous and well-connected MacDonalds of Largie in Kintyre. A fair face and a dowry had saved her – and the thing that had seemed her undoing – the ability to produce sons.

'Come away, Mistress,' Janet chivvied, 'they've gone now. And I've made you a flummery sweetened with extra sugar – been keeping it hid from those laddies – and a bowl of punch since you've lost the taste for tea.'

'Thank you Janet,' Marion smiled at the cheery round-faced woman who had befriended her the moment she had come to Balivanich. Her father had thought it best that she start afresh in Benbecula without servants from South Uist who might gossip and let slip the truth. But the practical and fun-loving Janet, guessing her predicament, had not judged her. It was she who had squashed any tittle-tattle among the house servants about the swelling of their mistress's belly so soon after her marriage and the seemingly premature birth of baby Ranald with his golden hair.

'We women will have a month of enjoying ourselves without the menfolk getting under our feet,' Janet declared.

'Amen to that,' said Marion.

'Or teasing us for singing love songs as loud as we like.' Janet steered her by the elbow back towards the house.

As they passed the steading and were crossing the farmyard, they heard the low thud of hooves again. Marion swung round. Had Ranald decided a month without his mother was as unbearable as she knew it would be without him?

She stumbled back across the uneven turf, her belly tightening at the sudden movement.

A stout Highland pony trotted into view, its black-clad rider stiffly upright in the saddle. Marion's spirits plummeted. Long before she could make out the severe expression on the jowly face, she knew who their unwelcome visitor was. From his black full-bottomed wig to his ill-fitting shoes, he was a government man, a Hanoverian. It would be no coincidence that he had come hurrying over the minute Milton had departed. He must have been keeping a watchful eye on the preparations – or else had a spy in their homestead. A chill of foreboding returned as Marion braced herself to welcome the missionary, Obadiah Gunn.

Chapter 3

'Good morning, Mr Gunn,' Marion addressed her visitor in English, 'I'm sorry your visit is wasted; my husband has just left on business.'

The missionary ignored her as he barked at one of the farmhands to help him dismount. The boy carried on sharpening a scythe. Gunn shouted louder. 'Stop what you're doing at once laddie. Don't you know I'm the catechist?'

The boy did not even glance up.

'He speaks only Gaelic,' Marion intervened.

'What dark ignorance Mr MacDonald keeps his peasants in,' Gunn blustered.

Marion turned to the boy and reverted to Gaelic, 'Peter, can you help the old fool off his horse or he'll be stuck there all day lecturing us on the catechism.'

Peter grinned and laid down his scythe. 'Aye, Mistress, and before that wee pony collapses under the weight of that fat *Sassenach*.'

Janet suppressed a giggle. Gunn shot them a suspicious look.

'*Sassenach*? That means southerner, doesn't it? What's he saying about me?'

'That we're honoured to have you visit us,' Marion said quickly. 'You'll take tea with me, Mr Gunn?'

'Tea Madam?' he sniffed. 'Don't approve of the stuff – or of this fad among ladies for drinking it – I don't allow Mrs Gunn to touch it. It stimulates unnatural desires. But I'll take a glass of brandy.' He grunted loudly as Peter helped him from the saddle. 'I have much I wish to discuss with you about your sons' religious education.'

Marion showed him into the book-lined dining-room which doubled as her husband's study. She did not want the man in her upstairs parlour throwing a critical eye over her personal things. She regretted that she was still wearing her loose morning-gown under her plaid, but it was comfortable and she had not expected visitors. While they waited for refreshments, Gunn strutted around the room peering at the prints of Scottish castles and French chateaux. He stopped and tutted in front of a portrait of a Clanranald chief dressed in full tartan regalia and weapons. Marion thought nervously of the small picture of the exiled Jacobite King James that hung above her husband's desk and gestured Gunn into a chair by the window. Janet brought in a tray loaded with oatcakes, cheese, eggs, the promised flummery, a glass of brandy and a bowl of punch.

'Call for me Mistress, if he has a fit of unnatural desires over the flummery.' Janet winked and left.

The missionary tucked into the food at once. Between mouthfuls he pontificated in his harsh Lowland English.

'You are aware, Mrs MacDonald, of my mission to these papist islands? All around I see ignorance and heathen practices – these people play games and get drunk on the Sabbath when they should be confessing their sins in the Kirk.'

'They work hard all week, Mr Gunn, they deserve– '

'Work?' he snorted. 'I've never known such an idle race. They spend half the summer running wild in the high pastures – aye, the lassies too – and half the winter sat around their smelly peat fires telling ungodly tales and singing in Erse.' A gob of oatmeal flew from his mouth as he spat out the word. 'It's the popery of their masters is to blame. The Clanranalds are openly Catholic even though it is against the laws of the land. It seems to make no difference that their chief is banished to France. How can this be, Mrs MacDonald? I'll tell you how; Clanranald's henchmen persist in the old ways too.'

Marion put down her spoon, the creamy flummery curdling in her stomach.

'Henchmen, Mr Gunn?'

'Aye, men like your husband.' His eyes were deep-set, his look distrustful. 'I can see how the heathens here look up to him – he could be such a force for good in God's work.'

'My husband is devout enough,' Marion defended, 'and our household is Presbyterian like yours.'

'But he does not come to Kirk on the Sabbath, nor does he encourage his peasants to do so. And you Madam fall far short of your duty as a mother – you neglect to bring your sons to Kirk or to my Bible lessons.'

Marion was stung. 'My husband is a busy man. And as for myself and my boys, we hold family prayers here in the house every day. I was brought up to do so. Remember that my father is minister of the Kirk in South Uist and very well respected.'

The missionary spluttered over his brandy. 'That old Episcopalian? He's not a true Presbyterian.'

Marion was offended. 'He took the oath to the Scot's Kirk and Queen Mary before I was born.'

'I know his type,' Gunn was dismissive, draining off his brandy, 'paying lip-service to Presbyterianism while still harbouring a love of bishops and prayer books and such idolatry – little better than the Papists in my opinion.'

Marion struggled to keep her temper. 'It's a wonder that you have not trained for the ministry yourself if others are so lacking.'

Colour flooded into his fleshy chin; she had found his weak spot. 'I did not have the patronage of an Erse-speaking chief to pay me through university or hand me a parish on a plate.'

He was a worm of a man but Marion regretted provoking him; she feared he could make trouble for Milton and the clan. She offered him more cheese. He waved it away, reached for the punchbowl meant for her and took a greedy slurp. His messy eating was making her nauseous.

'But I shall make sure my son Elijah becomes a minister; he will carry on my work of leading these people out of darkness.'

Marion thought of the missionary's weakling infant boy with his hacking cough and doubted he would survive childhood.

'What is it that I can do for you, Mr Gunn?'

8

He pulled at the linen tablecloth and used it to wipe his mouth. 'I am looking for somewhere to hold my catechism classes. My own house is too small and the Kirk roof leaks because the Clanranalds will not pay for its upkeep.' He looked around him. 'This room will do nicely. Your sons and their friends can sit around the table – the peasant children on the floor. I will instruct them in the rules of the Kirk – in English of course.'

'The local boys will not understand you,' Marion pointed out.

'Then they must learn.' Gunn banged down the empty punchbowl. 'This speaking of Erse is the main obstacle to the peasants becoming peaceable loyal subjects of King George and godly Presbyterians. While they persist in this barbaric tongue they cannot be trusted.'

Marion could take no more of his insults; she stood up and immediately felt dizzy. 'I'm sorry, but you will have to leave – I'm not feeling well.'

He hauled himself to his feet. 'Do I have your agreement, Mrs MacDonald?'

'You will have to ask my husband on his return,' Marion said.

'When will that be?'

'Not for a month at least.'

'A month? Why so long? His tack of land at Milton is only half a day's ride away.'

Marion's unease grew at his sudden interest. 'As I said, he has business to attend to and family to visit.'

'Ah, family. So he is going beyond South Uist to the mainland? Perhaps to his brother the priest in Arisaig?'

'His brother Donald is a Kirk minister.'

'And a Jacobite by all accounts.'

'No! You are misinformed.' Marion pulled her morning-gown tightly around her; she didn't like the way he was staring at her. She felt on the point of fainting. 'Janet will see you out, Mr Gunn. *Janet!*' she called.

Her cook must have been listening at the door for she bustled in at once.

'Your hat, sir,' Janet said in accented English, thrusting it at him.

'Stop by the dairy on your way, Mr Gunn,' Marion said, 'and take a cheese to your wife. Janet will you …?'

'Aye,' she nodded, steering Marion back onto a chair.

'I thank you,' the missionary said with a stilted nod. 'I hope I haven't tired you in your condition.'

Marion flushed. 'I'm fine.'

'You can send for Mrs Gunn when your time comes,' he said. 'She can sit and pray with you.'

'That's enough to keep the baby in the womb another nine months,' Janet muttered in Gaelic.

They went. Marion closed her eyes and didn't open them again until Janet returned.

'He's gone – with half the cheese of Benbecula.' She came over and put a cool hand on Marion's hot brow. 'You should lie down, Mistress. He's worn you out with his pompous words. Religious this and heathen that.'

Marion shivered, though she felt uncomfortably hot.

9

'I'm not sure religion's what he really came about at all,' she worried.

'What then?' Janet asked.

Marion dropped her voice to make sure no one overheard, 'I think he's spying on my husband – on all of us.'

'Spying for who?'

'Those who have banished our chief,' Marion whispered, 'who want to turn us into Lowland lapdogs.'

'That will never happen,' Janet assured, putting a firm hand on Marion's shoulder. 'As long as there are men like the Master to lead us.'

Chapter 4

Armadale, Isle of Skye

Milton stood in the bow of the boat and pointed. 'There, where those trees are growing. You can see the rooftop.'

'Where? I can't see it,' Ranald said impatiently.

Milton put an arm around the boy and crouching to his level, said, 'There, above the harbour.'

'That's not a castle,' Ranald cried in disappointment. 'Donald Gorm lived in a great big castle on a big rock on a high cliff. You said so.'

'He did,' Milton smiled, 'and the MacDonalds of Sleat still have their big castle at Duntulm on the north of Skye. But they also live here.'

'If I was Chief of Sleat I wouldn't live in that house – it's the same size as Uncle Donald's house – and his house isn't as big as our house.'

'Still, that's where they live,' Milton ruffled the boy's fair hair. 'And look at the mountains and the woods – good hunting grounds fit for a great chief.'

'Are we going to stay there long?' Ranald asked. 'Can we go hunting, Father, now cousin Ewen's taught me how to use a gun?'

'I doubt we'll be there long enough for that.'

'Please Father!'

'We've been away longer than planned; don't you want to get home and see your mother?'

Ranald frowned. 'Yes I do.'

'And so do I,' Milton smiled. They had been away two months and he fretted that Marion would give birth before they returned.

'But just one day's hunting first,' Ranald persisted.

Milton laughed. 'Perhaps.'

He was pleased at Ranald's appetite for sport and his bravery in competition. He would make a good leader of their people one day – on the battlefield if necessary – if their chief called them out. That's why he had given in to Ranald's badgering to be taken to visit their kinsmen at Arisaig where he could join in the rough and tumble with his older cousins, rather than be left at the old minister's house in South Uist. Angus had bawled in fury at not being taken too, but Marion's father had distracted the small boy by playing his fiddle and dancing a jig while the others rowed away from the shore.

At first, Ranald had been overawed by the towering mountains of the mainland and subdued after bouts of sea-sickness from the journey. But he was soon running after his older cousins – Ewen with his speed and story-telling being his favourite – and Milton had hardly seen his son for days on end.

His son. He gazed down at the golden-haired Ranald and felt a familiar twisting in his guts. He loved this boy as his own – always had – for the lad was easy to love. Yet sometimes, when the light caught his features, he saw a glimpse of Ranald's real father in the cut of his jaw, the straight

11

nose and the lock of unruly hair across his brow. If he could see it then Marion must too. She tried hard not to favour Ranald over their own son Angus, but it was clear that she loved him more. It made his heart sore for he knew that given the choice, Marion would rather be married to Ranald's soldier father than shackled to a man more than twice her age. At least her former lover was abroad fighting for the French so was unlikely to return – certainly not to the Long Isle – but Milton still felt uneasy as they lowered the sail and rowed into Armadale bay. Ranald's father came from the neighbouring township of Camas and they might bump into some of his kin. He would keep the visit brief. He had promised his brothers and their Clanranald kinsmen to carry a letter from their exiled chief to Chief James MacDonald of Sleat – head of the most powerful Macdonald clan. Then they would travel swiftly on.

To his delight, Kingsburgh, Chief James's young factor, was waiting to greet them on the shore. In his youth, Milton had fought alongside his father, now the son was turning out a wise and honest chamberlain for Sleat's many business dealings, including those on the Long Isle. Kingsburgh was throwing off his plaid and wading out in his shirt-tails alongside his men to help heave in the boat.

'Welcome Milton! Grand to see you. And this must be young Ranald?' Kingsburgh seized the boy and swung him through the air, chuckling at his protests that he could get ashore himself. A naked infant with jet-black hair and large blue eyes – a miniature Kingsburgh – was jumping around in the shallows in excitement.

'This is my son Allan,' Kingsburgh said with pride, 'he was the one to spot you off the coast an hour ago.'

'Go in the boat, Dada!' small Allan pointed, then slipped on seaweed and went head first into the waves.

Milton struggled towards him but his father just laughed.

'He swims like a seal – he'll bob up again, you'll see.'

Allan surfaced, spluttering and choking. Milton waited for the boy to wail with fright as Angus would do, but he scrambled onto sturdy legs and coughing, began staggering towards the boat again.

'No you don't,' Kingsburgh said, swooping to pluck his son out of the water and swinging him onto his shoulders.

Allan accepted this turn of events without protest, grabbing onto his father's thick dark hair and shouting out to a slim handsome youth hanging back on the dry rocks.

'Zander! Look at my boat!'

Milton said to his friend, 'Is this Alexander our young chieftain?'

Kingsburgh nodded and dropped his voice. 'He's living with us at the home farm; Sir James is not at all well.'

Milton strode forward and embraced the chief's son. Alexander flushed and gave a bashful smile, stammering out a greeting. But he responded at once to Ranald's chatter and talk of hunting. While the two fair-haired boys led the party off the beach and towards Armadale farm, Kingsburgh quietly explained the situation to Milton.

'Dr Beaton is treating Sir James for the ague, but the fever keeps returning. He sent to Edinburgh for a Dr Strachan who specialises in such conditions. He arrived two days ago but there's been no improvement.'

'I'm very sorry to hear it,' Milton said in concern, 'I'd hoped to speak to Sleat; I have a message from Clanranald which has newly come from France.'

Kingsburgh gave him a wary look. 'You are taking quite a risk, are you not?'

'If Clanranald has need of an envoy then I am honoured to be him,' Milton said proudly.

'Of course,' said Kingsburgh, 'and do you know its content?'

Milton thought of the heated arguing that had raged between his kinsmen over the past nights. A bundle of letters from their exiled chief had arrived unexpectedly, wrapped in linen and delivered by a passing packman. A French merchantman had slipped in under cover of darkness and anchored off Moidart but had gone by the dawn, no one knew where. The letters had been the touch paper to fierce wrangling over allegiance to the exiled Stuarts.

'We'll talk of this later,' Milton said, 'over a bottle or two of your best claret.'

'Indeed,' Kingsburgh agreed. 'Come away inside – my Florence will be delighted to see you.'

***

Milton was charmed by Kingsburgh's lively young wife with her mass of dark curls and easy chatter. She rushed about with a jangle of keys bouncing on her hip, giving orders to her servants to prepare beds with their best linen and pluck a brace of fowl for dinner. Her solemn-eyed daughter Ann followed like her shadow and buried her face in Florence's skirts when Milton tried to speak to her. With a pang he thought of his long-dead wife and the bright-eyed baby daughter who had lived a week and then followed her mother into the grave, taking his heart with her. How he longed for Marion to give him a daughter too.

It was much later, when Florence had bundled her children off to bed and presided over a tasty supper of trout in butter sauce, duck in gravy, barley cakes and currant jelly, washed down with ale and claret, that Milton and his host were left alone to talk of Clanranald's letters. The wind that had blown them to Skye had strengthened and now rain was battering against the shuttered windows and hissing onto the fire.

'My brother Donald thinks there has been too much bloodshed already in the Jacobite cause.'

'I tend to agree,' replied Kingsburgh. 'It's scarcely three years since the MacDonalds were cut to pieces in Kintail alongside King James's Spanish army – left high and dry when the southern invasion fell foul of those storms.'

Milton nodded. 'Yet you still call him King James?'

13

Kingsburgh, made bold by wine, thumped his chair arm, 'In my eyes he is our rightful king – a full-blooded Stuart! – no other has such a clear claim.'

'This is what my chief Clanranald believes too.' Milton leaned forward eagerly. 'What of your chief Sir James?'

Kingsburgh was about to answer when his wife burst into the dining-room waving her hands in agitation.

'Husband, quickly, there is someone at the door. Who could it be at this late hour? I don't like to answer – not with the bairns asleep – and I've sent the servants to bed. What if some brigand is planning to do the chieftain harm? – and you his tutor and he in our care–'

'Hush Florence,' Kingsburgh sprang up. 'It's you who will wake the bairns with your noise,' he teased. 'It'll just be some poor piper looking for shelter till the storm blows over.'

All the same, he nodded for Milton to follow. Florence hovered with a candle behind while Kingsburgh drew back the bolts to the solid door.

A weird half-light glowed in the late summer sky and the wind whipped out the candle flame. A tall bulky figure stood wrapped in a sodden plaid, his face hidden under a bonnet, his fine boots caked in mud. No itinerant piper, Milton thought.

'Greetings cousins!' the man marched boldly into the house, throwing off his heavy plaid. 'Mistress Kingsburgh, even in the dark your beauty shines like a lamp.'

The traveller pulled off his bonnet in a sweeping bow. As he turned, the dusk light caught his prominent features and the black eye-patch covering the hollow above his right cheek.

'Hugh *Cam*?' Florence gasped. 'Is it you?'

Milton stared in disbelief at the young soldier, conjured out of the storm like a bad omen; One-eyed Hugh. Hugh caught sight of Milton at the same time. For a moment he too was speechless with surprise.

'Aye, 'tis me, fair lady,' he replied with a jut of his chin.

Milton could only gaze in dismay at the appearance of the one man he hoped never to see – Marion's sweetheart, Ranald's father – Hugh MacDonald of Camas, kinsman of the powerful Chief James.

Chapter 5

As candles were re-lit and the fire stoked, the Kingsburghs attended to their guest, plying him with cold cuts of meat, a bowl of warmed rum punch and a flurry of questions.

Milton looked on while Hugh ate hungrily and answered between mouthfuls. He had sailed on the same French merchant ship that had brought letters from Scots in exile. News had filtered through that his cousin and chief, Sir James, was ill so he had insisted at once on travelling to Skye. Arriving at Armadale House, Dr Beaton had assured him Sir James was in good hands but warned him to lie low at Kingsburgh's as there were strangers from Edinburgh about the place.

'But you did not put ashore with Clanranald's letter to Sir James,' Milton scoffed. 'For I have it with me. That is why I am here.'

Hugh flicked him a challenging look. 'You may have one from Clanranald but I have more important ones for Sir James from King James's closest advisors.'

Milton was stung. 'From the exiled court in Rome? How can that be? I heard you'd been fighting for the French.'

'I've been in Rome. That's where I've just come from.'

'You've been to Rome?' Florence said in excitement. 'Is it very grand? I've heard that the Coliseum is the most–'

'Wife, please,' Kingsburgh held up his hand, 'let our kinsman speak.'

With a look of frustration, Florence hovered at Hugh's side, refilling glasses of wine.

'It is very grand,' Hugh smiled at his hostess.

Milton growled, 'even if you have letters from the court, Sleat will get a truer account of what is going on in Rome from his MacDonald kinsman than any of those puffed up courtiers.'

Hugh drained off the punch. 'I doubt it. I never saw Clanranald and his name was hardly mentioned – he appears to have little influence. But no doubt he has already written to you of the good news at the court, Milton.'

'Good news?' Milton flushed.

'A reason for celebration.'

'What reason is that?' Florence asked. Hugh paused, his expression gleeful. He glanced around the table; Milton could tell he was savouring the moment.

'Tell us man!' Milton said in irritation.

Hugh grinned. 'Queen Clementina has just given birth to a second son Henry – a brother for Prince Charles Edward – so the Stuart line is stronger than ever.'

Florence clapped her hands in delight and Kingsburgh said, 'that is heartening news indeed.'

'That is why,' Hugh went on eagerly, 'the King's advisors think now is a good time to take action.'

'What sort of action?' Kingsburgh frowned.

15

'A show of force from his Scots subjects to prove to King Louis of France that we still mean business. Stop him losing interest in the Stuart claim.'

'You mean another Rising?' Kingsburgh asked.

Florence gasped, 'Surely not so soon after–'

'Hush wife,' he interrupted.

'Yes, another push against the Hanoverians. King George is ageing and ill and still unpopular with many – in England too – and if the Highlands rose up first, the south would follow.'

'It would be madness without French backing,' Kingsburgh cautioned. 'Look what happened last time.'

'He'll back us if we return with pledges of support,' Hugh said impatiently.

Kingsburgh sighed. 'The timing is not good for our clan. Sleat is too ill to lead his men into battle, and young Alexander is still a boy.'

'He is twelve; I was a champion swordsman at his age despite having only one good eye!'

'He is a gentle soul,' Kingsburgh said, 'kind but immature for his age.'

'Then he needs toughening up,' Hugh was adamant, 'I'll give him some lessons while I'm here.'

'I am his tutor,' Kingsburgh said firmly, 'and I'll decide what's best for the chieftain.'

Hugh took a glug of wine, swallowing down his frustration at the factor's stubbornness.

'You are quiet Milton?' Hugh goaded. 'Does the news from Rome not please you?'

'The birth of any Stuart gives me pleasure but they are still exiled in Rome and no nearer to gaining the British crowns.'

'I disagree,' Hugh was dismissive. 'But perhaps you have as little stomach for a fight as your chief who has grown feeble in exile.'

Milton leaned across the table and thumped his fist. 'You will not insult Clanranald in my hearing. His letter to me was full of bravery.'

'I'm sure no insult was meant,' Kingsburgh said swiftly. 'Tell us what did Clanranald have to say in his letter to you, Milton?'

Scowling at his younger rival, Milton answered, 'He wanted his Clanranald kinsmen – both on the mainland and Benbecula – to find out what appetite there is among the clan for a show of support for King James.'

'You see,' Hugh crowed, 'there is a momentum abroad for ousting German George.'

'But,' Milton said gravely, 'my kinsmen are divided over the matter. We Clanranalds are not a rich clan and things were made ten times worse when half the lands were forfeit to the crown after the last Rising.'

'You sound like an Edinburgh shopkeeper,' Hugh was disparaging, 'putting your purse before the destiny of our true monarch.'

'That's easy for you to say,' Milton barked, 'you're nothing but a mercenary selling yourself to the highest bidder. You've turned your back on responsibility.'

'I had no choice,' Hugh cried, 'as a younger son I've had to make my own way in the world. No one's handed me a tack of land. But I'm a bloody good swordsman and I'll keep my skill sharp until my chief and king need me. And when they do, I won't think twice about how much it costs!'

'So speaks the word of arrogant youth,' Milton retorted. 'But clan leaders like me and Kingsburgh have our people and families to consider. We'll not risk our fighting men on a whim or let them be pawns in a political game between Rome and Paris.'

'You've gone soft in your old age, Milton,' Hugh taunted. 'Is that what a pretty wife does to an old man? How is the beautiful Marion by the way?'

Milton jumped out of his chair and launched at Hugh, seizing him by his damp shirt.

'Don't you mention her name!'

They tussled, knocking over a wine glass that splintered across the hard earth floor. Hugh landed a punch on Milton's jaw.

'Gentlemen!' Kingsburgh cried.

Milton, clutching his jaw, stood back panting.

'Oh, my best cut glass!' Florence exclaimed.

'I'm sorry,' said Milton, watched her picking up the shards of precious glass, her mouth a thin angry line. He cursed himself for being so easily riled.

Hugh dashed to help her, cutting his finger in his haste. 'I'll pay for a new set,' he insisted, 'I'll have them shipped from Venice – Venetian is the best, I'm told.'

'There's no need,' Kingsburgh said. 'A glazed goblet does the same job.' He motioned them all to sit down again. 'Florence will fetch another bottle and we'll drink a health to the new prince and forget our hasty words. We need time to think things over. We can't all be rushing about like the trade winds, Hugh *Cam*; you must learn a little patience.'

Hugh gave a sheepish smile. 'I can see why my cousin James chose you as tutor to his son; you're a wise man Kingsburgh.' He turned to Milton and held out his hand. 'Forgive me, I meant no dishonour.'

Milton hesitated then grasped his hand.

Quickly mollified, Florence poured a large measure of wine into the empty punch bowl and held it over the greasy water of Hugh's finger bowl. They all knew the significance of her gesture; the Jacobite code for the exiled Stuarts over the sea.

'To the new prince over the water!' she gave the Jacobite toast, handing round the quaich.

The men responded, 'To the Prince!' and drank in turn.

'And to kinship,' Kingsburgh added.

Milton and Hugh exchanged wary glances, then chorused, 'to kinship!'

'What prince?' a sleepy voice asked from the shadows.

They all turned at once to see Ranald standing in the doorway in his nightshirt. Milton's heart lurched. This was the moment he hoped would never come; when Hugh would catch sight of his natural son.

'What are you doing out of bed Ranald?' Milton demanded.

'I heard shouting.' The boy padded towards his father then stopped in his tracks. He gawped with fear at the man with the eye-patch and dishevelled hair.

'Who are you?' Ranald whispered. 'Are you a Barbary pirate?'

Hugh stared back at the boy, his good eye wide in astonishment. Milton felt his insides clench. Nobody spoke, but he knew what they must be thinking. Finally Hugh found his voice.

'Yes, and I eat small boys for breakfast.'

Ranald turned and ran out of the room screaming. Hugh barked with laughter.

Milton rounded on him. 'My Ranald is no coward.'

'I never said–'

'I promised him a day of sport tomorrow. He'll match any of your young Sleat MacDonalds at archery or pistol. And I bet he can outrun them all – including the chieftain Alexander.'

There was silence around the table. Milton wondered what had possessed him to issue such a reckless challenge. Hugh's eye glittered with a dangerous look.

'That I would like to see,' Hugh said. 'Clanranald versus Sleat it is.'

Chapter 6

Milton slept badly in the box-bed next to his son. He awoke groggy and disorientated to find the bedroom empty. He had supped too much claret; he could no longer drink as he used to. Dowsing his face in water from the china basin on the deep window ledge, he winced in the sunlight; the night storm had passed. Milton caught sight of the three boys outside in the sunshine.

Hugh was wrestling with them on the mossy slope; their squeals of laughter rang out like seagulls shrieking. Alexander and Ranald were wrapped around Hugh's legs, while a boisterous Allan clung to his back and pulled his hair. Ranald looked so happy; the sight was infuriating. The sooner he delivered the letter to Sir James and they could set sail again in good weather, the better.

Kingsburgh looked warily at his bad-tempered guest, as Milton quaffed a mug of ale and pushed aside his porridge.

'I'll come with you up to Armadale House,' he offered.

'No need,' Milton said. 'You have your duties to the chieftain. I'll take Ranald with me.'

'But the boys are expecting a day's sport.'

'They are?'

'It was your suggestion last night, remember? Clanranald against Sleat.'

Milton had a vague memory of rounding on Hugh's laughing face and issuing a drunken challenge. What a fool he was. All he wanted now was to whisk Ranald away from Hugh and sail safely back to Benbecula and Marion.

'There isn't time for that now,' Milton said. 'I want to take advantage of the fair weather.'

'You will disappoint the boys then,' Kingsburgh warned. 'Hugh told them at breakfast and they are as high as skylarks at the idea.'

***

Reluctantly, Milton agreed that while he and Hugh went to see Sir James at Armadale House, the boys would practise their running, rock throwing and shooting at targets.

'It might be too much for Sir James to have the boys visit too,' Kingsburgh advised. 'And you'll want to speak in confidence.'

Milton's boatmen were ordered to help set up the targets and gather rocks from the shore, before preparing the boat for sail. As Milton and Hugh set out for the chief's house, Ranald called out.

'Father, watch this!'

He picked up the biggest rock, his fair face straining pink with the effort. Balancing it between shoulder and chin, the boy frowned in concentration then hurled it forward. It landed a good four feet in front.

'Bravo!' cried Hugh, clapping. 'A champion thrower in the making.'

Ranald grinned. Milton, irritated by Hugh's quick praise and Italian exclamation, called back, 'I expect to see you throw better than that by the time I return.'

Ranald's smile faltered. 'Yes Father.' He trotted back to pick up the rock and try again.

Milton felt a surge of affection for his young son, realising how hard the boy was trying to please him. He would give him his due at the end of the games, but not flatter him with too much praise to make his head swell. Ranald would not grow up arrogant like his natural father.

The two rivals walked up the track from the farm towards the woods that sheltered Armadale House, neither speaking to the other. Today Hugh had shed his soldier's trousers and jacket and was wearing the garb of a Highland tacksman – plaid and homespun stockings – so as not to attract undue attention. They could hear the sound of gunshot as the boys practised in the distance.

'Ranald's a fine lad,' Hugh said, breaking the awkward silence.

Milton ignored the comment, not wanting to encourage talk of his son.

'Florence tells me that you have another boy, Angus,' Hugh persisted. 'And that your wife expects another.'

Milton flushed. 'Mistress Kingsburgh talks too readily of other men's business.'

They strode on, then Hugh asked more tentatively, 'Is – is Marion well?'

'Mistress Milton to you,' Milton snapped. 'And yes, she is well – very well – and happy with her life at Balivanich. We both are.'

'I'm glad,' Hugh said.

Milton gave him a sharp look but the young man's face was reflective not insolent. They walked on without another word but just as they came in sight of the house, Hugh put a hand on Milton's arm to stop him.

'I know your opinion of me is low, and I can't blame you; I often act with a hot head and speak before thinking. But you must believe me when I say I didn't know about Marion – about Mistress Milton – being with child when I left and went abroad to fight.'

Agitated, Milton threw off his hold. 'What nonsense if this?' he barked. 'My wife is a virtuous woman and I take offence at your insinuations. Ranald is my son and his fair looks come from his mother.'

Hugh's face twisted with sudden mockery. 'Come, come Milton. Anyone can see that the lad is the image of me. It's like looking in the mirror at my young self.'

Swift as lightning, Milton grabbed Hugh round the neck and drew his dirk, holding its blade to his throat. Hugh did not try to struggle.

'You stay away from my son and my family,' Milton hissed, 'and keep your vile thoughts to yourself. Ranald is mine, do you hear?'

'Aye, I hear,' Hugh said through gritted teeth.

Milton let him go.

They arrived at the house in hostile silence. Milton noticed how one wing of the modest two-storey dwelling was still a shattered ruin from when a government ship had bombarded it years ago. Perhaps the Sleat

MacDonalds were not as wealthy as people believed, or maybe the chief's heart lay not in Armadale but in the ancient northern fortress of Duntulm, as Ranald thought it should?

Just as they were being ushered indoors, the thud of horse's hooves grew louder behind. The men turned to see who rode in such haste. A bare-headed Kingsburgh came clattering into the courtyard, scattering hens and spraying up mud.

'Milton!' he cried. 'Come quickly.'

Milton's heart jolted at the panic on the man's face.

'What's happened?'

Kingsburgh wheeled around, sweating and ashen. 'I'll take you back. Just come.'

It was Hugh who jumped forward and seized the bridle. 'For God's sake, tell the man what's happened!'

'An accident,' Kingsburgh rasped, 'there's been an accident.'

Chapter 7

At low tide, Marion and Janet walked the beach below Balivanich, barefoot in the soft pale sand. Janet stopped to pick winkles and Marion eased herself down onto one of the glistening black rocks. The day was calm and the sea soft as a mantle, but she was restless and the baby twisted in the womb and wouldn't be still.

She pulled the creased letter out of her gown and read the brief message for the umpteenth time. Her family had been gone two months and she ached for them to return. The local boys fishing off the shore, the men repairing their boats and the women drying their washing on the stiff spiky grass only increased her longing for her own family life to resume.

'I'll not forgive him for this,' Marion said, waving it in the air.

'Aye, you will,' Janet replied.

'Fancy taking Ranald all the way to Arisaig; he's too young for such a journey.'

'It's good for him to get to know his cousins,' Janet said. 'And you can't keep him out of boats forever, Mistress. Not when we live on an island.'

Today her servant's plain speaking irked her. 'Did I ask for your opinion?'

Janet stood up and fished inside her apron. 'Eat this Mistress; it'll sweeten your mood.' With a grin, she held out a wedge of shortbread. 'It's flavoured with ginger.'

Marion wanted to protest but Janet's ginger shortbread was her favourite sweetmeat. In the early weeks of the pregnancy, it had been the only food that could quell her sickness. She took it with a nod of thanks, biting into the crumbly biscuit, revelling in the sharp-sweet taste.

'If they're not back by full moon in three days' time,' Marion munched, 'I'll get Lachlan to row me down to my father's and fetch Angus home. At least he will be company while my husband stays away – no doubt treating each day like a feast day with those wild Clanranald kin.'

Janet said, 'You'll need more than old Lachlan to row you to South Uist.'

'Why is that?'

'The heavy cargo you're carrying, Mistress. You'll need a crew of six at least.'

Marion snorted. 'I don't know why I put up with your saucy tongue Red Janet. If you weren't such a good cook, I'd pack you off home tomorrow.'

'And my mother would send me straight back,' Janet laughed. 'There's no room to squeeze a cat in my father's place.'

Marion felt chastened. She had seen Janet's home near Nunton once; it was no bigger than the hut where Milton kept his dogs, yet it had housed a dozen people or more. Janet's mother had lost five infants to smallpox and summer fever in the eight years that Marion had been in Balivanich. Janet's face was marred by pockmarks too, but she had survived the terrible disease that every mother feared.

Marion put out her hands for Janet to haul her up. 'Let's go back and break open a new canister of tea,' she smiled at her cook.

'Have you got the taste back Mistress?'

'No,' said Marion, 'but I know you haven't lost yours.'

Janet smiled back, knowing it was Marion's way of showing her affection.

They left the beach and laboured up the slope to the house. Panting, Marion stopped to draw breath. The baby kicked. Soon it would be time for her confinement. The bedroom had long been prepared; the linens and blankets looked out, the swaddling clothes pressed. She felt a thrill of anticipation for the event; she was strong and had never had trouble bringing her babies into the world. Janet would be there to help – she had delivered her two boys – and the Beaton midwife over at Nunton was on hand if they needed her.

Then there would be the luxuriant time of lying in bed for days feeding her newborn and been fussed over by Milton and the household. Kin and neighbours would travel from miles around to visit and bring gifts; the women would sit around in her parlour eating Janet's baking and cooing over the baby, while the sound of the men celebrating downstairs would ring up the stairwell. To Marion, the celebration of a birth was ten times more exciting than a wedding.

Weddings were wild affairs that could last for days, with too much drinking and bawdiness and the fear of fights breaking out among distant kin. At weddings all eyes were on the bride and groom to see when they would go to the master chamber. At her own, the guests had mistaken her sickness for the nerves of a young bride about to be bedded for the first time.

Marion shuddered at the memory. No, give her a birth any day, and the milky baby smell and crisp linens of a woman's bedroom.

'Someone's coming,' Janet said, breaking into Marion's reverie.

Marion shaded her eyes from the glare of pearly sky and squinted across the moor. Sure enough, a line of ponies were plodding into view.

Hurrying on, they were met by Peter at the end of the track.

'The Master's back!' he cried. 'I saw them from the hill.'

Marion shrieked with joy. 'Thank the Heavens!'

'And the Minister's with them too,' Peter grinned.

'My father?'

Peter nodded. 'I recognised his grey mare.'

'Oh, that's wonderful.' Marion felt tears of relief stinging her eyes. To see her dear father as well as her family would be a double cause for celebration.

'Quick Janet,' she ordered, 'we must get hot water ready and plenty of ale to quench their thirst. And make sure that there's enough flummery for the boys.'

'Aye, Mistress,' Janet laughed, 'but let's get you onto a seat first, before you burst.'

'Bring a chair outside,' Marion grinned, 'I must be here to greet my bairns.'

Big Alasdair, Milton's piper rushed for his pipes and struck up a welcoming tune.

Marion could hardly contain her excitement as the procession drew nearer. They disappeared into a dip and then emerged again closer. Her father led the way, his familiar faded bonnet dark against his silver hair. Her husband was further back with one of the boys wedged behind.

Janet returned with a stool and nagged her to sit down and wait in the shelter of the courtyard. Despite her eagerness to greet her family, Marion was breathless and glad to sit.

'Tell me what's happening,' she badgered Peter.

Her heart hammered in anticipation, as the youth dashed back and forth with news of their progress. They were passing the MacVurichs' place; they were nearly at the infields; they were over the burn. As her father's grey horse emerged round the side of the cattle byre, Marion heaved herself up.

He lifted a hand in greeting but his words were drowned out by the blare of bagpipes. She waved back and scanned the ponies for sight of her sons as the exhausted beasts stumbled across the uneven ground. The courtyard was suddenly full of snorting horses, servants rushing to help and children running around in excitement.

As Peter helped the old minister from the saddle, Angus leaned out from behind his father and screamed with delight as he caught sight of his mother.

'Mammy!'

Marion lumbered over, holding out her arms to him.

'Come here my wee lamb! Oh, how I've missed you!'

She glanced at Milton as he helped their eager son down. 'And you too husband,' she murmured.

He gave her a strange look and nodded. 'Wife,' he said, then glanced away, saluting his piper.

She was hurt by his lack of affection after so long apart, but Angus flung his arms about her neck and gave her a sloppy kiss. She buried her face in his dark hair and breathed in his boy smell.

'Goodness Angie, you weigh twice as much,' she gasped, 'has Auntie Agnes being feeding you venison pie and sticky cakes every day?'

'No Mammy, Aunt Agnes makes you eat black food. It's 'gusting.'

'Black food?'

'It goes on fire but she makes you eat it, even the burnt bits.'

Marion thought of her miserly sister-in-law. 'Oh dear, well, Janet has some treats ready for you and Ranald.'

Angus pulled back and shook his head. 'Not Ranald. He can't eat food in Heaven.'

Marion thought she had misheard over the noise of the pipes. 'What did you say?'

Angus looked suddenly unsure.

24

'Where's your brother?' Marion asked sharply, shaking him. She looked about her; people were still milling about and dismounting.

'Down Mammy,' he wriggled out of her hold, 'put me down.'

She almost dropped him on the ground as she swung around in a surge of panic. Her father was hurrying towards her as fast as his stiff legs allowed.

'Where's Ranald?' she shouted.

'Marion, my dearest–' His eyes glittered with tears.

All at once, she felt herself gripped in strong arms from behind.

'In the house Wife,' Milton ordered, 'and I will explain.'

She wrestled to be free. 'What have you done with my son?'

'Not here; you must sit down,' Milton barked, but his grip slackened.

She rounded on him. 'Tell me!'

He stared back at her, his expression harrowed. He looked exhausted, old. She saw him swallowing hard, trying to speak but unable to. The piping abruptly ended. Her heart stopped. Milton's face crumpled like a child's and he started to weep. She turned away from him, appalled.

'Marion,' her father spoke her name, his voice deep with compassion. 'There's been a tragic accident. Ranald was loading a gun; it went off by mistake. He died instantly without pain.'

Everything went quiet. All Marion could hear was the erratic thud of her heart pounding in her ears.

'No Father, Ranald doesn't have a gun. He doesn't know how to use one. He's a bairn.'

'He was a brave MacDonald. He died having sport with the young chieftain of Sleat.'

'Ranald was in Sleat?' Marion gasped, 'No, I don't believe you.'

'It's an honourable death, my daughter.'

'Honourable?' she wailed, pushing away his comforting arms. She turned on Milton. 'Can it be true?' But she knew from his weeping that it was. 'Where were you?' she accused. 'Why did you allow this?'

He flinched from her stricken face.

'Daughter,' the minister chided, 'you mustn't speak to your husband like that.'

'I'll speak how I want!' Marion cried. 'You said you'd protect my son but you let him die. I'll never forgive you!' Marion lashed out at Milton, pummelling his chest and arms with her fists.

Milton did not defend himself – he welcomed her blows – it was what he deserved. Better the physical pain than the mental torture of the past week. The horror of seeing Ranald with his face half-blown off, writhing in pain on the grassy sward would haunt him beyond the grave. He could at least spare Marion the truth of her son's slow agonised death.

Suddenly, Marion was seized with searing pain in her belly. She bent double, clutching at her skirts.

'Marion,' Milton said, reaching out, 'is it the child?'

'I don't care about this one,' Marion hissed, 'I only want Ranald.'

As her knees buckled, Janet rushed forward and caught her.

'Come away Mistress,' she urged, 'you must lie down now.'

Marion crumpled into her friend's arms and let out a howl of distress. Angus flew at her. 'Don't cry Mammy!'

But she shrank from her dark-haired son; he wasn't her golden boy. Marion clawed at the ground to get away from him, screaming for Ranald. She wished she could die there and then on the stony yard in front of Balivanich.

It took six of them to pull the resisting woman to her feet and carry her inside.

Chapter 8

That night, Marion went into labour. Already exhausted by the shock of her first-born's death, she had no energy for bringing her baby out. Janet sat by her bedside, cooling her brow with a damp cloth and singing encouraging songs, but her mistress seemed not to care.

She had screamed the house down for hours, refusing to lie down and insisting on Milton handing over Ranald's saddle-bag of clothing. Finally, she had curled up on her bed, crying into her dead son's shirt. Now she would speak to no one or answer their anxious questions.

'What can I do?' a distraught Milton demanded when Janet emerged for more water.

'Her birth pains are coming more frequently,' she whispered, 'but her look is feverish. I think it will be a difficult birth; we should send for Mistress Beaton.'

'I'll fetch her myself,' Milton said at once and was gone before anyone could argue.

He rode over to Nunton and ordered the midwife to leave her half-eaten supper to attend his wife. Mary Beaton knew the tragedy of Milton's first wife dying in childbirth and saw his desperation. She clung on fearfully as Milton galloped recklessly back to his farm.

'She's giving up,' Janet told the midwife in alarm.

'Not on my watch, she won't,' Mary said firmly and moved about the room, quietly giving orders and talking reassuringly to the unresponsive mother-to-be. She propped her up and gave her sips of a herbal concoction that calmed her racing heartbeat.

Marion was smothered in a red haze of pain. She wasn't sure if it was from her hard distended belly or the well of grief in her heart. Yet she could not believe what had happened; *would* not believe it. Ranald had been left behind by mistake; he was living happily with his cousins on the mainland learning how to hunt in the mountains. This autumn he would be old enough to need a tutor – perhaps her father could teach him? But then she wouldn't want him living away from her in South Uist …

Panic smothered her anew. Milton said Ranald was buried in the kirkyard at Armadale, but surely that was a cruel joke? Why had they been there, and so close to Hugh *Cam*'s home? Milton should have brought his body home so that she could bathe it and cherish it and put it in the ground where she could visit him every day; her darling little man!

'Breathe in deep,' said a calm voice, 'in and out, that's the way. Don't struggle. The baby's time has come.'

Marion felt another contraction grip her like iron hands. She whimpered, 'I don't want it.'

'It wants you,' said the midwife. 'It's pressing down now.'

Janet was still singing songs. Marion did not have the strength to tell her to stop; that only a lament would soothe her now. At least she did not have the prim Mrs Gunn sitting at her bedside reciting Scripture, as the missionary had wanted. Gradually she was feeling more detached from the pain; as if it was happening to someone lying next to her, a shadowy person she could feel rather than see.

Suddenly Marion yearned for her dead mother, the serene and beautiful Elizabeth, who had helped deliver Ranald but died shortly afterwards. A comforting thought flitted through her throbbing head; her kind mother would be there to receive Ranald in Heaven. He was not alone in the darkness as she was.

'Get ready to push,' Mary Beaton encouraged. 'When you feel the next pain, push down – and don't forget to breathe.'

Marion didn't want to push – didn't want to do anything – but her body was writhing and thrusting as if it had a will of its own. She screamed in agony.

'That's the way,' the midwife said, 'and again. In and out like the tide.'

'There's so much blood,' Janet gasped. 'Are we going to lose her?'

Marion shuddered. She was being engulfed by the sea; she was going to drown just like Ranald had. It was exactly as that witch Mairi MacVurich had foretold. But Ranald hadn't drowned had he? It made no sense. The witch had tricked her all along; it was only she who was going to drown. Drown in her own blood. She screamed and fought for air. She didn't want to die! She needed to live to see her baby son. Ranald would be returned to her in this new babe.

Janet held down her wild-eyed mistress while Mary Beaton urged the baby out, protecting the dark head emerging between Marion's juddering legs.

'Will she die?' Janet wailed.

'The saints will decide,' Mary Beaton said grimly. 'At least we will save the baby.' She pulled at the tiny shoulders and the baby slipped into her bloodied arms.

Marion went limp. Her breathing was ragged.

'Mistress!' Janet shook her with a sob. 'Please don't leave us. Your baby's born.'

Marion let out a groan. At once, there was an answering bleat from the tiny dark-haired baby that Mary was swaddling in a clean sheet.

'A lassie,' Mary beamed.

'Oh, the Master will be pleased,' Janet said and burst into tears.

Marion's eyes flickered open. 'A girl?' she whispered.

'Aye, Mistress Milton,' said Mary, 'and a bonny one for all the struggling.'

Marion closed her eyes again. Tears trickled down her exhausted face, but the women could not tell if they were of joy or disappointment.

Chapter 9

Marion's father baptised the new baby in a quiet ceremony at the house and christened her Flora. Marion sat propped up in bed watching, but felt completely detached, as if her father held someone else's child in his strong arms.

She was aware of the men reciting the Lord's Prayer, the baby squalling, Angus fidgeting and trying to kiss the baby, and then it was over.

When her father tried to hand her daughter for her to hold, Marion shrank into her pillows. The baby's crying set her teeth on edge.

'My wife is tired,' Milton said, stepping forward and plucking Flora from the minister's arms.

Marion saw the look of adoration on her husband's face, his craggy features softening as he smiled at the infant. Never had he looked on her like that. The thought made her tearful; how could he find comfort in the baby when she could not? Ranald had been dead only three weeks and yet her husband wanted a christening party. She had taken no part in organising refreshments for the day but she knew Janet would have prepared a whisky punch and the smell of baking had wafted in from the kitchens at the back of the house. The very thought made her nauseous.

Angus scrambled onto her bed and pulled at the covers. 'Get up Mammy.'

'Don't Angus,' she chided and dissolved into fresh tears.

Milton ordered his son off the bed. 'Come on Angie, we'll see what Janet's got for us. Leave your mother be.'

He left with the children, but her father lingered. He stood looking severe in his black clerical jacket and breeches, his long grey-white hair swept back from his hawk-like face. But when he spoke, his voice was tender.

'We all grieve for Ranald,' he said, 'but we must bear that grief together.'

'I can't bear it,' Marion sobbed.

'The Lord will give you strength to do so, daughter.'

She looked at him in despair. 'How is it possible to miss someone so much? I feel like my heart has been cut out.'

'It's because you loved him that much,' he replied gently.

Marion looked at his weathered, compassionate face. She knew his reputation as a hard man who would just as easily settle a dispute with his fists as with his Bible. But to her, he was like a warm, comforting plaid.

'Do you still miss my mother?' she whispered.

Her father nodded. 'Of course, every day. But the pain lessens.'

'I don't see how it will.'

'By being brave – every day.'

'I can't.'

'Then you are not your mother's daughter.'

He brushed her forehead with a kiss and left.

29

***

The next day, Obadiah Gunn came to arrange a baptism at the Kirk.

'The child is already baptised?' he cried.

'Aye, she is indeed,' said Marion's father, 'I carried out the sacrament myself.'

'That is most irregular,' Obadiah snapped. 'The thing isn't about to die, is it?'

'Her name is Flora.' Milton gave him short shrift. 'And our household is in mourning for our son Ranald. We didn't want any fuss.'

'Then I will stay and pray with the bereaved,' Gunn insisted.

'There's no need,' said Marion's father. 'The Lord prefers to hear prayers in Gaelic; God's own language.'

The missionary took instant offence, threatening as he left, 'this popery will be reported to the presbytery.'

'And the Lord preserve us,' Milton muttered in Gaelic, 'from *Sassenachs* in full-bottomed wigs.'

'Aye,' the minister snorted, 'he's a full-bottomed Whig, right enough.'

***

Despite her father's encouragement, Marion could find no appetite for life, and when he left to go back to his parish in South Uist, her black mood deepened. Her interest in food dwindled, she struggled to feed the baby and she could not even bear to have the affectionate Angus near her. It was Milton who got up in the night, hearing Flora's cries, and walked the floor with her singing Gaelic lullabies. When neighbours and kin turned up to visit with presents for Marion and the newborn, they were turned away from her parlour where she lay with the curtains drawn pretending to sleep.

Janet went in concern to her master. 'I'm frightened, sir. She's wasting away.'

Milton was at his desk. 'She just needs rest – it's only natural after childbirth.'

Janet noticed how he never referred to the loss of Ranald any more. 'It's more than that,' she persisted. 'She takes no heed of what's going on in the household. I can't run everything.'

Milton huffed with impatience. 'Surely you can manage a bit longer. Get one of your sisters to come over and help out if you must.'

'Well none of us can put the bairn to the breast,' Janet said boldly.

He gave her a sharp look. 'What do you mean by that?'

'Have you not noticed how quiet the baby grows? She's not thriving and her mother's milk is drying up.'

Milton was suddenly alarmed. He sprang from his seat. 'Why did you not say so before?'

Janet bit back a retort that surely he should have noticed. 'Sorry Master,' she muttered.

30

Pacing the room, he said, 'What should I do?'

'Flora needs a wet nurse.'

Milton flushed at this. 'Where do I … do we …?'

'We could send word to Nunton,' Janet suggested. 'I've heard that Mistress Benbecula is weaning her latest son and that her wet nurse will not be needed.'

Milton nodded. Benbecula was his cousin, senior to him in the clan but half his age. He was a bookish young man, though with an eye for bonny lassies if rumours were to be believed. His spirited young wife was from a powerful branch of Clan MacLeod on Berneray, an island to the north. Peggi MacLeod had borne Benbecula four children in five years, transformed Nunton into a comfortable modern house and still found time to visit the sick and dying on her black stallion. She had attempted to call on Marion but Milton's wife had made excuses not to see her.

'Thank you Janet,' he said, 'I'll send word to Mistress Benbecula at once.'

Peggi MacLeod rode by the following day with her eldest son clinging behind. Milton felt a stab of grief at the sight of the boy with red-gold hair whose name was also Ranald. Angus was immediately excited to have a playmate his own age and took him off to explore the farm.

'Welcome my lady,' Milton greeted his guest. 'Thank you for coming so swiftly.'

'Your concern for your wife does you credit,' Peggi smiled. 'Benbecula wouldn't notice if I rode stark naked from Berneray to Barra – unless I'd ridden off with his black tobacco and copy of Martin's *Description of the Western Isles*.'

Milton barked with laughter. She wasn't a pretty woman – her nose too large and eyes too deep-set – but her saucy grin and voluptuous mouth made her attractive.

'Come away Mistress Benbecula; Janet has tea ready.'

'It's time you called me Peggi, and I'm afraid I never take tea on a saint's day – only punch.'

'Is it a saint's day?' Milton frowned.

'It's always a saint's day at Nunton,' Peggi winked. 'It's the main advantage of marrying into Catholics.'

***

Marion could hear laughter below and wondered vaguely who could be calling. It was blissfully quiet in her bedroom; the baby lay in its cot making the occasional snuffle but never crying much. She felt she could exist in this twilight world forever, with nothing left to burden her. Marion had reached the comforting thought that the worst thing that could possibly happen had happened, so nothing else could hurt her again. If she could just be left alone …

The door swung open, letting a draught of cool air into the stuffy room.

31

'My dear Marion,' a woman swept in, discarded her plaid, strode across to the cot and plucked the baby to her ample bosom. 'I'm sorry I've neglected you these past weeks. I'm a worthless friend. But look at this wee poppet! I need a good peek.'

With Flora wedged in one arm, Peggi MacLeod drew back a curtain with the other. Marion winced in the sudden light.

'Mistress Benbecula?' she squinted at the intruder.

'Peggi please. We're practically the same age; I'll not have you making me feel like an old matron with your Mrs-this and Mistress-that.' She yanked at the other curtain and somehow unlatched the window and threw it open without dropping the infant.

Marion shivered at the blast of cold sea air.

'I'm not well,' she fretted, 'I can't see visitors. Milton shouldn't have let you–'

'Milton wanted to introduce me to your bonny wee daughter.' Peggi peered at the tiny scrap in her arms, pulling the shawl away from her wan heart-shaped face. 'Hello Flora, what a beautiful name, eh?'

The baby stared back at her with large blue-grey eyes – the colour of the Atlantic on a cloudy day – but did not make a sound. In concern, Peggi placed her little finger to the baby's rosebud lips but they remained tightly closed as if she had forgotten how to suck.

'Dearie me,' Peggi clucked, 'you're awful quiet for a Milton MacDonald – not like that noisy brother of yours. Well, we'll have to change that, bonny wee Florrie.'

She settled herself on the bed beside Marion and pulled back the cover to look her over. 'And we need to feed your mother up too – there's more meat on a crow.'

'Please,' Marion said in agitation, clawing back the cover, 'just leave me alone. The baby is fine.'

'The baby is not fine,' Peggi was blunt. 'She's disappearing in front of my eyes and so are you, my girl. This is what we are going to do. I shall send over my wet nurse today to tend to Flora – I can see that grief has dried your milk and no one can blame you for that. And you will concentrate on getting your strength back – you have the best cook on the island, so I'm told – I'll instruct Janet to feed you up.'

'There's no point.'

'There's every point. I'll not stand by and see my neighbour and friend waste away with melancholia.'

'Why should you care?' Marion said bleakly.

'Because I'm an interfering old wife who can't help poking my big nose into other people's business. If you die on me I'll take it as a personal insult.'

Marion looked at her in surprise. 'You're making fun of me?'

'No dearie, I'm making fun of myself.' Peggi took hold of Marion's clammy hand and squeezed it. 'Marion, I cannot imagine what it is like to lose a beloved son, but I know you have it in yourself to bear it. We island women do. And you *have* to recover, for the sake of your other children. You do see that, don't you?'

Marion's chin trembled as she fought back tears. 'I don't love it – the baby,' she whispered. 'I don't even think I love Angus any more. I resent that he lives when Ranald doesn't. I can hardly bear to have him near me. Isn't that terrible to admit? I'm not worthy of being a mother, am I?'

Peggi gripped her hand. 'You are a good mother,' she insisted, 'who is lost in the storm. But the storm will pass and the sun will return – I promise you that.'

Marion swallowed her tears. 'I wish I believed that.'

'If you like,' said Peggi, 'I will take Angus back to Nunton for a while. He can keep my Rana– my bairns company while you get your strength back. Agreed?'

Marion nodded, feeling a guilty wave of relief.

Peggi stood up and took Flora back to her cot. She kissed her button nose. 'You are as sweet as syllabub, wee Florrie.' And silently she prayed that the girl would prove a survivor.

As she picked up her plaid and threw it over her shoulders, Marion stopped her. 'Wait Peggi; do you believe in the power to curse?'

'Well cursing never seems to work on my husband,' Peggi joked.

But Marion did not laugh. She had fear in her voice. 'She cursed my sons and hoped they would drown; now one of them is dead.'

'Who said such a cruel thing?'

'Mairi MacVurich.'

Peggi felt a chill down her neck. She knew the young poetess and did not trust her. Mairi took offence easily. There was power in her strange-eyed look and she didn't doubt it could be used for mischief.

'That saucy besom?' Peggi said, shaking off the bad feeling. 'More gibberish flies out of her mouth than geese fly south in winter.' She almost added that Mairi had been wrong about Ranald drowning, but thought it insensitive. 'Angus will be safe with me, I promise.'

Marion nodded, her fear easing a fraction. She might resent Peggi MacLeod's bossy interference, but she trusted her with her son.

Peggi went and Marion lay back in exhaustion. It was the sound of two boys playing below her window that forced her out of bed and across to the window on shaky legs.

Her heart lurched in shock. There was Angus being chased by Ranald. She gasped and rapped on the window pane. The boys stopped and looked up. Angus waved and grinned. The other boy gave a half smile. He was ruddy-cheeked, round-faced and the hair, on second glance, was too red. Ranald Benbecula; not her Ranald.

Desolation swamped her. It would never be her Ranald playing below ever again. She crouched out of sight.

'Oh Ranald, my bonny bonny boy!' she wailed, and curled into a ball on the floor.

Chapter 10

The storms that autumn and winter were so severe that few boats crossed the Minch for weeks on end. The harvest of oats was blighted and a shipload of Benbecula's cattle was shipwrecked. Only one of the drovers survived; a reckless wiry youth called Donald Roy – one of the Baleshare MacDonalds – who clung to the shattered keel for two days and was rescued off Skye. When he returned in the spring to the delight of his family, who feared him drowned, he brought sombre news.

'Sir James of Sleat is dead. The funeral is to be held at Duntulm as soon as his kinsmen can gather.'

It was agreed that Benbecula and Milton would cross to Skye to represent the chief of Clanranald at the funeral of MacDonald of Sleat.

He clashed with Marion over taking Angus.

'The boy should be there to pay his respects – we are an important branch of the clan.'

'The seas are too rough still,' Marion fretted.

'We have the best boatmen in the Long Isle,' Milton declared.

'He has no mourning clothes fit for such an occasion.'

'Peggi Benbecula is having some made for him.'

This infuriated Marion. 'Am I to have no say in what happens to my son?'

Milton gave her a steely look. 'Aye, when you have him back in your household and behave like his mother.'

'I'm not well,' she protested.

'Then lie in bed and let the rest of us get on with life.'

She cursed him for his callousness, though only out of his hearing. Ranald's death and Flora's birth had driven them apart. Milton no longer came to her bed at night, but then she doubted whether she would have welcomed him if he tried. He had what he wanted from her – a healthy son and a daughter growing more robust as the days lengthened – so he had no further use for her, she thought bitterly.

Before the men set sail for Skye, Angus was brought home from Nunton to see her, dressed in his finery. He hesitated only a moment before rushing to her bedside.

'Mammy, I'm going on a big boat with Ranald Og and Donald Roy. Donald Roy's a cousin of the dead chief and he's going to march ahead of us in the big procession because he's more important. He says he'll probably get to carry the coffin too – 'cos only strong men like him and Father can do that job.'

'Well, well, this Donald Roy is very full of himself,' Marion said. 'Let me take a look at you.'

He stood, feet astride and hands on hips, mimicking his father. Marion's heart squeezed to see her five-year old dressed in kilt and fine blue doublet, his billowing shirt sleeves trimmed in clan colours, the bonnet sporting a buzzard's feather and making him seem taller. But then he had sprouted like a thistle since he had spent the winter at Nunton.

'You look a fine warrior, so you do,' Marion smiled at him. 'Come, let me kiss you.'

Angus hesitated, then did as she bid, throwing his arms about her neck with his old exuberance. She clung onto him, breathing in his smell. Her eyes pricked with tears. How she had missed him!

'When you return from the funeral, you must come home Angie,' she ordered. How could she not have wanted her affectionate son at her side?

He pulled away, his round face troubled.

'That is what you want, isn't it?' Marion asked.

Angus gave her a direct look. 'Can Ranald Og come and stay with us too?'

Her stomach tensed. 'I'm not sure Mistress Benbecula will want to part with her eldest son just to please you.'

'Then I want to stay at Nunton,' the boy said, his look stubborn. 'We play 'Castles' and Donald Roy is teaching us sword-fighting and they have a bardess who tells stories every night.'

'Which bardess?' Marion asked, fearing the answer.

'Mairi MacVurich,' said Angus. 'She sings like a skylark too – that's what Donald Roy says.'

'You stay away from that gypsy!' Marion cried. The boy pulled away in alarm. Marion caught his arm. 'I'm sorry, Angie. I'm not cross with you.'

He stood eyeing her warily.

'Listen, we'll ask your father to arrange for Ranald Og to spend some time here at Balivanich if that's what you want,' Marion promised. 'I just want you home.'

Angus brightened. 'And can Donald Roy come and visit too?'

Marion sighed, thinking of the wild youth from Baleshare Island across the bay who seemed to attract trouble wherever he went. 'I suppose so.'

Angus pulled away from her grasp. 'Where's Flora?' he asked.

'With Nurse,' Marion said, 'who's probably gossiping with Janet in the kitchen.'

'I've got a magic stone for Florrie,' Angus said eagerly.

'Let me see,' Marion smiled.

Angus dug it out of the small leather sporran hanging from his waist. He held out a smooth green pebble on the palm of his grubby hand.

'Will it make her wise and strong?' Marion teased.

'No,' Angus shook his head, 'it's to keep her safe.'

Marion's heart twisted. 'Where did you find it?'

'Ranald Og's Mammy gave it to me,' he said.

'Mistress Benbecula? Why did she do that?'

''Cos I had bad dreams. I put it under my pillow and the bad dreams went away. Ranald Og's Mammy got it from the Fairies – they make it work. Now Flora can have it so nothing bad will happen to her like it did to Ranald.'

Marion's eyes stung with tears as she watched him put it carefully back in its pouch. 'That's kind of you, Angie.'

Angus grinned then turned on his heels and dashed out of the room.

35

Marion covered her face with her hands. How ashamed she felt at her lack of attention to her son these past bleak months; leaving it to Peggi MacLeod to comfort the confused and bereft boy. And what of Flora, the baby she found so hard to love? She had neglected her too – punishing her for not being another son to fill the hellish void left by Ranald. Wee Angie had shown more concern and compassion for his baby sister than Flora's own mother had.

Forcing herself onto shaky feet, Marion pulled on her robe. She steeled herself to descend the stairs, clutching onto the wooden bannister. It needed a polish and the tapestry that hung in the hallway blocking out the draught needed the dust beating out of it. In her fog of grief, she had neglected all her duties.

She appeared in the kitchen like a ghost, her face pale as candle wax.

'Mistress!' Janet gaped; she was cradling Flora in her lap. Angus was standing over them, tickling the baby's chin and making her chuckle.

Janet stood up quickly and handed Flora over to her nurse. Marion felt a pang that she did not think to hand the baby to her.

'You shouldn't be out of bed Mistress. What is it you want?' Janet tried to steer her into a chair but Marion resisted.

'I would like to take tea,' she said, breathless at the effort of coming downstairs.

'In the parlour, Mistress?'

'Yes, if you will,' Marion nodded.

She came forward and rested a hand on Angus's dark head of hair while she looked warily at her daughter, propped on the nurse's hip. Flora gazed back at her with solemn eyes; she already had a mop of curls – lighter than her brother's – that framed her pink cheeks. How was it, Marion wondered, that one so small could give such a challenging look? She wanted to stretch out and touch her soft skin but was frightened the baby might protest and start to cry.

'And I want Flora brought upstairs too,' Marion ordered. 'From now on, she will sleep in my bedchamber.'

Chapter 11

After MacDonald of Sleat's funeral – a huge affair with chiefs from all over the Highlands in attendance to see 'the Knight' laid to rest – Milton lingered on Skye with his young son. He wanted Angus to meet his kinsmen from the mainland, as well as members of the more powerful and numerous Sleat MacDonalds, such as the Kingsburghs. It was important that his heir learnt from an early age the complex ties of blood and allegiance that bound them all together, for one day his kin might need to call on him for help – or he on them.

There was much discussion among the senior men about Sir James's young successor, Alexander, who was hardly out of boyhood. It was agreed that Kingsburgh as his tutor would continue to foster the lad, until he was old enough to go to St Andrew's university alongside the sons of Scotland's aristocracy.

It was an emotional meeting for Milton – the first time he had seen Alexander since the tragedy with Ranald – and the young chief seemed embarrassed by the old man's tearful embrace.

'When you visit your lands in the Long Isle,' Milton told him, 'you will be welcome at Balivanich.'

'Thank you sir,' Alexander said with a bashful nod.

'North Uist is just across the Sound from us,' Milton continued, 'and it would be an honour to have MacDonald of Sleat at our hearth.'

The youth looked to Kingsburgh for guidance.

'That is a kind gesture indeed,' Kingsburgh said, 'and when the time is right, Sir Alexander will make a tour of his lands in the Outer Isles.'

Later, Kingsburgh took Milton aside. 'What we spoke of last summer,' he said quietly, 'testing the waters for … for support of our friends in Rome?'

'Aye,' Milton nodded, 'I remember. My kinsman Benbecula is lukewarm. It is only eight years since the Clanranalds were burnt out of their home at Ormiclate and much of the land is still forfeit to the Crown. He will take a lot of persuading – though his young MacLeod wife is enthusiastic to the Cause.' Milton grunted, 'if anyone can persuade my kinsman to swap his books for his claymore, then it is Peggi of Berneray.'

'Aye,' Kingsburgh smiled, 'the Bernerays are a hardy breed, right enough. But now is not the time to be reckless,' he warned. 'It would be foolhardy for us Sleat MacDonalds to provoke a rising now with Sir James dead and the new chief too young to lead us. He must be given time. The poor lad is like a pup who has lost its master.'

Milton clapped a hand on Kingsburgh's shoulder. 'Well, if anyone can teach him how to be a leader of men, then it is you, young Kingsburgh.'

As Milton took his farewells and began the voyage back across the Minch with Angus, he thought with envy of Benbecula and his spirited wife and Kingsburgh with his warm-hearted Florence. He knew that Marion could hardly bear to have him near her; the drawn angry look on her face these past months cut him like a dagger and only deepened his

37

sense of guilt over Ranald. Returning to Skye and showing Angus where his older brother was buried had not brought relief; only a renewed feeling that he had failed to protect Marion's firstborn. Still, as the blue hazy outline of Benbecula grew clearer and he could make out the safe anchorage at Rossinish, his heart lifted. He would soon be reunited with his bonny daughter. Flora would raise plump arms to him in greeting even if his wife proffered a cool cheek.

***

Marion felt she had awoken from a dark spell. The moment she had decided to get up from her bed and live again, her energy and zest for life had returned. The house had been spring-cleaned from top to bottom; the rooms swept, the hangings washed, linens pressed and silver polished. Milton's bedroom was redecorated with red curtains around the bed and a matching counterpane with material ordered from a merchant in Stornoway on Lewis.

Marion had sent for Angus's belongings from Nunton and confided in Peggi Benbecula her son's request that Ranald Og come to stay with them.

'Perhaps he could spend the summer with us?' Marion asked, fearing a rebuff. 'He could take part in driving the cattle up to the summer pastures at Milton — he could learn much about droving from my husband.'

Peggi had considered her with her sharp-eyed look, then nodded.

'Every gentleman's son should be taught the skills of the droving,' she agreed. 'I don't hold with these Lowland gentry who squeal at the sight of good honest muck.'

'So you'll let Ranald Og come to us?' Marion brightened.

'I will plant the seed of the idea in my husband's mind,' Peggi smiled, 'until it grows into his own idea. Milton would be an excellent tutor to our boy — I'd be happy for Ranald Og to board with you.'

With Peggi's blessing, Marion felt a renewed sense of worth and optimism about the future. She was even growing to enjoy her daughter's company — Flora was inquisitive yet sunny-natured with ready smiles — and Marion kept on the wet nurse to ensure her baby thrived.

When word came through that Milton and his entourage had landed at Rossinish, Marion did the rounds of kitchen and dairy to make sure there was ample to eat and drink when the travellers arrived.

***

Milton did not hide his astonished delight at being met by Marion dressed in a fine blue gown with lace trimmings and yellow bows, cut low across her breasts. Her fair hair cascaded to her shoulders under a small lace cap and her face was flushed from spring sunshine and fresh air. He had not seen her look so well or so desirable since before her pregnancy with

38

Flora, and the smile with which she greeted him made his heart skip like a lovesick youth.

He seized her hand and pressed it to his lips. 'You look well, wife,' he smiled in return.

'The better for seeing you and Angie safely returned,' she answered.

'Angus has been a credit to the name of Clanranald,' Milton told her proudly. 'Many remarked on the boy's good behaviour at the funeral and his friendly chatter to all ranks – he quite charmed them, our boy.'

Marion felt a glow of pride at his words. 'I wish I had been there to see it, husband.'

Linking her arm in his he said, 'you may have your chance to meet the young chief and his henchmen sooner than you think.'

'Really?'

'Aye, young Sleat has promised to visit us on his next tour to the Long Isle.'

'That is grand!' Marion gasped in pleasure, thinking how long it was since there had been a chief on the island to honour with banquets and sports. Clanranald had been in exile since the time of her marriage, and the invalid Sir James had seldom ventured to his remote holdings on North Uist.

Encouraged by Marion's new warmth towards him and her effort to take back the reins of housekeeping at Balivanich, Milton climbed the stairs that night to her bedchamber.

She opened the door to his tentative knocking, dressed only in a loose bed-gown of fine linen. A single candle burned in its silver stick, throwing soft light onto the pale yellow hangings. From her crib, Flora snuffled in her sleep. Neither spoke as Milton cast off his plaid and stood half naked in his shirt. Eagerly, he pulled the ribbon that held up her gown and pushed it from her shoulders.

'My beautiful Marion,' he gasped.

She lay back on the bed as he threw off his shirt and straddled her quickly. His kisses were feverish and he was instantly aroused. Marion closed her eyes and imagined it was Hugh. She could not help herself. Milton had the vigour of a much younger man and she clung onto him, allowing him to pleasure her in frenzied love-making.

Afterwards, he lay back panting, an arm thrown possessively across her belly.

'I've missed our intimacy,' he murmured.

'So have I,' Marion whispered.

He propped himself up on his elbow and studied her in the weak light. 'Truly?' he demanded.

'Yes. I want us to be close again, like we were before …' She could not bring herself to say Ranald's name to him.

'Oh, Marion, my sweet lassie, that is what I want above all else too.'

He bent and kissed her again. Marion felt a wave of relief; she never again wanted to be as alone as she had been these past terrible months. She was still a young woman with needs and desires; she would not live like an old maid lying on her own in a cold bed every night. And she wanted more children. She would never be able to say this to Milton, but she craved being a mother again and she wanted a houseful of sons, so that every waking hour would be full of their noise and laughter. For Marion longed for the day when she would forget how much she adored her lost Ranald, and the pain would go away for good.

Chapter 12

1727

Flora's first clear memory was of being thrown high in the air by her father; his strong arms sweeping her off her feet and raising her up, tossing her into the sky. For a moment she felt like a bird soaring above his mane of grey hair and laughing face, then she was screaming as she fell and he caught her in his massive roughened hands.

'Careful Milton!' a woman had cried out. Looking back Flora thought it must have been her mother, for Marion was always chastising them for something. But she had no clear image of her mother's pretty fair face; only of her father's leathery cheeks and toothless grin as he held her tight and then flung her heavenwards again.

Her second strong memory was of her grandfather's funeral. The old minister was a shadowy figure in her life – a tall wiry old man with a loud sing-song voice – whom her mother must have loved more than any of them, because she cried for days on end and would not come out of her chamber. Janet had kept Flora away when she'd tried to go to her mother.

'Mammy's very sad, you must leave her alone.'

'But I want to kiss her better,' Flora had cried.

'Not yet little kitten.' Janet had pulled her away from the locked door and enticed her downstairs with the promise of crowdie, her favourite crumbly, salty cheese.

Flora grew used to these times when her bustling and talkative mother disappeared suddenly into what Janet called her 'black storms'. They came like bad weather, lasting for up to a week and then went. Everyone learnt to keep out of the way, to walk softly on the stair and not to make a noise below Marion's window. Sometimes, Milton would take Flora, Angus and Ranald Og – for young Benbecula spent more time with them than at Nunton – away to his tack of land on South Uist. At the farm at Milton, the children would help round up the cattle and steer them up to the summer pastures in the hills.

Flora loved to be outdoors – would have stayed all summer with the women and boys who tended the beasts if she had been allowed – and was never happier than when racing the other children or riding her own sturdy Highland pony.

'That lassie was born to the saddle,' Milton declared, proud that his daughter had learnt to cling onto a horse's mane before she was barely walking.

Best of all, Flora loved the company of her brother Angus and his friends; teasing Ranald Og, Lachie the boatman's son and the MacEachen lads from the neighbouring farm at Howbeg. Twice her age, the boys taunted her and ran off as often as they let her join in their games, but that never put her off. It made her the more determined to win. Her favourite MacEachen was fair-haired Neil. He was different from his darker-haired brothers and not as boisterous, but he was quick and strong and stood up to Ranald Og when he tried to lord it over them.

One summer day when they had been playing up on the crag and fishing in a small pool, a sudden downpour turned the rocky crevice into a treacherous torrent. The boys leapt across, but Flora was stuck on the far side, too small to make the leap. She clung to a spindly rowan tree above the waterfall and wailed for help.

'Jump!' Angus called.

'I can't! I'm stuck.'

'Silly Flora!' Ranald Og shouted. 'You shouldn't have come.'

The older MacEachens were already halfway down the slope, flinging stones at each other in the rain. Ranald Og ploughed off after them, ordering them to wait.

Angus hesitated, wanting to join the others but not sure what to do about his troublesome sister. Then Neil turned and saw what was happening. He scrambled back up the slope, pushing Ranald Og out of his way.

'Not much of a chieftain are you,' Neil challenged, 'if you can't even rescue your wee lass.'

'She's not mine,' Ranald Og retorted.

Neil gave him a withering look. 'She's your kin.' He leapt back across the swollen burn and held out his arms. 'Come on, Florrie, jump on my back.'

Flora slid down the tree and Neil hitched her behind him, grabbing her legs as she gripped him round the neck. They were now too heavy to jump and the stream was widening in the pouring rain, so Neil plunged barefoot into the racing water. Immediately the force of the water caught them and he lost his footing. As Neil went down, he twisted and threw Flora onto the heathery bank opposite. Angus was there to catch her and pull her to safety. Neil tried to stand up in the frothy water but the burn there was much deeper than he'd realised and he struggled against its pull. Flora watched in horror as their friend fought against the force of water that threatened to whisk him over the waterfall.

'Angus, help him!' she screamed.

Her brother whipped off his shirt and, holding onto one sleeve, flung it towards his friend.

'Catch hold of this Neilac,' he cried.

Neil launched himself with all his strength and managed to seize the shirt. Angus nearly toppled into the water as Neil yanked himself towards the bank. The shirt ripped but Neil was near enough for Angus to grab him and hold on while his friend hauled himself to safety.

The boys lay panting on the mossy ground, Neil's breeches and shirt drenched. Flora flung herself at Neil in relief.

'Oh Neilac, you're safe!'

Angus sat up in annoyance, pulling on his torn shirt.

'He nearly drowned 'cos of you! You shouldn't have come. That's the last time I let you tag along. Go and play with the girls.'

Flora looked at him in dismay. 'But I want to play with you,' she said, her chin beginning to tremble.

'Well you can't any more,' Angus was firm, 'you're not big enough. Isn't that right, Neil?'

'Aye,' Neil agreed, gently pushing Flora away and getting to his feet. 'Maybe when you're bigger and can keep up with us.'

'You don't want me!' Flora burst into sudden tears.

It was so unlike her to cry that the two boys stood and gaped.

'Come on Florrie,' Angus relented, 'you can still play with us – just not up here on the crag.'

'P-Promise?' Flora sobbed.

'Promise,' Neil answered swiftly and held out a hand. 'We'll give you a swing down the hill if you stop crying.'

Flora's tears subsided quickly. She grinned and held her hands up. With a boy either side, Flora skipped, jumped and stumbled through the wet heather back to Milton. They arrived bedraggled but happy, the harsh words forgotten. Even the scolding by Janet for the torn shirt and the state of Flora's dress, did not subdue them. Flora knew that whatever scrapes she got into, Angus and Neil would always be there to defend her.

***

Flora caught a cold and was confined indoors for several days. The house at Milton was little more than a summer bothy – a low-lying thatched dwelling of three rooms with a byre attached for the dairy cows – but Flora loved to sleep in the old box-bed in the corner of the kitchen with the smell of hay and animals wafting in from the cowshed. Her mother hated the place and never came on these summer trips to South Uist; Janet was sent to supervise instead.

At first Flora was listless and willing to lie close to the open fire, watching the servants cooking and listening to their chatter. They gave her hot milk and bannocks straight from the griddle and sang songs to soothe her. But soon she was feeling better and restless at the confinement. The boys had gone back up to the summer shieling to tend the cattle and Flora badgered her father to be allowed to follow.

'You can keep me company here, Florrie,' he smiled. 'I don't like being on my own.'

'Mother can come and then you won't be,' she suggested.

He looked suddenly sad. 'She is busy at Balivanich.'

'Why doesn't she like it here?'

'Your mother likes a comfortable parlour and lots of nice things about her.'

'But we have cows and dogs and hens in this house.'

'Yes,' Milton sighed, 'that's the problem. Your mother is not so interested in farming as you and me.' He pulled her onto his knee. 'But one day you, dear Florrie, will make a grand wife for some lucky gentleman farmer.'

'I'm going to marry Neil MacEachen when I grow up,' Flora announced.

Milton roared with laughter. 'That will be for your mother and I to decide.'

'Please let it be him, Father. He's very brave and kind to me and to cats, and Angus says he's like a brother to him – more than Ranald Og.'

'Neil's a fine lad,' Milton nodded, 'and the MacEachens are a good family.' He gently pinched her cheek. 'We will see.'

'Tell me a story, Father,' Flora asked, snuggling into his hold. 'Tell me the one about the fairy people and the white cattle that came out of the sea.'

He held her tight as he re-told one of the clan tales; she had heard it countless times before but loved to hear his deep, singsong voice repeat the familiar words. They were half way through the story when there was a drumming of hooves in the distance and a sudden commotion outside.

Flora slipped from her father's knee as he stood stiffly; she ran ahead.

Beaky-nosed Donald Roy sprang from the saddle. He ruffled Flora's chestnut curls in passing, and strode towards Milton.

'Sir, I bring news from Benbecula,' he panted. 'Is Ranald Og with you?'

Milton embraced him. 'The boy is up at the shieling with the other children. Is it grave news?'

Donald Roy nodded.

Milton, glancing at the curious faces of his farmhands said, 'Come away inside.' He motioned to Janet to bring refreshments for their messenger and led the way back into his chamber. Flora dodged Janet's hand and slipped in behind the men.

Donald Roy pulled off his bonnet and came straight to the point.

'Word has come from the Continent; Chief Clanranald is dead.'

Milton sank back heavily onto his wooden armchair. 'That is sad news indeed. And to die in exile away from his people – that is the worst kind of death for a chief.' Milton put his head in his hands. There was silence in the room and then Flora heard a low sob. Her father's shoulders heaved and she realised in shock that the noise came from him.

Donald Roy put a hand on the old man's shoulder. 'His body may be buried in foreign soil,' he said quietly, 'but his spirit will return to the lands of Clanranald, of that there is no doubt.'

Milton looked up, his face wet with tears. Flora crept forward.

'Are you crying Father?' she asked.

'What are you doing in here, lassie?' he croaked.

'I've never seen you cry before,' she said, shocked by the sight. She laid her head in his lap and reached her small arms around him in comfort. She felt his hand rest of her head.

'Flora,' he whispered, 'your chief has died. He was the father of us all. That is why I am full of sadness.'

Flora had never met this chief who was always spoken of with respect and awe, but she knew that he was the most important man to her father and the clan. Angus and Ranald Og said their chief had been chased out of Scotland by English soldiers in red coats and half the clan lands had been taken away. But they always spoke of the day when he would return and live again amongst them, free to be their leader once more. Now it seemed he never would.

After a moment, Donald Roy spoke. 'Benbecula asks that you make haste to Nunton and bring Ranald Og with you. The men of the clan are gathering to name the successor.'

Milton asked, 'is it to be as Clanranald decreed?'

'Aye,' Donald Roy answered. 'Shall I ride up and fetch the lad?'

'Thank you.' Milton nodded, disengaging himself from Flora. Donald Roy helped him to his feet. 'And bring Angus too.'

Donald Roy hesitated in the doorway. 'And young Neil MacEachen – should he come to Nunton? After all, he is a natural son of–'

'No,' Milton cut him off, 'I will not have Mistress Benbecula embarrassed at such a time.'

Donald Roy nodded and left.

Flora puzzled over this talk of the boys. 'Why is Donald Roy going for the boys, Father? Is there going to be a big funeral for the chief and they will have to carry him all the way to the grave like when Granddad Minister died?'

'No, my sweet,' Milton sighed. 'The chief is buried in a faraway land. The boys must go to Nunton to greet the new chief.'

'Can I come too?' she asked in excitement.

'Not this time.'

'That's not fair. Why can't I?'

'You must return to your mother and help prepare a welcome for our new leader.'

'Who is it Father? Who is the new chief?'

'Clanranald died without any sons,' Milton told her, 'so the chiefship goes to his nearest cousin: Benbecula.'

'Ranald Og's father?' Flora asked in surprise.

'Yes, Ranald Og's father.'

'Does that make Ranald Og very important now?'

'Aye, it does.' Milton smiled for the first time since the shock news. 'Though he already thinks he is.'

Flora slipped her hand into his. 'Can I still call him Ranald Og?'

'You may, while he remains in our household,' Milton said, 'but to the people of the clan he is now Young Clanranald and his father is the Captain.'

Chapter 13

Their time at Milton was abruptly cut short and the household returned to Balivanich on Benbecula. While Milton was sunk in sadness over the loss of the exiled Clanranald, Marion was enthused with a new energy in making preparations to entertain the new Clanranalds – in particular her friend Peggi MacLeod – and their rapidly expanding family. Flora listened to her mother chattering to Janet as they did their sewing.

'It's a great honour that the Benbeculas – I mean, the Clanranalds – continue to entrust their eldest to our care.'

'Aye Mistress, it is that. And the Master can make sure he doesn't grow too big for his boots.'

'Now Janet, I'll not have you criticising Ranald Og. He's growing into a fine figure and it's right that he should be proud of his position as chieftain.'

Flora piped up. 'I think he's a big bossy boots. He won't let me play with Angus any more.'

'Well that's no bad thing,' her mother said, 'your father has let you run wild this summer. It's time you learnt some household skills; isn't that right Janet?'

Janet winked at Flora. 'There's time enough for that. And Florrie is a great help at the milking – even with her wee hands.'

'I don't want them turning into rough maid's hands,' Marion objected, 'or she won't be able to hold a needle or show them off at the tea table. Flora, let me see your sampler.'

Flora held out her needlework for inspection; it was grubby from her efforts and she knew it wasn't good enough. She just didn't have the patience for sitting still.

'Oh dear,' Marion sighed, 'why do you pull the stitching so tight? Take out the thread and start that line again.'

***

News came through that the young chief of Sleat, Sir Alexander, was to take a tour of his property in North Uist that summer and while in the Long Isle, would call on the new Clanranald Captain in Benbecula.

'He's soon to go south to university at St Andrews,' Milton told them, 'and wishes to acknowledge our new chief before he goes. It's a fine gesture – one chief to the other – and bodes well for co-operation between the two MacDonald clans.'

'Will Sleat come with a large party?' Marion asked excitedly. Flora saw how the question seemed to irritate her father.

'Large enough,' he snapped. 'No doubt Kingsburgh will accompany him.'

'Kingsburgh,' Marion snorted. 'I hope we won't be expected to offer him hospitality.'

'Kingsburgh is my friend,' Milton barked, 'and you will show him and his family every courtesy if he should come here.'

Marion was suddenly tearful. 'He didn't keep my son safe, so why should I take care of him or any of his?'

'Don't blame him for Ranald's accident.' Her father looked furious.

'Then who should I blame?' her mother cried.

He stalked from the room without a reply. It was one of those baffling moments when her parents went from being happy to suddenly angry and shouting at each other. Flora and Angus usually ran off to their hideout in the byre and sat in the hay making up stories until they thought the argument over. But since Ranald Og had become Young Clanranald, Angus no longer came to the byre – Ranald Og told Angus it was too babyish – and so she had to puzzle their angry words on her own. She knew she had had an older brother called Ranald who had been killed in a shooting accident on Skye. It was sad of course, but then her mother had Angus and herself, and she didn't see why she should get so angry with her father all the time – or this Kingsburgh man who was somebody important to the Sleat MacDonalds.

Later, Flora found her father down on the shore gazing out to sea, leaning on a long stick that he used now for walking. She slipped her hand into his.

'What's out there, Father?' She always asked him this when they stood on the beach together.

'The Atlantic, daughter.'

'And what's beyond that?'

'St Kilda, the furthest of the Hebrides.'

'And what's beyond that?'

'More sea and more sea.'

'And what's beyond the sea?'

'A big land called America.'

She smiled. 'Tell me what America is like.'

'They say it's full of rivers and lochs the size of the sea,' he smiled down at her, 'and forests that go on forever.'

'What's a forest look like, Father?'

'You know the rowans and hazel trees that grow at the waterfall?'

She nodded.

'Well imagine that the whole island was covered in those and all you could see was the next tree; that's a forest.'

Flora felt a thrill at the idea of a land full of rowans.

'And who lives in the forest?' she asked, knowing what he would say.

'Wild Americans,' he grinned, squeezing her hand.

'Will we go there one day and visit them?' Flora asked.

'I'll get Lachlan to make a boat big enough to take us over the Atlantic, shall I?'

Flora nodded. 'As long as Angus comes too.'

'Of course Angie will come.'

'And Neil MacEachen?'

Her father hesitated then agreed. 'If Neil wants adventure then he had better come with us.'

***

Nunton was an imposing house dominating the shoreline of west Benbecula and Peggi MacLeod, now Lady Clanranald and known affectionately as Lady Clan, had laid on enough food and drink for a small army. She had sent to Balivanich to borrow their best chairs, extra linen and glassware so that they could seat all their visitors and guests at tables set for a lengthy banquet.

The Miltons went over to help, along with Donald Roy's family from Baleshare. Clanranald's brother Boisdale came up from South Uist, along with the MacEachens, while Lady Clanranald's kinsman, the mighty MacLeod of Berneray – nicknamed the 'Trojan' for his martial strength – came with his vast family.

Flora was ecstatic to see the MacEachen boys and was soon running around with them on the grassy sward marked out for sport and competition.

When Sir Alexander and the Skye entourage arrived to the noisy blast of their own pipers, Flora, Angus and their friends rushed with curiosity to see these rival MacDonalds. Sir Alexander was tall and lanky, with blond hair tied back under a bonnet decorated with three eagle's feathers, denoting his chiefly status. Flora thought he had a kind face which blushed easily, and he looked far too young to be a chief.

There was much greeting and speechifying to which the children soon got bored; they ran off, followed by the handful of children who had come with the Sleats. One of them, a stocky black haired boy, with a broad lively face, challenged one of the MacEachens to arm-wrestle. The stocky boy won easily. Angus, who vaguely remembered him from old Sleat's funeral on Skye, took him on but was beaten too.

'Anyone else want to try?' the Sleat boy grinned. 'Or are all you Long Islanders as weak as old wives?'

'What's your name?' Neil demanded, stepping forward.

'Allan of Kingsburgh,' he said proudly.

'I'll race you to the beach and back,' Neil challenged.

They hared off, leaping hummocks of stony ground and tufts of marram grass, as they sprinted away.

'Come on Neilac!' Flora and Angus yelled, while his brothers jumped up and down, whistling and shouting him on. 'Show that Skye boy who's best!'

Neil was the faster on the way down but as they turned and headed back up the slope, Allan gained ground. They came in neck and neck, hurling themselves across the rope that the boys held up as the finishing line.

'Neil won!' Angus cried.

'No he didn't,' one of the Skye boys protested. 'Allan touched the rope first.'

'Neil had his foot over the line before that,' Flora shouted.

Allan swung round and laughed in derision. 'Lassies can't judge.'

'Yes they can!' Flora went pink with indignation. 'My eyes are twice as good as yours.'

Allan rushed at her with staring eyes. 'Like this you mean?' He deliberately crossed his eyes and fell over. His friends hooted with laughter.

Flora lashed out. 'Well you're a cheat and I hate you – and my mother hates your father – I heard her say so, 'cos he let my brother Ranald die!'

There was a sudden silence. Allan looked at her in astonishment, picking himself up.

'That's a lie,' he said, blushing. 'I don't even know your brother. And nobody calls me a cheat.' He shoved at Flora.

'Leave my sister alone!' Angus hurled himself at Allan and a fight erupted between the rival packs. They rolled on the ground, punching and kicking. Flora was suddenly afraid; she backed off but was knocked over in the melee and skinned her knees.

Eventually, servants from the house came out and broke up the fight, hauling the boys to their feet and cuffing them for their lack of hospitality to their guests. They were summoned inside and scolded affectionately by Lady Clanranald.

'Boys will be boys,' she snorted, 'and it seems Milton's girl enjoys a bit of sport too, eh Florrie? I was just the same, wasn't I Donald?' She waved across at her cousin, the Trojan.

'Aye Peggi, we lads were all afraid of you,' he chuckled.

Her remarks diffused the tension and the banquet got under way. It lasted for hours, the servants replenishing the dishes of fowl, venison, hare and herring as soon as they ran out. In between courses there was entertainment; Clanranald's piper and harpist both played and the Clanranald's young daughter Penelope played a duet on the spinet with her mother Peggi. Flora was entranced that a girl of five, the same age as her, could be so clever and make such a beautiful sound. Then Penelope was requested to sing a French song that she had newly learnt.

No sooner had she finished than Milton announced that Flora would sing too.

'But in the Gaelic, Florrie,' he ordered, 'in honour of our two chiefs.'

Flora was taken by surprise. She looked down the long table of guests and felt overawed.

'Come lassie and stand by me,' her father beckoned. She heard her mother murmur something about not being prepared, but Milton ignored this.

Flora went nervously to her father's side. The songs she knew by heart were lullabies that Janet had crooned over her, or the working songs that she heard around the farm and that the women sang when they sat spinning or making cloth. Perhaps the Captain and Sir Alexander would like one about cows at milking time? Her mouth felt suddenly too dry to sing. People were staring at her. She wanted to run from the room.

Just then Flora caught sight of Allan Kingsburgh's smirking face. He just thought her a silly Long Isle girl who couldn't even fight; well she'd show him that she could sing in front of all these important people. She was proud of being a Clanranald MacDonald.

Flora lifted her dainty chin, pushed back her curls and began to sing. The last murmurings died away as her clear sweet voice filled the dining-hall with an ancient song about hunters and mermaids and then a lullaby about cows returning home in the evening. As she finished, the room erupted in applause and the thumping of tables. Even her mother was smiling with pleasure which made Flora's insides feel warm.

She pulled a face at Allan who still seemed to be laughing at her, and went to join her brother and Neil. After further eating and a lot more wine drinking, Clanranald called on his young bardess, Mairi MacVurich to recite a poem.

Flora, growing bored with the banquet, watched the poet rise slowly to her feet and sweep down the hall in her plaid like a queen. Mairi, with her mane of red hair and her different coloured eyes, fascinated Flora. For some reason she was never invited to Flora's home at Balivanich, even though she and her old infirm father were some of their nearest neighbours. Flora thought Mairi was probably one of those magical mermaids – a silkie – that take on human form so they can live on land for a while.

Mairi stood with eyes closed and Flora wondered if she had fallen asleep standing up. Then all of a sudden, she threw up her arms, opened her eyes and began to chant. All the men were staring at her, transfixed, as she recited her poem in a voice that rose and fell in rhythm with her waving arms. It was as if they had fallen under a silkie's spell, Flora thought. The women didn't look the same. Her mother's face was angry and Aunt Peggi was putting her arms around Penelope as if she was worried the silkie might steal her away.

Mairi's poem went on for ages about the greatness of the Clanranalds, how good they were in battle and generous in feasting. Then just when Flora thought it was coming to an end, the bard turned to Sir Alexander and stared praising him and his ancestors until he was as red as a lobster. When it finally came to an end, people pushed back their chairs, stood up unsteadily and raised their glasses to toast both Mairi and the chiefs.

In the noise and confusion of the toasting and pushing back tables for dancing, Flora and some of the other children took the chance to escape from the dining hall. Outside it was still light, though the sky was a golden colour from the evening sun. Tomorrow there was to be a day of sport and music and more feasting before the Sleat party travelled on to North Uist. Flora and Angus would share a cramped bedroom with the Clanranald children; the MacEachens would bed down in the stables.

They ran around in the twilight playing hide and seek till it grew dark, nobody bothering to call them in or send them to bed. The sound of piping drifted out of open windows as the adults danced inside. When it was Allan's turn to hunt them down, Flora ran after Angus and Ranald Og to hide.

'You can't come with us Flora,' Ranald Og said, 'you'll give us away.'

Flora expected Angus to speak up for her, but he just shrugged and ran off after his friend.

Neil appeared at her side. 'Come on Florrie, I know a good place.' To her delight, he grabbed her hand and pulled her after him.

At the back of the kitchen buildings and outhouses there was a door leading down into the cellar. It was dark and damp; full of musty-smelling barrels and caskets.

'I don't like it,' Flora hissed, 'I think a witch might live here.'

She heard Neil snort with amusement and then say, 'It's a secret way in.'

He fumbled forward, Flora clinging onto his jacket, and pushed open a tiny door at the back of the cellar. 'Careful, there are steps up.'

They inched up a wooden spiral staircase, Flora's heart thumping in fear and excitement. She clutched his hand tightly so he couldn't let go. The only light came from the dim cellar below. She heard Neil lift a latch and then they were stepping into a room hardly bigger than a cupboard with a small window that let in a patch of twilight. Flora could make out a narrow bed, a table and chair. It smelt musty like the cellar.

'Where are we?' she gasped.

Neil shushed her and guided her to sit on the bed. Flora wasn't sure whether she felt happy at being with Neil or frightened that they would never be found. She became aware of adult voices close by but couldn't work out where the people could be; there didn't seem to be another door to this strange room.

She recognised Aunt Peggi's loud laugh and thought she heard her mother's voice. But there were men's voices too; Ranald Og's father and a younger man's, perhaps Sir Alexander?

'They're behind the panelling,' Neil whispered, 'in Captain Clanranald's study. There's a door in the panelling but it's hidden by a bookcase.'

'This is a secret room?' Flora whispered, feeling a thrill.

'Aye, it's called a priest's hole – somewhere to hide him if any government men come spying on us Catholics – or that interfering Obadiah Gunn.'

'I wish we had a priest's hole,' Flora replied, 'so me and Angie could hide from Mr Gunn when he comes to give us Bible study – and his son Elijah who smells of cabbage and picks his nose.'

Neil suppressed a laugh. 'You can't have a priest's hole 'cos you're Presbyterians.'

'Well I still want one,' Flora said. 'Anyway, how do you know about this place?'

After a moment Neil said, 'Sometimes Ranald Og's father invites me to stay. He's teaching me Latin and Greek.'

Flora peered at him in the dark. 'Just you and not your brothers?'

'Just me,' Neil said.

51

Flora thought about this for a bit. 'Maybe it's because you're the brainy one in your family.'

'Maybe,' he replied, and she could tell that he was smiling.

***

Sitting at Clanranald's fireside, Marion thought how much she had enjoyed the day; she could not remember the last time they had been to such an important gathering and spent hours feasting and chatting. It made her realise how isolated she had become at Balivanich where they hardly ever entertained – Milton was always so distracted with business – and she had lost the appetite for sociability since Ranald's death. But today, her joy at being with others had been rekindled, especially dancing with young men of the clan nearer her own age than her elderly husband. Even the sight of Mairi MacVurich showing off and flirting with Sir Alexander had not spoilt her fun. She had to admit a twinge of disappointment that the entourage from Sleat had not included her dashing Hugh *Cam*, but then she had no idea where her former lover was these days or with whom he might be living.

Emboldened by the claret that she had drunk, and with her husband still lingering in the dining hall with the pipers, Marion decided to ask.

'Sir Alexander,' she smiled, 'I wonder how the Sartle MacDonalds from Camas are? They used to travel with your father when he came to the Long Isle.'

'Sartle Senior is well thank you,' Alexander replied. 'He is helping with the planting of more trees around Armadale.'

'And his younger brother Hugh?' she pressed.

'Hugh *Cam*?'

'Yes; is he still soldiering?' she asked.

'He is,' Alexander nodded, 'with a Scottish regiment in the French army. But I haven't seen him since–' Abruptly he broke off, his fair face flooding with colour.

'Since when?' Marion asked, thinking how handsome he was when he blushed.

He began to stammer. 'W-when there – when there w-was that terrible accident – w-with young Milton.'

Marion felt thumped in the stomach. 'My Ranald?' she gasped. 'Hugh was there when my son was shot?'

The Clanranalds fell silent beside her.

'Y-yes,' Alexander said. 'Well, he didn't actually see it happen. Kingsburgh went rushing to get Milton you see – and Hugh *Cam* was with him.'

Marion was stunned. Hugh had been there – had met his own son – yet Milton had never told her. Had Hugh guessed that Ranald was his? Alexander felt he had to fill the silence.

52

'We did what we could for him – but he was too injured – we made him as comfortable as we could – Hugh knew about gunshot wounds – he stayed with him till the end.'

'Till the end?' Marion cried. 'How long did he suffer?'

'No more than a c-couple of hours.'

'Hours!' Marion shrieked, pushing back her chair. It toppled over.

'My dear,' Peggi rose, 'you mustn't get distressed.'

Marion fended her off. 'Tell me please Sir Alexander,' she demanded, 'exactly what happened.'

'Best not,' Peggi warned.

'I just want to know,' Marion pleaded, 'no one has ever told me. *Please*?'

Alexander stood and faced her; he looked nervous but his blue eyes shone with compassion.

'R-Ranald was eager to do sport that day – we both were. He was better than me at the stone throwing; I was better at archery. He was impatient to show how good he was with a gun.' Alexander swallowed before continuing. 'Kingsburgh wouldn't let him handle the squibs of gunpowder – thought him too inexperienced – so he was loading Ranald's gun for him.'

'So it was Kingsburgh's fault?' Marion cried.

'No,' Alexander was quick to defend his tutor. 'I handed Ranald my gun so that he didn't have to wait – he was so keen to show us all – and then it went off in his hands …' The young chief looked close to tears. 'The fault was mine, Mistress Milton. I'm truly sorry.'

Marion let out a yelp of pain. Peggi rushed and gripped her round the shoulders.

'It's no one's fault – it was an accident,' she said firmly.

Marion gritted her teeth. 'And where was my husband?'

At that moment, Milton stepped unsteadily through the door. He had supped long and hard.

'Where was I when?' he grinned drunkenly at them.

Marion turned on him. 'When my Ranald was shot!'

Milton's smile vanished. He looked at the others aghast.

Alexander answered for him. 'Milton was seeing my father on important business – but he came straight back as soon as he was told.'

'And Hugh *Cam*?' Marion's voice quavered.

Milton answered before Alexander could. 'Hugh came back with me from the big house. We did what we could.'

'He took hours to die,' Marion said, almost choking. 'You lied to me Milton! And you never told me that Hugh was there!'

He saw the bitter anger in his wife's eyes and knew in that moment he had lost her for good. But the brave part of him knew he could offer her a slim reed of comfort, so he forced himself to go on.

'Hugh held Ranald and comforted him as if he was his own. He stayed with him till the end. Ranald died in his arms.'

Marion let out a howl, and pushing her way past him, fled from the room.

Chapter 14

'I don't want to go home,' Flora complained when her brother eventually found her and Neil emerging from the cellar.

'You have to,' Angus said. 'Mother's taken ill and you have to go with her.'

'I heard them shouting about our brother Ranald,' Flora told him. 'Is that why she's ill?'

Angus shrugged. He rarely talked about Ranald to her. She trailed along behind him.

'Who is Hugh *Cam*?' she asked.

'Don't know,' Angus said.

'He's the best swordsman in the whole of Skye and he fights for the French,' a voice rang out behind them. It was Allan. 'Got you!' He flung his arms roughly around her.

'Get off!' Flora shouted in irritation. 'The game's over. I have to go home.'

'Oh.' Allan let go but carried on walking beside them.

Flora couldn't resist asking. 'Why is he called Hugh *Cam*? Has he really only got one eye?'

'Yes,' Allan said, 'he wears a patch where he should have an eye.'

'Then how can he be good with a sword if he only sees half of everything?'

Allan laughed. 'Only a daft girl would say that. He can see just as well with one eye as everyone else sees with two.'

When Angus and Neil laughed too, Flora pushed Allan as hard as she could and then ran ahead to find her mother. He was probably the most annoying boy she had ever met; even more so than Ranald Og.

***

The good weather broke that night – the wind had whipped up on their ride home in the moonlight – and by daybreak the rain was horizontal. The games at Nunton were cancelled and the Sleat chief and his party left early for North Uist. Flora was pleased to see her father and Angus return, though both seemed subdued.

'Ranald Og will not be staying with us any more,' her father announced. 'He has reached the age where he needs a tutor to teach him Classics. Captain Clanranald has all the learning and books that his son needs now. I have taught him the ways of our people, so my job is done.'

Flora didn't like him sounding so sad, but when she tried to climb onto his knee and ask for stories to make him feel better, he waved her away. 'Not now, Flora.'

The bad weather seemed to bring on one of her mother's 'black storms' and Flora found herself confined to the house but unable to play in the light and airy upstairs parlour where her mother lay behind shuttered and curtained windows.

Even after the sun returned and a light breeze chased the clouds away, life did not return to how it had been. Her mother's 'storm' lingered for weeks and her father took himself off to the farm at Milton and didn't come back till the drovers gathered to herd the cattle onto boats at Rossinish in late summer.

Worst of all for Flora, Angus chose to spend most of the summer over at Nunton with Ranald Og and rarely came home, which meant that the MacEachen boys didn't come visiting either. She was left hanging around the farm or helping the women in the dairy. Sometimes she would persuade Peter-the-Stables to ride out with her on one of her father's small ponies and trot up the eastern hills that overlooked the Minch. On a clear day, she could see all the way to Skye and she couldn't help wondering about tiresome Allan Kingsburgh, and the mysterious Hugh *Cam* and her dead brother Ranald who was buried far from home.

As the oats turned golden in the fields, Milton announced over dinner, 'I'm going to accompany the drovers as far as Glenelg.'

'Can I come too Father?' Angus asked eagerly.

'And me,' Flora squealed.

'Not you,' Angus was dismissive. 'Girls can never be drovers.'

'I can,' Flora declared.

'Neither of you will be coming,' Milton said. 'Angus, I have arranged for you to join the Clanranald boys for schooling at Nunton.'

Marion looked up for the first time. 'Nunton? He's too young.'

'I'm nearly ten,' Angus said proudly.

'Old enough to be needing more knowledge than I can give him,' Milton said firmly. 'And from what I hear, he's practically living with the Clanranalds already.'

Flora thought her mother would object but with a sigh she dropped her gaze and said no more. Flora hated the silence between her parents.

'Where's Glenelg?' she asked.

'On the mainland opposite Skye,' her father said.

'Will you see the Kingsburghs?'

'I might well.'

But this seemed the wrong thing to say, for Marion snapped. 'You're too old for the droving. What are you thinking of, leaving us alone without a man in the house?'

Milton reached for his stick and hauled himself to his feet. 'My dear wife,' he said, 'I doubt you'll even notice I'm gone.'

***

Flora and Angus rode with their father up to the hills in South Uist to help with the rounding up of the cattle. Flora loved the sight of dozens of the small sturdy beasts – a patchwork of tan, cream and black – jostling and swaying down the glen. Their bellows of protest rang out in response to the whistles and calls of the drovers. Peter-the-Stables had been chosen to go for the first time and was running around eagerly, slapping the flanks of those that stopped to munch.

'One day soon I'll be going too,' Angus declared, dashing off after Peter and copying the older boy.

When Flora tried to follow, Milton called her back.

'Stay with me Florrie; they'll trample you.'

All day, her father barked out orders and pointed with his long stick. It took most of the day to bring them down from the pastures and by nightfall, Flora noticed how her father was limping and wheezing from the effort.

That night Milton took his children back to Balivanich and made final preparations for leaving early the following morning. Marion, accepting that her husband was determined to go on the drove, made an effort to lay on a large supper of trout and game and hens eggs.

Flora was encouraged by the way her parents spoke to each other over the meal. Her father made compliments about the food and her mother asked about the cattle. Maybe, when her father returned, they would be happy again and there would be no more 'black storms'.

As dawn broke, Flora heard her father moving around in his chamber below. When she heard him go out, she scrambled out of bed, anxious that he should not slip away without saying goodbye. Pulling on her woollen dress, she followed.

Outside there was no sign of him. She searched the stable but his horse was still there so she knew he hadn't gone far. She couldn't find him in the byre or the dairy. Eventually, she found Big Alasdair the piper at his door waiting to pipe his master from home.

'He's away down to the shore, Miss Flora,' he told her. 'Saying his farewell to the seals,' he chuckled.

Flora waved and scampered down the track towards the beach. Running through the tall marram grass, she followed her father's limping footprints over the soft dunes. The sand was rose-pink in the early light and the sea beyond rippled in the dawn breeze.

To her delight she saw him standing at the water's edge rubbing himself dry with his plaid. He had been in the sea with the seals! He was singing them a rowing song as their heads bobbed up and down with curiosity.

She called to him from the top of the dune. 'Father!'

He turned; his craggy face caught in the morning light, showed surprise and then pleasure. She waved.

'Florrie!' he cried. He hitched his plaid around him and, reaching for his stick, raised it in greeting.

She jumped down the dune, her bare feet sinking into cold powdery sand. She loved it when she had her father to herself and his smiles and words were just for her.

Crossing the beach she saw him drop the stick. He looked puzzled as if he hadn't meant to let go. He clutched his arm.

'I'll get it!' Flora cried, running closer.

He let out a strange noise like bagpipes deflating. He pitched sideways and crumpled onto the sand. Flora wondered if this was a game. She bounded up to him. He was lying awkwardly, face upwards, eyes staring.

'Father? What are you doing?'

She crouched down, frightened by his silence. She thought she heard a soft sigh escape his lips; they were bluish from the cold sea.

She shook his shoulder. 'Get up Father, please!'

But he did not move and did not reply. She sat there, waiting for him to end the strange game and get up.

Chapter 15

The funeral of Ranald MacDonald of Balivanich and Milton brought mourners from the length of the Long Isle and beyond. It was a huge affair with a dozen pipers and a procession of Highland gentry from the ranks of Clanranald, as well as that of MacDonalds of Sleat and MacLeods of Berneray.

Special mourning clothes were made for Marion and her children, cattle were slaughtered for the funeral feast and vast quantities of venison, fowls and salmon were procured, along with casks of whisky, port and French wine.

'The merchants will do well out of us,' Flora heard Marion's dry remark to Janet.

But her mother refused to let her husband's kinsmen take over the organising of the wake or the hospitality. 'This is still my house,' she told Lady Clanranald firmly, 'and I will be the one to see that my husband's funeral feast befits his high station in the clan.'

'Good for you Marion,' Peggi approved, 'call on me for any help you might need.'

When Obadiah Gunn came by to offer condolences and criticise her for not allowing him to take part in the service, Marion rounded on him.

'My husband's brother, Reverend Donald, is coming from Arisaig to take the service and if that's not good enough for you, then you can complain as much as you like to your mealy-mouthed presbytery.'

'But madam–'

'I don't have time for your carping words, Mr Gunn,' she cut him off. 'And don't pretend you are sorry at my husband's death – you didn't have a good word to say about him when he lived and breathed. So kindly leave my house and don't bother coming back.'

Flora and Angus gazed, open-mouthed, as the missionary stalked away in high dudgeon.

'That's the last we'll see of the Full-Bottomed Whig,' Angus crowed.

But the look Obadiah threw them, made Flora worry he had overheard his disparaging nickname.

Flora watched the frantic activity around the house and farm with a sad heart. Somehow it felt like her fault that her father had fallen over on the sand and not been able to get up. Perhaps if she hadn't waved and called out to him, he might have lived? But she couldn't talk about it to anyone – not even Angus – in case they blamed her too. So she stayed quiet.

On the day of the funeral, her spirits lifted to see the MacEachens arrive. Neil gave her a shy hug. 'I'm very sorry Florrie; I know how much you'll miss him.'

She cried as she watched the men of the clan lift her father's coffin and carry him from his chamber and out of Balivanich for the last time. Big Alasdair led the procession from the homestead and the noise of pipes drowned out the wailing of the women as they stood in their low doorways, wrapped in plaids against the buffeting wind.

She saw Mairi MacVurich rush from her cottage and throw something – a briar rose? – onto the coffin, raising her arms and chanting words that were lost in the din.

Flora followed a short way, until Janet fetched her back. They stood on a low hummock gazing at the sea of people who lined the wayside or joined the procession to the burial ground. The hum of pipes and sorrowing could still be heard after the funeral party was out of view.

Later, when the men returned and the funeral meats were brought out and the wine and whisky was flowing, there was much reminiscing about Milton. Flora hunkered behind a dining-room chair with Angus and Neil, listening to tales of her father's strength and bravery.

'Aye, a man you'd always want at your side,' said his brother Donald.

'And a man of justice,' said Captain Clanranald.

'Sometimes rough justice,' laughed the Trojan. 'I remember the news travelled all the way up to Berneray that he'd strung up a tenant of his who'd murdered their wife.'

'Aye, he did that with his own bare hands,' nodded old MacVurich. 'Roped him up and left him swinging in the wind for a week.'

'And no one in Balivanich has murdered his wife since,' grunted Donald.

They raised their glasses once again and toasted their departed kinsman.

The wake went on long into the night. The candles burned down as the men carried on drinking and talking, breaking into melancholy song and weeping drunken tears for Milton.

The next day most left, but a handful of senior kinsmen – led by Clanranald and his brother Boisdale – stayed on to decide the family's future. They were left closeted in Milton's chamber, going through his papers and making a reckoning of the heavy costs of the funeral. Flora heard them arguing, and every so often they would emerge to demand more whisky punch and food.

'What will happen to us?' Flora asked her mother.

But Marion, who had risen to the challenge of mass hospitality for the funeral, had retreated to her bed in exhaustion and could not answer her anxious questions.

'Will we stay on here or go to Milton?' Flora persisted.

Marion sighed. 'I don't know – it is out of my hands.' Then added, 'but it is the custom for a widow to be returned to her own kin.'

Flora pondered this. 'Does that mean Uncle Archibald at Howbeg?'

But she got no further answer. She and Angus crept off to their old hideaway in the byre and discussed it.

'If we go to Howbeg at least we will be near to the MacEachens,' Flora said.

Angus pulled a face. 'I don't want to live at Howbeg – it's cold and Aunt Agnes never gives you enough to eat.'

Flora had no memory of her uncle's house; they had last visited at the time of Grandfather Minister's funeral.

'I think we will stay on here,' Angus was optimistic. 'I am the heir to the lands here and at Milton.'

'But you aren't old enough, are you?' Flora worried. 'You can't tell people what to do.'

'I will be soon,' Angus said in hope.

Over the next couple of weeks, men appeared around the homestead, sizing up the stock and making a note of the number of cows in calf, milk cows and yearlings. A week later, as the weather turned stormy and autumnal, they returned and drove off large numbers of the beasts. That same week, Marion packed them off with Peter for a day to collect mussels at low tide. When they returned the house was bare of furniture. Flora rushed from room to room. She clattered upstairs and found her mother packing clothes into a trunk. The yellow curtains and bed cover were gone, as were the carved tea table and the fire irons.

'Where are all the chairs? And Father's pictures?' Flora asked.

'Are we moving house?' Angus demanded.

Marion bowed her head and let out a sob. They rushed to her and put their arms around her.

'Tell us Mother,' Angus urged.

Marion pressed her hand against her mouth and gulped. She swallowed her tears and taking a deep breath, put her arms around her children.

'There was a sale at the house today. People came and took things away. The family needs money to pay for Father's funeral – and – and to provide for us in the future.'

'Is that why the cattle had to go?' Angus asked.

Marion nodded. She pulled them towards the bed and sat them down either side of her.

'Angus, your father's kinsmen have decided that you will still go to live at Nunton as your father wanted and be schooled with the Clanranalds. It's a great honour and they are being very generous to provide for you until you come of age.'

'Why can't I stay here with you and Flora?' Angus protested. 'I'm the man of the house now and this is where I should be.'

Marion smiled sadly and squeezed him to her. 'In time you may be able to take on the tack at Milton. Clanranald is generously keeping that tack of land in your name. But not here.'

'Not here?' Angus puzzled.

'Balivanich was only your father's under a wadset – a loan,' she explained. 'It must now be farmed by someone else who can take on that loan.'

'Who?' Angus asked.

Marion shrugged. 'That will be for the Captain to decide, but I've heard rumour that it might be one of the Baleshare MacDonalds – maybe Donald Roy.'

Flora struggled to take it all in. 'So we can't live here any more?'

'No,' her mother said, 'we can't. That is why we are packing up and flitting.'

61

'Where to?'

'You and I are being given a home by my brother Archibald – your uncle at Howbeg. And Aunt Agnes.'

'I don't like Aunt Agnes,' said Flora.

'You will have to try.'

'Why can't Angus come with us? I don't want him to go to Nunton without me.'

Marion grew impatient. 'It's not for you to say what you want, Flora. It has been decided and we are lucky that I have a brother who is prepared to take us in with little more than the clothes we stand in!'

Flora felt her stomach begin to ache, like it had in the days after her father died. Tears sprang to her eyes. This was her fault; Angus was being sent away and her mother had only a few clothes to stand in, all because she had made her father fall over on the beach and die.

***

A week later, Uncle Archibald, a genial red-faced man with sparse fair hair and a red beard, came to collect them. The farm and house were being turned over to a new tenant, Murdo MacDonald, a piper and distant kinsman of the Baleshares and Donald Roy. Marion bustled around packing two saddlebags of clothes for her son while Angus and Flora went around the homestead saying goodbye to their neighbours.

They were hugged and kissed and had oatcakes pressed into their hands for the journey. Big Alasdair gave them each a penny to bring them luck.

'Got the head of old King James on them,' he winked. 'Keep them next to your heart, young Miltons, but don't tell that weasel Gunn that you've got them. He'll have my Jacobite head on the chopping block, so he will,' he joked.

Hardest of all was saying goodbye to Janet.

Flora threw her arms around the cook's waist and breathed in her smell of baking and peat fire.

'Why can't you come with us Janet?' she cried.

'Like your mother said; your aunt and uncle have their own cook. Lady Clan has been kind to me and given me a job in the kitchens at Nunton so I'll be keeping an eye on your brother for you.'

'Will you come and see us?'

'If I can.'

Outside again, Flora clung onto Angus. 'I don't want you to go,' she sobbed.

'I have to,' Angus said, hugging her quickly. There were tears in his eyes. 'Look after Mother.'

Marion broke down when her young son embraced her. She clung on until Archibald pulled her away.

'You're making it harder for the boy,' he chided.

As Angus mounted his pony, Big Alasdair struck up a lament on the pipes. Flora gripped the skirts of her distraught mother, but Marion seemed not to notice her. She stretched out her arms to her son and wailed. Only Archibald gripping her shoulders prevented her running after him as Angus trotted down the track and turned along the shore towards Nunton.

Soon after, Flora was perched in the saddle behind her shaking mother, the sight of Janet and the kitchen maids waving, blurred by her tears. All the while her father's tall piper continued to play a haunting air as they passed beyond the infields and the settlement of cottages, following Uncle Archibald's packhorse.

At the final rough stone house with its heathery thatch, Flora felt her mother tense. Out of it stepped Mairi MacVurich. She darted towards them and grabbed the pony's bridle.

'Let go,' Marion said, startled.

'I wish you well Widow Milton,' the young woman said, 'even though you did not invite me to give the eulogy to your husband as custom demanded.'

'I don't want your good wishes,' Marion said, yanking back the bridle, 'or your eulogies.'

The bard stared up with a malicious smile. 'I'll run Balivanich well for you.'

'What's that supposed to mean?' Marion demanded.

'It means I will soon be the mistress here.'

Marion snorted in disbelief. 'In your dreams maybe.' She kicked the pony into a trot.

'Yes in my dreams,' Mairi cried, running along beside them. 'I will be betrothed to Murdo MacDonald by the time the rowans are bare.'

'Murdo wouldn't be so foolish,' Marion was dismissive. 'Eulogies are no good for housekeeping.'

'It will be so,' Mairi shouted as they pulled ahead, 'because I have seen it, Widow Milton, I have *seen* it!'

Flora twisted round to see Mairi shaking her fists at them, her red hair wild and writhing in the wind. They soon caught up with Uncle Archibald.

'What did that lassie want?' he asked.

'Nothing,' Marion said stonily, 'she is quite unstable.'

But all the long ride to Howbeg, Flora could not get the image out of her head, of the young poet and her angry fists.

***

Aunt Agnes was waiting up for them. In her brown woollen dress, mittens and severe linen cap that hid every strand of hair, Flora thought she looked far too old to be married to Uncle Archibald.

The house was long and low with tiny windows covered in sacking and earth floors with no rugs.

'There's broth in the pot,' Aunt Agnes said. 'Marion, you will share a room with me; Flora can go in with the maids.'

63

Flora expected her mother to protest at them being separated.

'Thank you Agnes,' she said in a tired voice. 'I'd like to go straight to bed.'

She kissed Flora on the head and followed Agnes out of the room. Flora sat at the table on a hard chair and ate the thin soup that her uncle doled into a wooden bowl. It tasted fishy and very salty. The single candle guttered in the draught that came through the unpanelled stone walls. She put down her horn spoon and swallowed back tears. She wanted Janet and her rich warm broth; she wanted her mother who had disappeared with the frightening Aunt Agnes; she wanted Angus who she might never see again – and she longed for her father to be alive and turn everything back to how it was before he fell over on the sand.

'What are you crying for lassie?' Aunt Agnes reappeared through the gloom. 'Eat up and get to bed. You'll need to be up bright and early to help the girls in the kitchen. Isn't that right Archibald?'

'Yes dearest,' he said. 'Eat the soup Flora.'

'I d-don't want it,' Flora said, gulping down tears.

'Straight to bed then,' her aunt ordered. She hauled her out of the chair. 'Follow me.'

Seizing the candlestick, Agnes held it aloft and dragged Flora through to the adjoining room, leaving Archibald in the darkness. The room had a large fire in the middle, set inside an old millstone, its embers still glowing. Cooking pots were arrayed around the circular hearth. In the shadows, dark shapes shifted and stirred.

'There's a mattress over there with a nice warm blanket. Go and lie down like a good lassie.'

She held the candle up long enough for Flora to find the pile of heather her aunt called a mattress and lay down. Aunt Agnes and the candle retreated, plunging her in darkness, save for the fire that glowed red like an angry monster.

Flora pulled her plaid around her and curled up as small as she could. The rafters creaked as the wind howled and she could hear mice scrambling overhead. Was this the Hell that Mr Gunn relished telling them about in their Bible lessons? Perhaps it was her punishment for killing her father? She groped for the smooth green pebble in her skirt pocket that Angus had given her as a baby to keep her safe, and gripped it in her hand. She willed it to protect her broken family and bring them together again.

Flora buried her head in her plaid and dissolved into tears.

Chapter 16

It seemed that no sooner had Flora fallen asleep on the scratchy heather bed than she was being shaken awake.

'We have to clear the bedding, lassie,' a grey-haired woman with a wheezing chest told her. 'Pile it in the corner and then you can help fetch some peats for the fire. I'm Betty the cook and you do as I tell you.'

Flora got to her feet, woolly-headed, wondering where she was. There was a weak light from the hole in the roof above the central fire where the smoke was supposed to go. But a strong draught of air was gusting in from the open door and sending the smoke billowing around the room.

'Be quick about it,' Betty ordered, 'I've breakfast to make.'

Flora yawned and rubbed her eyes. A skinny youth staggered through the door with two pails slopping with water.

'Rory, be careful!' the cook scolded as he dumped them down. He shook long hair out of his eyes and peered at Flora.

'Are you the Milton lass?'

Flora nodded, a lump forming in her throat.

'Lost your tongue?' Betty asked. 'Aye, well, you've just lost your father so I suppose that's no surprise.' She prodded Rory. 'Help her move the bedding and bring in some peats before the Mistress starts ringing her bell. Else we'll all be in trouble.'

Numbly, Flora copied what Rory did. Outside, he showed her the peat stack and they loaded up with blocks of the aromatic turf.

'Are you staying here for long?' Rory asked.

'No,' Flora said. 'I'm going to tell my brother Angus to come and fetch us.'

'Aye,' Rory nodded in approval. 'You shouldn't be with the servants, it's not right.'

Flora didn't understand what he meant. She just wanted to be together with her brother and mother again, but it was too difficult to explain.

She helped Betty stoke up the fire and fill a pot with water to boil, and when the cook began to mix the oatmeal to make cakes, Flora said, 'let me. I can do that. Janet taught me.'

Betty raised bushy eyebrows but handed over the mixing while she heaved the iron griddle onto the firestones. Together they cooked the oatcakes, Flora rolling and flattening them into neat circles with her small hands while Betty threw them onto the hotplate and toasted both sides.

An imperious ringing began in the adjoining room.

'Just in time,' Betty wheezed. 'You can take them in lassie. Where's that Kate with the milk? Rory go and fetch her.'

The cook transferred the cakes to a cracked china plate, its blue pattern almost worn away, and Flora carried them carefully next door. To her dismay, her mother was not there; only her aunt and uncle were sat at the breakfast table. Uncle Archibald smiled.

'These look good, Flora.'

'I made them,' Flora gave a shy smile. 'Where's Mother?'

'In bed,' Aunt Agnes sniffed with disapproval. 'She is complaining of a headache.

'I want to see her,' Flora said, alarmed.

'Well she doesn't want to see you,' her aunt replied. 'Now sit down and your uncle will say grace.'

Flora wanted to dash from the room and find her mother; but somehow knew this would make her aunt crosser.

Uncle Archibald was half way through grace when the door swung open and a young woman hurried in with a tray of drinks.

'Sorry Mistress,' she gabbled, 'Isla was in a mood and I couldn't get near for her kicking and only a trickle would she give me but there's plenty ale–'

'Quiet,' Aunt Agnes snapped. 'The Master is saying grace.'

The maid blushed and apologised, hastily offloading the tray.

'Thank you Kate,' Uncle Archibald murmured, with a nervous glance at his wife. The dark-haired Kate retreated.

'Continue Sir,' Flora's aunt commanded.

After grace, Flora watched Aunt Agnes pouring out ale from a jug for her husband and herself. A third cup, she half-filled with milk and handed it to Flora. The milk was still warm from the cow and tasted smoky, reminding her of Balivanich. Her eyes smarted with tears. Her uncle and aunt began munching on dry oatcakes; there was no butter or jams or cheese to go with them. They ate in silence, Flora trying to swallow down the dry mixture for which she suddenly had no appetite.

'Please can I have some more milk?' she asked.

'No you can't,' said Aunt Agnes. 'We must leave some for your mother.'

'Can I take it in to her?'

After a pause, her uncle said, 'that would be helpful, wouldn't it dearest?'

'I don't approve of eating and drinking in bed,' pronounced Aunt Agnes, 'but just this once.' Pouring out another half cupful of milk, she handed it to Flora with a single oatcake. 'If you spill it, there will be consequences.'

Not knowing what this meant but just happy to be given permission to go and find her mother, Flora nodded and carried them carefully, ducking under the curtain that hung in place of a door. The next room was a small sparsely furnished bedroom-cum-study that smelt of her uncle's tobacco. Beyond that, Flora found a room crammed with furniture and provisions; a large dresser full of pretty plates, chests of drawers, padlocked trunks and a box-bed in the corner with heavy dark green curtains. Next to it, she saw her mother's purple-blue plaid draped over a chair and a pale slender arm trailing below the curtain.

Mother!' Flora cried, rushing forward and nearly slopping the meagre milk ration onto the dark rug by the bed.

'Flora?' her mother's voice was a whisper.

Flora thrust forward the milk and oatcake. 'I made the oatcake. Will you eat it? And the milk is tasty; I've had some.'

'Thank you Flora. Just put it down for the moment.' She sounded sad.

66

'Are you ill again?' Flora asked anxiously.

'Tired,' Marion sighed.

'How long do we have to stay here Mother? I want to go home.'

'This is our home now,' her voice hardened.

'No it's not,' Flora said stoutly. 'I don't want to stay here.'

'Don't make trouble for your aunt and uncle,' Marion pleaded, 'we've nowhere else to go.'

Flora felt her stomach cramp with sudden pain. 'Why can't we go to Nunton and be with Angus?'

'Because I'm a widow and you are just a girl.'

Flora was baffled by this nonsensical answer. She wanted to climb in next to her mother and feel her arms around her keeping her safe. But just as she was about to ask, there was an impatient ring of Aunt Agnes's bell.

'Best go and help your aunt,' said Marion.

Flora swallowed her panic. 'Yes, Mother.'

'You're a good girl Flora,' her mother whispered as she turned away and faced the wall.

Flora trailed out of the room as the bell rang insistently once more.

***

The first days at Howbeg that seemed to stretch forever soon turned into weeks and then months that whipped by like racing clouds. Flora's days were full of activity about her uncle's small farm. She would rise early and help Rory fetch water from the burn, make breakfast with Betty and milk Isla the cow with Kate. She learnt how to darn woollen stockings, make porridge, bake barley bread, plant kale, churn butter, make candles, trim the wicks of oil lamps, gather berries, make jelly, cut heather, gut fish and patch clothes.

She stopped asking her mother when they would be leaving and quickly accepted that she slept in the kitchen with the servants – preferred it – to sharing the dark claustrophobic box-bed with her mother and aunt.

At times when she felt pangs of homesickness for her past life, Flora would retreat into the dairy – it was little more than a windowless bothy compared to the one at Balivanich – and sit crying on the milking stool with her face pressed into Isla's warm flank. The cow, so truculent and moody with Kate, was always patient with Flora and produced twice as much milk for her small firm fingers.

Kate the maid was kind and often sneaked her extra bits of cheese or crowdie from the dairy, behind the back of their eagle-eyed mistress. Flora picked up Kate's milking songs and love songs, and often they would work together and sing in unison.

'You have a beautiful voice Miss Flora,' Kate was admiring. 'You should be singing in Lady Clan's parlour not a Howbeg cowshed.'

Flora just found this funny; it was more than a year since she had been to Nunton for Sir Alexander's visit and her memories of her old life were fading fast. She knew her mother received letters from Angus telling her about his new life of lessons and sport at the Clanranalds' home, but he had only come to visit once on a hunting trip with Ranald Og. Angus had been grandly dressed in tartan doublet and hose, and Flora had been unexpectedly tongue-tied at his teasing.

'Florrie, do you always run around in bare legs like a gypsy?'

She had wanted to show him Isla and how good she was at milking but Ranald Og had been impatient to get away. Her mother had been tense and weepy; one minute lavishing Angus with kisses and the next bemoaning her situation and chiding him for neglecting her.

'I write every week,' Angus had answered helplessly. 'What else can I do Mother?'

The boys had not lingered. 'We'll be staying over at the MacEachens if you want to visit, Florrie,' Angus had told her in parting.

Flora had longed to go but her aunt had dismissed the idea at once. 'The MacEachens don't want to be bothered with you lassie; not when they are entertaining the chieftain.'

So Flora had not gone to visit. But that autumn, Kate the maid began courting a boatman from the MacEachens' homestead. He was a genial man called Ronald Oar because of his great rowing strength and when he came visiting, Flora followed him around asking about Neil MacEachen and keen to show off her skills in the dairy.

'Leave them alone,' Rory, the outdoor servant, teased.

'Why do they want to be alone?' Flora asked bemused.

'Cos courting couples do.'

Kate became fretful and moody that winter, cooped up indoors during fierce gales and short dark days when Ronald Oar could not visit. So when spring came, Flora was glad to see Kate's mood lift and hear her cheerful announcement.

'Ronald and I are betrothed to be married.'

'Will you have a big wedding? Will the MacEachens come?' Flora asked, knowing that Kate's parents had died of smallpox so she would need other guests. 'I'll make crowdie for you and Rory can give you some of his whisky he makes up the back—'

'Wheesht!' Rory stopped her, scowling behind his wild hair.

'We can't afford a big wedding,' Kate gave a rueful smile. 'But you can be there Miss Flora – and some of your crowdie would be just grand.'

Betty the cook warned, 'that's if the Mistress allows. Have you asked the Master's permission to wed?'

Kate shook her head.

'Well you'll have to lassie – they took you in when you were orphaned.'

Flora overheard the argument a few days later when Kate went seeking permission.

'You're too young to be marrying,' Aunt Agnes was dismissive.

'I'm seventeen, Mistress.'

'Precisely.'

'Master?' Kate appealed to Uncle Archibald.

There was silence and Flora could imagine him scratching his red beard in indecision.

'Seventeen is young to be starting a household of your own; perhaps wait a year or two–' he said.

'Far too young,' Aunt Agnes cut in. 'And where would you stay? There is no room for this laddie here. Do you really want to live in an upturned boat on the shore? Don't look so surprised, I make it my business to know who is courting my maid. Ronald Oar is as poor as a fieldmouse.'

'But I love him, Mistress.'

Aunt Agnes snorted. 'You'll soon grow out of that. Now dry your eyes and get back to work. The Master and I know what is best for you and we'll not let you make a fool of yourself over some burly boatman. When the time comes for marriage, we'll choose one of our farm boys who can give you a cottage and where there will always be work for the pair of you.'

Kate cried all night and would not be comforted. Flora crawled over and whispered. 'Does Ronald Oar really live in an upside-down boat?'

'Go away; I don't want to talk about it.'

'I wouldn't mind living in a boat,' Flora said. 'You could eat fish every day and talk to the seals 'cos they're really humans that have been turned into sea creatures.' Flora leaned closer still and whispered, 'And you wouldn't have to share the heather with snoring Betty and Rory who shouts in his sleep.'

Kate gave a sniff that was half a laugh.

'I'd miss you if you went away to Ronald Oar's boat though,' Flora added.

Kate reached out and put her arms around Flora, pulling her close. She did not say anything, but the older girl held onto her as Flora fell asleep cupped in her warm embrace.

The next day Kate was gone. No matter how much Aunt Agnes rang her bell or stormed around the house shouting for her maid, Kate did not appear. News came a few days later that Kate and Ronald Oar had been wed in a hand-fast marriage – promised to each other in front of witnesses – but without the full blessing of the church.

Rory told a wide-eyed Flora and astonished Betty that he'd heard pipes playing down by the shore along from the MacEachens' homestead and seen flaming torches lighting up the beach where Ronald and his friends were dancing jigs with the new bride.

'I wish I'd been there to see it,' Flora cried in envy.

'I never thought she'd be so foolish,' Betty snorted. 'She can't come back here now. Come winter she'll be wishing for a heather bed under this roof.'

Surprisingly, Flora's mother was the only one in the household who seemed pleased at Kate's rash decision. Her dull eyes showed a spark of interest when Flora told her the details.

'Good for her,' Marion smiled. 'It's a brave lass who follows her heart and doesn't care what others think.'

Flora imagined doing the same with Neil MacEachen; they would live in an upturned boat on the shore, catching fish and making fires on the beach to cook the shiny mackerel.

'If I lived in a boat I'd take Isla the cow with me and have milk every day to go with the fish and make crowdie and Neil would go hunting for hares–'

'Neil?' her mother interrupted.

'Neil MacEachen,' Flora said, 'that's who I'm going to marry.'

She didn't like the way her mother laughed at this suggestion but then Marion unexpectedly put an arm about her and kissed her head.

'Neil's a fine boy. A good choice.'

Flora's heart lifted in joy to receive one of her mother's rare smiles. Too often Marion sat alone, thin and pale, in Aunt Agnes's cramped chamber half-heartedly sewing and mending clothes. Occasionally her mother would venture out at twilight to climb the hillock behind the house and Flora would follow. But Marion never answered her questions and Flora was left to wonder what her mother was thinking as she gazed east across the far Minch to Skye.

Yet Marion's interest in the eloping Kate soon waned and she put up little objection to Flora's workload being increased because of the absent maid. When winter arrived once more with howling storms rushing in from the Atlantic, the rain poured under the ill-fitting kitchen door, turning the floor to a sea of mud and leaked through the heather roof spitting at the smoking fire.

Betty's wheezing chest grew worse, making it difficult for the cook to lift the heavy pots. Rory and Flora did what they could to help, but sometimes Flora felt so dizzy from the fetching and carrying that she was curled up asleep on the damp heather bed before suppertime. Her appetite lessened as her worry for Isla increased. The cow's milk began to dry up.

'There's not enough hay put by,' Rory complained, 'we're running out of feed. And the oats and barley were planted too late.'

Aunt Agnes berated Uncle Archibald for his useless husbandry and for sitting about reading his books while they starved.

'We'll not have enough to see us through to the spring,' she cried, 'and us with two extra mouths to feed!'

'I could sell my silver brooch,' Marion offered.

'Your brother can sell his books first,' Agnes glared at her husband.

'I'll call on MacEachen.' Archibald said in agitation, 'he's helped us out before.'

'The shame of it!' Agnes cried. 'You will not go cap in hand to our neighbours.'

As punishment, Rory was forbidden to lay the fire in the master's chamber or replenish the candles so that Archibald could not waste precious peat or tallow on frivolous reading.

Isla was bled and the cow's blood mixed with oatmeal to provide nourishment. They eked out the meagre supplies in the storeroom.

Then one spring day Ronald Oar appeared with a basket of fish.

'My Kate sent them,' he told Betty. 'It's been hard for the farmers this winter, but the fishing's good when we can get out.'

'Why didn't Kate come?' Flora asked. 'I'd like to see her.'

He was shocked to see how thin the girl had become, her hair dull and matted, though her eyes still shone with interest. He smiled bashfully. 'Kate's keeping to the house. Our baby's due any day now.'

'That's grand,' Betty said, 'and you thank her kindly for the fish.'

'Can I see the baby when it comes?' Flora asked.

'Of course you can.'

Flora sought out her mother at once to tell her the news about Kate's baby, but to her disappointment, her mother no longer seemed interested in Kate or any stories Flora had to tell. Marion kept increasingly to her bed as she had in the bad times at Balivanich and Flora feared she would never get up again.

It was another month before they heard that Kate's baby had been born; a daughter also called Kate. Flora did not know what babies liked, but chose a horn spoon from her small box of trinkets kept from Balivanich. Deciding not to tell anyone where she was going in case they stopped her, Flora set off alone across the hill to Howbeg beach.

She remembered the effort of climbing the boggy slope, her too tight dress hitched up as the peaty bog sucked up to her thighs. And she remembered thinking that it had never taken so long to reach the top; it felt as if rocks were tied to her legs and pressed down on her chest. Then a buzzing began in her head and she had to sit down, and as she did so, the world went dark.

***

It was Neil MacEachen who found Flora in the heather at dusk, ice-cold and limp as a rag-doll and raised the alarm. He had been out on the hill with his father's spyglass watching a naval ship off-shore, fascinated by the sudden detail of rigging and the faces of sailors working on deck.

Neil raced down to Archibald's farm and found Rory. Between them the two boys carried Flora back to the house. Betty ordered them to lay her on the heather bed and fussed about making an infusion of herbs. Neil was horrified to think that this damp and primitive dwelling was where Flora lived; his father's cattle were housed in more weather-proof byres. He had heard the Howbeg MacDonalds lived modestly and didn't invite visitors but he had not guessed at this hidden poverty. Now he felt guilty for not having called on Flora or kept an eye on her as Angus had asked him to do. Eleven years old now, Neil had thought it babyish to be friends with a girl barely seven.

Flora opened her eyes at the sound of her mother's voice and saw Marion's pinched face frowning above her.

'Flora! What possessed you to run off like that? Where were you going?'

'Mother,' Flora tried to smile.

71

'I was so worried,' Marion fretted. 'You could have died–' She jammed a hand over her trembling lips.

'To see Kate's baby,' Flora whispered, 'wanted her to have my spoon.'

Marion crouched beside her and stroked her brittle hair. Her daughter's pretty eyes were tinged with blue shadows like bruises to her sallow skin. Shame overwhelmed her to think she had brought her child so low, skivvying for the bullying Agnes when she should be learning how to dance and play the spinet. She had given up caring what happened to herself – would have welcomed a quick decline in health and an early grave to follow where her husband and son had gone. Everything had been taken from her and she hated being beholden to others; the daily humiliation of doing her sister-in-law's bidding and watching her brother Archibald being diminished by each scolding too.

But not everything had been taken from her; she still had Flora, her bright, resilient, exasperating daughter. Even as she chastised her for her naughtiness in running off, Marion wanted to crush her to her breast in relief that she was alive.

'Neil found you,' Marion told her, 'you've him to thank you're not a corpse for the crows.'

For the first time Flora noticed a boy standing in the shadows behind. He was too tall for Neil, his shoulders thicker and his hair curling around the neck of his jerkin.

'Neil?'

'Aye, Florrie,' the boy grinned and stepped forward. Even before she saw the glint of his brown eyes, she knew his voice. He squatted on his haunches and took her hand. 'I thought one of the Little People had escaped from the dun,' he teased, 'but it was only you.'

Flora gave a weak laugh of delight. 'The Little People aren't real.'

Neil gasped in mock shock. 'Don't say that Florrie or they'll put a spell on you.'

'Enough talk of spells and fairies,' Marion interrupted brusquely. 'Flora needs to rest and it's almost dark. We don't want your family worrying about you as well Neil.'

He stood up. 'Will I come over and see you in a few days?'

'Yes please,' Flora smiled.

'I'll bring some crowdie and oatcakes,' he promised.

'Just wait there a moment Neil,' Marion said, 'and I'll fetch you a small reward.'

'There's no need–'

'Please.' Marion gave him such a pleading look that he nodded. She returned after a few minutes and steered him outside. Glancing around nervously, she murmured, 'take this – I want you to deliver it to Nunton – please don't speak of this to anyone.' She tucked a folded piece of paper – a page torn from a printed book – into his jerkin. 'And make sure it gets to Lady Clan and no one else. Can you do that for me, Neil?'

'Of course,' he reassured. 'I won't say a word.'

When he appeared the following week, he was met by Agnes MacDonald.

'The girl has a fever and isn't well enough to see you.'

Neil's fear rose. 'Shall I send for Dr Beaton?'

'There's no need to fuss. Her mother is tending to things.'

'Can I not just see her for–'

'No, a visit would over-excite her.'

'I've brought her some food,' Neil said, feeling quite helpless.

'I shall deliver it,' Agnes said, holding out scrawny hands. Reluctantly he gave her the parcel. Neil tried to peer beyond the waterlogged yard to the house behind for any sign of Flora's mother but there was neither movement nor sound from the dismal dwelling. There was no way of telling Milton's widow that he had delivered her note to Lady Clan.

'Tell her I came, won't you, Mistress Agnes?'

'May I speak plainly, young MacEachen?' The woman was stony-faced. 'It's best you stay away laddie. The girl doesn't want reminding of a past life she can't have any more. She and my husband's sister live on charity now and I don't want you filling her head full of fancy ideas. She has a life of plain honest work ahead of her. She can never be a match for you.'

Neil flushed at the brazen words, embarrassed she should think his interest in Flora was anything other than childhood friendship. He retreated down the track, stopping at a stunted hazel tree to glance back, but Flora's aunt still watched him so he hurried away. For days afterwards he agonised over whether to return to Howbeg farm and each time he set out, Mistress Agnes's bald words of warning made his courage fail.

This did not stop him slipping over the hill from Howbeg House after lessons were over and crouching in the heather, observing the farm. When, after a couple of weeks, he saw Flora out and about doing chores, he felt relief that the fever was past. He watched for her making any attempt to leave the farm or seek him out, but she never did. Perhaps she was resigned to her new life and did not want to see him?

Summer returned and Neil heard from Ronald Oar, one of his father's boatmen, that Flora had taken to visiting his wife and baby in the long light evenings.

'Kate's always had a fondness for Miss Flora,' said Ronald, 'and wee Katie cries when she leaves.'

But while Neil pondered whether he should seek out Flora on one of her visits to her friend – just to make sure she was content with her life – something quite unexpected happened at Howbeg farm.

Chapter 17

Even though it was past midnight, twilight still seeped through the hole in the thatch where the last wisps of smoke rose from the kitchen fire. The short nights of May made Flora restless; her spirits had rallied now that she could stay out of doors longer in the fine weather and slip away to the shore to visit baby Katie. She adored the gurgling, sunny-natured baby girl and liked to stagger around with her swaddled to her chest in imitation of mother Kate, singing lullabies.

She closed her eyes, softly humming a song that their former cook Janet had taught her about a father going to the hills to hunt while the cows were milked. An image came sharply of her own beloved father and she felt tears prickle behind her lids.

Suddenly there was a loud hammering at the front door. Flora sat bolt upright.

'Open up!' a man's voice boomed. 'Open up at once or I'll take a broadsword to it!'

The pounding on the door continued. It sounded like several fists.

Rory struggled to his feet. Betty cried out, 'It's robbers; don't open it.'

'I must go to protect the Master,' Rory said, fear in his voice.

Flora scrambled after him.

'Stay where you are, lassie,' Betty gasped. Rory turned and pushed Flora back. As he pulled open the door into the dingy hallway, the front door shook as the intruders beyond heaved at it with their shoulders.

Betty began to wail.

'Get the door open, MacDonald of Howbeg,' a man bawled, 'or I'll shoot through it.'

Flora saw her uncle emerge from his room, a plaid thrown hastily around his nightshirt, his spindly hairless legs shaking as he hurried to the door. The servants stood clutching each other, unsure what to do.

'Who are you?' her uncle croaked. 'Please don't harm us.'

'Just open the door and face me like a man!' the stranger bellowed.

'I won't till you tell me who you are and why you are here,' Archibald said querulously.

Agnes appeared in a dark woollen gown over a voluminous linen nightdress, her hair hidden in a large white cap. Flora had never seen her so flustered as she crept to her husband's side and clung to his arm.

'Don't let him in,' she hissed. 'Offer him your silver drinking cups if he'll leave us alone.'

'Is it money you're after?' Archibald cried. 'We are not wealthy.'

'You can have the silver cups,' Agnes called, her voice thin and high.

'I don't want cups – I want a woman!'

Agnes stifled a sob, cowering behind her husband. 'We must lock ourselves in the storeroom,' she panicked.

'Give me Marion of Balivanich and I'll leave you in peace,' the man bargained.

'My sister?' Archibald said in alarm. 'Certainly not.'

74

'Husband!' Agnes berated. 'Do you want us all murdered?

'Unlock the door,' ordered Marion.

Flora saw her mother step out of the dark doorway beyond Agnes, her woollen plaid pulled tight around her. She had a strange feverish look in her eyes.

'No Mother!' Flora screamed.

But Marion was already pushing her way past the others and fumbling with the large rusty iron key. Archibald tried to stop her.

'Sister please–'

Marion fended him off and pulled back the bolts with a strength Flora had not seen in her before.

The door flew inwards, nearly knocking her off her feet. Armed men pushed inside. Agnes and Betty screamed.

Flora watched in horror as an enormous man with a thick mane of hair and a patch over his eye, stormed into the hallway and seized her mother with one huge hand, brandishing a long dirk in the other.

'Hugh *Cam*?' Archibald gasped. 'Is it you?'

'Stand back!' he ordered. The household cowered in fright.

He turned to Marion. They stared at each other long and hard, neither speaking. Flora knew he must be a notorious pirate. He would kill her mother with the long knife or sell her into slavery.

'Come,' he ordered.

Her mother did not resist. Flora threw herself at Marion. 'Don't hurt my Mammy!' she wailed. 'Don't take her away.'

'Who is this?' the pirate demanded.

Without taking her look from the man's, Marion put an arm around her daughter. 'This is my Florrie.'

The pirate's severe face was disbelieving. He turned on Archibald in fury.

'You keep your own niece like the lowest skivvy? The daughter of Milton? Shame on you!' he thundered.

Archibald looked ashen. Agnes rallied. 'We offered her a home when no one else would.'

'A home?' he said in contempt. 'I've seen better dungeons. Marion and the lass are coming with me.'

Marion turned and gave Agnes a look of triumph. Flora was full of confusion. Her mother seemed quite willing to go with this terrifying man. The next instant, the man lunged at her, sweeping her up effortlessly in one arm and throwing her over his shoulder like a sack of oatmeal.

Flora gasped, her breath trapped in her chest. Behind the man she could see three other dark figures in bonnets with dirks drawn. She began to howl in fright and kick her legs.

'Please don't harm them,' Archibald cried, flapping his hands ineffectually.

The man barked with savage laughter. 'Harm them? I've come to rescue them.'

He spun around and Flora thought she would fall. She clung to his leather jerkin. He tipped her into the arms of another man.

'Mother!' Flora yelled.

'Be careful with her Hugh.' It was her mother's voice; she sounded more excited than fearful. 'Let me gather some clothes.'

'There is no time for that,' the pirate replied, 'we must catch the tide.'

He seized her hand and pulled her after him.

Flora knew then that she had been right; these were Barbary pirates who were going to take them away for ever. She would never see her brother Angus again, or Neil MacEachen, or Kate and baby Katie. She screamed and tried to pummel the man who held her pinned in his arms. But her mother did nothing to try and save them.

'Wheesht girl,' Marion called, 'we must be quiet. No one's going to hurt you.'

Flora didn't believe her. She thought her mother was just trying to be brave. The chief pirate led the way down the track towards the shore. He had enveloped her mother in his plaid and she could no longer see her. In the eerie half-light of the night, Flora glimpsed a boat bobbing at the water's edge. Further up the beach was Kate and Ronald's boathouse. This was her last chance to save her mother and herself. She opened her mouth and began to scream. The man who carried her, clamped a rough hand over her mouth. Flora could hardly breathe.

Hugh the pirate suddenly swept Marion off her feet, waded out into the sea and tipped her into the boat, where a slim, shadowy figure helped her sit. Hugh came back for Flora. She bit him hard on the hand. He didn't even flinch.

'Come you little wild cat. I'm your mother's friend; One-eyed Hugh. Surely she has talked of me?'

Flora wailed, 'Mother doesn't know any pirates!'

Hugh barked with laughter. 'Does she not? Well I'm no pirate. I'm a soldier and am going to protect you.'

He swung her effortlessly into the arms of the figure on board.

'Here, Donald Roy; take the wild lass.'

Flora stared at the youth who held her. A large beaky-nosed face grinned down at her. Her cousin Donald Roy from Baleshare.

'Are you captured too?' Flora gasped.

Donald Roy laughed. 'No lassie. Hugh *Cam* is a cousin of mine. I'm here to help row you away.'

'Are we going to Baleshare?' Flora brightened. If so, she would be close to Angus at Nunton.

Donald Roy just laughed and shook his head as he leapt over the side to help push the boat off the sandbar. As the men rowed away from the shore, Marion pulled Flora under her arm and they clung tightly to each other. The wind lifted and they left the lee of the land for the dark ocean; Donald Roy ran up the sail. The boat rocked.

'Where are we going?' Marion finally asked, releasing Flora from her hold.

Hugh *Cam* stood over them, legs astride, his rugged face in shadow.

'To Skye.'

Marion's voice wavered. 'I thought we would be going to Lady Clan at Nunton? Was that not her plan?'

Hugh crouched down beside her and seized her arms. 'I'll not risk the cautious Clanranald sending you straight back to your brother. Lady Clan knew when she called on my help, what I would do.'

Marion said in a breathless voice. 'And what will you do?'

His large mouth twitched in a smile. 'You're mine now, Marion. I've dreamt of this day.'

Abruptly, he grabbed her head in his hands and planted a robust kiss on her lips. Flora watched in horror. She had never seen any man – not even her father – kiss her mother in such a way. It made her stomach curdle. But her mother did not rebuke him or push the frightening man away.

***

Flora woke with the sun in her eyes. She was cradled in her mother's lap. Huge cliffs rose out of the sea to their left; birds shrieked and circled overhead while a stiff breeze whipped them forward.

Last night had not been a terrifying dream; One-eyed Hugh and his crew were still there and the land was equally overwhelming and unknown.

'MacLeod country,' Hugh told her, holding out an oatcake. 'Have some breakfast.'

Flora pushed it away, feeling nauseous.

'Don't be rude, Flora,' her mother chided. Marion's face was tilted to the sun, her fair hair lifting in the wind. She looked happy again, the way she did at Balivanich after the 'black storms' had left her.

Hugh sat down beside her. 'I don't much like being in a boat either,' he smiled. 'Don't worry, before the sun dips, we'll be safe on dry land in the protection of my chief.'

Flora wanted to ask who his chief was but could not speak. Her lips were clamped and dry, as if a bad fairy had sewn them together in the night. Hugh began to tell her stories about adventures in France as a soldier. She didn't want to listen – she was determined not to like him – but she could not help being intrigued by his talk of French palaces and Stuart Kings. She closed her eyes and slept again.

***

It was dark and the stars were hidden by cloud when they made land. Donald Roy carried Flora ashore. She clung to him mutely, her skinny arms around his neck. Marion walked ahead. They were taken to a house but Flora could hardly see its outline; she kept her worried eyes fixed on her mother. They were shown into a small room with a box-bed, a table and chairs and a fireplace with a proper chimney where a peat fire smouldered. There was cold chicken, barley bread and dishes of milk awaiting. Flora could not eat, though her stomach growled with hunger.

Marion put her to bed behind the curtain, but Flora fretted that she could not see her mother and climbed back out, curling up by the fire. She would stay awake and keep watch over her mother because she still did not trust the loud-voiced Hugh *Cam* with his one flashing blue eye and sudden bursts of laughter.

Flora awoke much later. The fire was out and the room pitch black.

'Mother?' she called in alarm. 'Mammy, where are you?'

'In the bed, Florrie,' Marion answered drowsily. 'Do you want to climb up?'

Flora hesitated. Relief flooded through her at the sound of her mother's calm sleepy voice. Someone had wrapped a woollen blanket around her and she had long since grown used to sleeping on a firm earth floor rather than a lumpy, itchy mattress hemmed into a box-bed.

'No,' Flora yawned and lay back down. As her eyes grew used to the dark she saw that an ember of peat still glowed in the grate giving a trace of warmth and light. The smell of peat was comforting. She lay, staring at the fire, mesmerised and half asleep.

Presently, her mother made small murmuring sounds in her sleep. The box-bed creaked. Flora glanced over and thought she saw the curtain move in the draught. The creaking continued; her mother groaned restlessly. Flora nearly called out again but didn't want to wake her. The noises went on until the ember flickered and died. Then came a long low sigh – a man's sigh? – and a short time later, the even breathing of two people sleeping.

Chapter 18

The scandal of Hugh *Cam*'s kidnap of Marion spread up the Long Isle like the burning of heather in springtime. Even the gentry of Skye could talk of nothing else when they gathered in each other's parlours. It eclipsed all talk of the young Stuart princes over the water or the price of cattle or grandiose plans to transform Edinburgh into an Athens of the north.

Flora was oblivious to all of this. She soon grew accustomed to their new home – a modest farmhouse on the water's edge looking across at the huge purple mountains of the mainland – and spent her time helping around the farm that belonged to One-eyed Hugh's brother. Her mother, who would disappear for long hours with the boisterous Hugh, often found her daughter milking in the dairy or helping with the spinning. She quickly learnt new Gaelic songs from the servants. What Marion didn't know was how much of her day Flora spent combing the shore or climbing the steep cliffs looking for birds' eggs.

One day, a florid-faced woman called to see Flora's mother, bringing an older girl and a stocky, black-haired boy who looked familiar. The girl was left in charge while the mother went in to take tea with a flustered Marion.

'Still think you can climb like a boy,' the boy grinned. 'Saw you up on the crag.'

Allan Kingsburgh; Flora remembered that annoying boy from the celebrations at Nunton over two years ago. She recognised his startling blue eyes and the way his left cheek dimpled when he smiled.

'Bet I can still outrun you,' Flora pouted.

'Bet you can't.'

'Race you to the beach.'

'I'll give you a head-start,' Allan condescended.

'Don't need it,' Flora scoffed.

'You must stay here with me,' ordered Allan's older sister Ann.

They both ignored her and tore off across the springy turf towards the shore. Flora was ahead until they got to the rocks, then lost ground as Allan vaulted easily over the sharp boulders and landed on the beach first.

'I win!' he cried. 'Girls are slow as pack ponies.'

Flora sank on the pebbly shore heaving for breath. She still had not totally regained her strength after her winter fever. White phlegm smeared her lips. She retched.

'Are you all right?' Allan peered at her.

Flora nodded; she didn't want to admit how winded she felt. Allan leapt over to the stream that tumbled out of the hillside behind and came back with fresh water cupped in his hands.

'Drink,' he ordered.

Flora slurped, though most of the spring water had seeped through his fingers. It tasted of peat – or maybe his earthy hands. They sat getting their breath back.

'How is your brother Angus?' Allan asked. 'I liked him.'

'I hardly see him any more. He lives at Nunton and takes lessons with the Clanranalds.'

'I hate lessons,' said Allan.

'I wish I could learn things,' Flora sighed. Only then would her brother and young Clanranald and Neil MacEachen let her be one of them, she thought.

'Whatever for?' Allan asked in bafflement. 'Girls don't need books.'

'Yes we do,' Flora cried. 'My father used to read me stories about kings and battles. Now he's dead but I'd still like to read them.'

Allan laughed and poked her in the ribs. 'You're a strange lass.'

'And you're a stupid boy.' Flora jumped up, annoyed at his talk.

Shortly afterwards, Allan was scolded for disobeying his sister and summoned home.

'It was that wild girl's idea,' Ann accused in disapproval.

'No it was mine, Mother,' Allan insisted. Flora felt a stab of guilt at being rude to him until he stuck his tongue out at her behind his mother's back as he left.

The visit brought an end to their peaceful existence. Flora overheard Marion and Hugh in heated conversation.

'We cannot go on like this Hugh,' her mother protested, 'I've had no invitations to call on the neighbours since we came to Skye. Only Florence Kingsburgh has dared to visit and she couldn't wait to tell me we're the talk of the island. Is it true?'

'Florence likes to gossip – she means no harm.'

'I refuse to be an outcast – I don't deserve it. I didn't ask for this.'

Hugh snorted with laughter. 'You came willingly enough.'

'You promised to marry me! Now you've had your pleasure you're no doubt planning to disappear abroad again and I'll be left all alone!' Marion burst into tears.

'My darling, don't upset yourself. Come here.' He held her tight and kissed her head. 'I will never leave you again, I promise. We shall be married. Why do you think I brought you to Skye?'

'Then why do we have to wait?'

'So I can ask my kinsman and chief his permission to take you as my wife.'

'But you don't need young Sleat's permission,' Marion sniffed, 'and neither do I.'

'I need his blessing and patronage,' said Hugh. 'We can't live on a soldier's pension – I need a position of importance in the clan and land to go with it. That is why we need to wait for Alexander to return from university so I can persuade him in person of my thinking.'

'No doubt he's heard of my abduction even in far off St Andrews.'

'That was the whole idea,' Hugh chuckled. 'Present him with a *fait accompli*, as the French would say.' He kissed her loudly. 'And in the meantime we can have our sport.'

'But what if I should become with child, Hugh?' Marion fretted.

'I would like nothing better,' he declared. 'And our case will be all the stronger. Alexander will be only too happy to make our situation blessed in marriage if there is a babe on the way. He still feels guilt at the death of young Ranald.'

'And so he should,' Marion trembled.

'Darling Marion,' Hugh chided, 'you must let go your grief for the lad, or it will eat you up like a parasite. We shall have many more sons together, you and I.'

'Oh, Hugh, how I want us to have another son. But I want Angus with us too.'

'From now on you will have whatever you want, my beautiful Marion.'

Flora heard them kissing. She slipped away, pondering their strange words and excited by talk of Angus coming to be with them. Soon they would be a family again.

***

Marion and Hugh were married in a quiet ceremony later that summer. Autumn came, the drovers went south with their cattle and Hugh *Cam* took his new family back to the Long Isle where to the astonishment of all he had secured the tack of land at Balivanich. Flora could hardly contain her excitement.

'Are we really going back home?' she asked for the umpteenth time.

'Yes,' her mother reassured with a broad smile as big as her daughter's. 'Hugh *Cam* has arranged it all. He will keep an eye on the Chief of Sleat's business in North Uist and stand guardian to Angus. Your stepfather is a very important man. The chiefs of both Sleat and Clanranald take note of what he says.'

'And we can go back to our old house again?'

'Of course – it is Angus's right to have the tack of Balivanich as well as Milton.'

'But what about the people who have been living there? Will they stay in the house too?'

'Certainly not,' Marion snapped. 'Mairi MacVurich and her tribe of tinkers can go back to their own place. Her husband Murdo is a useless farmer and knows nothing of rearing cattle. He should stick to mending tools.'

They found the house in a filthy state, the walls damp and the roof leaking. Chickens had been roosting in Milton's old study. Marion broke down and wept.

'It's like a midden! She's done it to spite me, the wicked witch!'

'Nonsense,' Hugh laughed, 'she's a saucy wench who knows nothing of keeping house. We'll soon have it put right.'

He sent for help. Janet returned and brought two of her sisters to clean the house. Hugh employed a team of carpenters, stonemasons and farmhands to make the house and its farm buildings watertight. New furniture and pictures were sent for from Edinburgh, brocades and linen from Inverness, wallpaper and mirrors from Holland and wines and brandy from France. Whatever Marion wanted, Hugh supplied. For Flora a spinet was bought.

'I will teach you,' Marion promised, though never did. She just grew fatter and hardly left her bedroom where she ate bowlfuls of cream sweetened with bramble jam.

So Flora taught herself and wiled away wet afternoons picking out tunes by ear. She was happy to be back at Balivanich and be reunited with their old cook Janet; she was less wary of Hugh *Cam* and grew to miss his loud voice and barking laugh when business took him away. She was soon calling him Father.

Her happiness would have been complete if only Angus would come home too. Bafflingly, her brother stayed away at Nunton.

'He's too busy being educated,' Marion would explain with an impatient sigh. 'The Clanranalds want him as the chieftain's companion.'

But Flora noticed how Angus sparked with Hugh whenever he made duty visits to the house. Hugh would give him bear hugs and back slaps and was eager to offer advice. Angus quietly resisted.

'Don't you like Father?' Flora asked him when she got him alone for a rare moment.

'He's not my father,' Angus scowled. 'He's my mother's husband.'

'I used to be frightened of him,' Flora admitted, 'but he's kind and funny. He makes me feel safe when he's around. I wish you would come more often.'

'Doesn't sound like you need me,' Angus said, his look fierce.

Flora flew at him and wrapped her arms around his waist. 'I do! I always will Angie.'

He let her hang on to him for a moment and then he pulled her arms away. 'That's a babyish name. Don't call me that again.'

***

As they prepared to celebrate their first New Year back at Balivanich, Marion gave birth to a tiny baby with a fuzz of fair hair. They called him James. Marion fretted he was too small and premature to survive, but Flora delighted in her new brother and helped Janet with his swaddling and sang him to sleep in his cradle. Hugh strode around with his son in his arms, as proud as could be. They held a christening party fit for a prince with gallons of punch and wine to toast baby James, and invited all the gentry from South Uist up to Berneray to feast on roast mutton, goose, fish and venison for a week.

Two years later, a sister was born. Annabella was as sunny-natured as her brother James. A further two years brought another daughter Florence – who soon became known as Tibby – and then two more sons, Sorley and Magnus, followed in successive years. The house at Balivanich rang with the cries and laughter of Hugh and Marion's growing family. Flora was happy to play nursemaid to her half siblings and was endlessly patient. She sat up through the night if one of them was teething and soothed them if they woke wailing from a bad dream. To her they were as much her own flesh and blood as Angus, with whom she had grown shy as their contact dwindled.

Angus was a strapping lad of sixteen and had been to the mainland with the drovers for the past two years. He was strong with a smouldering temper like his father Milton, and fiercely loyal to the Clanranalds who had brought him up. He was a passable scholar but his interests and strengths were physical. Flora sometimes mused how alike her brother probably was to the dark-haired rumbustious Allan Kingsburgh.

She had long given up hoping that Angus would live with them at Balivanich and instead enjoyed the attention of her affectionate stepfather – she played the spinet while he sang lusty songs in French – and he defended her against her mother's carping.

It baffled Flora how Marion could find fault with her life at Balivanich. It was obvious how much Hugh *Cam* adored his wife and family, but she fretted whenever he went away.

'I can't sleep when he's not lying next to me,' she complained. 'Flora, you must keep me company.'

Yet, she scolded Flora for tossing restlessly and babbling in her sleep, and turfed her out of bed.

She relied on Flora to help with the younger children, yet it worried her that Flora was approaching womanhood without the polished skills expected of their class. At fourteen, Flora was still running around the farm in bare feet and riding bareback like a wild boy.

'She'll be a spinster for ever,' Marion cried at Hugh, 'Why didn't Milton leave her with a dowry? She's more equipped for the dairy than the parlour.'

'Florrie will make a good match, my darling,' Hugh soothed, 'I'll see to that.'

'But you must provide for Annabella and Tibby. You can't lavish the same on Flora. Anyway, you are much too spendthrift.'

'Stop worrying,' Hugh grew impatient. 'Flora has natural charms – she's turning into a beautiful young woman – and she learns quickly.'

'What do you mean by natural charms?' Marion said in suspicion. 'Does she flirt with you?'

'Don't be ridiculous. I merely meant that any young gentleman of the clan will be happy to marry her.'

'She must go to Nunton,' Marion announced abruptly. 'Lady Clan will make a lady of her.'

'But you can do that,' Hugh pointed out, 'if you pay her a bit more attention.'

'Well, I think she should go to Nunton where you can give her a bit less attention!'

'Sometimes you are impossible, woman!' Hugh slammed out of the parlour.

It came as a complete surprise to Flora, when Lady Clan sent for her from Nunton. She was to join her household and be schooled in music and dancing with the Clanranald daughters. Flora greeted this with her usual calm acceptance. She would miss her family, but Angus would be at Nunton and she had heard that Neil MacEachen was being taught Greek there by Clanranald. She went with a flutter of excitement.

Her young brothers and sisters screamed and threw tantrums at her going. Bafflingly, Marion clung to her and wept the loudest, although Lady Clan had told Flora that the whole idea had been her mother's.

Chapter 19

1738

'Come quickly Pen!' Flora dashed into the girls' bedroom. 'There's a boat in from the mainland – it's bound to have letters.'

She whipped the sewing from Penelope's knee and pulled her up.

'Careful of the needle,' her friend protested, resisting Flora's pull long enough to place the fine needle safely into a pin cushion. But Flora could see the excitement in Penelope's deep-set brown eyes and the smile she could not smother on her full mouth. Each day she looked more and more like her vivacious mother, Lady Clan, but without her impetuous nature.

'There's bound to be word from the drovers,' Flora winked. 'They must be at Falkirk by now.'

'When has your brother ever put pen and paper together for me?' Penelope snorted.

'Angus may not be a man of letters,' Flora admitted, 'but Donald Roy will send news about them all.'

'Aye, and probably in Latin verse.' Penelope rolled her eyes.

'What it must be like to have *two* men swooning over you,' Flora teased, as they clattered downstairs and across the large hallway. 'And one of them first cousin to Lord MacDonald of Sleat.'

'Donald Roy can be very sweet,' Penelope said.

'And very eligible,' Flora added.

'But I couldn't marry him.'

'Because you love my brother more?'

'No,' Penelope shook her head, 'because of the size of his nose.'

'What?' Flora frowned.

'Well with my big nose and his enormous one – imagine what the poor children would look like?'

Flora burst into laughter. Arm in arm and giggling, the friends went tripping down the drive towards the harbour.

'And what about you and the Priest?' Penelope asked. 'Are you still intent on winning him away from celibacy?'

Flora flushed. 'Neil MacEachen and I are just good friends – I look forward to his letters – but I don't expect anything to come of it.'

'Well perhaps his heart's not really in the church. He only lasted a year at the Scots College in Paris.'

Flora tried not to let her hopes soar. 'Yes, but he's settled to his studies at the Catholic College in Arisaig. I just wish he would come back to the Long Isle for a visit.'

Penelope squeezed her arm. 'What a pair of hopeless lasses we are. You're in love with a trainee priest and I've lost my heart to a lad who's only got eyes for prize-winning heifers.'

Flora laughed and squeezed her arm in return. From the moment she had come to Nunton two years ago, Penelope, the Clanranalds' eldest daughter, had befriended her and shared everything.

'Thank the saints! You'll be an ally against my eight brothers. Call me Pen.'

They were the same age and both loved singing, dancing and riding. Flora taught Penelope to make syllabub as light as mist, the way Red Janet made it; Penelope helped Flora to improve her reading and letter writing. They were inseparable. Flora loved Nunton; it was even more noisy and lively than Balivanich. Clanranald was hospitable but when it all got too much, he retreated to his book-lined study to smoke and read, while Lady Clan thrived on entertainment and family life.

After evening meals, she insisted on each of them singing, playing an instrument or reciting a poem.

'Come Flora, you next. You have the voice of a linnet.'

'What does a linnet sound like, Mama?' Ranald Og had teased her. 'You've never heard one.'

'A linnet sounds like Flora,' Lady Clan replied with a laugh.

Every night, Penelope's mother would come to the girls' bedroom and sing songs to the younger girls, Louisa and Mally, say prayers, tuck them up and kiss them goodnight. Then she would come to the bed the older girls shared, hug them and kiss their foreheads.

'May your dreams be sweet ones,' she would smile and Flora would fall asleep happy and full of anticipation for the day ahead.

The first few months at Nunton had been blissful because her brother Angus had been there and Neil MacEachen came often to visit. Clanranald was teaching both Neil and Ranald Og Greek and Latin. Angus had dropped out of these classes and Flora noticed how Neil was becoming a closer companion to Ranald Og, the heir to their clan. While her brother went about the estate with the chamberlain learning the business of farming, Neil and Ranald Og would stay closeted with Clanranald discussing Plato, religion and politics.

Flora loved it best when Neil would bring out his violin and play for them all to dance. He looked so handsome, an intense look in his brown eyes, his high forehead and lean face framed by fair wavy hair, a secret smile playing on his lips when he caught her look. He rarely danced himself, preferring to make music. As the evening ended, at the bidding of Lady Clan, he would calm her over-excited children with haunting slow airs. A dreamy look would steal across his face and Flora always wondered what or whom he thought about in those moments.

She found it impossible to ever get Neil alone; he was kind and polite to her, but she suspected he merely saw her as a childhood friend; Angus Milton's pestering little sister. Until the day he came to leave.

Flora remembered every detail. She had been practising the spinet in Lady Clan's parlour. Lady Clan called Penelope away to help sort some linen and left them alone.

'I shan't be coming here for a while,' Neil said.

'Oh?' Flora's breathing stopped.

'Captain Clanranald has given me this great opportunity to study in Paris – he is paying for me to attend the Scots College.'

'How kind of the Captain. H-how long will you be gone?'

'Perhaps three years.'

Flora burst into tears.

'Florrie,' Neil said, putting a hand on her shoulder, 'don't be sad. This is what I'm called to do – to go to France. I'm doing this to make Clanranald proud.'

'But it's such a long time,' Flora tried to control her emotions. 'And isn't the Scots College for training priests?'

Neil nodded. 'I'm not sure yet if that is the life for me but that is what I intend to find out.'

'But you won't be able to marry!'

Neil took her hands in his; strong, supple musician's hands. 'Flora, I am very fond of you but you are still so young.'

'I'm in my fifteenth year and a woman!'

He smiled with affection. 'I can see that. But I don't want you to waste your womanhood waiting for me. By the time I return you will no doubt be married to some young buck from the clan.'

'I shan't,' Flora insisted, trying to hold back further tears.

He touched her cheek gently and brushed away a tear with his thumb. 'You must forget about me, sweet lassie. My duty is to a higher calling than marriage.'

He raised her hand and kissed it. As he stepped back, Flora felt panic rise in her throat.

'Will you write to me? Let me know how you are getting on. *Please*.'

Neil hesitated, his brown eyes shining with some emotion she could not fathom.

'I promise to write,' he smiled.

She watched him walk away, tall and straight-backed, and disappear through the doorway without looking back.

That had been over a year ago and Flora's sadness had not lasted. Life was too busy and full of fun at Nunton: dancing and singing lessons, cookery, needlework, poetry and riding. Lady Clan involved her in all the social occasions and Flora loved it when her mother came visiting with young Annabella to take tea with the Clanranald women and Flora would proudly show off her skills by presiding over the tea table. Her mother spoke dotingly of her growing family. Flora thought with a pang that things were more harmonious at Balivanich without her but she was glad to see Marion happy.

Flora's life at Nunton was spiced with extra excitement when the mail boat arrived from Skye or the mainland with a letter from Neil in France. She treasured all six letters she had from him. They were full of lively observations about the French and France, and his fellow students. He seemed to spend most of his time with the Scots abroad which made Flora wonder if he was homesick.

Then news had come to Captain Clanranald that Neil had left Paris and transferred to Arisaig where an unofficial college for training Catholic priests was run. What did this mean? Flora was still waiting to hear from Neil, who had not written to her since his return to Scotland.

'Look!' Penelope stopped in her tracks, half way to the sheltered harbour. 'That man …'

Flora shaded her eyes with a hand against the pearly glare of the autumnal sun on the wide expanse of water. A tall figure in blue bonnet and curly hair was leaping from the boat onto the stony pier.

'It's him!' Flora gasped. She kicked off her dainty shoes, picked up her skirts and ran ahead.

***

Neil MacEachen looked around at the familiar landscape of white beach and boggy moorland studded with small lochs and strips of tilled farmland. He breathed in a lungful of the salty clear air; nowhere smelt quite as sweet. He was home.

'Neil!'

He turned to see a young woman flying towards him, barefoot and skirts high revealing shapely legs. She looked as if she would run straight into him – he braced himself to catch her – but she stopped just short.

'Flora?' he stared.

'Aye,' she grinned, blushing and suddenly self-conscious. She dropped her skirts and smoothed them down. Neil couldn't help noticing how her figure had filled out. She pushed auburn hair out of her dark-lashed eyes.

'We came hoping for letters,' she panted, 'but this is better by far. I can't believe it's you!'

He smiled, reached forward and taking her hands in his, said, 'And I can't believe how you have turned into a beautiful woman in the short time I've been away.'

'It's been ages,' Flora cried. 'I'm surprised I recognise you at all.'

'I haven't changed that much, have I?'

She scrutinised him. 'Older and wiser, I'd say.'

He laughed. 'Not too old I hope.'

Penelope caught up with Flora and greeted him eagerly too. 'I hope you have come for a long visit, else Flora will be impossible to live with.'

'Stop it Pen!' Flora flushed crimson.

'That depends on your father,' Neil said. 'I have much to discuss with the Captain.'

'How intriguing,' Penelope arched her brows. 'Are you going to tell us first?'

'Miss Milton!' a shout from behind interrupted their conversation.

They turned to see the portly figure of the elderly Obadiah Gunn arriving round the bend on a mule, his thin son Elijah following on foot, laden with bags.

'Good day, Mr Gunn,' Flora said.

Neil caught the look of irritation on her face as the catechist struggled to dismount.

'Put those down, boy,' Obadiah snapped at his son, 'and help me off.'

In his hurry, Elijah dropped a bag. It split and oatmeal spilled out.

'You clumsy oaf!' Obadiah smacked his head as if he were a small boy and not a man of twenty.

Elijah's sallow face turned pink. 'Sorry,' he mumbled.

Flora went at once to help retrieve the oatmeal. 'Most of it will be fine,' she smiled. Elijah gave her a grateful look as he took the strain of his father's weight.

'Don't fuss Miss Milton,' Obadiah said, 'the boy must learn the consequences of his carelessness. He will have less to eat when he gets to his lodgings in Aberdeen.'

'You're returning to the university?' Flora asked Elijah.

'Yes, it's my second year–'

'Well, if it isn't MacEachen!' Obadiah interrupted. 'What a surprise to find you back on Benbecula.'

'Mr Gunn,' Neil greeted him, 'you look in good health.'

'The Lord shines on the righteous,' said Obadiah, ignoring Neil's outstretched hand. 'I thought you had gone to live with the Papists in Paris?'

'I stayed long enough to become fluent in French and improve my Latin.'

'Latin?' Obadiah sneered. 'The language of popery. I see no use for it. English is the language of progress and enlightenment.'

'Strange then that you choose to live among the Gaels,' Flora said with spirit, 'if you yearn to speak the language of the *Sassenach*.'

He gave her a sharp look.

'It has long been my calling to bring the light of the Protestant faith to the godless of these islands and to discourage the use of Erse. Wouldn't you agree, MacEachen,' he turned his imperious look on Neil, 'that we should be encouraging the common people to be loyal and obedient subjects of our Protestant King George?'

Neil knew Obadiah was trying to provoke him. 'You mean that German-speaking monarch in London?'

'Aye,' Flora joined in, 'you'd do well to start with teaching King George to speak fluent English before you try teaching it to our people here.'

Elijah gaped at her. No one teased his father about such things. Obadiah turned his annoyance on Penelope.

'I hope, Miss Clanranald, that you hold your monarch in more reverence than your friends?'

Penelope smiled. 'The sunshine has gone to their heads and they are just having sport with you, sir.'

'Then they are foolish,' Obadiah scowled. 'You should all know where your loyalty lies – and it's not with the French or that nest of Jacobite traitors they harbour in Paris. Wouldn't you agree, Miss Clanranald?'

'I know nothing of politics,' Penelope said airily.

'Well, I hope for your sake that your father takes more interest. Tell him from me to ignore treacherous advice or the temptation of Papist foreigners,' Obadiah said with a distrustful glance at Neil. 'It would be ill for you all if Clanranald should lose his lands and go into exile like your previous chief.'

Flora protested, 'you have no right to question the loyalty of the Clanranalds. They are the kindest, most peaceable family on the Long Isle.'

'Everyone is in danger of temptation, Miss Milton,' Obadiah lectured, 'even the mighty at Nunton.' He turned on Neil and demanded. 'Do you bring letters from France for the Captain?'

'I have come from Arisaig not France,' Neil said, keeping his temper. 'And yes, I bring letters from his kin. But most of my baggage is full of buttons, ribbon and thread for the industrious Lady Clan. Please excuse us, kind sir, I must go and make myself known to my patrons.' He turned to Elijah and shook his limp hand. 'Good luck in Aberdeen with your studies.'

Elijah mumbled his thanks.

'Come ladies,' Neil ushered the women ahead of him. Flora and Penelope gave hurried curtsies.

'Goodbye Elijah,' Flora smiled and turned away.

Only Neil noticed the look of adoration on Elijah's pinched face as he watched Flora go. The young man was still squinting myopically at them as he stood in the departing boat, hoping for her to turn around and wave. But Flora had forgotten all about Elijah by the time they reached the house; her heart was bursting with happiness at Neil's surprise return.

Chapter 20

To Flora's delight, Neil stayed on at Nunton through the winter to tutor the younger Clanranalds. He seemed in no hurry to return to Arisaig and by early 1739 had abandoned the idea of entering the church.

'It's obvious why,' Penelope teased her friend. 'You've made him realise how impossible it would be to remain chaste.'

'Pen!' Flora swiped her with a cushion.

'It's true. I've seen the way he looks at you. I bet you ten merks he'll be proposing marriage as soon as you turn seventeen.'

'Do you think so?' Flora gasped. 'I don't like to hope too much. He's never hinted that he loves me.'

'Wasn't it his idea to teach us French in the afternoons? Just an excuse to be with you, I'm sure of it. And isn't he always suggesting that you accompany him on the spinet when he plays violin?'

'That just proves his love of music, nothing more,' Flora sighed.

'Florrie!' Penelope cried. 'Don't you realise how attractive you are to men? I wish I had a fraction of your looks.'

Flora looked at her in astonishment. She always thought of herself as quite ordinary and overshadowed by her self-confident friend.

'I think you must be as short-sighted as Elijah Gunn,' Flora snorted, 'if you think I'm prettier than you.'

She dismissed the idea as fanciful but was secretly pleased at the suggestion that her feelings for Neil might be reciprocated. She lay awake at night trying to imagine what their first proper kiss would be like; not a brotherly peck on the cheek or forehead but a lingering of lips. Flora was impatient for each day to start so that she could gaze upon his handsome lean looks and listen to his lilting voice. Best of all was when she could sit and hear him sing or play his violin, for he seemed to be playing just for her. Yet, for all he was kind and affectionate towards her, Neil never declared his love or spoke of a future together. Whenever she pressed him on how long he would stay as the Clanranald's tutor, he would smile and shrug evasively, 'that is up to the Captain.'

Spring came, and another baby to swell the Clanranald household; a fourth daughter whom they christened Margaret but was swiftly called Peggi like her mother, Lady Clan. She was baptised in the kirk under the watchful eye of Obadiah Gunn but one evening, shortly afterwards, Flora saw a man arrive by boat and disappear down the cellar steps. She suspected he was a priest from Barra or the mainland, come to give the baby a Catholic blessing in the secret room that Neil had shown her years ago. The next morning, the boat was gone and the mysterious visitor was never mentioned.

Then Flora's stepfather, Hugh *Cam*, appeared one early summer's day with news from Skye.

'My chief, Sir Alexander of Sleat, is to marry again!'

'That is good news indeed,' Lady Clan cried. 'The poor man deserves a piece of happiness.'

Flora thought how sad and lost the Skye chief had looked on his last tour of the Long Isle the previous summer, though his first wife had died over six years ago in childbirth. Their baby son had gone to his grave shortly after his mother and the young chief had been heartbroken.

'Tell us,' Penelope urged, 'who is the lucky bride? Is she one of the MacLeods of Dunvegan?'

Hugh shook his head. 'Guess again.'

'A MacLeod of Raasay?' Flora joined in. 'They have lots of daughters.'

'Yes,' Penelope agreed. 'I bet five merks it's one of them.'

'No.'

'A Mackenzie?'

'Cameron of Locheil?' said Lady Clan.

'Mackinnon of Strath?'

Hugh continued to shake his head at each suggestion.

'A MacDonald of Glengarry?' Flora brightened.

'All wrong,' Hugh grinned. 'She's not from the Highlands at all.'

'A Lowlander?' Lady Clan gasped in dismay.

'Well he has spent all winter away from Skye,' Neil piped up.

'Has he?'

'Neil is right,' Hugh nodded. 'Sir Alexander has been courting one of the beauties of Edinburgh society – Margaret Montgomerie – one of Lord Eglinton's seven daughters.'

'Aristocracy then,' Penelope said in approval.

'But will she settle on Skye?' Lady Clan was dubious. 'These society lassies might know how to drink coffee and dance a gavotte but they can't ride through a storm or deliver a calf.'

Penelope rolled her eyes at her mother's comment. 'Is she very beautiful?'

'Very,' Hugh grinned.

But where will they live?' Lady Clan fretted. 'Armadale House is little more than a farmhouse – she'll be used to luxury – and Duntulm Castle is half falling down.'

Hugh said eagerly, 'Sir Alexander has been building a mansion at Monkstadt in the north of the island in preparation for a new wife.'

'So he won't be abandoning us for a life in the capital?' Neil asked.

'Quite the contrary,' Hugh reassured. 'Sir Alexander is not suited to city life and to be frank, he chose Lady Margaret out of all the others because she agreed to live on Skye. She seems just as eager to become the wife of a Highland chief.'

Neil nodded in satisfaction. Flora wondered why he should seem so interested in the marriage plans of Lord MacDonald of Sleat. Would it spur him on to make plans of his own? She hardly dared to hope.

'Will there be a big wedding?' Penelope asked in excitement.

'The biggest on Skye this century,' Hugh grinned. 'Sir Alexander wants to impress upon his Lowland in-laws that no one in the land can match the hospitality of a Highland chief.'

'Will we all be invited?' Flora gasped.

Hugh winked with his one good eye. 'I think that can be arranged,' he chuckled.

Penelope and Flora squealed with delight. 'I've never been to Skye before.' Penelope clapped her hands. 'We'll need new dresses, won't we Mama?'

Lady Clan smiled broadly. 'Indeed we will. These Lowlanders will be turning their heads with envy when the Clanranalds step ashore at Monkstadt.' Then she laughed the infectious throaty laugh that Flora loved so much and they all joined in.

***

It was late summer when the Clanranald and Balivanich households set sail across the Minch for Skye in a small flotilla of open boats. Flora was happy to be reunited with her family – her mother was excited at the prospect of mixing with the MacDonald elite, though anxious at Hugh's insistence that the younger children be left at home.

'James can come – he's a sensible lad and Angus can take him under his wing – but let Janet spoil the rest for a few days,' Hugh had insisted. 'Monkstadt will be bursting at the seams as it is. It'll do you good to cut the apron strings and enjoy yourself.'

'I must at least have Annabella with me,' Marion had insisted. 'I can't be without my little buttercup.'

Hugh had relented but Flora guessed that he had wished to have his wife to himself for once.

For Penelope's sake, Flora was glad that her brother Angus had agreed to delay joining the drovers in their southward migration until after Lord MacDonald's wedding, and he was in high spirits. Frustratingly, Neil chose to travel in a companion boat with the Baleshare MacDonalds – Donald Roy and his older brother Uisdean – and during the day for much of the voyage, Flora only caught glimpses of them, deep in conversation.

But the crossing was calm and the cliffs of Skye could be seen from far off. Lachie, son of her father's old boatman, led the rowers and they sang lustily as they pulled towards shore. She was soon distracted by Penelope's gasps of wonder at the sight of the gleaming new mansion at Monkstadt standing tall amid ripening fields of golden oats. Disembarking at the harbour of Kilbride, they were piped ashore by Sleat's elite MacArthur pipers and boatmen rushed to lift them to safety.

The land seethed with people arriving off boats, servants shouldering luggage and provisions, Highland ponies carrying the elderly or infirm guests, and local barefoot children running around in excitement at the unusual spectacle. Flora was as wide-eyed as the children, the nearer she drew to the vast house. It stood three stories tall and ten rooms wide, freshly whitewashed and fitted with casement windows that glinted and flashed like jewels in the late summer sun. She had thought Nunton the grandest of houses until she set eyes on Monkstadt; it was fit for royalty. Did all Lowland nobility live like this? She wondered.

The Clanranalds were ushered into the vast mansion but as Flora followed Penelope in the melee, Hugh *Cam* pulled her back.

'I've just been told we are staying with Sir Alexander's chamberlain,' he smiled, 'come and meet Kingsburgh.'

Flora and Penelope exchanged looks of panic. They had been inseparable for over two years.

'Can't I stay with Pen?' Flora pleaded.

A flash of annoyance lit Hugh's face. 'You are a Milton and I am your guardian not Clanranald. It is a great honour Kingsburgh does us to offer his hospitality – he is the most powerful man in the Skye clan.'

'But I thought the Kingsburghs lived in Armadale in the south of Skye?'

'They do but they also have the tack at Kingsburgh near here – it's their family home.' His look softened in a smile. 'I'm sure you and Miss Penelope will survive without each other for one night.'

'Go Flora,' Penelope said, gently disengaging their arms. 'It'll be nice for your mother and Annabella to have you for once. We'll all meet at the wedding soon.'

Flora vaguely recognised the burly, genial man in MacDonald plaid who greeted them. She knew she had met the Kingsburghs when she was a little girl living on Skye for a brief time before her mother had married Hugh *Cam*, though her memory of that time was hazy. The one Kingsburgh she remembered clearly was the restless, dark-haired son Allan who had delighted in teasing her and challenging her to races. Her clearest memory was beating him in a race to the shore.

'It's a pleasure to meet you again, Miss Milton,' Kingsburgh said, his smile genuine. 'We hear great things of you from your stepfather when he travels to Skye on business. You do the name of Milton and Balivanich .proud.'

Flora blushed, quite taken aback by the compliment. 'I'm just an ordinary Long Isle lassie,' Flora smiled, 'and any accomplishments are a reflection on my parents not me. But thank you for your kindness.'

'Charming as well as pretty,' Kingsburgh chuckled.

It was nearly an hour's ride and the sun was waning as they reached Kingsburgh House. It was an attractive two storey farmhouse set among trees with a view across fertile fields to a large bay.

Florence, Kingsburgh's wife, bustled out to greet them and whisk them inside to a cosy parlour. As she fussed around them, Kingsburgh at once began pouring brandies for Hugh and himself.

'What a long day you've had,' Florence exclaimed, 'you must be exhausted. Marion – may I call you Marion? – I feel we're old friends – I'll send hot water to your bedroom or would you prefer to eat first? And this must be wee Annabella – aren't you a pretty wee thing?' She kissed the girl on her fair curls. 'I think we should eat first, husband, don't you?'

A slim, dark-haired woman appeared at her side. 'Mother, let them get settled first. I'm Ann,' she gave a short curtsy to Marion and Hugh then turned to Flora and fixed her with an assessing look. 'You must be Flora.'

'Aye, I am,' Flora smiled and stepped forward to kiss her cheek but Ann did not respond.

Florence cried, 'goodness me! Is this the wild lassie who used to skim stones and rush about with my Allan? Haven't you grown up?'

'Who used to rush about with me?' A deep voice sounded behind the door and then a man strode in.

For a moment, Flora thought it must be one of the herdsmen; he was dressed in rough breeks and a homespun shirt with half its buttons missing, his mane of black hair loose and tangled, and his face weather-beaten.

'Laddie!' his mother shrieked. 'You can't come in here with those filthy clothes. Don't step on the carpet. We have guests–'

He paused to yank off his dusty boots, then continued barefoot, thrusting out a hand to Hugh *Cam*.

'Good to see you again, sir.' He took Marion's hand and kissed it, winked at Annabella, ruffled James's hair and clasped Angus by the hand. 'Welcome Angus Og.'

He turned to Flora, his vivid blue eyes registering surprise then appreciation as he looked her over. He gave a short bow and grinned. 'I challenge you to a stone-throwing contest or a race, Miss Milton. Though these days I'd have to give you a head start, I imagine.'

'I don't need any special treatment,' Flora quipped back.

'Careful Allan,' Angus laughed, 'she still runs like the wind.'

'That I would like to see.'

Flora felt her cheeks go on fire at his bold look. He might look like a grown man – she tried not to stare at his broad chest through the tatty shirt and his hairy legs – but he was obviously still the aggravating boy that she remembered.

'I no longer run races like a child,' she said, attempting a withering look and turned to Ann. 'Are you still good at knitting? I remember you being so quick with your needles.'

'Oh she is,' Florence answered before her daughter could reply. 'My Ann has such nimble fingers – she can knit, sew, spin like a fairy.'

'Mother,' Ann protested, squirming at the praise. 'Let me show our guests to their rooms.'

'Of course,' Florence agreed, 'and I will have supper prepared the instant you want it. Allan, you must go and change at once.'

'I will,' he smiled but did just the opposite, joining his father and Hugh by the quaich of brandy.

The women were taken upstairs. Annabella was to sleep with her parents on a truckle bed in a pleasant room overlooking the bay; Flora was to share a bed with Ann. Ann looked as unenthusiastic about this as Flora felt. The older girl hardly spoke to her except to reprimand her, 'I hope you aren't going to be rude to my brother all the time? We Kingsburghs are important folk among the Sleat MacDonalds – and our clan ranks above your Long Isle Clanranalds.'

95

Flora sparked, 'I too am related to Lord MacDonald of Sleat through my mother.'

Then she felt bad for having risen to the girl's baiting; she should have defended the kind Clanranalds instead. They might be the chief's family of a smaller, less wealthy MacDonald clan, but they were matchless in their loyalty to their people and their clan traditions.

The look of disdain that Ann gave her made Flora realise that whatever she said, the haughty Kingsburgh daughter would still look down on her as an inferior being from the Outer Isles.

Flora, anxious not to say anything that might provoke derision, stayed quiet at the evening meal and made excuses to retire upstairs early with Annabella. She feigned sleep when Ann came to bed – the girl pulled half the covers off her – and wondered if Penelope was feasting or dancing with the Sleats and their guests. Where was Neil staying? Was he sharing a room with Ranald Og? She lay restless and impatient for the wedding morning to come.

Chapter 21

Hugh *Cam* and Kingsburgh began the day with whisky at breakfast. Marion and Florence fussed that they would be drunk before the ceremony.

'Before, during and after!' Hugh roared with laughter at their disapproval.

Flora did not see Allan. Her mother said, 'Angus has gone with young Kingsburgh to inspect the cattle. They were up at dawn.'

The women made ready together; Flora in a sky blue gown with lace trim and white stockings, her mother and Annabella in matching yellow dresses decorated with blue ribbon and pearl buttons. Even Ann became animated as they discussed the bride and her Lowland family.

'I've seen Margaret Montgomerie,' Ann preened. 'She's small but very pretty.'

'Then they will have beautiful children,' said Marion.

'She's not much older than me,' Ann replied, 'and they say she's keen on society life. Don't suppose she'll be rushing into motherhood and confinement.'

'And is there someone chosen for you?' Marion asked.

Ann gave a coy smile. 'I am being courted by a Mr Macalister.'

Flora was intrigued. 'That's not a local name is it?'

'They are a well-respected and prosperous family newly come to Skye. Mr Macalister sees to Lord MacDonald's business in Trotternish – he's Sir Alexander's factor around here.'

'Is he handsome?' Flora asked in excitement. 'Will he be at the wedding?'

'Yes to both questions,' Ann nodded. With a condescending look, she added, 'perhaps we can find a suitable husband for you among the guests – though you are still rather young.'

Flora laughed. 'Oh, I'm not looking for a suitor.' She exchanged knowing looks with her mother.

'Florrie has lost her heart to Neil MacEachen,' Marion explained.

'Is that the MacEachen who went to France?' Ann raised disapproving eyebrows. 'Isn't he a known Jacobite?'

'Many of us in the Long Isle have sympathies for the exiled Stuarts,' Flora retorted.

'Well please don't say such treasonable things in front of Mr Macalister or Lord Eglinton's party,' Ann said brusquely.

A warning look from her mother, made Flora swallow down a defence of herself and Neil. They hurried out to the waiting horses.

She had to look twice to see if she was mistaken, but it was Allan who came forward with a fistful of pink and white roses. His dark hair was well-groomed and pulled back into a queue, showing a handsome full-featured face with a strong well-shaven chin. He was immaculately dressed in kilt, white linen shirt, velvet doublet, plaid across broad shoulders and sword buckled at his hip.

'Roses for all the prettiest women at the wedding feast,' he offered them round. 'I've clipped the thorns so you can wear them in your dresses.'

Marion cried in delight. 'How thoughtful.'

'He grows them himself,' Florence said proudly.

'Let me,' Hugh said quickly, taking the rose from Allan and tucking it into the bodice of his wife's low-cut dress, caressing the tops of her breasts as he did so.

Flora saw a knowing smile pass between her parents that made her blush. She caught Allan's amused look as he held out a white bloom. 'This will match the lace of your dress perfectly, Miss Milton.'

She took it quickly and slipped it through a ribbon in her hair instead. 'Thank you.'

'My pleasure.'

Why did his dimpled grin make her feel so childish and gauche? Flora thought in annoyance. Just let him wait till Neil chose her as his dancing partner, then Allan would stop treating her as a girl to be teased.

***

Flora had never seen so many people gathered together in such finery; they could have outshone any court in Europe, she felt sure. All the clans from across the Highlands appeared to be represented – many of them by their chiefs or heads of important branches – as well as Lowland nobility and men of business in velvet breeches, silver-buckled shoes and fancy wigs.

She could not help staring in wonder at the array of silk and satin dresses – crimson, moss green, claret red, salmon pink and royal blue – and the elaborate hairstyles, bejewelled headdresses and dainty shoes.

The bride was almost hidden in swathes of white silk, ribbons, bows and jewels, her hair hidden in a powdered wig that made her look older. She looked pale and overawed as she took dainty halting steps towards the slimly handsome Sir Alexander, waiting anxiously for her at the other end of the great hall. It was too crowded for Flora to see much but when the pipes struck up in deafening unison, she knew the marriage ceremony was done.

Penelope found her. 'Isn't this exciting? I love the rose in your hair – it suits your chestnut curls. Where is that brother of yours? I hope we can all sit together.'

The friends made sure that they did.

In the feasting that followed – both in the hall and at trestle tables set up in the courtyard – huge trenchers of beef, venison, haddock, fowl, hare and shellfish were constantly replenished, together with bowls of gravy, green vegetables, anchovy sauce and plates of tongue, boiled eggs and barley cakes. All was washed down with vast amounts of brandy punch, claret and porter.

'Do you see that man at top table?' Penelope pointed out a distinguished man in red tartan and neat wig, his face animated and cheeks flushed.

'That's Chief Norman, MacLeod of MacLeod from Dunvegan Castle. And the woman to his side with the dark hair and the sour look? That's his wife. They've been estranged for years but now they're back together again.'

Flora stared, fascinated to see the head of a rival clan whose ancestors had fought her own MacDonald ones. 'She doesn't look very happy.'

'I'm not surprised,' Penelope's eyes lit with the fire of gossip. 'Chief Norman still has a mistress in Edinburgh from when he and Mrs MacLeod were living apart. You see that lad over there with a fresh face and curly hair sitting with the MacLeod children? That's Alex, Chief Norman's illegitimate son from this other woman.'

Flora's eyes widened in shock. 'Never!'

Penelope nodded. 'It's true – MacLeod of Dunvegan's quite open about it – dotes on Alex more than his own heir, so they say. And there's a second son born to this mistress but he's not here.'

'How do you know all this?' Flora gasped.

'The Unish MacLeods told me – they're from the next peninsula round from here – arrived in a horde at breakfast. That's Tormod, the eldest son over there.' Penelope pointed to a plump-faced young man who was drinking deeply from a silver bowl. 'He's a bit full of himself – you would think he was the heir to Dunvegan Castle the way he boasts about his closeness to Chief Norman.'

Young Unish caught them staring at him. He winked back with an inebriated grin.

'Tormod said Chief Norman has only repaired his marriage to please Sir Alexander, 'cos his wife is a relation of Lord MacDonald.'

'Why would he want to curry favour with Sir Alexander?'

'Business interests, I suppose.'

Their chatter was interrupted by the drumming of fists on the wooden tables and Kingsburgh rose to announce a toast to the bride and groom. This was followed by speeches and a long eulogy in Gaelic from MacDonald's senior bard about the greatness of Sleat and the beauty of Margaret Montgomorie. The bride sat looking bemused until someone translated for her.

A harpist played while the tables were cleared and puddings and sweets were served. Then when everyone was sated with food and drink, the pipers struck up once more and led the wedding party outside to dance. The weather held and a light breeze kept the midges at bay. The dancing began sedately with the bride and groom leading off the dancers. Flora looked round in frustration for Neil. She had hardly set eyes on him all day; he seemed always in deep conversation with others.

But to her delight he appeared at her side as the fiddlers struck up a reel.

'Will you do me the honour of dancing this jig with me, Florrie?'

'I'd like nothing better,' Flora smiled, her heart leaping as he took hold of her hand.

The dancing soon became fast and furious, all pretence at decorum gone, as the sun sank into the sea beyond the distant Outer Isles and the noise of revelry rang through the cooling air. Flora and the Long Isle girls kicked off their restricting shoes, hitched up their full skirts and tucked them into their girdles.

When the matrons scolded their immodesty, the young bride, Lady Margaret, threw off her own shoes and picked up her skirts too.

'This is so much fun!' she cried in her Lowland English, her petite face broadly smiling.

As darkness fell, flaming torches were placed around the courtyard so the dancing could continue. Flora warmed to the young bride – she hardly looked older than her or Penelope –and had the same zest for dancing and fun. Lady Margaret called for the musicians to play a Lowland tune.

'It's so popular in the Capital,' she cried, her voice high-pitched and excited.

Sir Alexander spoke to the bemused fiddlers, suggesting a reel with the same tempo while his young wife organised the dancers into pairs in a huge circle. The Lowland guests all knew what to do and soon had the Highlanders following their footsteps in a progressive dance where the men handed on the women to the next partner. The fiddlers played increasingly fast and Flora's head began to spin at the speed at which they had to move on to the next man, the flames of the torches blurring into streaks of light.

Strong arms came around her waist, steadying her and pulling her to a broad chest. Flora laughed then gasped as she came face to face with a grinning Allan of Kingsburgh. He had discarded his doublet and plaid and was pressing her firmly to his body.

'At last Miss Milton! I thought you were never going to dance with a Skye man.'

'I don't choose to,' she gave a breathless answer as they crossed arms and turned each other.

He laughed as he twirled her under his arm. 'I see Neil MacEachen is my rival.'

'No, he's not,' Flora quipped, 'because there is no contest.'

'What does the Uist boy have that I don't?'

Flora smirked. 'Sophistication, knowledge of the world, speaks French like a native, plays violin better than anyone I know, writes courtly letters–'

'And is he as strong as this?'

The next moment Allan was lifting her off her feet as they spun right out of the circle and into the blackness beyond the torchlight. He pinned her in his arms, his face coming so close to hers she could see the devilment flash in his blue eyes. His look left her dizzy and breathless.

'And can your courtly Uist boy give you kisses like this?

'What are you doing–?'

Flora's protest was silenced by Allan's mouth coming firmly down on her half parted lips. Shock ripped through her at his lusty enthusiastic embrace. Suddenly he wasn't gripping her any more as his hands went around her face, caressing her neck and hair, sending tingles of excitement down her body. She had no idea kissing could be like this.

'Allan, are you there? Come out of the dark so I can see you.'

Ann's imperious voice made them break apart. Flora could feel Allan's warm breath on her forehead and see the heaving of his chest as he debated whether to answer his sister.

'I know you're there Allan; I saw you leave the dance. What are you doing?'

Allan swore softly under his breath.

'Mother and Hugh *Cam*'s wife want to go home,' Ann persisted. 'You are to accompany them. Allan, are you listening?'

Allan ran a finger across Flora's cheek and gave her a rueful look.

'I'll come back,' he whispered.

The thought sent Flora into a panic. What was she thinking of allowing the annoying Skye man to take advantage of her like that?

'Don't,' she hissed, pushing him away. Then before he could stop her, she ducked sideways and ran back towards the dancers. Ann gave her a disapproving look as she sped past – how shaming that Allan's sister had followed them – but Flora fled before she could be questioned.

Chapter 22

The wedding celebrations lasted all week. There were games and tournaments during the day, then more feasting, music, poetry and dancing at night.

Flora avoided Allan at all costs. Each morning, she came down to breakfast once she knew he had left to check on the cattle and she spent as much time up at Monkstadt with Penelope as she could. It made her hot with shame to think how he had tricked her in the dance to get her alone and then forced his kisses on her. On the few occasions they sat at the same table or passed on the stair, she caught his amused, slightly baffled look. He tried once to get her to dance with him but she feigned tiredness and he never asked again.

'Don't you like young Kingsburgh?' Penelope asked. 'He seems interested in you.'

'No, he's not,' Flora said hotly, 'and I'm not the least bit interested in him. He's uncouth with the manners of a cowherd.'

Penelope's eyes widened in surprise. 'Angus likes him. Says Allan is full of ideas for the farm and has a way with animals.'

'Like I said,' Flora pouted, 'a cowherd.'

To Flora's relief, her friend let the matter drop and they did not mention him again. Soon, Allan was ignoring her too, throwing himself with vigour into arm-wrestling and tug-of-war competitions, and dancing with MacLeod of Dunvegan's pretty young daughters. She watched this with a strange feeling in the pit of her stomach that she told herself was relief. She returned to filling her daydreams with thoughts of Neil and it was like the sun bursting out from behind clouds whenever he sought her out and paid her attention. True feelings of love she thought she understood; the queasiness in her stomach when she thought of Allan's embrace left her confused and annoyed.

Gradually, the guests from the mainland began to leave and the numbers to dwindle. Marion, pining for her other children, nagged Hugh to return to the Long Isle. Flora too was growing homesick and tired of sharing a bed with the critical Ann who never missed an opportunity to belittle her.

'I'm surprised you've stayed this long – Mr Macalister thinks your family have rather taken advantage of my father's hospitality – but then he doesn't understand you Long Isle folk.'

'Meaning?' Flora bristled.

'Well, you so seldom travel beyond the Outer Isles that it's a huge event for you, isn't it? Once in a lifetime, I imagine.'

Flora bit her tongue. She found the fussy, chinless Macalister a bore and wondered what Ann saw in him. But she seemed to hang on his every word and absorbed his opinions as her own, so it seemed they were suited.

Flora's only worry was that Neil might stay on at Monkstadt for he seemed to have quickly attached himself to the close group of young gentry around Sir Alexander and Lady Margaret. It was already clear that the chief's new fun-loving wife thrived on the company of other young attractive people. She was constantly calling on Neil to play French airs on his violin.

The following morning, the boat to take them back to Benbecula came into the bay below Kingsburgh House. The Kingsburghs went down to see them off, Allan carrying young Annabella piggy-back and making her squeal with delight as he raced across the pasture.

To Flora's joy, Neil was standing tall at the bows of the open boat to wave them aboard. He greeted Kingsburgh and Florence with a respectful bow, and exchanged nods with Allan.

'Lady Clan has asked me to accompany Miss Milton safely back to Nunton,' Neil called.

Flora blushed with pleasure but Annabella cried out, 'I don't want Florrie to go back to Nunton. Why can't she live with us?'

'Don't fuss, my buttercup,' Marion put arms up to lift her from Allan's back.

'But I want her to stay with us!' Annabella wailed and pushed her mother away.

Flora went quickly to intervene. Briefly her look met Allan's as she said, 'I'll take her.' With one swift movement he had the girl off his back and was steadying her on the ground. Annabella flung her arms around Flora.

'You are much in demand,' Allan murmured, his smile sardonic.

Flora held his look. 'We Long Isle folk are clannish, that's all. We always stand by each other.'

She thought she saw something in Allan's expression change – was it regret? – and he seemed on the point of speaking when his sister said briskly, 'best not keep Mr MacEachen waiting. Goodbye Flora.'

The next moment all about them were taking their farewells, shaking hands and embracing, saying thank you for the hospitality and clambering on board.

Flora kissed Florence on the cheek. 'You've been so kind to us, thank you. I hope someday we can return the favour.'

'It's been a pleasure,' she beamed, 'come again dearie.'

Allan and his father waded into the shallows to help them leap into the boat. Flora handed over Annabella to Hugh *Cam* and then tucked up her skirt and splashed into the sea, determined not to be helped, but Allan blocked her way. For a brief moment, his strong warm hands went around her waist as he lifted her clear and passed her over to Neil. Flora reached out quickly and grabbed Neil's hands; he hauled her aboard.

'Morning Miss Flora,' one of the bonneted boatmen said, as he helped her to sit in the rocking boat.

Flora peered at the familiar looking man. It was the MacEachens' rower from Howbeg, husband of kind Kate who had befriended Flora after her father died.

'Ronald Oar?' she gasped.

'Aye,' he grinned.

'How is Kate?' Flora cried. 'And wee Katie? Do tell me!'

'Both grand. And Katie is not so wee. She's ten and working in the dairy for the MacEachens.'

Flora was so excited to get news of her old friends that the boat was well out from the shore before she realised it. She looked back to see Kingsburgh and Florence still waving them away. Ann and Macalister were already retreating to the house. There was no sign of Allan. He must have stridden off quicker than the others, impatient to be back to his cattle and his plants. She felt a twisting sense of relief. Turning her head towards the Outer Isles and breathing in the salty air, she caught Neil observing her.

'Happy to be going home?' he asked lightly.

'Very,' she smiled.

'Good,' he smiled back.

***

Allan scrambled quickly up the rocky cliff-face by Peindoun. From this vantage point he could see the flat topped mountains of MacLeod's Tables away to the south; to the north-west he could see all the way to the end of the loch where it flowed into the Minch and open sea.

MacEachen's boat passed right below him, the rowers pulling hard against the incoming tide. He didn't think it was a coincidence that Neil MacEachen had appeared this morning to whisk Flora away to Benbecula. Flora was too trusting to see that the man was sly, wheedling his way into everyone's confidence, learning their secrets. Allan, like a fool, had allowed Neil to ply him with too much brandy. He had confessed his infatuation with Flora MacDonald, the Milton lass; he remembered babbling about her soft skin and her bewitching blue-grey eyes.

He stared down at the boat bobbing and lifting on the waves, the singing of the rowers carried up to him amid the screeching of seabirds. Flora's dark hair was writhing in the breeze, its auburn tints catching in the sunlight like skeins of red thread. He felt his chest constrict with longing. Neil was sitting close-by her, leaning towards her to catch her chatter. Allan was too far away to see the expression on her face but he imagined her adoring look at the attentive MacEachen.

'Flora is destined to marry within the Long Isle,' Neil had warned off Allan. Or at least that was Allan's hazy memory of their conversation during the drinking binge. Neil had clapped him on the shoulder like a comrade-in-arms and said, 'you'll be expected to make a great match, young Kingsburgh – one that will bind the Skye clans together forever. The Chamberlain's son and the Chief's daughter. The time will come soon enough when we must stand united for the greater good of our people and our country.'

Allan had no idea what he was talking about, except that he was left with the strong impression that he had been rebuked for making a play for Flora. Obviously Neil wanted her for himself.

He watched until the boat shrank to a distant speck and the sails were unfurled, whipping the vessel quickly out beyond the cliffs of Skye. With a deep sigh, Allan forced himself to turn away. The droving couldn't come soon enough. Only the physical exertion and the camaraderie – the jesting and hard drinking – of being on the road with the other men would quench his thirst for the unattainable Benbecula girl.

Chapter 23

Flora's happiness at Nunton was short-lived. Within a month of returning, it was announced that the Clanranald's eldest son, Ranald Og, would be going to Paris to finish his education.

'You're going too, aren't you?' she confronted Neil after his daily French lesson with the younger Clanranalds.

Neil collected up the children's slates and chalk. He waited for them to clatter out and then turned to Flora and said, 'walk with me to the shore.'

Her heart did not stop hammering as they donned plaids and left the house; anxiety gripped her. Neil did not speak until he was sure that they were out of hearing.

'It will be much easier for Ranald Og to settle into life in France if I am there to help him. I can make introductions and ensure no one takes advantage of a young Highland chieftain who has never left the Isles before. The Captain has asked me to go and keep an eye on his son.'

'So once he is settled,' Flora asked in hope, 'you will return to the Outer Isles?'

Neil regarded her. 'I will stay for as long as he needs me there.'

'But he could be away for years studying!'

'Aye, he could.'

She gazed into his lean handsome face, trying to fathom his thoughts but his expression gave nothing away.

'You feel nothing for me, do you?' she said unhappily. 'If you did, you would not be able to bear the thought of being apart for so long.'

Suddenly he reached out and placed his hands on her shoulders, his face earnest.

'Dearest Florrie, you have a special place in my heart, you must believe that.'

'Then why do you keep leaving me?' she challenged. 'I'm old enough now to know my own mind – old enough to be promised in marriage – yet you still treat me like a child. Do we have an understanding, Neil, or not?'

For the first time she had unsettled him. His face clouded.

'I haven't chosen the path I take – it is chosen for me. I wish I could marry you now and give you the life you desire but I can't.'

'I don't understand,' Flora said impatiently, 'I thought you had turned your back on becoming a priest?'

'I have,' he insisted, 'but I have difficult work to do. I can't tell you what it is; you just have to trust me that it is for the good of our clan.'

Flora searched his face. 'Will you be in danger?'

He did not answer. She reached up and touched his cheek. 'Oh Neil,' she gasped, 'are you working for the Jacobites in France? You are, aren't you?'

He glanced around, fearing she might have been heard. 'Shush.' He put a finger to her lips.

Flora held onto it and kissed it. All at once, he was tilting her chin upwards and gazing at her with fierce brown eyes. He dipped his head and brushed her lips with his own. Fleeting and elusive as the touch of a butterfly, it left Flora yearning for more.

'One day,' he promised, 'when the rightful King James is back on the throne of Scotland, I will be one of his most trusted nobles and richly rewarded. Only then can I offer you marriage, Flora.' His look bore into her, willing her to comprehend. 'Until then, my life will be one of travel and danger – I will not put you at such risk – you do understand that, don't you?'

Flora nodded, tears welling in her eyes. Her heart was so heavy she could not speak.

'Will you wait for me, Florrie?'

She gulped down tears. 'You know I will, Neil. You've had my heart for as long as I can remember.'

He squeezed her hands in his and smiled at last. She wished she could hang onto his touch forever, but by the time they came in sight of Nunton once more, he had dropped his hold and pushed her gently ahead of him up the path.

***

1740 came with bitter winds and the news that Ranald and Neil were settled into life in Paris. Both Penelope and Flora found the house quiet without Ranald's boisterous teasing and Neil's genial presence. Angus spent more time away too. Flora returned from a visit to her mother with news for Penelope.

'Angus is building a large house down at Milton,' Flora said to her friend.

'Really?' Penelope could not hide her curiosity. 'But there is a perfectly good house at Balivanich which will be his one day.'

'Angus doesn't want to be beholden to our stepfather. He wants to take on the tack at Milton himself and live there full-time.'

'Oh,' Penelope's face fell. 'So he wants to go and live in South Uist rather than spend time here.'

Flora flung an arm around her. 'Don't be glum, Pen. It's obvious he's doing it for you.'

'For me?'

'He's building a house for a bride,' Flora grinned. 'A modern house fit for a chief's daughter.'

Penelope covered her blushing cheeks with her hands. 'Did he say so?'

'Not in so many words,' Flora admitted, 'but I'm sure that's what he intends.'

'What does your stepfather say? I thought he liked Angus to keep an eye on Balivanich when he's away travelling on Sir Alexander's business.'

'Hugh *Cam* understands and won't stand in his way.'

Flora did not want to dwell on the wrangling at Balivanich. Marion and Hugh were increasingly at loggerheads. She accused him of neglecting her and his family and being at the Sleats' beck and call; he complained

107

that she was becoming a recluse, neglecting her duties as his hostess and locking him out of her bedroom. Flora was glad that she had resisted Annabella's pleading for her to go and live with them. Balivanich was becoming a battleground. She tried to keep the peace when she was there but this just enraged Marion.

'You always take his side!' she railed. 'Just like you did with your father. I don't know what I'd do without my Annabella to comfort me.'

None of this did Flora relay to Penelope – she did not want anything to put her off becoming her sister-in-law – but she did admit that the house at Milton would not be built overnight.

'My brother has laid the foundation stones and will have the walls built this year. But it won't be roofed till next and likely furnished the year after that.'

'I know,' Penelope sighed. 'It all depends on how well the cattle do at the sales – I'm quite aware of that. I'm prepared to wait.'

Flora laughed. 'They should have named you Patience not Penelope.'

So when Hugh came one day in early summer with a request from Lady Margaret that the young women visit Monkstadt, both friends jumped at the chance.

'Between you and me,' Hugh confided to them and Lady Clan, 'I think Lady Margaret is finding Skye life a little dull after wintering in Edinburgh. She wants some young pretty friends to keep her entertained while Sir Alexander goes about his business.'

'Well we can't let the poor Lowland lassie grow bored, can we?' Lady Clan said dryly. 'Heaven forbid she should spend one evening without someone to sing her little ditties and carry around her fan.'

Hugh chuckled. 'I knew you would understand. My chief will be forever in your debt.'

The crossing was rough; Penelope seemed unaffected but Flora was ill the whole way. On arrival, she was put to bed and took two days to revive. After that, Lady Margaret lost patience and she was summoned to her parlour to take tea.

'Goodness you look like a little ghost.' She pinched Flora's cheeks to force some colour into them and waved for Penelope to pour tea. 'Not like that, girl. Don't put that awful local milk in mine – tastes like meat – can't imagine how anyone can drink the stuff. Squeeze a slice of lemon with one of those silver sugar spoons. Now stir in the sugar. And no drinking out of the saucer. You would have thought your mothers would have taught you the etiquette of the tea table by now. Drink little sips, Flora. There's nothing like China tea to make you feel better.'

At first the friends were a little overawed by the eagle-eyed attention from young Lady Sleat and had to concentrate hard to understand her high-pitched quick-fire English. But they soon grew used to her and realised she lavished the same bossy attention on all the young gentry who visited from across the island.

The summer sped by, and they became unofficial ladies-in-waiting to their patron, helping her dress, choosing fabrics from tailors summoned from Inverness, and attending balls at other grand houses, such as Dunvegan Castle and Raasay House, the homes of MacLeod chiefs. Lady Margaret needed constant entertainment. Flora learned new tunes on the spinet and was summoned in the night to sing her to sleep.

'I can't sleep when Alexander is away,' Lady Margaret fretted.

She reminded Flora of her mother. Marion had been just as vivacious and attractive to men in her young days – by all accounts – yet there was a neediness and lack of confidence under Margaret's brittle beauty. Flora cared for Sleat's young bride as gently as she had her mother in her 'black storms', soothing her to sleep with Gaelic lullabies. It did not matter that Lady Margaret made no acknowledgement of Flora's nocturnal vigils and chided her for yawning at breakfast; it was just her way. The Lowland heiress might be spoilt and demanding, but she was hugely generous – she showered them with clothes she'd hardly worn – and full of fun.

The one thing both Flora and Penelope found trying was Lady Margaret's constant attempts to match-make on their behalf.

'That Captain Malcolm MacLeod from Raasay is such a handsome man, don't you think, Flora? Cuts such a dashing figure on the dance floor. Captain's pay in the military too. And if you marry him, we will practically be neighbours. Raasay is so much easier for me to visit than Benbeck – or wherever it is you come from.' She waved a dismissive hand towards the sea.

'Benbecula,' Flora corrected.

'Yes well, I can't pronounce your funny Gaelic names. Alexander is always trying to get me to visit our estates out there,' she said, 'but wild horses wouldn't drag me. Look how sick you were, Flora, after the voyage. I would simply die.'

For a time, Lady Margaret tried to push Penelope towards MacLeod of Unish.

'He's an ambitious young man. Alexander says Unish has the complete confidence of MacLeod of MacLeod. Practically running his business operations while Chief Norman potters around planting the most outlandish species in his walled garden at Dunvegan. Unish is not the best looking of men, I grant you, but you'll never want for the nice things in life, Penelope.'

Flora saw how hard Penelope tried to hide her irritation but quietly resisted any attempt to pair her off with the chubby, florid-faced Unish.

Flora braced herself for the moment she would meet Allan of Kingsburgh again. The weeks went on and it never happened. She learned that, after the Sleats' wedding, the Kingsburghs had returned to Armadale in the south of Skye to take up the duties of managing the MacDonald estates from there. Ann – married swiftly to Macalister that winter – was already expecting their first child. The Macalisters had stayed on at Kingsburgh.

'They are really quite a dull pair,' Lady Margaret complained, 'not nearly as much fun as the other Kingsburghs. But then she's heavy with child and I expect that changes your mood for the worse.'

It was at Dunvegan Castle that Flora finally bumped into Allan – almost literally – in a melee of people in the great hall.

'Miss Milton?' his eyes widened in surprise. He took in her elegant low-cut dress and elaborately-styled ringlets.

'Sir,' Flora said, heart thumping at his sudden appearance filling the doorway. He seemed broader than a year ago, his chin more stubbled and eyes more knowing. She saw colour spread into his jaw and felt her own cheeks burn.

'You're with Lady Margaret's party?' he asked.

'Yes.'

'I didn't know you were back on Skye.'

'I've seen your sister.'

'She didn't say.' For a moment they stared at each other, both awkward. Then he gave a flash of his teasing smile. 'I must say, I'm surprised. Didn't think anything would entice you off the Long Isle back to Skye.'

Flora gave a snort. 'Who better to teach your chief's wife our Gaelic ways than a Long Isle lassie?'

Allan threw back his head and laughed. 'Flora, I–'

'Allan? Oh there you are!' a girl's voice interrupted him. A slim, fair-haired young woman of no more than fifteen pushed her way to his side. She put a possessive hand on his arm, curling delicate fingers into the soft linen of his sleeve. She flicked a look at Flora.

'This is Miss Milton of the Clanranald clan,' Allan said swiftly. 'And this is Amelia, Miss MacLeod of Dunvegan.'

Flora greeted Chief Norman's daughter. 'I remember meeting you last year at the Sleats' wedding.'

'Really?' Amelia said. 'There were so many people, weren't there? I hope you don't mind if I take Allan off your hands. He promised me the next dance. I hope you enjoy your evening here at Dunvegan, Miss Milton.'

'Thank you.' Flora smiled as she watched the petite girl steer Allan's square bulk into the throng. He threw her a look – either pleased or embarrassed – as he went.

She had no further chance to find out what Allan was going to say to her, as Miss Amelia kept him by her side for the rest of the evening and he seemed happy to be there. Flora danced with Captain Malcolm MacLeod – a genial witty man – and got nods of approval from Lady Margaret. But she did not want to give him false hope that he could be her suitor and made excuses to leave the dance floor.

Flora pushed her way quickly out of the hall and went to seek fresh air on the deserted gun court overlooking the sea.

'What a delightful sight; Miss Milton alone under the stars.'

Flora spun round at the deep voice, fleetingly thinking that Allan had followed her out after all. But it was the portly MacLeod of Unish who joined her at the parapet, panting from his exertions on the dance floor.

'Am I spoiling a secret tryst?' he leered.

'No,' Flora said, 'I merely came for air.'

110

'Good.' He stood very close; she could smell the sweat on him. 'It's a fine view at night, isn't it? Especially when it's too dark to see all the hovels that cover the hillside.'

'Hovels?' Flora frowned.

'The hordes of cottars,' Unish sniffed. 'Chief Norman allows too many hangers-on – widows of pipers and cripples who can't till the land – he feels he has to keep them all.'

'Isn't that the job of a chief to look after his people?' Flora asked tartly.

'How very old-fashioned of you, Miss Milton.' He gave her a condescending look. 'The landowners of the south don't have this problem. If people won't work, they don't get housed, simple as that.'

'Perish the day when our people are treated so callously,' Flora said with distaste.

'All very well for you to say, Miss Milton, but how do you think your fine clothes and your warm bed are paid for?' He leaned close. She tried not to wince from the sour smell of stale wine on his breath. 'All these fancy balls and entertainments you attend with your MacDonald kin – it is the same for Lord MacDonald – our chiefs need a fortune to keep them and us in this style of living. They can't afford to pay for the weak and feeble too.'

Flora recoiled in disgust, pressing back against the cold stone. 'And what do you suggest? Send them off to the colonies like slaves?'

He hesitated and then smiled. 'An interesting thought.'

Flora let out an angry exclamation and he quickly added, 'not slavery but they should be encouraged to migrate to the towns where there is commerce and employment – or if they are too lame, then they can seek alms from the rich burghers. Just because they share our surnames, doesn't give them the right to an easy life of indolence.'

'Easy life?' Flora cried. 'Our clanspeople work their fingers to the bone to bring food from the soil and fish from the sea. Every winter they endure great hardship – close to starvation some years – but they do so without complaint. And do you know what keeps them going? She pushed him away from her, her eyes blazing with indignation. 'It's the code of our ancestors – knowing that however old or frail they might get after a lifetime of endurance and service to their clan, they will be looked after by the next generation – above all by their *chief.*'

She stood shaking at her outburst. Unish's smug look had turned to one of dark fury.

'I won't be lectured to by a Long Island girl whose people still live in the Dark Ages,' he snapped. 'Our chiefs are turning to the south for political power and for their pleasures – Lord MacDonald included – and those pleasures are expensive. Sooner or later, they will have to choose between the old life and the new – they can't afford both. And I know which one I would rather have.' He swept her with a look. 'And I can see from your finery that you, Miss Milton, would prefer a life of indulgence too.'

'Not at the expense of my people,' Flora retorted.

Suddenly, he grabbed her chin in his hand and hissed. 'You might act all high and mighty, but you're no different from me – you have wants and desires – I saw you last summer kissing in the shadows with young Kingsburgh and then acting all lovesick over MacEachen. You like a man's embrace, don't you?'

He lunged at Flora, forcing his lips on her. She froze in horror. His mouth was wet, his breath overpowering. She pushed at him to no effect. He plunged a hand into her bodice and squeezed her breast. As he took a breath, Flora bit down hard on his fleshy bottom lip.

Unish swore and loosened his hold. She raised her hand and slapped him hard on the cheek. He gave her a stunned look. Before he could react, Flora ran for the open door back into the castle.

'You'll regret that, you little vixen!' he shouted after her.

Chapter 24

Sleep eluded Flora. She crept out of the cramped upper room in the Castle keep that she and Penelope were sharing with other female guests. The dancing and revelry had gone on till late but she had kept in the shadows after the unpleasant encounter with Unish, anxious to avoid him.

Servants were yet to stir in the kitchens below but she saw a door ajar and weak daylight beyond – some kitchen boy must have gone to collect firewood – and she slipped out too.

A pink dawn was flooding over the castle walls that thrust up from the rock. Last night, the sea had lapped up to the rocky promontory but now the tide was out. Flora clambered down uneven stone steps roughly hewn in the rock and slipped on seaweed; hitching her skirts high, she waded across the icy stream cascading into the bay, making for the mossy bank and wood beyond.

She gazed in awe at the high trees, their tops swaying and rustling in the breeze, the leaves on the silver birches already tinged with the orange of the autumn to come. In all her life, Flora had never seen so many trees in one place and they drew her like a siren. Soft light filtered through the leaves and birdsong filled the air – not the mournful cry of seabirds but the happy trill of small darting birds.

'Beautiful, isn't it? You don't feel the wind at all in here.'

Flora whipped round in fright at the man's voice, eyes wide. The intruder was a dark bulky shadow, wrapped in a plaid.

'Who–?' she gasped, fearing Unish had followed her.

The man stepped closer and the pearly light fell on Allan's handsome face.

'Sorry, I didn't mean to frighten you.' He stopped, unsure. 'I thought I'd have the woods to myself.'

Flora's pounding heart eased; she let go a long breath. 'I thought you were someone else.'

'Sorry to disappoint.' His look was quizzical. 'Who were you expecting?'

'No one. I couldn't sleep.'

'Neither could I.'

She looked more closely at his unshaven chin and tousled hair loosened from its queue. He was still dressed in his best trews.

'Doesn't look like you've been to bed at all,' she said wryly.

'I haven't,' he admitted. 'And you look like you've just stepped out of it.'

Flora pulled her plaid more tightly about her, aware that she was only dressed in shift and underskirts, her legs and feet bare and still wet from the stream.

'Like a wood fairy,' Allan teased. 'Quite bewitching.'

Flora blushed. 'I shouldn't be out here.' She stepped away.

'Don't go.' Allan followed. 'Let me show you around MacLeod's plantation first. It's one of the wonders of the world – or at least of Skye,' he grinned.

She hesitated.

'And you'll taste the best berries in the kingdom, I promise.'

Flora glanced back at the Castle; all was still quiet.

'Just for a few minutes,' she relented.

***

'These are ash,' Allan touched the tree trunks as they walked through the shadows, 'and those over there are birch.'

'Aye, we even have those on the Long Isle,' Flora said with the twitch of a smile. 'Battered and leaning like drunkards, but I can recognise a silver birch.'

'Sorry,' Allan gave a sheepish smile.

'But what's this one?' Flora stopped under its spreading branches, admiring the fluted leaves turning from green to copper.

'Beech,' said Allan. 'Chief Norman keeps pigs that thrive on beech nuts.'

'Pigs?' Flora asked in surprise. Many on the islands thought pigs unclean and refused to rear them.

'MacLeod is very progressive,' Allan explained. 'He reads a lot about new ways of farming and is passionate about putting the land to better use. He thinks we should be growing more food – not just for the people but for the cattle too. If we introduced turnips like they do in the south, we could keep our cattle healthy through the winter. You wouldn't believe the size of beasts that are fed on turnips. And he wants to introduce potatoes; fill a man's stomach twice as fast as oatmeal.'

Flora watched him, admiring him for his enthusiasm.

'Sounds like root vegetables are your passion too?'

He laughed. 'I can see from your look you think that's mad.'

'No, just unusual.'

'It's the cattle I care about.' Allan's face lit up as he spoke. 'They are the gold of our islands. The city folk can't get enough of our Highland beef. All our prosperity lies in good healthy herds. If we can feed them here with better crops instead of having to drive them south to be fattened up for market, then they will be worth twice as much. MacLeod sees that. I'd like to do the same for Sir Alexander at Sleat.'

Flora thought how handsome he was when animated, his blue eyes flashing and cheeks dimpling as he smiled. How her father would have loved to talk cattle rearing with this man; droving had been in his blood too.

'Will you be going on the drove this year?' she asked.

'Of course. I can't wait to go.'

'Doesn't your father want you on Skye learning the business of the Sleat estates?'

114

Allan gave a dismissive wave. 'Time enough for books and ledgers. I'm learning what's important for a gentleman farmer.'

'But won't Sir Alexander expect you to take over from your father as chamberlain one day?'

Allan scrutinised her. 'Is that what Lady Margaret has been saying about me?'

'No,' Flora blushed under his gaze. 'We've never discussed you.'

'No, of course not.' He gave a short laugh and looked away. 'Let me show you the nursery before we go back.'

'Nursery?' Flora's mind was suddenly filled with an image of babies wrapped in linen and squalling infants with faces like Allan's.

He glanced back and grinned as if he had read her thoughts. 'Chief Norman's plantation – his baby trees.'

Feeling foolish, Flora followed him, her bare feet sinking into the cool soft mulch of soil and leaves while Allan's heavier impatient tread snapped on twigs. They came to a high wall with no windows or roof, only a door. Pushing through it, Flora realised it wasn't a house at all, but a large enclosure planted with uniform rows of trees. It was so sheltered and still that midges danced in the dawn light and clung about them. She pulled her plaid over her head and covered her mouth. Allan seemed unbothered by the biting insects.

'Chief Norman is growing these for his people – he wants them to plant trees around their homes to give shelter from the wind for their animals and give them a source of food – rowan berries, elderberries and hazelnuts – and over there,' Allan pointed, 'alders. Excellent for making brooms and strong implements like ploughs.'

Flora stared in amazement. 'If there were trees like this on the Long Isle, they'd be chopped down for firewood.'

'That's been the problem here,' Allan said impatiently. 'Once there were forests all over the island – if our bards are to be believed – but the trees were cleared for fuel and hunting the deer. We need to plant again – it might not benefit our generation but our children and children's children will reap the reward of our far-sightedness.'

His keen-eyed gaze was boring into her again and she went hot under her plaid at his talk of children. He was standing very close and it was so still and quiet in the walled nursery that she could hear his breathing. She was suddenly aware of how alone they were, how he could so easily pull away her plaid and plant another kiss on her lips if he so wished. Her heart thumped at the prospect.

She swallowed. 'You promised me berries, remember?' She hoped her voice sounded calmer than she felt.

He stared at her as if he had not heard, then abruptly wiped a hand over his face, aware of midges for the first time.

'Aye, over here.'

She followed him to the far wall and a mass of towering fat-leaved brambles. Ducking down, Allan reached in and filled a hand with blood-red berries. He offered them to her.

'They don't look ripe' Flora frowned, still holding her plaid in front of her face like a veil.

He took one and ate it. 'They're supposed to be red not black. They're raspberries. Try one.'

Flora let go of her plaid and picked a berry from his large calloused hand. Slowly she put it in her mouth. Sweet tangy juice flooded her tongue; tiny seeds lodged in her teeth. Sweeter than a bramble and more flavour than a bilberry.

'Delicious,' she murmured and reached for another.

Allan's face broke into a grin of delight as they shared out the handful.

'Chief Norman brought cuttings from an Edinburgh garden,' he told her.

Flora picked at a seed in her teeth with her tongue and licked her fingertips.

'His mistress's garden?' she asked.

Allan gave her a shocked look. 'How would you know about such things?'

'Everyone at Monkstadt was talking about it last year. That handsome boy Alex is his illegitimate son, so they say. I thought Chief Norman made no secret of it?'

'Suppose not,' Allan grunted. 'People are too quick to let their tongues wag though. MacLeod might have an eye for the ladies but he's not a bad man. He's never happier than when experimenting in his garden or with his family around him.'

Flora shot him a look. 'Is that why you so readily defend a MacLeod?' she teased. 'Because you expect to join his happy household?'

Allan flushed. 'I don't know what you mean.'

Flora laughed. 'Miss Amelia of Dunvegan is what I mean.'

His colour deepened. 'And what of her?'

'You hardly danced with anyone else last night.'

'I'm glad you noticed.' He took a step closer. 'Surely it didn't make you jealous?' His mouth twitched in a smile.

'Not at all,' Flora pouted.

'I was jealous of Captain Malcolm,' Allan said, his voice suddenly serious.

'Were you?'

'When I saw him stop dancing to drink with Unish I looked for you to dance a minuet but couldn't find you.'

'I don't believe you,' Flora gulped, her heart racing. She shouldn't be feeling like this; young Kingsburgh meant nothing to her.

He tipped her chin upwards so she had to look into his blue eyes; they had lost their playful teasing and gleamed with naked desire.

'Believe this,' he murmured and bent to brush her lips with his.

He kissed her slowly, his mouth tasting of berries, his tongue flicking between her teeth to find hers. This was not the robust horseplay of his embrace at Monkstadt but something far more sensual and languorous that made her heart thud erratically and turned her insides molten. She kissed him back, craving his taste and the feel of his strong mouth exploring hers.

Her plaid fell to her shoulders as his hands cupped her head and he pulled her against his firm body.

'I knew you felt the same,' he rasped as his lips moved over her face, each kiss delivering tiny shocks to the pit of her stomach. 'You only pretended to dislike me, didn't you?'

He nibbled his way down her neck and pulled at the ribbons that tied the neck of her shift. His tongue licked at the opening; she felt his warm breath between her breasts. Her heart banged. She ought to stop him. She had never felt so aroused. Something this exquisite couldn't be wrong, could it? She could hear her own breathing coming quicker as if she were out of breath.

Allan paused, his eyes dark pools of longing, and smiled down at her.

'I'm glad you're over that sneaking Neil MacEachen. He could never make you happy.'

The sudden mention of Neil was like a slap to the face. Flora gasped and pulled away. 'Don't say that!'

Allan laughed and pulled her back. 'I'm sorry, I shouldn't have mentioned him. I meant nothing by it. Give me another of your sweet kisses, Florrie.'

'I'm not your Florrie,' she snapped, a hot wave of embarrassment engulfing her. What was she thinking of allowing herself to be lead here by this scheming man? He was shameless in his pursuit of women; happy to court Amelia MacLeod yet take advantage of a chance encounter with her too. Goodness knows how many other lassies Allan had seduced; he certainly was no novice when it came to lovemaking, Flora was sure.

She pushed him off and clutched her plaid to her throat.

'Neil would never treat me with such lack of respect. He's a true Highland gentleman.'

'He's a French spy,' Allan was scathing.

'That's not true,' she glared. 'He's the bravest man I know – and the most loyal. He puts his people and his country before mere commerce and the price of cows.'

Allan's smile vanished. He gripped her arm. 'Are you promised to MacEachen?'

'Let go of me!'

'Just answer my question.'

'Aye, I am. I promised Neil I'd wait for him, however long it takes.'

Abruptly, Allan let go of her. They stared at each other for a long moment. Flora felt angry and bewildered, wishing she was out of his reach.

He gave her a mirthless smile. 'What would MacEachen say if he knew you were here in your night clothes, embracing a Skye MacDonald?'

Flora turned puce with shame. 'A gentleman of the Sleat clan would never tell him,' she whispered.

'But a man who thinks only of the price of cows might,' Allan said.

'Please don't,' Flora begged. 'Please don't tell anyone.'

She saw the glint of devilment in his eye and feared he would boast to his fellow drovers about seducing her. He could so easily ruin her reputation and her dream of marriage to Neil. How could she have been so reckless?

'I never meant for any of this to happen,' she said more boldly, refusing to be intimidated by his look. He glanced away first.

'I misjudged the situation,' Allan said curtly, 'I'm not used to being rebuffed like this – usually I'm attuned to mutual attraction. I beg your forgiveness.' He gave a mock bow and swept his plaid back over his shoulder, ushering her out of the nursery.

They didn't speak a word as they walked back through the woods, until the castle loomed into view, towering over them in early morning sunlight.

'You're safe from here,' Allan said, his look once again mocking.

Flora nodded, feeling relief. He turned and made off into the woods again, leaving her alone. Hurrying inside the castle, she was suddenly aware of midge bites itching all over her neck and arms. She scratched them, revelling in the temporary relief that it brought, but the discomfort returned almost at once, worse than before.

The bites lasted for days, plaguing her fair skin and a constant reminder of her foolish encounter in the woods, like a madness coursing through her blood that kept her awake at night and gave her no peace during the day.

Chapter 25

Lady Margaret grew contrary. She ordered up syllabub with chopped chives. She could no longer bear to drink claret or tea and refused to let her ladies-in-waiting drink it in her presence as the very smell made her nauseous. She was tearful and moody and snapped at those around her for being too quiet or too noisy, too dull or too boisterous.

A concerned Sir Alexander sent for the doctor who diagnosed what Flora and Penelope already suspected; Lady Margaret was with child.

The Lord of Sleat was overjoyed but full of anxiety for he had lost his first wife and baby in childbirth eight years previously. There was to be no travelling beyond Skye until the baby was born and no wintering in Edinburgh, he ordered.

'I can't stay here at Monkstadt,' his wife declared, 'the miasma from the farmyard is making me ill. It's too windy and too cold; I can't possibly spend the winter here.'

Sir Alexander compromised on taking her to Armadale in the south of the island where their other home, though less grand, was sheltered and the climate more temperate.

Flora had not been since the time Hugh *Cam* had taken – some say kidnapped – her mother and her, and lodged them near Armadale until young chief Alexander had given Hugh and Marion permission to marry and secured Hugh a position in clan administration. It was where she had raced Allan across the beach in childish rivalry. Full of apprehension, Flora prayed that the drovers had already left for the mainland with their cattle and she wouldn't have to face him.

The area of Sleat in the south of Skye was more magnificent than Flora had remembered. As they sailed around the west of the island, the jagged peaks of the Cuillin Mountains – like a fairy-tale fortress – gave way to slopes of rich pasture and green meadows, tumbling waterfalls and rigs of ripe oats ready for harvest. Putting into harbour at Armadale, the hills of Sleat were overshadowed by the massive purple mountains of the mainland that loomed over the narrow stretch of sea in between. Armadale House was set amid lush grazing and a young plantation of beech and elm that made Flora think uncomfortably of Allan and his passion for trees.

After a few days of settling in, Flora was thankful to discover that the drovers were already on the road driving the cattle to Kylerhea where they would swim the beasts across to Glenelg on the mainland. Word came that they would wait on the Skye side till after the full moon, to catch the tide at its lowest.

'Can cattle really swim?' Lady Margaret was disbelieving. 'I want to see it.'

She badgered her husband until he relented and a small boatload of the chiefly couple and their young companions set sail around the south of Skye to the narrow rushing waters by Glenelg.

The sight of a hillside of restless, bellowing cattle moving together in a patchwork of brown, black and beige, stirred poignant memories for Flora. For a moment she was back in childhood, riding with her father in the cattle drove on the Long Isle. Closing her eyes, she could imagine that the whistles and Gaelic calls were those of her father, her brother Angus and their men.

The chief's party disembarked on the Glenelg side and picnicked on a beach while they waited and watched. There were dozens of men and scores of cattle amassed on the far side. Flora too was intrigued to see how so many beasts would cope with the crossing. The stretch of water was narrow but the current was fast flowing, despite the low tide.

It happened like an army on the charge; one minute the cattle were stamping, lowing and jostling, the next they were cantering into the shallows, whipped on by men wielding birch twigs. The spray was tremendous, the noise rolling around the mountains as rank after rank plunged into the chilly waters.

'How thrilling!' Lady Margaret stood and clapped her hands. 'They really can swim. Who would have thought such ungainly animals could turn into fish.'

The sea seemed to boil with bobbing heads. Small boats were rowed along beside, encouraging and cajoling. Flora looked for Allan but there was no sign of him. The first wave of cattle came clattering ashore, eyes wide, with bellows of relief or triumph. Some had their tail roped to the head of the cow behind. The men got busy herding them together.

The swim continued with wave after wave of cattle. The wind was rising and the current growing stronger. Sir Alexander fretted that they should set sail for home; a storm was growing rapidly in the west. The main body of cattle had safely thrashed their way out of the sea onto the Glenelg beaches. A few straggled behind, skittish with nerves

Suddenly there were urgent shouts from across the water. Flora peered. There was a commotion on the far side; men pointing out into the middle. Two cows were in difficulty.

'One is dragging the other down,' Penelope gasped beside her.

'They must be roped too tight together,' Flora guessed.

'Oh dear,' said their mistress, 'I suppose it's to be expected that one or two will drown.'

'If they do,' Flora said, 'it could mean starvation for some family this winter. Everyone relies on these animals getting to market.'

'Well,' Lady Margaret huffed, 'it's not worth anyone risking their life over.'

'Someone is,' Penelope cried and pointed.

On the far shore, a burly figure was stripping off his plaid and shirt. Naked, he plunged into the choppy waves and struck out towards the struggling cows. His dark head bobbed and sank and bobbed up again.

Flora put a hand to her chest. 'It's Allan Kingsburgh.'

Penelope threw her a look of panic. 'Are you sure?'

Flora nodded, speechless with sudden fright. Few islanders could swim and those who could would be no match for this treacherous straight.

Lady Margaret called out. 'Go back, it's not safe! Alexander, do something! Send a boat out for him.'

Sir Alexander was seized with indecision. He looked on in alarm. Allan had reached the drowning beasts and was hanging on. With the swell, they kept disappearing from sight. A boat set out to help. For a long terrible moment, there was no sight of either Allan or the cows. Flora could hardly breathe. Dread clawed her stomach. She didn't want him to die.

'Please don't drown,' she whispered. Penelope must have heard; she squeezed her hand.

Then the sea hurled the cows upwards again. Allan was clinging onto the tail of the one in front while holding up the head of the one behind. He was near enough now for them to see the strain on his face, the tautness in his neck and arms. He was keeping them all above water with supreme effort.

The boat reached him. One of the drovers threw a rope over the first cow and helped pull it ashore. Allan came swimming in with the second one. Sir Alexander rushed to haul him out of the water. Flora watched as Allan leaned, hands on knees, gasping for breath and choking with salt water as the chief slapped him on the back. They were too far away for her to hear what was said, but Alexander's relief was palpable, hugging young Kingsburgh like a brother.

'Goodness me,' Lady Margaret exclaimed suddenly, 'you girls shouldn't be looking so closely. Though young Kingsburgh is very manly, I must say.'

Flora flushed and glanced away. The other women laughed, skittish with relief. When she next sneaked a look, Allan had been given a plaid to wrap around his exhausted body. He came towards them, dark hair dripping and clinging to his shoulders, grinning bashfully.

'Lady Margaret, please forgive my state of undress – I hadn't expected a welcoming party of young ladies.'

She giggled. 'Well, it certainly added to the excitement of the expedition, didn't it girls?'

Allan flicked Flora a look – amused or challenging, she wasn't sure. She didn't know where to look, trying not to stare at his muscled hairy legs and broad chest. Their embrace in the walled garden when he had pressed her hard against him seemed only moments ago. The thought made her hot with shame.

'Well done for saving the cows,' she managed to say.

He gave her a brief nod, kissed the hand of the chief's wife and padded off to join his fellow drovers.

***

121

On the way back to Armadale, Flora sat feeling queasy in the rocking boat, listening to Lady Margaret berate her husband.

'It's all very heroic saving cattle, but he could easily have drowned. You should have stopped him. Young Kingsburgh is one of your top gentry and should be acting as such – not rushing about the land like a common drover.'

'It's just our way,' Alexander tried to explain, 'we all have to learn the jobs and traditions of the clan – even the chief has to. I lived with the Kingsburghs like a son so that old Kingsburgh could teach me–'

'I know all that,' she interrupted, 'but I don't see why it's necessary.'

'It is necessary my dearest. In time, if our child is a boy, he will be fostered by Kingsburgh or Allan too.'

'We'll see about that,' Margaret was dismissive. 'Allan must be sent away to learn the business side of things. Edinburgh is full of good lawyers and men of learning who can teach him. Knock some of the wildness out of him too. Then he'll be a perfect match for Amelia MacLeod.'

Chapter 26

1741

That spring, Lady Margaret gave birth to a strapping baby boy. He was christened James and was doted on by both his parents. Flora saw Allan at the celebrations; he was courteous but distant, keeping out of her way. It was hard to believe that the intimacy of that dawn meeting in Dunvegan had ever been. Flora wished that she could be friends with him – she missed his enthusiastic chatter – without the awkwardness of what they had let happen between them. She still turned hot with embarrassment whenever she let herself think about his kisses. He had spoilt things for them both.

'I didn't enjoy his attentions,' she had protested to Penelope when her friend had wheedled a confession out of her. 'You do believe me, don't you Pen?'

Her friend had given her a funny look and shrugged. 'If you say so.'

'I do say so. It's Neil I love.'

'Perhaps it's possible to love more than one man at the same time.'

Flora gave her a sharp look. That was an uncomfortable thought. 'But I don't love Allan – in fact I don't even like being in his company – he makes me feel awkward.'

'Stay away from him then,' Penelope advised.

So Flora did. It was made easier by Lady Margaret's decision to return to Monkstadt in the north of the island for the summer.

'Sir Alexander spends all his time away on business,' she complained, 'so I might as well be left alone in a comfortable house than one that's little more than a farm cottage.'

Now that there was a baby in the household and the Sleat chief was often absent, the lavish entertainment of the previous year had diminished.

'I wish we could go home for a bit,' Penelope said one day, as they took baby James outside for fresh air while his mother rested. Flora delighted in carrying him about; he was an engaging, smiley infant. 'Don't you?' Penelope sighed.

Flora followed her friend's gaze to the thin blue smudge of islands shimmering in the haze across the Minch; the Outer Isles. She missed her family and the Clanranalds but knowing that Neil was far away in France, she had no great desire to return. She kept up a correspondence with her absent suitor and delighted in his descriptive letters of life on the Continent. Neil, in turn, seemed pleased that she was making herself indispensable in the Sleat household.

'Not really,' Flora admitted, surprising herself at the thought. 'I'd miss this wee pet too much,' she nuzzled the baby and kissed his button nose, making him giggle.

'I'm homesick,' Penelope said, her eyes welling with tears. 'And I miss Angus. He's hardly ever written since I've been away. Do you think he's courting someone else?'

'Of course not,' Flora defended her brother, 'he's not like that.'

'Because I would never look at another man and it would break my heart if he's found another lassie,' Penelope dissolved into tears.

Flora quickly shifted James onto her shoulder and put a comforting arm around her friend.

'Och, don't upset yourself Pen. Angus thinks the world of you.'

'I won't be happy until I see him and hear him say so.'

Flora hugged her. 'Then perhaps you should ask Lady Margaret leave to visit your mother.'

Penelope brightened. 'Will you ask for me? She listens to you and you're not afraid to speak your mind. I'd come back, of course.'

'If you think it would help,' Flora agreed, trying to hide her dismay. She didn't think that her friend would return – not once she was back at the centre of the large and loving Clanranald family.

***

Penelope left in mid-summer. Lady Margaret complained bitterly at her ingratitude and made it quite clear that she would not countenance desertion from both her Long Isle maids-in-waiting. But Flora was happy to stay and said so. The chief's wife lavished more attention on her for a while, though she showed signs of jealousy over Flora's obvious attachment to the young chiefling James.

'Put him down and come and play the spinet for me,' she ordered, 'it soothes my headache.'

The one visitor that Flora dreaded was Unish. He came whenever Sir Alexander was at home as if he was keeping watch on the comings and goings of the Sleats.

He never attempted to get Flora on her own but she felt uneasy under his scrutiny and his derogatory remarks about Outer Islesmen; they were savage and uncouth, they ate pig meat, believed in fairies and their women were sly as witches.

'I'm jesting, of course,' he would smile and make Lady Margaret laugh at his outlandish claims. But Flora knew he meant to insult.

During that summer, a portrait painter who had been studying in France, came visiting the noble houses on Skye. Lady Margaret was thrown into a panic when her husband insisted that she sit for a full-sized portrait.

'But I've nothing new to wear,' she cried, 'and I still can't squeeze into my ball gowns since the baby.'

Flora knew this to be untrue but suggested she had something made up from the bolt of India chintz cloth with its bright birds of paradise that had been ordered from London last year.

'Blue and yellow suit you, madam,' Flora encouraged.

This pleased Lady Margaret and she at once appointed herself patron of Thomas the young painter, inviting the gentry from all around to come to Monkstadt and have their portraits done.

'All you young ones must have miniatures to give to your intendeds,' she enthused.

Unish came. Kingsburgh paid for his daughter Ann to be painted (her husband Macalister thought it vain and an unnecessary expense). The MacLeod chief was away from Dunvegan but sent his daughters Amelia and Anna.

Donald Roy arrived from Baleshare in the Outer Isles on his way to the mainland and entered into the spirit.

'Make sure you don't make my nose as big as it really is,' he grinned, 'or no young lady will have me.'

Flora was delighted to see someone from home and quizzed him for news.

'Lady Clan is delighted to have Penelope back – though she won't be truly happy until Ranald Og returns from France.'

'Will that be soon?' Flora asked.

Donald Roy shrugged. 'He is learning useful skills.'

'Swordplay and fighting you mean.' Flora was dismissive.

He flashed her a look. 'And how would you know that?'

Flora reddened. 'Neil MacEachen writes to me.'

Donald Roy raised amused eyebrows. 'Does he now? Then you will be better informed than me, Miss Flora.'

She quickly changed the subject. 'And my parents – are they well?'

Donald Roy hesitated. 'Hugh *Cam* is in rude good health.'

'And my mother?' Flora felt a surge of concern.

'She keeps very much to the house. I haven't seen her for a while but Lady Clan visits – and your brothers and sisters thrive.'

'Perhaps I should return?'

'No, you mustn't worry. Lady Clan would call for you if you were needed. Your mother just enjoys a quiet life.'

Flora felt sure he was holding something back but his smile was reassuring and Lady Margaret appeared so they stopped talking of the Outer Isles.

The liveliness of the previous year returned briefly to Monkstadt while the young of the various clan branches came to sit for their portraits. Flora thought the miniatures that Thomas produced were all rather similar and not particularly lifelike, but she enjoyed the bustle about the house and the laughter among the guests.

One day, returning from picking bog myrtle to make scent for her mistress, she recognised Allan's sturdy black horse, Whisky, drinking from the yard trough. Her heart lurched. She could not resist peering through the large casement window where the painter worked. Allan was sitting for him.

Flora wasn't going to go near the painter's room but she just happened to glance in on her way past.

'Flora!' Allan called. 'Come and keep me company or I'll go mad with sitting still.'

'You are not sitting still,' Thomas complained.

Flora could not help a smile as she stepped into the room. What harm was there in being sociable. Allan's broad shoulders were straining at a too tight doublet, his thick neck cut by a linen ruff. His long dark hair was pulled into a neat queue.

'Lady Margaret insists I have this done,' said Allan fidgeting.

'Aye, she is very keen on miniatures,' Flora smiled.

'You must show me yours.' Allan turned to look at her. Her insides jolted; she had forgotten just how blue his eyes were.

'I haven't had mine done.' Flora exchanged awkward glances with Thomas. She had told the painter that she could not pay for a portrait. It irked her that she had no money of her own but she would not ask her stepfather to pay for such a frivolous item when he had a large family of his own to support.

'Please sir,' Thomas lost patience, 'look back towards the window. It won't take long if you would just hold that pose.'

Allan rolled his eyes. 'Flora, come and stand by the window so I can see you to chat to.'

'No, Miss Flora not there,' the painter complained, 'you are blocking the light.'

Flora moved to the other side and watched. Allan was being painted with his face in profile. Thomas had already caught the strong jaw, straight nose and high forehead. But he was struggling to capture the fullness of the firm mouth – it was portrayed as too thin – and the sideways pose did not do justice to the handsome lively eyes.

'Tell me what's being going on at Monkstadt,' Allan said, glancing sideways. 'How do you fill your hours now that your friend Pen has escaped back across the sea to safety and away from us Sleat MacDonalds?'

'I fill them very easily,' Flora said, holding up sprigs of bog myrtle.

Allan looked round and grinned. 'I thought it was you who smelt so sweet.'

'Please sir, look away,' Thomas cried. 'And don't speak, just for a few minutes.'

'Flora, you must do all the talking,' Allan tried to hold still.

She told him about Donald Roy being a guest and the MacLeod girls coming over from Dunvegan, watching for his reaction at mention of Amelia.

'We all went out in a boat to fish and then we cooked mackerel on a fire by the shore and Donald Roy composed *An Ode to a Very Dead Fish*.'

She could tell by the way Allan's dark eyebrows went up that he was longing to say something but he resisted. His fingers drummed on the chair arm. Flora told him stories about baby James.

126

'I'm singing him the lullabies of the Outer Isles and can't wait to teach him the legends of the Clanranalds, so he knows about real bravery,' Flora teased, enjoying his frustration at not being able to answer back.

Finally Thomas relented. 'You can go now, sir. I can finish this off without you.'

Allan leapt out of the chair, pulling at his necktie.

'Come on Flora, I need air. Show me where you picked the myrtle.'

She led him away from the house and the shore to where the land began to slope up towards the high pastures. She didn't want to dwell on why she had agreed so easily to his request. Bees hummed over wild flowers; the air was sweet with the scent of early bell heather.

'I love coming here,' she mused, 'it reminds me of childhood summers – going with the animals up to the shieling when my father was still alive.'

Allan studied her. 'My father said Milton was a great man.'

'Did he?'

'Aye, he said your father was well known far beyond the Long Isle for his strength and leadership.'

Flora's throat tightened. She felt a wave of loss for her long dead parent.

'And they say he was one of the best cattle breeders of his day – at least for an Outer Islesman,' Allan added with a smile.

'He could teach you Skye boys a thing or two about droving,' Flora said with the twitch of a smile. 'How not to tether cattle so tight they nearly drown in the water.'

Allan laughed. 'Ah, Glenelg. Well there's nothing you don't know about me now, Miss Milton.'

Flora flushed at the sudden memory of Allan wading naked out of the sea.

'We should be getting back,' she said, 'Lady Margaret will be wondering where I am.'

He put out his hand. 'I didn't mean to embarrass you. Stay a bit longer. Tell me about your father and your trips to the shieling.'

Against her better judgement, Flora allowed him to steer her onto a dry tuft of heather and found herself talking of long ago. She felt an easing of her sadness over her dead father by recounting tales of him. It was so long since she had spoken about such things – her mother hated any mention of their past life – and yet Allan made it so easy to talk about it all. She made him laugh about her attempts to keep up with her brother Angus and the older boys and her fury when they tried to leave her out of their games.

'And was Neil MacEachen one of these wretched lads?' Allan asked, squinting at her in the sunlight.

'Neil always stood up for me,' Flora admitted.

'So that is why he is special to you?'

Flora felt uncomfortable; she did not want to think about the grown-up Neil just at that moment. She liked talking to Allan – he was so easy-going and interested in people's lives – but his tone turned mocking at mention of Neil.

'Yes,' she said, her look defiant. 'He has always been kind to me.'

'Kind?' Allan snorted. 'Kindness is for nursemaids. Marriage should be based on more than that.'

'Who said anything about marriage?' Flora felt flustered.

'I thought you were promised to MacEachen?'

'I am – we are – just not yet. When I'm older.' Flora scrambled to her feet.

'So there's hope for me yet?' Allan was on his feet at once.

Flora stared at him in astonishment. Was he teasing her again?

'You?' she gaped.

'Is that such an outlandish idea?' he challenged. 'I may not have MacEachen's fair looks or silver tongue but I have lands and standing in the Sleat clan.' He blocked her way. 'I'm not hundreds of miles away in a foreign country – I'm right here, Flora. And I know how to make a lass happy.'

He didn't try to touch her; he just stood close, his look bold and his body tensed.

Flora swallowed. This was not what she wanted to hear; she desired him only as a friend. Yet standing so close, her body felt mutinous, shaking at his words, craving another touch of his lips and warm hands.

'I think about you all the time, Florrie.' His look bore into her.

Flora shook her head. 'Please don't say that.'

'It's true. And I know you feel something for me. Given time I think you could learn to love–'

'Your family would never allow it,' Flora cut him off. 'You must marry the MacLeod heiress. Lady Margaret has told me often enough.'

'I won't let a Lowlander decide my future,' Allan was dismissive.

'A man of your position has no choice. You will do whatever your parents and chief decide.' Flora held his look. 'And they will never choose a lassie from Benbecula with hardly a dowry to scrape together, no matter how noble my ancestry.'

Allan touched her cheek. 'Are you saying that you would consider marriage to me if my family did not stand in the way?'

Flora flinched at the contact. Her heart drummed at his intense look. She forced herself to look away. 'There is no point discussing what cannot happen.'

'Anything can happen if you want it badly enough,' Allan cried. 'Look at Hugh *Cam* kidnapping your mother so that she had to marry him. Run away with me, Florrie!'

She stared at him, open-mouthed. He was full of pent-up eagerness, his look full of devilment – almost feverish. Flora still couldn't be sure he wasn't just toying with her, playing one of his jokes. It was madness to even think about being so reckless. He would have his sport and then send her packing back to the Long Isle while he accepted whatever match his father decreed.

'I could never do that,' she insisted. 'I'm not the type of lass who goes looking for adventure.'

'I don't believe that. You came to Skye like a shot.' He brushed hair back from her face making her skin tingle. 'And you wandered into MacLeod's woodland at dawn without a second thought about your safety.'

'I regret that now.'

'I don't believe you.'

'You must.' Flora turned away in agitation. Her feelings for him were so confused. She craved his physical presence yet wanted to get away from him; she drank in his seductive words but didn't trust his motives.

Suddenly there was a shout from right behind. Flora jumped in fright. Donald Roy appeared out of the heather clasping a book.

'Fell asleep. Woke at the sound of voices.' He strode forward and clasped Allan by the hand. 'Good to see you, young Kingsburgh. What are you doing with my fair kinswoman? Nothing that will cause me to have to challenge you to a duel, I hope?' He guffawed at his own joke.

'Nothing at all,' Allan smiled, 'more's the pity.'

Donald Roy shot Flora an enquiring look.

'We were doing nothing more illicit than collecting bog myrtle for Lady Margaret,' she gave a trembling smile, linking an arm through his. She felt thankful at his solid presence while her head still reeled at Allan's words. 'You weren't eavesdropping, where you?'

'My mind was on higher things,' he grinned, waving the book with his free hand. 'Virgil's poetry.'

Allan grunted. 'Give me a bawdy Gaelic verse any day.'

The men chatted as they returned to Monkstadt, Flora trying to steady her heartbeat and stop herself dwelling on Allan's proposal. Or was it a proposal?

Later, making ready for dinner, she decided it had been a spur of the moment idea of his to elope, not a plan at all. She avoided his looks across the dining table at dinner. She mustn't allow herself to be caught alone with him again. It was too much temptation. While she was under the care of the Sleats she must do nothing that would anger her patrons or damage her reputation. Without a proper dowry, the good name of Milton was all she had to protect her. Flora went hot at the thought of how careless she became in Allan's company; how ready to risk her future for one of his kisses.

After a sleepless night, Flora resolved to put Allan from her thoughts and to give him no further encouragement.

***

Two days later, Thomas the painter sought her out.

'You are to sit for me. It's my last commission before I move on to Argyll.'

'I told you before–'

'It's paid for.'

'Really? Who by?'

Thomas waved a hand. 'An admirer.'

'Really! Who is it?'

'I'm sworn to secrecy.'

Flora immediately thought of Neil; after all, the painter had recently come from France. She was touched and a little astonished at the gesture; Neil never seemed to have much money to spare. She sat for Thomas, finding it no hardship to sit in repose, letting her mind wander to a hundred different places. The men had gone hunting into the hills for deer. It was a relief. She wondered who would be the best shot. Allan might have the advantage over Donald Roy because of his knowledge of the land. Allan! Could he be the admirer who was paying for this? The thought made her quite flustered. Surely not? She must stop thinking about him … She would force her mind elsewhere.

What was really happening back home in Balivanich? Was her mother very unhappy? She should probably return for a visit soon. She missed her sisters and brothers. It was strange how Hugh *Cam* had not come to Skye this year to report on Sleat's business in North Uist. Or had he been but avoided visiting her at Monkstadt?

Unish. He had left very abruptly the week before boasting of some important business that could not wait. Some trade with the colonies that would bring him a lot of money. She was glad he was gone; he made her feel uncomfortable and was sure he dripped poisonous words into her mistress's ear about her. Lady Margaret always grew more critical of her dress and deportment when Unish was around.

'It's done,' Thomas said.

Flora was dragged back from her reverie, amazed at how long she had been sitting there. She rose stiffly and went to see the miniature. A handsome young woman with chestnut hair and large eyes stared back at her. He had managed to convey the shifting colour of her eyes – the blue-grey that was almost green – and the cupid's bow of her pink lips against the pale skin. The silk tartan bodice revealed a more buxom chest than she thought she had and the look was too bold, too sensual for her.

Flora nodded. She didn't want to hurt his feelings. This woman was not her but it was a fine depiction of a genteel Highland lady.

'Thank you,' she smiled, 'it's one of the nicest miniatures I've seen.'

Thomas grinned with pleasure. 'And you were one of the most perfect sitters I've had. Such stillness and calm in one so young – the perfect artist's model.'

Flora laughed. If only he knew how her thoughts had raced around like wild cats all the time she had sat so still.

***

'So I hear you sat for Mr Thomas after all,' Lady Margaret said as Flora brushed out her mistress's hair before bed.

'Yes,' Flora blushed, thinking how she had in vain badgered Thomas to divulge her admirer's name. She wondered if Lady Margaret knew. But the woman had her eyes closed and a dreamy expression on her face as Flora brushed away. 'Something to send your young man, eh?'

Flora paused, brush in hand. She had a guilty thought that Donald Roy might have said something about her being with Allan up on the hill, over-hearing his wild talk of running away with her.

'My young man?'

'Keep brushing! Yes, that one in France – what's he called? – the MacEachen boy.'

'Oh, Neil,' Flora said in relief.

Lady Margaret swivelled round. 'Who did you think I meant? Goodness me, you've gone quite pink. Do you have some other suitor I know nothing about?'

'No no,' Flora said, beginning a rapid brushing. If Allan had paid for her portrait then it was obvious Lady Margaret was ignorant of it.

After several minutes, her mistress said, 'that's enough. I'm tired now.'

Flora lingered as she pulled fine fair hair from the brush. She plucked up courage to ask the question that had nagged her for days.

'Is Allan of Kingsburgh promised to Miss MacLeod of Dunvegan?'

'As good as.' Lady Margaret eyed her. 'Amelia was delighted with his miniature. The sweet girl is head over heels with the young buck.'

Flora went crimson. 'He gave her his portrait?'

'Of course.' Lady Margaret laughed. 'She positively squealed with delight when he handed it over. Such a touching sight.'

Flora gulped down disappointment. Of course Allan hadn't paid for her portrait; why go to that expense when he was courting another? Within seconds she felt anger flare. All this time she had been struggling to overcome her desire for Allan – fighting the temptation to rush to him and say she would run away with him right now – he had been playing the willing suitor to the chief's pretty daughter.

Allan had only been toying with her affections after all. She felt furious with herself for being taken in by his passionate words once again. Flora tore at the brush and flung loose hair on the flames.

'Are you all right, girl?'

'Yes, I'm fine, my lady.'

'I know you must miss your handsome MacEachen. It's so romantic though to have a lover in a distant land making his fortune. We'll arrange to have your miniature sent to him at once – just to remind him of what he is missing at home. Don't want him getting too comfortable and settling down in France now, do we?'

'No,' Flora said. Guilt burned her cheeks. It must have been Neil who had made the romantic gesture after all, hoping she would send the portrait to him. How could she have contemplated giving up her noble Neil for the womanising Allan?

All the following week, Flora made a point of avoiding young Kingsburgh, deliberately snubbing him when he made attempts to speak to her. She made sure she was never left alone with him.

131

Eventually he gave up and left Monkstadt. The next she heard of Allan was from his sister at a harvest ball.

'He's gone to Edinburgh to learn business from an eminent lawyer,' Ann preened. 'Our Allan is destined for great things in the clan – perhaps even beyond Skye and the Highlands. Sir Alexander might even be grooming him for political life – he can be so persuasive about things he cares for passionately.'

Don't I know it, Flora thought, managing a tight-lipped smile.

She told herself the emotion that overwhelmed her was relief. She wouldn't have to think about Allan again or worry about coming across him socially for a long time. Life would be tranquil and happy at Monkstadt.

Then – abruptly, destructively – a tragic scandal that no one had foreseen erupted amongst them, shattering the lives of the Skye aristocracy.

Chapter 27

The woman ran out wildly from the gorse bush. Screaming, incoherent and babbling, she tore at her hair, seemingly quite mad.

'Taken them, taken them all! Please stop them – I beg you – lady of my chief!'

She was covered in cuts from the gorse, her worn clothes ripped. She threw herself at Lady Margaret's horse, making it whinny and jump.

Lady Margaret recoiled in fright. 'Stop that at once, you'll make me fall!'

The woman paid no heed, wailing and beseeching, trying to grab at the noblewoman's skirts.

'Flora, help me!' Lady Margaret cried. 'She's deranged.'

Flora scrambled down from her pony and grabbed at the distraught woman. The woman fought her off but Flora clung on trying to calm her.

'It's all right, I've got you. You're safe. Tell me what's happened. Quiet now. Leave Lady Sleat be. She doesn't understand your Gaelic tongue. You are frightening her. Speak to me.'

The woman fixed her with eyes full of horror. 'They came in the night. Flaming torches. Beat me to the ground.'

'Someone attacked you?'

'Said they would set fire to the thatch if I didn't give them what they wanted.'

The woman crumpled against her, sobbing.

'Who did? Who did this to you?'

'The Knight's men.'

Flora gasped. 'Sir Alexander's men? They attacked you? Surely you're mistaken.'

The woman screamed, 'they took my babies! Took my sons – both my bonny boys!'

Lady Margaret pulled her horse away. 'What is she saying? Why did you mention my husband to her?'

Flora hesitated then said, 'She says Sir Alexander's men attacked her and took away her sons.'

'Why would they do such a thing?' her mistress demanded. 'She's a lunatic.'

Flora tried to get the woman to sit in the heather but she clawed at her dress and would not let go.

'Why did they do this to you?' Flora kept asking, but the woman wept so much she was incoherent.

'Where has she come from?' Lady Margaret asked, bewildered. 'There's no village near here. She must be a witch or making the whole thing up. I need to get back to Monkstadt and see baby James. I hate being away from him for more than a day.'

Flora looked at her in disbelief. They had been away visiting the MacLeods in Raasay for nearly a week while Sir Alexander was in Edinburgh on business and her mistress had been content to leave her son in the care of a nursemaid. But the strange woman was making Lady Margaret agitated.

'We can't just leave her here alone,' Flora said.

'Well we can't take her with us.' Her mistress glanced behind, fretful. 'Look, the servants will catch up in a few minutes. They can see to her – bring her to the house and give her something to eat. It's obvious she's a vagrant.'

Flora tried to explain all this to the woman. 'The servants will help you. You can see them at the brow of the hill. My mistress wishes to ride on ahead.'

Abruptly the woman let go. Her look of desolation stopped Flora's breath.

'My babies,' she sobbed. 'Too late. Why won't you stop them?'

'You must come to the house and tell everything to Sir Alexander, then it can all be sorted out.' Flora forced an encouraging smile. 'If these men have done wrong, your chief will punish them and get your boys back.'

The woman flopped on the ground and buried her head in her arms, refusing to look up or be comforted.

Flora remounted and followed her mistress, gulping down her upset at leaving the woman behind. At the crest of the next hill, she glanced back. The servants with the baggage mules had reached the gorse bush. The woman had vanished.

***

Rumours began to blow around the island like thistle seed. A large sailing ship had been seen anchored off the north of Skye a few days previously. Some said it was a commercial brig; people leaving for the colonies and a new life. Others maintained it was a prison ship collecting men from the gaol in Portree. Still others said it was a merchantman hired to take indentured servants to jobs in the Americas. People were missing. Children had run away. Stowaways had been discovered and put ashore in Ireland.

Flora could not rid her mind of the distressed woman and her fevered story of men with flaming torches carrying off her young boys. Had this anything to do with the strange rumours of the dark ship; the Ship of the Men as the gossip-mongers now called it, because of the disappearing islanders? With each day, her guilt increased. She should have done something for the desperate mother.

The atmosphere at Monkstadt was tense and brooding. Sir Alexander spent most of his time at Armadale but when he visited there were raised voices in the private chambers.

'You're keeping me in the dark. What is going on? No one is visiting me.'

'Nothing's going on. It's not the season for visiting.'

'Tell me about this wretched ship.'

'There's nothing to tell. It was business.'

134

'What sort of business?'

'A commercial arrangement with MacLeod.'

'MacLeod of Dunvegan? Then I'll ride over there and ask him what's going on if you refuse to tell me.'

'No you won't Margaret. His wife is dying. You'll leave him be. And stop interfering with things that don't concern you.'

'If it affects me and my son – your *heir* – then it is of my concern. I will be told!'

'They were criminals,' Sir Alexander snapped. 'We were ridding the place of rotten apples. The colonies are happy to take such people and put them to work. Unish arranged it all.'

'Well why didn't you say so before? I don't see the need for such secrecy.'

When Flora heard that Unish was involved, her heart froze and dread clawed her insides. She knew of the practice of shipping convicts to the New World to be put to work on the American plantations but something was different about this. She was plagued by the memory of Unish on the gun court at Dunvegan bemoaning the numbers of islanders dependent on his chief; deriding them as hangers-on living a life of indolence.

And what do you suggest? Send them off to the colonies like slaves?

Flora's disdainful reply – and Unish's malicious smile – now haunted her. Surely he had not taken her seriously? Sir Alexander would never allow such a thing, nor would Chief Norman; Allan admired him as a good family man. Sir Alexander had talked of 'rotten apples' being transported away, but what of the rumour of women and children disappearing?

They took my bonny boys! Flora could not rid her mind of the screaming woman.

Early one autumnal morning the household were woken by banging on the main door and shouts in the courtyard. Flora looked out to see half a dozen militiamen gathered below.

The place erupted in noise and confusion. 'We've come for Lord MacDonald. We have a warrant for his arrest.'

Lady Margaret began screaming. 'How dare you. Get out of my house!'

Sir Alexander appeared white-faced but calm. 'Please do me the courtesy of waiting outside while I say goodbye to my wife.'

The officer nodded and withdrew.

'It's all a mistake, my dearest. Please don't be upset – you must let me go.'

She clung to him. 'I won't let them. You've done nothing wrong.'

He turned and gave Flora a pleading look. Flora rushed to her mistress's side and put her arms about her rigid body.

'The sooner you let him go, the sooner this will be sorted out,' she coaxed.

Sir Alexander extracted himself and kissed his wife on the forehead.

'How long will this take?' she cried. 'What should I do?'

'Stay here and carry on as normal.'

'Normal? Nothing is normal any more. I can't bear it here without you!'

'I'm so sorry Margaret.'

The look of regret on his boyish handsome face made Flora's heart squeeze. Then he was following the arresting officer out of his mansion and out of their lives.

***

Flora was so worried about her mistress – she refused to eat and could not sleep – that she sent word to her stepfather, Hugh *Cam*, for help. A week later, he appeared at Monkstadt with grim news. Newspapers from the south were circulating with the shocking news that a shipload of kidnapped islanders had foundered on the coast of Ireland. Many had made it ashore to tell their tale of being forced at gunpoint to leave their homes and be herded onto a sailing ship.

'Ordinary women and children among them,' Hugh *Cam* said, his one good eye glaring with indignation.

'It must be a mistake,' Lady Margaret insisted.

'No mistake,' Hugh said, throwing down the newspaper, 'it names dozens of them – some as young as ten.'

'My husband knew nothing of this,' she trembled, 'nothing. It must have been MacLeod's doing. He is behind this.'

'That may be true. Sir Alexander certainly never mentioned such an enterprise to me else I would have done all in my power to stop him.'

'You must follow and find out where they have taken my husband.' Lady Margaret sat shredding a handkerchief in her lap. 'I can't bear the thought of him in some prison–'

'It won't come to that,' Flora said. 'My stepfather will do all he can.' She threw him a beseeching look. 'Perhaps Kingsburgh will know by now where they have taken him. He sent word from Armadale that he would travel to Edinburgh for a lawyer if necessary.'

'Kingsburgh,' Lady Margaret said with distaste. 'He should have looked after my husband better. Always boasting of their special relationship – his foster father – what good has it done Alexander?'

'Kingsburgh is a good man,' Hugh *Cam* defended. 'Neither of us will allow any lowland court to take our chief from us. We'll take up arms if needs be.'

Flora saw from his determined look that he meant every word.

***

The days that followed were an unbearable waiting game. Messages came from Hugh that both chiefs, Sleat and Dunvegan, had been taken to Inverness for questioning. Lord Forbes, a powerful judge had them in his keeping.

'A Government man' Hugh called him. Flora knew this was code for saying he was a Hanoverian so not disposed to look kindly upon Highland

136

chiefs taking the law into their own hands. She kept her doubts hidden from her anxious mistress.

Locally, news came of the trickle of islanders making it back from Ireland and the traumatic voyage. But it appeared that many were unaccounted for. Perhaps they had travelled on, taking their chances on another ship to a new life or maybe they were stranded with no way back. Flora never stopped wondering what had happened to the two young brothers snatched from this very area. She prayed that they had been safely returned to their bereft mother.

Abruptly, a month later, Hugh reappeared with Sir Alexander. Lady Margaret almost fainted, flinging herself at him with relief.

'Are you really free? What's happened? You look ill. Is it over?'

'It's over,' he promised.

The MacDonald chief was pale and haggard; he broke into a fit of coughing when his wife tried to question him about his ordeal.

'I just need to rest, my dearest.'

'Of course you must. We'll leave Skye and winter with my parents in the south.' She latched onto the idea. 'Best to get away from here until it's all blown over.'

Her husband looked too exhausted to argue.

'What of Chief Norman?' Flora asked.

'He has been freed too,' said Hugh.

'So it was all a misunderstanding?' she frowned.

Her stepfather gave her a warning look. 'No one is to be prosecuted,' he said. 'Now let us leave Lord and Lady Sleat in privacy.'

Later, sitting by the fire in Hugh *Cam*'s guest room, he explained further.

'It was all the fault of that schemer MacLeod of Unish – he saw a way to get rich quickly by selling his people. But the money for the ship had been raised in the names of MacLeod and Sleat.'

'Did they know anything about this?' Flora asked.

Her stepfather stared into the flames. 'Who knows? They say not.'

'Do you believe them?'

'It doesn't matter what I believe. My only concern is to protect my chief.'

'Well if a staunch Hanoverian like Forbes thinks there is no case to answer then they must be innocent.'

Hugh did not reply, his look troubled. 'Are you keeping something from me?' Flora asked.

'Forbes has let them go but at what price?'

'Meaning?'

'Meaning that he extracted assurances of loyalty to King George for dropping the matter.'

'That doesn't sound such a hardship, surely? They have to do that anyway.'

Hugh grimaced. 'The Hanoverians don't trust us Highlanders. They will go to any lengths to tie our chiefs' hands. Forbes thinks he has them under his thumb now.' He took a swig of his wine. 'At least no real damage has been done to Sir Alexander; it was MacLeod's man who did the deed.'

'But what about the poor people involved? That woman who lost her boys – I'll take her image to my grave.'

'Then blame Unish,' Hugh grew cross. 'He exceeded his powers out of greed and his own advancement.'

'Has he been arrested?'

Hugh shook his head. 'He's disappeared. MacLeod must have warned him. Rumour has it he's been banished abroad and Chief Norman will throw him in Dunvegan dungeon if he dares show his face again.'

Flora shuddered. 'I feel so guilty.'

'Don't be ridiculous. You mustn't blame yourself for those boys.'

Flora unburdened to him about her argument with Unish at Dunvegan over a year ago.

Hugh reached out and squeezed Flora's hands in his. 'Dear daughter,' he said, 'you have nothing to be ashamed of – you stood up for your own people and challenged his selfishness.' He gazed at her fondly. 'You are loyal and brave and I couldn't be prouder of you.'

Her eyes blurred with tears at his kindness. 'Thank you Father,' she smiled.

'Come home, Florrie,' he urged. 'Your mother misses you. Lady Margaret has had you to herself for too long.'

Flora sighed. 'I don't think she wants me to go south with her anyway. She seems set on getting away from people who remind her of the scandal.'

'Then her loss is our gain.' His one eye glinted as he smiled.

Suddenly Flora was overwhelmed with longing to get back to Benbecula, to her family and friends. Skye no longer held the attraction that it had. Things had soured at Monkstadt. She quelled the thought that life here had lost its zest ever since Allan had left so abruptly for Edinburgh.

***

Lady Margaret put up a token resistance to Flora's going.

'That's all the thanks I get for giving you such a good start in society, is it? You were just a country mouse when you came to me, remember that. Who will see to my dressing – and no one does my hair like you do. I'll just have to train someone else, I suppose.'

'I'm very grateful, my lady,' Flora said, 'but my stepfather thinks it best if I return to the Long Isle while you are away.'

'Well don't think you can skip back again whenever you feel like it. I'll no doubt have other young ladies to assist me. In fact I might be better bringing girls from the Lowlands who understand me and can't gossip with the servants in Gaelic behind my back. Yes, you're better suited to someone like Lady Clanranald who doesn't mind a lady's maid who runs about the hills in bare feet. Don't think I didn't notice.'

138

Before Flora left, she went in search of the woman who had lost her sons to the Ship of the Men. She combed the cottages along the shore from Monkstadt up to the abandoned castle of Duntulm at the top of the peninsula, but couldn't find her. As the autumn squalls blew in from the Minch and soaked her to the skin, she carried on searching, visiting remote bothies and isolated farms. No one had heard of such a woman.

Flora began to doubt whether she had ever existed. Had she been a figment of their imagination? Perhaps her mistress had been right and the woman had been a witch conjured up like a bad omen of the tragedy to come.

She gave up.

When the moment of departure came, Lady Margaret clutched her in thin arms and wept.

'Take care, Flora. You must write to me and tell me how you are. I want to know about your boy in France and how you get on. You will tell me, won't you?'

Flora hugged her back and promised to keep in touch. She left the island wrapped in mist, only the rocks at shore level showing. Briefly, the clouds parted as the rowers pulled out of the loch. Monkstadt stood gleaming white in a brief shaft of sunlight, then it was swallowed up and Skye disappeared from view.

Chapter 28

Largie, Argyllshire, 1745

'You can't keep her at home forever, Marion; unless you want her to be an old maid.'

'There are worse things,' Marion snorted. 'Marry in haste and repent at leisure.'

'You don't mean that. You've had two fine husbands.'

Flora paused on the stairs outside her Cousin Elizabeth's chamber; she had gone in search of more thread for their sewing. Was she the old maid they were talking about?

'One was an old man and the other is ...' her mother sighed, 'well you know what he is.'

'He's a man of great standing in the clan,' Elizabeth reminded, 'and a good father to your brood. But he can't be expected to keep Flora in his household for much longer – his own daughters will be needing suitors before long – so it's time you found Flora a husband.'

'She's set her heart on Neil MacEachen of Howbeg,' Marion sighed. 'It was a bit of a blow when he didn't return from France with Ranald Og last year.'

Flora wanted to burst through the door and shout out that Neil had written to her of his plan to return very soon, but he had sworn her to secrecy. How she longed to tell someone.

'MacEachen's a bit of an adventurer, isn't he?' Flora could hear the disapproval in her cousin's voice. 'She'd be far better suited to a farmer or merchant – someone who would find merit in her household and dairy skills – and who wouldn't mind the lack of a large dowry.'

'When the time comes she will marry a gentleman,' Marion said stoutly. 'My Florrie has breeding and gentility that would be wasted on some shopkeeper. She gave that po-faced minister Elijah Gunn short shrift when he proposed marriage to her last year.' Marion snorted with amusement. 'Quite put out he was, but she was having none of it. Flora can be stubborn when she wants.'

'A minister would have been suitable,' said Elizabeth. 'Like your own father.'

'Gunn is not a patch on my father! He commanded respect. Gunn is a sneaking little man. Flora was quite right to turn him down.'

Flora, deeply embarrassed to be the subject of her cousin's forthright opinion, couldn't help a smile at her mother's defence. She had grown close to her mother in the years since returning from Monkstadt. She knew Marion relied on her too much for companionship and in running the household – Flora was like a mother to her half-siblings, always intervening in family squabbles – but it was a small price to pay for seeing her mother's spirits revive.

Flora had settled into the role without complaint, though sometimes she was wistful for the carefree days when she and Pen had been at the centre

140

of Lady Margaret's entourage and mixing in Skye society. But last year her best friend had finally married her sweetheart Angus and moved into their new homestead at Milton in South Uist. Her brother's dream of developing the tack of land that their father had so loved had been realised and Angus was relishing building up his cattle farm.

Life was routine and uneventful, but Flora was content enough while she waited for Neil to return. Only the uneasy relationship between Marion and Hugh marred Flora's happiness. Deep down, she was sure they loved each other, but they could not show it. Her mother nagged him and threw accusations if he so much as looked at another woman. Hugh was too quick to lose his patience and told her it was her fault if he stayed away. Flora cared for them both and tried to keep the peace. Since Angus had married and moved down to Milton permanently, Hugh seemed to be making more effort to please his wife. Perhaps the sight of the newly married couple made him remember his passion for Marion. But to Flora's dismay, her mother remained suspicious and thought it a sign he was hiding something.

When Cousin Elizabeth from Largie on the mainland had sent for Flora to help out at the birth of her tenth child, Marion had seized the chance to go with her and visit her family. A month had turned into two but Marion had kept making excuses to stay. Flora knew she was avoiding returning to Hugh.

Now overhearing their gossip, Flora realised it was time they returned to Balivanich. It was up to her to prise her mother from Elizabeth's comfortable house, or else Hugh *Cam* might give up on her completely. Besides, Flora was determined to be back on the Long Isle when Neil came sailing home. She must be bold.

'Here is your thread, Cousin Elizabeth,' she said, hurrying in. 'I couldn't help overhearing your remarks about marriage.'

Elizabeth's plump face coloured. 'You weren't meant–'

'I know I wasn't and I shouldn't really have stood their listening but I couldn't help it. You see, I have heard from Neil MacEachen quite recently. It was among the letters that arrived last week.'

Marion's mouth fell open. 'You never said.'

'No, but now I have. You seem so concerned for my maiden state that I want to put your minds at rest. Mr MacEachen will be returning from France very soon. He wishes that I be there when he does. No doubt he will want to speak with my stepfather about our future, so I think Mother that it's time we should be going back to Benbecula. Don't you agree, Cousin Elizabeth? You've been very kind to have us to stay for so long.'

The older women gaped at her. Flora swallowed, holding her nerve.

'Well,' Elizabeth said, 'I suppose high summer is a good time to travel.'

'Quite so,' Flora nodded, 'and I know my sisters and brothers will be longing to see you, Mother. We never intended to be gone this long.'

'That's true,' Marion said. 'I do miss my darlings.'

Flora left them to discuss travel arrangements and hurried away to find her maid Katie. The boatman's daughter from Howbeg, who had willingly become Flora's maid these past three years, had been pining for home for weeks; she would be overjoyed to be packing up and heading for the Outer Isles.

Shortly afterwards, a letter came from Hugh urging them to return home. The rumours that had been flying about all summer of a French invasion against King George in England appeared to be true. Word was reaching the islands that a French force was amassing. Local militias were already being recruited. Travel would become more difficult.

Amid conflicting reports of whether the south of the country was really under attack or not, Cousin Elizabeth bade them an anxious goodbye and God speed.

***

Sailing up the west coast, they broke their journey at Arisaig with Flora's elderly Uncle Donald but the men were preoccupied with talk of war and the atmosphere tense.

'What does it mean for us?' Flora asked her Uncle Donald and Cousin Ewen.

'No one wants war with France,' said Ewen. 'This is a quarrel with the English. We should take no part in it.'

'It is for our chiefs to decide,' Uncle Donald replied.

The boatmen were keen to move on the next day and sail straight for the Long Isle without stopping. Passing Skye, Flora gazed at the hills of Sleat in the distance. She knew from her stepfather that the Kingsburghs still lived at Armadale and that Allan had returned from Edinburgh and was helping run the Sleat estates. There had been no word that he had married Amelia or anyone else. Flora was sure Lady Margaret would have written to tell her if there had been such a grand clan wedding. Her former patron had sent letters spasmodically for a couple of years; baby James was walking and talking, Chief Norman's wife had died but young pretty Ann Martin was his constant companion and chaperone to his daughters. The last missive told her that Ann Martin had given birth to a daughter, then the letters had stopped. Perhaps because her replies were so poorly written – Flora was embarrassed at her lack of style – or Lady Sleat found the content too dull.

News had come last year that a second son had been born to the Sleats. Sir Alexander was overjoyed to be a father again and the baby was named after him. Scanning the horizon for a glimpse of Armadale, Flora wondered if the young chieftain James was being fostered by the Kingsburghs in the old tradition or whether Lady Margaret had succeeded in keeping her adored son with her instead?

She imagined Allan helping to teach the boy to run and jump and hurl stones, to recite Gaelic poems, ride bareback and fill his head with the legends of his ancestors and love of the land ...

Flora shook her head to rid it of such thoughts. What was she doing? She had managed to bury any lingering feelings for young Kingsburgh long ago; she had hardly thought about him in years – well perhaps months. It was just being so near to Skye conjured him up; his intense blue gaze, his mane of black hair and his broad smiling mouth.

Flora let out a long sigh, trying to banish Allan from her mind again. Her mother, who had been looking anxiously for signs of invading ships, was watching her.

'Are you feeling unwell?' Marion asked. 'You look a little strange.'

'My stomach's just upset from the journey.'

'But the sea couldn't be calmer.'

Flora turned from her mother's searching look.

'I understand,' Marion said softly, with a squeeze of her hand. 'It's the thought of seeing him again at last, isn't it? Your MacEachen.'

***

Balivanich was deserted of men. Annabella and Tibby came rushing out to greet them with hugs and breathless news.

'Papa's at Nunton – James too – the Captain summoned them. It's a council of war, James said.'

'War?' Marion gasped.

'James is just being dramatic,' said Flora, 'he's itching to join the army. Where are the boys?' She looked around for her youngest brothers in an attempt to distract her mother.

'Playing at sword fighting,' Annabella rolled her eyes.

Their cook Janet – her fading red hair the only sign of ageing – welcomed them with a meal of poached salmon, barley cakes and a bowl of frothed cream and honey.

Flora was happy to see her mother revive with her favourite food and her family around her again. Marion kissed the boys and fussed over them fighting with real swords and pulled Magnus onto her knee although he insisted he was too old for cuddling.

'I'm never going away again and leaving you for so long,' Marion declared, tearful at being reunited. 'I'm just thankful you're both too young to be called up in a fighting force.'

But there was consternation when Hugh returned late that night with their eldest son James. Marion's pleasure at Hugh's warm greeting vanished at his sombre words.

'War is coming one way or another.'

'War with the French?' Marion gasped.

'Or the English,' Hugh murmured.

'I don't understand–?'

'Word has come to Clanranald that the fleet setting out from France is in support of Prince Charles Edward and a Jacobite force.'

There was a stunned silence. Flora's heart began to thud. 'Who brought this news?' she whispered.

'MacEachen.' Hugh eyed her steadily. 'He's at Nunton.'

143

She felt herself blushing. How long had she longed to hear of his return? Yet she was almost frightened of meeting him in case he had cooled towards her. It had been six long years.

Marion fretted, 'What do the Clanranalds think? Surely it would be madness to come out again for the Stuarts. Look what happened the last time – the Sleats and Clanranalds lost half their lands – and you went into exile Hugh, don't you remember how terrible it was?'

'Of course I remember, but the choice is not mine. We'll do whatever our chief tells us and we won't shirk a fight.'

'So the Captain is in favour of supporting the Prince?' Flora asked.

Hugh grunted. 'Not as much as his brave wife. Lady Clan would lead us into battle tomorrow given half a chance.'

Marion snapped, 'I hope you didn't encourage her.'

Hugh ignored this. 'I must leave in a day or two for Skye and convey messages from Clanranald to Sir Alexander.'

'And Papa said I could go too,' James said, his fair face eager.

'Oh husband,' Marion cried, 'must you take James?'

'He's sixteen and old enough to be of use to his chief,' Hugh said, then softened his voice. 'Don't worry my dearest – I'm sure we won't be gone long.'

***

Exhausted as she was, Flora could not sleep. At dawn she rose, dressed and walked the short distance to Nunton. She could not bear to wait any longer to see Neil; she must know what was in his heart. His letters had been affectionate yet lacked the ardour of a man in love. But then he might have been cautious in case they were read by others.

Lady Clan welcomed her warmly.

'I'm so glad you are safely back, lassie. We are entering troubled times – but great times, I feel sure.' She could barely suppress her excitement. 'We women must be strong if our men are to be called away. But I know you have not just come to see me, Flora. Wait in the parlour and I will send for MacEachen. I shall allow you a few minutes alone together.'

Flora thought her heart would drum right out of her chest it was banging so hard. She paced the room, glancing out at the sea beyond the casement window, each minute passing like ten.

'Florrie.'

She spun round at the familiar voice. 'I didn't hear you come in,' she gasped.

Neil crossed the room without a sound, his tall frame slightly stooped. His wavy hair was receding at the temples and there were new lines around his eyes; white creases in skin that the sun had turned the colour of honey. His brown eyes were watchful as if he hardly recognised her.

After a moment's hesitation, he took her hand and raised it to his lips, planting a courtly kiss on her trembling fingers.

144

'*Enchanté*,' he smiled. 'You have grown into a beautiful woman, my dear. Your portrait did not do you justice.'

Flora was immediately tongue-tied. He seemed so much older and worldly-wise with his polished formal manners. It was like a stranger before her, not the passionate Highlander she had yearned for all these years. He must have sensed her awkwardness, for he led her gently to a two-seater sofa and sat beside her. While she brought her breathing under control he talked about his joy at revisiting Howbeg, his kind welcome by the Clanranalds and the changes he noticed in six years of absence. He spoke of everything except the reason for his return.

Flora found her voice. 'My stepfather says you brought a message from the Stuart Prince. Is there to be another Rising?'

'It seems likely.'

Fear flared at his words. The older generation still talked with bitterness at all they had lost thirty years ago – the butchery and land-grabbing. But there was excitement in Neil's eyes.

'Is that what you want?'

'It's what I yearn for, Flora. Our rightful King restored and our country taking back power from that German imposter in London.' His face lit up as he talked. 'I long for the freedom to pray as a Catholic and to live freely in Scotland and not have to eke out a living as a mercenary for a foreign monarch, however sympathetic.'

'But there will be civil war,' Flora said.

'There is an appetite for change,' Neil insisted. You'll see. It's just a matter of persuading the larger clans to support us. Everyone who meets Prince Charles knows that he will make a fine king one day.'

'You've met him? What is he like?'

'There is no one more noble and brave. He has already proved himself a soldier and leader.' Neil's eyes shone. 'And he has the Stuart belief in his destiny as our ruler – and the Stuart charm.'

'Is he really coming to Scotland?' Flora felt a quickening of excitement.

'He is on his way with a large French force. We must rally for him too. He is relying on us Scots to lead the way in ousting the fat Hanoverian in London. That's why Hugh *Cam*, Ranald Og and I must go to Skye at once to persuade Sleat and MacLeod to back the Prince.'

'You're leaving again so soon?' Flora could not hide her dismay.

'Don't look so sad.' He took her hand in his. 'I have no intention of repeating six years away from here again.'

'So are we still …?' Flora went pink at having to ask.

'My heart is promised to you forever, *ma cherie*. Never doubt it.'

'So we can be married soon?'

'Soon; when the Stuarts are back in power. I will be well rewarded for my loyalty and we will have a wedding fit for a lord.'

Flora's heart sank. 'Why wait when things are so uncertain. I don't ask for anything grand.'

'But that's what you shall have. When the time comes we shall have a royal prince at our wedding.'

Flora could see he was single-minded in the Jacobite Cause and had no time for a swift marriage. She could do nothing but wait. Yet she craved reassurance.

'Kiss me to prove you love me,' Flora challenged.

His eyes widened at her boldness. Then he smiled, leaned towards her and kissed her lips. When he drew back, Flora put her hands around his lean jaw and held onto him, opening her mouth and kissing him with more vigour. She felt light-headed – she had dreamed of this moment – and desire began wash through her. She willed him to touch her more intimately but he pulled away.

His brown eyes surveyed her. 'Where did you learn such passion?' he demanded.

Flora forced away the unwelcome memory of Allan's sensuous mouth on hers.

'In my dreams of you,' Flora teased.

He smiled. 'Oh Flora, I had forgotten how much I'd missed you.'

'Please come back to me soon,' she urged. 'I want to be wed and have children and our own place. That's what you want too, isn't it?'

'Of course.'

Lady Clan did not leave them alone for long. Flora stayed for breakfast and then left, reassured that Neil still loved her. Only later, as she watched Hugh and James make ready to leave for Skye, did she ponder Neil's reasons for returning. Never in his list of wants had he actually said that he had returned for her.

Chapter 29

Dunvegan, Skye

'*All* the ships wrecked?' Chief Norman asked, horrified.

'Most before they even got out of port – a freakish storm,' said Captain Malcolm, the bearer of shocking news that the French fleet was no more.

'This changes everything,' Norman declared. 'We need the French army to back us.'

'It could be lies put about by the Hanoverians,' Neil was scathing. 'I've heard no such news.'

Allan said, 'you've been on the Outer Isles so you wouldn't have. Malcolm's come from the barracks at Fort William.'

Neil gave him a dismissive look. 'Exactly – a hotbed of government troops and propaganda.'

'Highland troops,' Allan sparked, 'with no reason to lie.'

'It's a setback,' Hugh intervened, looking around at the dozen gentry crammed into the high tower room that MacLeod used as a study. 'But the French won't give up easily. They will still send us arms and money for the Cause. We can raise an army for the Prince.'

'The mainland clans will join us,' Ranald Og said eagerly. 'My kinsman Glengarry is keen, and Cameron of Locheil. Atholl will bring out his troops and the Jacobites to the east – Lovat and Gordon.'

'And the men of the Long Isle will follow the Prince to a man,' Neil said.

'You speak for the Islesmen though you haven't lived there for years,' Allan mocked.

'They will follow Clanranald and Berneray if asked.'

'And will the Presbyterians of Lewis do that too?'

Kingsburgh stayed his son with a hand on his shoulder, baffled by his antagonism to MacEachen. Perhaps it was the man's air of arrogance; he had been holding court all morning, the names of royalty and French expressions tripping off his tongue.

'It will be for the chiefs to decide and for you young men to follow,' Kingsburgh cautioned.

'And what do you think, Kingsburgh?' Sir Alexander, plagued by indecision, asked his foster-father.

'It is a heavy responsibility to bear, taking our people into battle against other countrymen – not just our traditional enemy in England but fellow Scots, even Gaels. I'm old enough to remember the terrible losses we bore in 1715 and '19 and the hardship that followed.'

Kingsburgh spoke quietly but everyone fell silent to listen to his opinion. 'The Government will be merciless if we rise again and fail.'

'We won't fail,' interrupted Ranald Og.

'Our support is stronger this time,' Neil said.

'Let him speak,' MacLeod ordered.

Kingsburgh continued. 'They are already trying to curb our power with their military road building and barracks. The Hanoverians fear us and will need little excuse to subdue us further. Yet some of our young men are benefiting from the army commissions they hand out.' He glanced at Captain Malcolm. 'They give much needed jobs and pay.'

'The Stuarts will do that tenfold for their supporters,' Neil retorted. 'Prince Charles will come with gold if that's all that concerns you. Let's not be held back from action by worry over sinecures for running local militias.'

'My father is no lackey of the Government,' Allan scowled, clenching his fists.

The room erupted in arguing. MacLeod held up his hand for silence.

'So Kingsburgh, you think we should not risk our men's lives and our own livelihoods for the Cause?'

'I'm not saying that,' Kingsburgh replied. 'There is much that would be better for us in the Highlands under a Stuart monarch – especially if King James chose Edinburgh for his court and brought back some powers from London – allowing our culture and economy to flourish again.'

He looked at them all with sombre eyes. 'But failure would be terrible for us Gaels – the *Sassenachs* would occupy us for generations to come.'

'Tell us what you would do,' Sir Alexander urged.

'It is too early to say one way or the other without more facts. It's crucial to know what support is still coming from the French and from the Prince's Jacobite allies elsewhere. If he is well supported, we could act swiftly from the north and march on Edinburgh. I have no doubt we could secure Scotland for the Stuarts – England is an unknown.'

'There is much discontent with German George south of the border too,' Neil was quick to add. 'If they see a mighty army bearing down on London, they will join us.'

'And there is rumour,' said Hugh, 'that many Irish could be called upon to fight for a Stuart and a Catholic one at that.'

'That worries me,' Mackinnon of Strath spoke up, 'that this could be seen as a religious war. Most of us aren't Catholic and don't want to go back to Catholicism.'

'That is not King James's intention – nor that of his heir Prince Charles,' Neil said. 'His faith is a personal choice. The Prince has told me that he would never interfere with the reformed church in Scotland.'

'As a Catholic you would say that,' Allan murmured.

Neil shot him a look of irritation. 'When you show you are prepared to do more than herd cattle and instead risk your life for king and chief then I'll take more heed of your sniping.'

MacLeod snapped, 'Farming is every bit as important to us chiefs as soldiering, don't forget that, young MacEachen. I think it's time we all shared a bowl of punch to calm our tempers. We will think on your wise words Kingsburgh and await further news from France.'

Allan took himself off to the woods to calm down. What had got into him? He was ashamed of his petty point scoring with MacEachen. The man was insufferable with his French affectations but he had far more idea of what was going on beyond the isolation of Skye and the likely strategy of the Jacobites. Neil had done nothing to deserve his hostility and yet he, Allan, had delighted in goading him.

He wandered among the bluebells, stopping to lean against a silver birch. He was assaulted by the memory of being there that magical dawn when Flora had come stepping through the trees like a wood sprite, hair loose about her slender shoulders, a look of wonder on her pretty face. It was then that he knew the physical ache she provoked in him was more than just passion; he had fallen in love with the Milton girl.

Allan pulled the tiny miniature from the leather pouch he kept on his belt, the one he had paid the painter Thomas to copy from the larger one. He knew that Neil possessed Flora's official miniature, even though it was he, Allan, who had secretly paid for Flora's sitting. He had hoped she would give it to him – he'd been sure she'd felt something for him – but Lady Margaret had told him how keen Flora was for the absent MacEachen to have it; Lady Sleat had already instructed him to give his own one to Amelia MacLeod.

He sighed. Amelia was now of marriageable age and if he did not ask MacLeod for her hand soon, he knew he would miss his chance of a prestigious match. She was a beautiful young woman. So why was it that he still hankered after a Long Isle lass with no dowry or land to her name? A lass too proud and impetuous for her own good who did not return his feelings. He thought once that she had desired him too, but she had waited six years for another man. Soon MacEachen would have her as his wife.

The thought cut through him like a dirk. That was the real reason he disliked the man from Howbeg; Neil had known Flora all his life and had captured her heart in childhood. Allan knew he could not compete with that. He looked again at the impression of Flora held in his palm. The lustrous hair and mesmerising eyes – the look both bold yet dreamy – and the sweet heart-shaped face filled him with futile longing.

Allan tucked it away once more. Why bother with affairs of the heart when the future of their people was so uncertain? A sense of dread flooded through him. Whatever side MacLeod and Sir Alexander decided to take, there would be bloody civil war. Turmoil was coming to their island; only the scale of it was yet unknown.

Chapter 30

Balivanich, Benbecula

'I insist on speaking to One-eyed Hugh and not you,' Reverend Elijah Gunn said to Marion. He stood in the downstairs parlour, where Katie the maid had brought him, shaking with nervous excitement. He ignored Flora's attempts to greet him.

'Hugh of Balivanich is not here,' Marion glared, affronted by his rudeness.

'Where is he?'

'About his business as usual.'

'I heard he has gone to Skye with that Papist MacEachen.'

'Then you know more than I do.'

'There is talk of treason in the islands, and our British Navy has captured French frigates carrying arms to the rebels. I hope your husband is not in any way involved?'

'My husband is a peaceable man – he swapped his claymore for a factor's pen when he married me.'

'I know that you people keep weapons hidden in your byres. Your pretence at loyalty to the British Crown is hypocritical, Madam.'

Flora tried to diffuse the tense atmosphere. 'Would you care for a bowl of punch, Reverend Gunn?'

'I don't drink liquor.' His look was resentful. She knew he would never forgive her for rejecting his proposal. 'And I hope you don't either.'

'So the bottles of claret that are taken to the manse after dark are filled with water, I suppose?' Marion retorted.

The minister's pale face flushed with indignation. 'That is for communion.'

'Of course.' Marion's look was disdainful.

Flora winced. Her mother was making things worse. She didn't trust Gunn; his wheedling of information out of his parishioners was more dangerous than his gout-ridden old father's bullying had been.

'Will you take a seat, Minister?' Flora smiled.

'No, this is no social call. I came to speak to your stepfather to give him a chance to prepare for communion.' He gave a sour look. 'To atone for his sins.'

'Then you will have to return when he does,' Marion was brusque.

'I shall. And it would be best for you all if he confesses swiftly.'

'My husband is a loyal subject and I resent your insinuations, Sir.'

'I am not talking about loyalty to the Crown but to a higher King,' Gunn replied. 'Your husband has broken his oath before God.'

'I don't know what you mean,' Marion said. Flora saw panic in her look.

'His marriage oath is what I mean,' Gunn said, his expression pious. 'I'm surprised the daughter of a minister would allow such lax behaviour in her husband.'

'I don't want to hear your nasty tale-telling,' Marion said in alarm.

'Especially with another married woman,' he went on. 'If they do not repent, they will be excommunicated.'

'How dare you!'

'Oh I dare, Madam. I will no longer stand for such sinfulness in my flock.'

'I've heard enough. Flora, see Reverend Gunn to the door please.'

'You must know who I mean, Mistress Balivanich. She has been flaunting her affair for months.'

'You will not besmirch my husband's name in his house. I shan't listen.' Marion shook.

'It's time you went, sir.' Flora opened the door wide; angry at how upset he was making her mother.

'She is a boastful wench. But the world will soon see them for the licentious adulterers that they are.'

'Get out!' Marion cried.

Flora took the minister by the arm but he shook her off as if her touch was contaminated. At the front door he turned on her and hissed, 'you Miltons think you are above the law but you are not above God's law. I am only doing my duty by pointing out the sins of your errant stepfather.'

Flora did not trust herself to speak. The man had turned out as unpleasant as his father Obadiah. He hesitated.

'However, there may be a way to forgiveness – of keeping One-Eyed Hugh from the humiliation of the penitent's stool – and that's if you were able to reassure me that he is not involved in the fermenting of rebellion. If you could tell me where he is and with whom he consorts …'

Flora flashed him a look of contempt. She wanted to shout at him never to return to their house again but knew that would only make him the more vindictive.

'As my mother said,' Flora kept her voice level, 'my stepfather is going about his everyday business.'

Elijah Gunn glared and jammed on his black hat. 'You are as vain and foolish as your mother. You would have been quite unsuitable as a minister's wife.'

Flora closed the door, not waiting to see him ride away. Marion was working herself into a temper.

'The gall of the man! He's the worst gossip on the island – they should clamp an iron scold over his wagging tongue!'

'You mustn't get so upset.' Flora steered her into a chair and called for Katie to bring her a drink of milk. But her mother continued to rant.

'It was bad enough when his pompous father used to come and lecture me on my children's education – he'd sit in this very room stuffing his face like a hog on Janet's cooking and listing my failings as a mother – but this is ten times worse. How dare he call my husband an adulter– I won't even bring myself to say it in my own home! It's lies, pure lies!'

Flora took the bowl of milk from Katie and nodded for her to go. She coaxed her mother to sip. Marion was shaking so much, drops of warm milk splashed onto her dress. But gradually she calmed down.

'Oh, Florrie,' she whispered, 'what if it's true?'

'It won't be.' Even as she said it, Flora felt anxiety grip her.

'He wouldn't do that to me, would he?' Marion fretted. 'He wouldn't take up with a local woman? And a married one at that.' Her eyes flooded with tears. 'Whose wife would do such a thing?'

Flora did not answer. A horrid suspicion wormed its way into her mind. There was one family that Elijah Gunn hated more than theirs – hated with a passion – the Catholic Clanranalds. Was it possible that he saw this as a way of discrediting them all? She knew that Hugh and Lady Clan were close friends and enjoyed each other's company. Surely they had not taken their attraction to each other beyond flirtation? It was rumoured that Captain Clanranald had a roving eye but Lady Clan would draw greater censure.

She hoped for all their sakes that her wild notion was wrong.

'You know who it is, don't you?' Marion gasped. She clutched Flora's hand. 'Tell me!'

***

By the time Hugh and James returned the following week, Marion had made herself ill with speculation. Flora had kept quiet about her suspicion of Lady Clan. She wanted to talk to Neil about everything but he had gone straight to Nunton to report on their Skye meetings.

But Hugh was dismissive. 'I can't believe you allowed that toad of a man to poison you against me.'

'So it's not true that you have taken up with a married woman?' Marion demanded, not caring that Flora, James and Annabella sat at the dining table with them. Flora saw how her siblings squirmed.

'I'll not be questioned like this in front of my family,' Hugh snapped. 'There are far more pressing affairs to consider than the minister's gossip. We could be at war in a matter of weeks.'

James chimed in, 'Prince Charles Stuart has set sail with a force from France. They think he will head for the Isles to avoid the Navy.'

Flora gasped. 'But we'd heard the French fleet was destroyed?'

'Prince Charles has other support. Neil says he's bringing men and supplies.'

'All we know for sure,' Hugh said grimly, 'is that the Prince is on his way.'

'What does that mean for us?' Marion worried.

'It depends what Sir Alexander decides.'

'Will you have to go and fight? I can't bear the thought of you going away and getting killed.'

'Don't think the worst, Mother,' Flora said.

'And where Father goes, I go too,' James declared.

'No! You're too young,' Marion cried.

'I'm sixteen. Father was fighting abroad at my age.'

'Don't let him, Hugh,' she appealed.

'If our chief calls on him then it will be an honour.'

'How can you say that when that man was responsible for my Ranald's death!'

'Don't bring that up again Marion,' Hugh protested.

Flora broke in. 'So you will be fighting for the Prince? I know that's what Neil wants.'

'Most likely but Sleat has not declared for either the Prince or the Government yet,' Hugh said.

'Because he is weak,' Marion retorted, 'and cannot make up his mind.'

James chided. 'Mother, do not speak of our chief with such disrespect.'

'I don't want you to go either,' Annabella was close to tears at the arguing.

The bickering was interrupted by knocking at the door. Katie came in, her fair face troubled.

'There's someone at the door for you Master.'

'Who?'

Flora's heart leapt, hoping it was Neil with news of the Prince.

'A woman,' Katie mumbled, throwing Flora a pleading look.

Flora sprang up. 'Let me see to it.' She could not bear to see the stricken expression on her mother's face.

Before she could reach the door, a woman barged in.

'I'll not be kept waiting like a servant.' Her plaid fell away from her head revealing a tangle of long hair, still the colour of copper despite her middle age. Mairi MacVurich, the bardess.

Flora heard her mother gasp. The colour drained from Hugh's face.

'What is the meaning of this intrusion?' he demanded.

'You know fine well,' she flashed him an angry look.

'If you have come for news of the King across the water,' Hugh blustered, 'you had better go across to Nunton and ask the Clanranalds.'

'I know that the Prince is come,' Mairi boasted, 'I see him in my mind's eye. I don't need any man to tell me what I already foresee.'

Hugh seemed paralysed by her bold gaze.

Flora moved between them. 'My brother James will see you home, Mistress Mairi. It is late and whatever concerns you will have to wait until tomorrow.'

For a moment, Mairi scrutinised her with her strange eyes of different colours. Flora felt winded but stood her ground.

'Well, this daughter of Milton shows more guts than all your brood, Hugh *Cam*,' Mairi sneered. 'And you.' She pushed Flora aside. 'Why have you not come to me as you promised? I shouldn't have to come seeking you out at Balivanich.'

'What nonsense is this?' Hugh found his voice.

'You would deny me in front of your wife after all the sweet words you've poured into my ears these past months?'

'You?' Marion gasped. 'It can't be *you*!'

Mairi's face lit with savage pleasure. 'Did I not warn you years ago to keep a watch on your husband?'

153

Marion looked at Hugh, appalled. 'Tell me she lies.'

'If you deny me,' Mairi threatened, 'I will put a curse on you and all your family.'

Hugh launched himself at her. 'Out of here now,' he ordered.

'Don't lay a hand on me,' she warned.

'Hugh,' Marion cried, 'tell me the truth!'

He faced her. 'It was nothing – a quick dalliance. She bewitched me. It was over months ago.'

'Over?' Mairi screamed. 'It will never be over.'

Marion put her hand to her mouth to stifle a sob. Annabella rushed tearfully to her side. Hugh turned on Mairi.

'How dare you come here and threaten me and my family. I never want to see you anywhere near my house again.'

Mairi flew at him like a wildcat, scratching at his face with sharp fingernails.

'I am your family now!'

Flora tried to grab her; James reached for her other arm. She wrestled them off with surprising strength. As she did so, her plaid dropped to the floor. Underneath she was wearing only a simple shift. Her breasts bulged like full udders. Her belly swelled against the tight linen gown.

Everyone froze. Flora could not stop staring at Mairi's swollen girth.

The bardess tossed back her hair. 'Everyone knows Murdo has not been able to give me a child,' she said, her expression defiant. 'It's yours Hugh Cam.'

Chapter 31

Three days later, Neil came at dusk to tell them that the Prince had landed on the tiny island of Eriskay, two islands to the south. Flora had no chance to speak to him in private, just threw him a longing look as he set off into the gloom with Hugh. They were going to meet up with Angus at Milton and Boisdale further south. James was ordered to stay and look after the household.

'No doubt that prying Gunn will be watching,' Hugh said, his face gaunt from sleepless nights and wrangling with his wife. 'We don't want to draw his attention more than necessary.'

But Flora knew he was keen to be gone and put himself at a distance from the mess he had created at Balivanich. She knew he was remorseful over his affair with Mairi – he had said so umpteen times – but Marion was beyond listening. Flora had never seen her mother so bitter or upset.

'I can't believe you would do such a thing,' Marion had railed. 'Right on our doorstep – right under my nose – could it not at least have been far from my sight? Now all my family are having their faces rubbed in the sordid affair – and all the neighbours – how they will be laughing at me behind my back – the shame of it! And with that strumpet. The very thought of it is like a knife in my heart!'

Nothing Flora or her stepfather could say made the slightest difference. Marion wore herself out with tears and shouting. After Hugh left, she sank into despair, locked herself in her chamber and would answer to no one – not even a weeping Annabella. Flora and Janet despaired.

'She won't eat or drink,' Flora worried. 'It frightens me. It's as if Mairi has sent her mad.'

Janet sighed. 'Long ago, that wretched girl cursed your mother. My mistress has been fearful all her life for the safety of her sons and her marriage.'

Flora waited impatiently for Neil and Hugh's return. The days went by with no news. She worried that they would leave to follow the Prince and not bother to come home first. But she saw how James paced down to the shore each day and knew that Hugh would not join up without his son. After what Janet had told her, Flora now worried for her brother's safety. At least Sorley and Magnus were too young to go to war. But what of her dearest brother Angus? Would he be compelled to fight too? Waiting helpless and in ignorance was worse than the actual knowing.

***

Hugh returned without Neil, his mood troubled.

'The Prince has sailed for Arisaig and Clanranald's mainland estates,' he told them. 'Neil and Ranald Og have gone with him to rally support.'

'You saw the Prince in person?' Annabella asked in excitement. 'Is he very handsome?'

Hugh gave a brief smile. 'Very. And charming too; so I'll be keeping you away from him, my bonny lassie.'

'Father!' Annabella blushed and giggled.

James was impatient. 'So what happens now? Do we go too?'

'We'll leave soon for Armadale and put ourselves at Sir Alexander's service.'

'That's grand!' James whooped. 'I'm going to fight for the King over the water!'

'That is not certain,' Hugh cautioned.

'Why is that?' Flora asked.

He let out a long sigh. 'Prince Charles Edward has only a handful of men with him.'

'A handful?' James frowned. 'A hundred, two hundred?'

Hugh briefly closed his good eye. 'Seven.'

'Seven hundred?'

Her stepfather shook his head. 'Seven men – and himself.'

'But more will follow?' James frowned.

'That is the Prince's fighting force from the Continent,' Hugh said grimly. 'He is relying on us for the rest.'

'That would be folly, surely?' Flora gasped.

'Clanranald thinks so,' said Hugh, 'and has already told him so. But the Prince is full of optimism. It's hard not to let it infect you. He is a passionate young man.'

'Armadale you said?'

They all swung round at the sound of Marion's voice. She had slipped into the room on bare feet, her gown hanging loose on her thin body, her face wan and eyes dark-ringed yet still beautiful.

'You are going to Armadale, husband?'

He nodded, his look wary, fearing an outburst.

'Then we shall go with you.'

'Marion, dearest.' He moved towards her. 'It will be safer for you all here. Skye will soon be crawling with government troops if the Prince makes a call to arms on neighbouring Arisaig.'

'Safer?' she repeated, her mouth turning down in disgust. 'I shall never be safe while I live within sight of that witch.'

Hugh flushed. 'She can't hurt you and I will never speak to her again, I promise on the lives of our ch–'

'Don't say it,' Marion hissed. 'I want only one promise from you, Hugh; that you will take me away from this place. I refuse to live here when that witch's brat is born. If you won't take me to Armadale then I will leave you and take the family to Cousin Elizabeth in Largie.'

'Wife, be reasonable,' Hugh pleaded, 'Skye will be in turmoil. Let me go first and see how things are. I will speak to Sir Alexander about securing a different position – perhaps another tack of land closer to Angus at Milton. You would like that, wouldn't you?'

'I will not stay on the Long Isle,' Marion was adamant. 'I want to return to Armadale where we were first married – where we were happy.'

'But,' Flora pointed out, 'the Kingsburghs run the tack at Armadale and live in the farmhouse, Mother.'

Marion did not take her gaze from Hugh as she answered. 'I'm well aware of who is there. That is where I wish to live. The Kingsburghs have a perfectly good home in Trotternish.'

Flora felt dismay at her mother's callousness towards their fellow MacDonalds.

Hugh bowed his head. This calm, steely-minded Marion seemed to unnerve him more than the ranting deranged wife he had fled from just days ago.

'I will see what I can do,' he agreed.

'Good.' Marion gave a wintry smile, turned and padded out of the room leaving her family staring after her in shock.

***

By the time Mairi's baby was due, the islands were in upheaval. Clanranald, appalled by the Prince arriving virtually alone, decreed his clan would stay at home.

'It's madness to even think of risking our lives for such an escapade. It's doomed before it starts without French backing.'

Lady Clan was scathing. 'Victories are not won by sitting at the fire smoking tobacco and drinking porter. This young man needs our support. Imagine if it was our Ranald asking for help; would you not give it within the blink of an eye?'

'But he is not Ranald Og.'

'Well, I for one will support him,' Lady Clan declared.

'I never doubted that you would,' Clanranald said, retreating to his fug-filled library.

Encouraged by his mother, Ranald Og rallied a company of men from the Long Isle for the Jacobite army. His father did not try to stop him going.

'Keeping a foot in both camps,' Hugh snorted when discussing the Clanranalds with Angus and preparing to sail for Skye.

'So you won't be going to war?' Flora asked her brother anxiously.

'Not unless the Captain changes his mind and calls us out. Pen is pleased,' Angus smiled. 'She wants me at home when our first born arrives.'

Flora gasped. 'That's wonderful news. How soon?'

'Turn of the year or sooner. I hope you will come and help Pen in her confinement, Florrie?'

Flora gave an embarrassed glance at her stepfather.

Hugh cleared his throat. 'Your mother and sister may be removed to Skye by then.'

Flora added swiftly, 'But I'll visit in the spring, I promise.'

Shortly afterwards, Hugh and James had left for Skye. In August, news spread like heather fires that Prince Charles had raised his banner at

Glenfinnan in Lochaber, the land of the Camerons, and that warriors from all over the Highlands were swelling the ranks of his army. They had taken Hanoverian troops prisoner near Fort William. Marion fretted about Hugh and young James. Then rumours reached them from Lady Clan that neither Sir Alexander nor Chief Norman had given their support to the Prince.

'Surely that can't be true?' Flora was baffled. 'James went away full of talk about joining the Prince.'

'Talk is all it amounted to,' Lady Clan said angrily. 'The Skye chiefs withholding their men will be a serious blow to the Cause. What cowardly sign does that send out to the rest of Scotland?'

'At least it means our men might soon come home,' Marion said, 'and we can all get on with our lives.'

'My dear Marion, whatever happens,' said Lady Clan, 'our lives will not be the same as before.'

'You're right,' Marion sighed. 'I just want to be gone from here.'

Lady Clan left, exchanging regretful glances with Flora.

Their men did not return. Angus brought a letter from Hugh. Independent companies of soldiers were being recruited by MacDonald of Sleat and MacLeod of Dunvegan. Local militias were also being set up under the leadership of Kingsburgh.

"I've secured James a commission as an ensign. It's a fine opportunity for the lad but tell your mother she mustn't worry. Sir Alexander's men will be doing nothing more than coastal defence and checking passes. But the government pay is good."

'Government pay?' Flora queried. 'So they will be fighting for the Hanoverians?'

Angus nodded. 'I think he's trying to tell us that the Skye chiefs are already under pressure from the Government to lend active support – not just abstain from helping the Prince.'

'So James could end up fighting Ranald Og and Neil MacEachen?' Flora was horrified.

'Oh why did Prince Charles ever decide to come?' Marion cried.

*** *

The summer waned as they waited tensely for more news. Would the Rising peter out before it really began? How many had gone with the Prince? Flora hoped for word from Neil but none came. She found herself wondering if Allan was among the MacDonald men newly recruited for the Hanoverian side. His father was being active for Sir Alexander's militias and a letter from Hugh told them that he was also in charge of two local units. Flora read it with her mother.

'But he doesn't say when we can join him on Skye,' Marion fretted.

'No,' Flora said, 'just that they are both well.'

By October, newspapers were arriving on the Outer Isles with astonishing news. Lady Clan came rushing from Nunton.

158

'The Highland army has taken Edinburgh!' she cried. 'The Prince is at Holyrood Palace. He's been there since mid-September. A Stuart reigns again in Scotland! Can you believe it to be true?'

Flora scoured the paper. 'And taken without bloodshed. Thank goodness.' Relief engulfed her.

'The Jacobites saw off the Hanoverians at some place called Prestonpans,' Lady Clan crowed. 'The enemy turned tail like whipped dogs. If we can take Edinburgh so easily, then the rest might fall like a pack of cards.'

Other stories flew around that autumn. MacLeod had sent a force to the mainland to challenge the Gordons east of Inverness. The ranks of Skye men, discovering that they weren't to fight for the Prince, put up a half-hearted show of arms and quickly melted away west to their homes.

Edinburgh society was rejuvenated with dances and parties in honour of the charming Prince Charles; the ladies of the city were flocking to his lively court and swooning at the sight of swaggering bare-kneed Highlanders in their warlike plaids and bonnets. Was Neil enjoying adoration from the sophisticated young women of the Capital? Flora plagued herself with the thought. Yet the more successful the Prince, the more likely it was that Neil would return triumphant and marry her.

November storms came and Marion badgered Flora to put pressure on her stepfather and write to Hugh too demanding that he remember his promise to take them to Armadale before winter set in.

'I can't be marooned here another winter,' she despaired. 'If he is to be in charge of men in Sleat then I must be with him.'

Late one evening, the sky black and moonless, a loud hammering on the door sent Marion into a panic.

'Who can that be?'

'Open up, quickly!' a man's voice bellowed in Gaelic.

They found a distraught Murdo on the doorstep. Marion shrank from the sight of Mairi's cuckolded husband, his face ghostly in the flickering light from their lamp.

'Please Mistress Flora, come and help,' he babbled. 'I know you have the way with babes.'

'Babes?'

'With bringing them out.'

Flora tensed. 'I'm no midwife,' she protested.

'You have the touch with calves and you've helped others.' He was close to tears. 'I'm losing my Mairi. For pity's sake, help me!'

Her mother looked horrified as Flora pulled on her plaid.

'I have to go Mother,' Flora said in English, 'look how distressed the poor man is.'

'Wait!' said Marion. She called for their servant Peter and ordered him to go with her daughter. 'Take the lantern and see that no harm comes to Florrie. Katie,' she bade Flora's young maid, 'you go and help your mistress too.'

Stumbling through the dark to Murdo's cottage, Flora was met by the cloying stench of blood amid the peat smoke. Mairi lay writhing in the box-bed, eyes rolling in terror. Gone was the haughty woman who had boasted of her affair with Hugh in front of Marion and her family. Her hair was lank and stuck to her face – a face lined with pain and age – and she screamed in agony.

'Get it out of me! I want to die.'

On quick examination, Flora saw the baby was in the dangerous breach position. She ordered Katie to fetch water to bathe Mairi's brow.

'Hold onto your man's hand and squeeze hard when the pain comes,' Flora said.

'The pain never goes,' Mairi panted. She fixed her with a crazed look. 'Will I die? Don't leave me. I don't want to die.'

'You won't die,' Flora said, her voice calm but heart racing in fear. There was so much blood on the bed that she doubted either mother or baby would survive. 'Sing to your wife,' she encouraged Murdo.

'Sing? I can't sing.'

'You're a piper – you have tunes in your head – hum a tune.'

Flora could think of no other way to distract Mairi from her pain. It had helped her Cousin Elizabeth through childbirth so it was worth a try now.

While Murdo croaked a tune and Katie wiped the sweat from Mairi's face, Flora felt for the baby and tried to manoeuvre it round. But the baby was ready to come. Mairi seemed sapped of any strength to bring it out.

'Breath shallow – small breaths – panting breaths,' Flora encouraged. 'Feel the pain come like waves on the shore. Wait for the big one. Can you feel it coming, Mairi?'

'No,' she wailed, 'it's all one big tide.'

'You will. When it comes, blow like the wind and push with the wave. Come on Mairi.'

The contractions began to come more frequently and Mairi sobbed in distress. Flora encouraged and cajoled but the baby did not come. Time ground on. Flora saw the woman was giving up. Her eyes were closing. The birthing contractions were gripping her but she was doing nothing to help force out the baby.

Fear dried Flora's throat. She was losing the battle. In desperation, she pressed down on the hard belly, feeling for the head.

'Don't give up on me, Mairi. Call yourself a MacVurich? Your ancestors are turning in their graves with shame. No one will remember you – except as the bardess who didn't even have the courage to bring her baby into the world. Mairi the coward!'

Mairi's eyes snapped open. 'Don't you call me that,' she hissed.

'The last of the MacVurichs – never again will they be bards to the Clanranalds – because you couldn't be bothered to fight. Your child will never sing of the Stuart kings returning to Scotland. All because you gave up!'

'I'll never give up,' Mairi panted.

'Then push hard,' Flora commanded.

Mairi roared and pushed. Flora grabbed at the baby's feet and pulled, shouting encouragement. Murdo raised his voice and sang as if his lungs would burst while his wife clawed at his hand and screamed.

'Again,' Flora cried, sweat dripping from her brow in the fetid air. 'And again.'

The birth seemed never ending but just as Flora was despairing, the baby tore its way out of Mairi's body.

Frantically, Flora cleared its mouth, pinched a bloodied leg and made it cry.

'Hear that, Mairi?' she smiled, eyes smarting with sudden tears. 'Your baby lives.'

The mother lay heaving for breath, too exhausted to lift her head.

'What is it?'

Katie beamed. 'A wee lass – and a bonny one.'

Flora gazed at the bloodied baby, the tiny face creased and pink with indignation and thought it anything but bonny. She wrapped Mairi's daughter in a cloth and placed her gently by her side. Mairi's eyes shone with sudden tenderness as she gathered the baby into her weak arms. Murdo stood looking on and wept openly. Flora squeezed his shoulder. She admired him for his loyalty and devotion to the contrary bardess. She had no doubt that the piper would accept the lass as his own.

Flora and Katie set about cleaning up mother and baby, coaxing Mairi into feeding her infant.

'What will you call her?' Katie asked.

'Wee Mary,' Murdo said at once, 'after her beautiful mother.'

On the point of leaving, Flora paused to watch. The baby was latched onto her mother's breast, bright button eyes gazing up, trusting and blissful. Emotion welled in her chest. Katie was right; the baby couldn't have been more bonny.

'Thank you, Flora, daughter of Milton,' Mairi smiled, catching her look.

Flora nodded and ducked out of the room. Mairi's lilting voice followed her. 'You are destined to be the greatest of all MacDonalds that ever came forth from the Long Isle.'

Flora rolled tired eyes at Katie. Even in childbirth and near death, the bardess could not help being dramatic. 'Typical MacVurich,' she said with a tired smile.

Katie looked thoughtful. 'Or she has the second-sight, Mistress,' her maid murmured as Peter led them homewards.

Chapter 32

Hugh came for Marion and the family at the end of November. Somehow, he had persuaded Sir Alexander to appoint him as his factor in Sleat and grant him the tack of land at Armadale. Flora wondered what he had promised his chief in return for ousting the Kingsburghs. Had her stepfather promised not to slip off to join the Prince as other kinsmen – Donald Roy for one – had done?

Hugh sensed her disquiet at the deal. 'The lease on Armadale was up for renewal in December anyway,' he assured. 'Kingsburgh has been given full control of Sir Alexander's lands in the north of Skye and he's happy to be returning to Trotternish. It's better for him to run the militias from there too – more central – while my men are to be based at Kylerhea which is handier for Armadale.'

Marion busied herself in packing up the house. Janet and Katie would go with them, Peter too. Her mother was feverish with impatience to be gone as if the years at Balivanich had meant nothing. Her only regret was the distance she would be from Angus and Penelope and their eagerly awaited first child. But Marion avoided all talk of babies; Flora saw the haunted look on her mother's face whenever she overheard the servants chatter about Mairi's red-headed infant.

Before they left, Flora went down to the shore and stood on the beach facing into a westerly gale, saying her silent farewell to her childhood home. Here was where she had stood chattering to her father about America, and later, where she had seen him keel over into the wind when his heart gave out. Just down the shore was where Neil had returned with his Jacobite dreams – dreams that appeared to be realised as the latest news was of the Prince's army marching deep into England. Flora comforted herself with the thought that once she was Neil's wife they would return to the Long Isle and live again on Benbecula or South Uist; perhaps even taking on the tack at Balivanich. And even if they settled elsewhere – Arisaig or Edinburgh – she would always return to visit Angus and Pen.

She had said an emotional goodbye to Lady Clan at Nunton the previous day.

'I feel sure we are on the verge of a great victory for the Stuarts,' Lady Clan had declared with optimism. 'And a new golden age for us island clans. We have been ignored and put upon for too long by a distant and hostile government. All that is about to change.'

Then she had clasped Flora in a tearful hug. 'You will always be like a daughter to me, Flora. Take good care of yourself, dear lassie.'

On the spur of the moment, Flora called in to see Mairi on her way home from the beach.

Baby Mary lay swaddled in a crude crib made out of an old box for carrying bagpipes.

'Hold her if you like,' Mairi encouraged.

How did the woman know that was what she craved? Flora gently reached down and plucked the sleeping infant from the heather-lined nest. She cradled her in the crook of her arm, enjoying the weight and warmth of her small body, feeling the breath in the baby rise and fall like tiny bellows. Mary smelt of milk; her pink mouth twitched. Suddenly she opened her eyes. Flora tensed, expecting her to start crying, but the baby just gazed at her with solemn dark eyes.

'She knows you, Flora of Milton. Mary knows you saved her life – and mine.'

Flora gave a laugh of embarrassment, kissed the tiny nose and put her back.

'I'm sorry you are going,' said Mairi. She looked tired yet content; her red hair was pulled back and the lines of suffering on her face had softened. 'I didn't mean for all this to happen with Hugh *Cam*.'

Flora eyed her. 'Oh I think you did.'

Mairi looked about to protest then her gaze slid away. 'I've always been jealous of your mother. I wanted what she had and now I've got it.'

'No you haven't,' Flora said. 'My stepfather will never come to you again. It's my mother he loves.'

'Hugh *Cam*?' Mairi frowned. 'I don't mean him. I mean you.'

'Me?'

'Aye, I wanted a daughter like you – beautiful and brave – the only woman I've met who doesn't fear me.' Suddenly she smiled and her eyes flashed with their old fire. She placed a possessive hand on the baby. 'And now I have my Mary.'

Flora felt a wave of envy that quite took her by surprise. How powerful motherhood must be if it could turn the wilful and restless bardess into this contented cat of a woman.

'You will know what it means to be a mother, Flora of Milton. You will know a man's love and have a bonny daughter of your own one day.'

Thinking of Neil, Flora turned away blushing at the bold words, elated yet embarrassed that Mairi could so easily read her thoughts.

'Goodbye Mairi and take good care of the wee one,' Flora hurried out.

Mairi's rich laughter followed her. 'Aye, you'll bring forth many bairns from your marriage bed, so you will!'

***

Hugh and his family arrived at Armadale at the beginning of December – a day of snow flurries – to find the Kingsburghs still at the house. A sudden early snowfall two days previously had delayed their departure.

Furniture was piled at the door and a relay of numb-fingered servants was carrying boxes and linen baskets of possessions down to the shore to waiting boats that bobbed in the icy water next to the one in which Flora's family had just arrived.

'I'd offer you tea,' Florence said, 'but the china is packed away goodness knows where. Would you like to come inside?'

163

Flora blushed at the woman's kindness towards them; she doubted she would be so welcoming if put in the same position. Her mother, thrown by the situation, was speechless. Kingsburgh appeared with a cursory greeting – there was a tension between the men – and Flora felt a new wave of guilt at their taking over at Armadale.

'We'll go to Sleat House,' Hugh said quickly, 'I have business with Sir Alexander anyway.'

Kingsburgh nodded, his relief palpable as he ducked inside once more.

'We'll be gone soon,' Florence said distractedly. 'Mind that chest boys!'

Flora's younger half-brothers were slipping around on slushy snow, hurling snowballs at each other and getting in the way. Hugh called them over but they were too excited to obey.

'Can I help you?' Flora asked. 'Is all the packing done?'

'Well thank you–'

'The packing is done.' Ann Macalister waddled out, hugely pregnant. 'We don't need your help.'

'Ann,' Flora smiled, 'I didn't know you were here.'

'Well someone had to come and help my mother dismantle the house – there is so much when you've lived in a place this long.'

Flora flinched at her hostile look. 'Of course,' she answered lamely.

'Ann dearie, you shouldn't be carrying that stool,' Florence fussed. 'Let the servants take care of all this.'

There was a sudden howl from behind. Flora turned to see Sorley clutching his cheek from a snowball.

'Sorley!' Hugh bawled. 'Stop fighting your brother.'

'It wasn't me threw it! It was him.'

A burly man, sleeves rolled up, strode towards them laughing. Flora thought it was a boatman; he had the powerful chest and upper arms of a rower. But the moment he pushed a dark lock of hair from his eyes she knew, with a jolt, it was Allan. Gone was the boyish look of four years ago; his face was lean and weathered, the jaw shadowed with bristle and dark hair sprang from the neck of his shirt. Only the blue eyes under thick eyebrows danced with familiar devilment.

He grabbed both boys in his strong arms and swung them around. 'That'll teach you for not doing as your father tells you,' Allan grinned, dropping them in a pile of snow.

They scrambled to their feet squealing and flinging themselves at his legs.

'Enough,' Hugh ordered, pulling his sons away and clasping Allan by the hand. 'I remember when you used to clamber over me, young Kingsburgh.'

Allan laughed, clasping him back. 'I learnt fighting from the best.' He turned and greeted Marion and her daughters with a bow. 'Mistress Balivanich; Flora, Annabella. And this must be Tibby.'

Flora nodded, heart thudding at his direct assessing look. She felt as breathless as if she had run up a mountain.

'Mistress of Armadale now,' Ann said, resentful.

164

'Quite so,' Florence said, looking flustered.

Flora thought with alarm that Allan's mother was about to cry. Her own mother seemed turned to stone; her face had lost all colour and she was staring at Allan strangely.

'Shall we go up to the Sleats' house, Mother?' Flora said, taking Marion gently by the elbow. 'You look exhausted from the journey.'

'Take my horse,' Allan offered at once. 'It's slippery under foot.' Without waiting for an answer he disappeared to the stables and came back leading a chestnut mare.

'You don't have Whisky any more?' Flora asked.

He shook his head. 'He went lame on a hunting trip. I had to–' Allan broke off and looked away.

'I'm sorry,' said Flora.

'Now I have Berry.' He stroked and patted the mare.

'Why Berry?'

Allan flicked her a look. 'Because this beautiful beast has a taste for berries – the sweeter the better.'

Flora coloured, wondering if he too thought of that time in Dunvegan's garden when he pressed raspberries to her lips. She turned to see Ann eyeing them with suspicion.

'Be quick about it, brother. We leave on the next tide.'

Hugh helped Marion onto the horse while Allan swung a giggling Tibby in front of her mother and Annabella behind. Allan clicked his tongue and the mare began to walk forward. Hugh swung Magnus onto his back and followed. Flora took Sorley's hand. He broke away.

'I want Allan to give me a piggy-back.'

'He's needed here,' Ann said.

Allan ignored this. 'Jump on laddie. I'll not be long,' he called to his sister.

Away from the farm, Allan fell into step with Flora. 'How are you?' he asked.

'I'm well thank you.'

'You certainly look it,' he smiled.

Flora laughed. 'You look in rude good health too.' It unnerved her to have him so close, their arms brushing as they knocked into each other on the treacherous path. 'I'm sorry that we are taking over your home. You mustn't think badly of my parents – there are reasons.'

'I know,' Allan eyed her. 'There has been talk.'

'Oh dear.' Flora was dismayed. 'They hoped to escape the gossip – make a fresh start.'

'Then that is what they must do. But you Flora; do you not mind leaving the Long Isle? You could have stayed with your brother, could you not?'

'Oh I don't imagine I will be staying long on Skye. Once I am married–' She broke off. He gave her a searching look.

'So you *still* wait for MacEachen? If I was him I would have wed you long ago. He must be a fool or a saint to be so abstinent.'

Flora gasped at his impertinence. 'Well you are not he,' she retorted. 'My Neil has rallied to his King's Cause. When he returns victorious we will be wed straight away.'

Allan glanced about. 'You should be careful. Such talk is not welcome in Sleat.'

'I'm not afraid to speak it.'

Allan suppressed sudden amusement. 'Miss Milton, little did I know that tranquil exterior hid the passionate heart of a Jacobite.'

'Don't mock me, Allan. When the Prince enters London, the Sleat MacDonalds will soon change their tune.'

Allan's look darkened. 'I wish it were that easy. I fear there will be no fairy-tale ending for your Prince. If he had come with French backing the Skye chiefs would have gone with him. Even now if France would send support …'

They walked on in silence. Flora spoke first.

'Why have you not joined one of Sir Alexander's companies? Even my brother James at sixteen has a commission.'

Allan said dryly, 'someone has to run the chief's farms. I intend to stay out of the army as long as possible.'

She shot him a look. 'You surprise me. I thought you would have been one of the first to join up – you were always fighting as a boy.'

'Wrestling and competing yes,' Allan said, 'but I have no appetite to go to war against my fellow Gaels.'

Flora nodded. 'That I understand.' As they approached the Sleat homestead, she asked, 'What will happen to us all, Allan? The Rising is happening so far away and yet I am daily anxious that the news will be bad.'

He stopped and met her look. She was struck anew by how vividly blue and full of vitality were his eyes. Her heart fluttered.

'I wish I knew. If I could take away your worry I would, but my mind is troubled by the same doubts, Florrie.'

She gulped at the use of the endearment. Sorley piped up.

'Are you in love with my sister?'

Flora saw Allan's jaw redden. Then he laughed and swung the boy down. 'You wee scamp – I've been in love with your sister since she first tried to beat me in skimming the stone.'

'Ugh!' Sorley pulled a disgusted face.

'Don't listen to him,' Flora retorted, 'he's just teasing me as usual.'

Allan gave her a mocking bow and grinned. 'Look after your sister, Sorley, and don't let her rush off after handsome Prince Charlie.'

Flora pulled a face at him. He laughed and blew her a kiss. Exasperated and unsettled, she turned and hurried out of the cold.

Chapter 33

Skye, 1746

Arctic winds blew all winter and brought unaccustomed snow even to sheltered Sleat, keeping Marion and her family housebound. Hugh came and went, bringing news when he could; battered copies of the pro-Jacobite *National Journal* telling grim news of the Highland Army's retreat from England. It seemed that Allan's premonition of bad fortune for the Prince was coming to pass, yet stories were conflicting. In January, a victory at Falkirk for the Prince was reversed by withdrawal from Stirling after a failed siege in February. Edinburgh awaited the return of the Jacobites but they went to Perth instead.

'There's talk of the Prince and his generals at loggerheads,' Hugh reported.

He took Flora aside. 'King George's younger son, the Duke of Cumberland, has been put in charge of pursuing the Prince. From what I've heard he's an arrogant young man, keen to prove himself. If the Prince's army retreats to the Highlands to regroup, the fighting will come to our door.'

'What are you saying?' Flora asked anxiously.

'That James's company may be put into battle,' Hugh said. 'But keep it to yourself; there's no point worrying your mother about any of this yet.'

'Of course not. Do you know where James is now?'

'He's still safe at Kylerhea but there's talk of men being needed to reinforce the garrisons at Fort Augustus and Fort William.' Hugh paused, eyeing her, then said, 'Young Kingsburgh is one of them.'

Flora blushed. 'Allan has finally joined up?'

'Yes, Sir Alexander made him a lieutenant. Old Kingsburgh is proud as a cockerel though Florence hates her son being from home. Maybe it'll finally help him cut the apron strings and find himself a wife, don't you think?'

'It's no business of mine.' Flora turned away, annoyed at how talk of Allan and marriage made her cheeks burn.

***

In late March – seed time – the atrocious weather eased and men who mysteriously hadn't been seen in Sleat for six months began to reappear. Hiding their Jacobite cockades and broadswords, these supporters of the Prince got down to planting their spring crops and mending their thatched roofs. Stories seeped out like peat smoke; the Prince was ill, they hadn't been paid for a month, the remnants of the army was somewhere near Inverness.

Then to Flora's joy and astonishment, a letter came from Angus on South Uist containing a message from Neil that had been smuggled back to the Long Isle with a retreating Clanranald soldier. She fell on the short correspondence written in Gaelic. Neil was bullish about the Jacobite's chances; the withdrawal was planned, they were consolidating in the north and had captured the garrison at Fort Augustus. Once they had Fort William then a port would be secured for French supplies. The Jacobites could hold out for years in the Highlands if necessary while France put together a fighting force to come to their aid. She mustn't be downhearted at stories in the newspapers; they were just there to sap morale. The Cause was still very much alive.

Flora's initial euphoria at hearing at last from Neil was followed swiftly by doubt. There was no mention of his trying to get to see her – or even fond words of endearment to ease her longing – but then he thought her far away on the Long Isle. He was putting himself in enough risk writing to her. Flora was desperate to talk to someone about it all but did not want to add to her mother's anxiety. Annabella was too immature as a confidante and Katie was in love with a young clansman who might unwittingly pass on information.

Flora was tempted to confide in her stepfather – he had done the same with her – but she did not want to bring trouble to their home. Hugh was in the government's pay and it might be putting him and their family in danger if a Jacobite letter was found in her possession. So she memorised every word and then put it to the candle in her bedroom and watched it burn to ashes.

* * *

Allan surveyed the damage done to the barrack walls. The Highland Jacobites had come swiftly in the night and laid siege to Fort William but the following day a cannonball from the ramparts had landed with a deafening blast amid the besiegers. When the smoke had cleared, Allan saw the carnage of bloodied bodies writhing in the mud. The screams of the dying still rang in his ears. The attackers had retreated.

'We've orders from Cumberland,' his captain, a fresh-faced MacDonald from Cuidrach near Kingsburgh, told him. 'We're to punish the folk of Lochaber for this.'

'Punish?' Allan frowned.

Cuidrach shrugged. He looked pale and anxious as he handed the message over.

Allan read it with mounting disgust. 'Seize their cattle and set fire to their homes? Does he think we're still living in the Dark Ages that we'd do something so savage?' He thrust the missive back at Cuidrach, his lip curling. 'It's revenge for the Jacobites humiliating him by taking Fort Augustus so easily. I'll have no part in it.'

For his defiance, he was locked up and given only water for three days by a Lowland officer.

On a reconnaissance out from the fort a week later, Allan was appalled at the scene of devastation in the surrounding countryside carried out by the regular troops; Lowland Scots who despised them all equally. Cottars sat stunned in the rain, their houses still smouldering and byres empty. The keening of the women and the smell of scorched animal flesh haunted Allan and gave him no peace. What if such a fate should befall those of Clanranald and other MacDonalds who had defied their chief and followed the Prince? Anger churned inside him that Gaels like himself should be asked to do such coward's work. This Cumberland must be the devil indeed.

***

Flora sprang up at the sight of Hugh's stunned face. 'What's happened?'

He stood in the doorway in the late April twilight unable to speak. He had been away for days with the militia. Rumours were rife of a terrible battle near Inverness and the Prince's army fleeing.

Marion trembled. 'Is it James?'

'No, the lad is safe.' His wife's fear made him find his voice. 'It's – there's been – our kinsman Baleshare needs our help.'

'Donald Roy?' Flora gasped. 'Where is he?'

'In the boathouse. I brought him over from the mainland. He's injured but alive.'

'Then we must bring him to the house,' Marion insisted.

'The servants mustn't know who it is,' Hugh said, 'someone might talk.'

'What do you mean?' Marion worried. 'Is it dangerous having him here?'

'Come on Mother,' Flora said, 'I'll fetch linen and water; you get the medicine chest.'

They hurried down to the shore. Hugh lit a lamp in the dank bothy. Donald Roy lay wrapped in his plaid on the hard floor. His face was grey and glistening; he tried to smile.

'Angels,' he rasped, 'I must be in Paradise already.'

'It's his foot,' said Hugh.

Flora recoiled in horror at the sight of the bloodied wound under the filthy makeshift bandage; the flesh torn and bone showing. She struggled not to retch.

'Pass me the water, Flora,' Marion said. 'First this needs a clean. You'll not be dancing many jigs for a while, Donald Roy.'

Flora was in awe of her mother's calmness as she took control and set about the task of washing and dressing the bullet wound, making their old neighbour laugh even as he winced in agony. Marion gave him laudanum for the pain.

Later, when Flora had fetched food and a bottle of porter, the soldier began to tell them of his escape; the battle on Culloden Moor a week ago had been lost in an hour, the Highland army shot to pieces by the devastating fire-power of the government troops.

'No one told us to charge,' Donald Roy said angrily. 'We MacDonalds stood slashing our swords at the heather at our lack of action. When the order finally came it was too late – the Redcoats were lined up like ants with their deadly muskets. It was slaughter.'

Flora saw the horror in his look as he relived it.

'What of the Prince?' Marion asked. 'Does he live?'

'He survived the battle, I know that much. We saw him ride off.'

'We've been sent orders to be on the alert for deserting Jacobites,' Hugh said grimly. 'Cumberland wants men like you rounded up. The Government is tightening the noose.'

'Tightening the noose you call it?' Donald Roy hissed. 'I call it cold blooded murder. They didn't take prisoners – they butchered them there on the battlefield and went after the ones who escaped. I took to the high passes but I saw the smoke from the burning houses – they are laying waste to everything. The things I have seen. I crept out at night to find milk – found this shieling – every one of them with their throats cut – even the children–'

'That's enough man,' Hugh protested.

'Oh mercy!' Marion clamped hands to her mouth.

'I'm sorry.' Donald Roy collapsed back. 'Forgive me.'

'What of the others?' Flora whispered, full of dread. 'Ranald Og and Neil MacEachen?'

Her kinsman's eyes brimmed with tears. 'I don't know. We all got separated.'

Marion laid a hand briefly on his prone body. 'I can't imagine how you walked all that way with your foot like that. You must rest. In the morning, Hugh will decide what to do.'

***

Within days, news was confirmed of the Prince's defeat at Culloden. London was celebrating the news of Cumberland's victory with bells and lighted windows. The *National Journal* complained that those who did not illuminate their windows had had them smashed by a Hanoverian mob.

Hugh was summoned by Kingsburgh. He had instructions from Sir Alexander via Cumberland that the Skye militia had to mount a thorough search of the island for the Young Pretender.

'The Prince has eluded the troops on the mainland,' Kingsburgh said, 'so they think he must be heading west – perhaps to rally support again – more likely to find a ship that will take him to safety.'

'What about our Jacobite kinsmen?' Hugh said stonily. 'Are they to be hunted down too?'

Kingsburgh was brusque. 'I have no more appetite for this task than you, Armadale.'

Hugh flinched at the title, a reminder of how he had taken the tack of land from the older man.

'I have more important things to attend to than playing hide and seek around Skye,' Hugh mocked.

'Quite so,' Kingsburgh nodded, 'that is why I am sending you to the Long Isle with two of our companies to carry out a search there.'

Hugh's one eye flashed in annoyance. 'The Long Isle? You'd banish me there? This is all about revenge for Armadale, isn't it? You know how it will distress my wife if I return to Benbecula–'

'This is not about you!' Kingsburgh snapped. 'This is about protecting our people. Do you know how huge the reward is for the Prince's capture? Thirty thousand pounds! Several fortunes for most Highlanders.'

'That jumped up Englishman thinks he can bribe us into betraying a royal Stuart?' Hugh cried. 'We care nothing for his blood money.'

'I quite agree – but that is how vengeful the Hanoverians are – they want him caught at any cost. Cumberland is spitting blood that his enemy has escaped and he's just as keen to round up any Gael he can – not just the ones who fought for him but the ones who harbour him or his fighters too. Sir Alexander has seen with his own eyes the butchery on the mainland carried out by the Redcoats – unspeakable horrors.'

Kingsburgh leaned close, his voice a hiss. 'I hear you have a wounded man sheltering at Armadale – one that Cumberland would itch to get his hands on. Tell me one thing, Hugh; are we agreed that we don't wish to deliver such men on a plate to butcher Cumberland?'

Hugh nodded, his jaw tight. 'Of course.'

'Good. Then you will understand when I say that it's in our best interests to dilute our forces here on Skye and send two bands of militiamen to the Outer Isles, just in case a certain royal gentleman and his henchmen might have gone into hiding there.' Kingsburgh eyed him. 'You will take your time searching and in your own good time, send back reports to me of how you are getting on – and how you will need another month or so for further searches. Are we agreed?'

'Agreed.' Hugh gave a tense smile. 'You are a good man, Kingsburgh. I'm sorry for what happened between us.'

'That is in the past,' Kingsburgh replied. 'What matters now is that we are both working in unison to keep Sir Alexander as our chief. He has a difficult path to tread keeping Cumberland happy and his murdering dogs at bay – if they suspect him of being weak and too lenient to his own kind they won't hesitate to clap him in irons too. The Hanoverians hate all us Highlanders whether we fight for them or not. But we have to be seen to be doing their dirty work.'

'I understand,' Hugh replied.

***

'Donald Roy has gone,' Flora told Hugh on his brief return to Armadale. 'We don't know where.'

'He thought that staying was putting us in danger,' Marion said. 'Are we in danger Hugh?'

Flora noticed how anxious her mother had become since Donald Roy's departure; the village was full of talk about parties of soldiers arriving at

171

night by boat and setting fire to whole settlements along the west coast, driving out their animals and raping their women. Marion kept her daughters close and jumped at every sound outside.

Hugh put on a brave face. 'There is nothing to fear at Armadale. Sir Alexander would not allow any harm to come to you or the family. But it is as well that young Baleshare has chosen to move on.'

'But what if they should find him; these *Sassenach* soldiers that we hear about?' Flora fretted.

'Donald Roy is a tough man,' said Hugh, 'even with a bad foot he could probably outrun most ordinary men. He can take care of himself.'

When Hugh confessed that he was being sent to the Long Isle, Marion grew distressed.

'Why does it have to be you?' she railed. 'You want to go, don't you? You can't wait to get back to Balivanich.'

'It's not true. I promise you I won't go there. You have to trust me. It's Kingsburgh's orders.'

'Kingsburgh! Why should you have to listen to him?'

'Because he is in overall charge of the Skye militia; you know that.'

'You are more important to Sir Alexander – you should be the one to stay on Skye and protect us.'

'Mother,' Flora tried to calm her, 'you mustn't get upset. Father has a job to do. The sooner he goes and does it, the sooner he will return to us.'

'Then we shall go with you,' Marion said in desperation.

'Wife, you know that cannot be! It's almost impossible to travel about the islands now – everyone is under suspicion and must carry papers to prove that their journey is necessary. You will be much safer here.'

The tense atmosphere in the house lasted until Hugh left two days later. Flora went with him to the shore to see him off. The early May sunshine warmed her bones, yet she shivered with foreboding.

'If you hear anything of Neil,' she asked shyly, 'will you get word to me somehow?'

Hugh nodded. 'Of course, if I can.' He kissed her forehead. 'Look after your mother for me – and the children.'

'You know I will, Father.'

Hugh smiled. 'I count myself lucky to have such a level-headed lassie for my eldest daughter.'

Flora's eyes pricked at his fond words. She would always be grateful that he treated her as one of his own.

'Send my love to Angus and Pen – and a kiss for baby Angie – tell them I long to visit.'

With a brief nod, Hugh clambered on board and waved a farewell. As Flora retreated to the house, she saw her mother standing, forlorn and beautiful, watching her husband sail away.

Chapter 34

'You are to take these shirts of Sir Alexander's and deliver them to your brother at Milton,' Lady Margaret beamed.

Flora was still reeling from the sight of her former patron sitting drinking tea with Marion in their parlour. Annabella and Tibby sat wide-eyed at their noble guest. Lady Margaret had not visited Sleat since they had come to live there, preferring the luxury of Monkstadt. Her face and figure had filled out since Flora had last seen her. A scowling fair-haired infant with a runny nose and dressed in baby skirts, clung to her legs; the Sleats' youngest son Alexander. To Flora's disappointment, the older Sleat boy, the sunny-natured James, was being fostered at the Kingsburghs' for the summer. She tried to concentrate on Lady Sleat's outlandish request.

'To Angus?' Flora asked, astonished. 'In South Uist?'

'Of course in South Uist,' Lady Margaret laughed. Her mood was skittish as if she had been drinking claret, eyes shining with excitement.

'What would Angus be doing with Lord Sleat's clothing?' Flora was baffled. 'They make their own linen—'

'Goodness me, girl! Questions, questions. You're as impertinent as ever you were.'

'Sorry, ma'am,' Flora flushed. 'Of course I'll gladly take them. I'm longing to visit my new nephew. Was it Pen who begged the clothing? Perhaps she hasn't been able to grow enough flax this year.'

Flora caught her mother's pleading look and stopped. Marion was tense as a coiled spring.

'This has nothing to do with flax growing!' Lady Margaret could hardly contain herself. 'This is my idea – my contribution if you like.' She raised her eyebrows in a knowing gesture. 'My contribution to the *Cause*. There is money there too and newspapers to keep him informed.'

Flora exchanged wary glances with Marion. When no one spoke, the chief's wife said in exasperation. 'Oh, you must guess who I mean? The shirts are for the Prince.'

'Prince Charles is in South Uist?' Flora exclaimed.

'Well, somewhere on the Long Isle – has been for weeks it seems. He is suffering greatly – exposed to the wind and rain – hunted like an animal by naval patrols. The least I can do is send a few shirts to keep him clothed and dry, don't you think? But you mustn't breathe a word of this to Sir Alexander – he must never know. He would hate me risking my life in such a way.'

'Yet you wish my daughter to risk hers?' Marion spoke at last.

Lady Margaret was dismissive. 'How can it be a risk for Flora when she will just be going to visit her brother? It's the perfect excuse.'

'She will still need a pass from the military,' Marion pointed out.

'I have one; written out by your husband, no less.'

'Hugh has agreed this?'

'Yes. It was Armadale who suggested Flora.' Lady Margaret's look was triumphant.

Marion gaped. 'Are you saying that Hugh knows of the Prince's whereabouts?'

'He knows Prince Charles is somewhere on the Long Isle – everyone seems to know – apart from Cumberland.'

'And Angus too?'

Lady Margaret waved a hand. 'If not then Lady Clan will make sure that the shirts get to the right person and that he knows whose gift they are. It's the least I can do for the brave tragic Prince.'

Marion looked deathly pale. 'Kind as your gesture is, Madam, it seems that the risk Flora would take for a handful of shirts is too great.'

Lady Margaret flashed a look of annoyance. 'I think Flora will think it worth it once she knows who else is keeping the bonny Prince company in his hardship.' She turned to Flora. 'Armadale says that young MacEachen is there. He asked me to tell you.'

'Neil?' Flora gasped. Her heart began to pound.

'Yes, your young man,' Lady Margaret smiled. 'So, will you be my secret envoy?'

'Of course I will,' Flora said without a moment's hesitation.

***

It was a rain-lashed crossing but Flora relished the salty air and the sight of the South Uist hills lit in a brief shaft of sunlight and covered in June flowers – a myriad of yellow and white stars. All seemed as she had left it, except for the distant ominous sight of government frigates emerging out of the mist, circling the Minch.

The welcome at Milton was joyous. Flora embraced her brother and fell into a hug with Pen who would not let her go.

'I've missed you so,' Pen said tearfully.

'Come on, show me your son,' Flora insisted.

Penelope took her into the bedchamber where baby Angus lay sleeping, swaddled and content. Flora stroked his plump pink cheek, marvelling at its softness.

'You make bonny babies,' she smiled at her friend.

For the next few days, housebound by torrential rain, Flora enjoyed being at Milton and catching up with her brother and sister-in-law. She was besotted with her new nephew; cuddling and playing with him and making him giggle.

'You're a miniature of your daddy, so you are.' She tickled his chin.

Yet there was tension underlying their happy reunion. They spoke in hushed tones about the fugitive Prince.

'Neil took him up to Lewis a couple of weeks past,' Angus spoke about his old friend, 'trying to find a boat in Stornoway to get him away.'

'That was brave,' Flora said, her stomach clenching at the thought of Neil in such danger.

'But someone betrayed them – troops were waiting – they had to take to the heather. It was thanks to Campbell of Scalpay that they weren't both arrested. Campbell turned the soldiers away when they tried to land on Scalpay. By the time they returned, Neil had got the Prince away by boat.'

'Who betrayed them?' Flora demanded.

'We think it was Elijah Gunn,' said Pen. 'He's been sniffing around trying to find out what he can.'

'He hates all Jacobites but he loathes Neil especially,' Angus said. 'He would love to deliver him up to the Hanoverians.'

'He's still bitter that you rejected him in favour of Neil,' Pen explained.

'Where is Neil now?' Flora asked, feeling guilty that she made Neil's situation even more risky.

Angus and Pen looked around nervously as if the walls were listening.

'He could be anywhere – he's urgently trying to get messages to the French to send a rescue ship – and to keep the Prince hidden.'

'Mother is trying to keep them both fed and healthy,' said Pen, 'sending food and clothing. She knows where they are but she doesn't want to attract too much attention – or put us in danger by telling us. It was easier when they hid in the mountains, but South Uist is too full of naval raiding parties now. Hugh *Cam* advised Neil to lie low in Benbecula – the fords between the islands are too well-guarded.'

Under cover of stormy weather, Angus rode to Nunton with the parcel of shirts and delivered them to his mother-in-law, Lady Clan. Flora had wanted to go with him in case there was a chance Neil might be there but Pen had worried.

'What if the Reverend Gunn spots you both together and starts asking awkward questions? He might be suspicious that you are suddenly on the Long Isle, Flora. How will you explain fancy shirts and money? Let Angus go alone – it's not unusual for him to be visiting Nunton on business.'

In frustration, Flora had agreed.

Angus returned the following day with Hugh *Cam*. Flora's initial delight at seeing her stepfather turned quickly to fear at his words.

'Word has got back to Cumberland that the Prince is trapped on the Long Isle. General Campbell landed a large force of dragoons in the north a few days ago. They are doing a thorough sweep from Berneray southwards down the Long Isle. The General has sent orders that I am to meet him in North Uist. I'll try and delay him but my time is running out.'

'What do you mean, Father?' Flora asked.

'My militias have turned a blind eye for over a month,' said Hugh, 'we can't continue to do that now that word is out about the Prince being here. If the General is being sent to comb the north, mark my words, there'll be other regular troops arriving in Barra and the south before the week is out. The Prince will be caught between the jaws of the Hanoverian cat.'

'What can be done?' Pen fretted. 'Is my mother aware of the danger?'

Hugh and Angus exchanged looks. 'Aye,' Angus nodded. 'Your mother has a plan. I think it's madness.'

'That's for Flora to decide,' said Hugh.

'Me?' Flora was baffled. 'What could I possibly do?'

'Lady Clan wants me to take you to her without delay, Flora.' Hugh fixed her with a keen eye. 'She wants you to meet Prince Charles.'

***

That night, Flora crossed from South Uist to Benbecula, perched up behind Hugh on his pony. The guards at the crossing – Hugh's own militiamen – asked no questions. By the time they reached Nunton they were drenched and frozen. Lady Clan ushered in Flora with relief and quickly found her dry clothes and ordered up warming food.

'I feared you would not come,' she said.

'And miss the chance of meeting a royal prince?' Flora said with a wry smile.

Lady Clan shot Hugh a look. 'Have you not told her the plan?'

'Not everything – I thought it best you did,' Hugh murmured.

'I know you think I can help the Prince in some way. Tell me what it is you want me to do,' Flora urged.

'Every day that the Prince remains on Benbecula the danger for him grows,' said Lady Clan, 'and for all of us.'

'I know that,' Flora grew impatient, 'Angus has told me how Neil only just escaped capture on Scalpay.'

'The situation is worse now that the Navy is landing regular soldiers to begin a hunt in earnest. We need to get the Prince away from the Long Isle as soon as possible. The only real chance of doing that is if we disguise him in some way so that if he is stopped he might not be recognised.'

'Such as dress him up as a government Redcoat?' Flora suggested.

'Something more original,' Hugh said, with the ghost of a smile. 'As a woman.'

'As your maid,' said Lady Clan, 'or some kind of servant.'

'You'll travel back to Skye with him – with *her*,' Hugh explained, 'and hand him on to Lady Margaret at Monkstadt. She seems more than happy to help him.'

Flora stared at them in stupefaction. 'My maid?'

'Aye,' said Hugh. 'No one will question your return to Skye back to your mother. You've simply been visiting your new nephew but have become alarmed by the sight of so many troops and wish to go home.'

'So they're not going to think it odd that I'm travelling with a manly oversized foreign-sounding maid,' Flora snorted in disbelief. 'He'll be found out at once, then what?'

'We'll work on a good costume,' said Lady Clan.

Flora's head spun. She would never get away with such a plan; no wonder Angus thought it madness.

'And when my papers are checked, how do I explain this outlandish servant?'

'I shall provide you with a pass,' said Hugh, 'and for the servant – I'll give authorisation.'

'You'd put your name to this?' The full realisation of the danger they were being swept towards, left her winded. 'If the Prince is unmasked, you'll be arrested for treason.'

'We all will,' said Lady Clan. She exchanged wry smiles with Hugh.

It struck Flora that they were enjoying this; the high stakes and the intrigue. How could they? She was suddenly angry at their recklessness.

'Think what that would do to Mother if you were arrested,' Flora cried. 'Why would you risk everything for this man? He's brought nothing but trouble since he came to Scotland. What about your loyalty to Sir Alexander? He's supposed to be helping the Government. What happens when it's discovered his own kin were plotting to get the Prince away? How can you ask me to do this? What about *my* safety?'

Flora felt sick with fear; she buried her head in her hands. She was consumed by the spectre of all her family being rounded up and dragged away in chains for their collusion. Baby Angie would be left orphaned or worse still, impaled on a bayonet – a horror that Donald Roy had witnessed on his escape from vengeful Redcoats.

She felt Lady Clan's arms go around her. Flora burst into tears. The chief's wife stroked her hair and rocked her like a child.

'I know it's frightening,' she crooned, 'and we won't make you do anything that your heart is telling you not to.'

Flora leaned against her, comforted by her hold.

'It's a desperate plan, I admit it,' she went on. 'I would take him myself but I wouldn't get further than Balivanich before they stopped me. I'm being watched.' Lady Clan sighed. 'If we can just get him to Skye, he might have a chance of getting away to Arisaig on the mainland. That's where Neil thinks a French boat will try and find him.'

'Neil?' Flora lifted her head. 'Does he know of this plan?'

'Yes dearie, he does. When Neil heard you'd taken the risk of bringing shirts from Lady Margaret, he was most impressed.'

Hugh grunted, 'it was MacEachen came up with the idea.'

***

They waited till twilight the next day before Lady Clan slipped out with Flora, armed with a basket of food and medicines.

'If we're stopped, we'll say I'm visiting a sick child at a remote shieling.'

The rain had eased to a light drizzle but mist lay over the low-lying bog giving them cover. Flora knew blindfold the undulations in the land and the web of lochans that led them east to remote Rossinish on the coast. Yet she was full of trepidation. To be responsible for the Prince's safety weighted her down like a grinding stone. What would her stepfather and Lady Clan think if they knew the truth that she was only agreeing to meet the Prince so she could see Neil? But perhaps they guessed that.

Leaving the track they ploughed on through rough heather and bracken, their rain-soaked plaids and skirts dragging their steps. Flora carried her shoes, squelching along in bare feet. The light was fading from the sky as they dipped down towards the shore. Suddenly a figure loomed out of the mist; a bearded man with a bonnet pulled low over his eyes.

'Ladies,' he bowed, 'what a heart-warming sight.'

'Neil?' Flora gasped, recognising the voice rather than the man.

'Flora,' he smiled, clutching her hands in a clasp of welcome. His fingers were icy cold. 'How glad I am to see you.'

'And I you,' she beamed. Her heart raced to touch him again. She was bursting with things she wanted to ask but he was swiftly turning away and leading them across the shore. He stopped at a tumble of old stones and glanced around. At once Flora knew where they were; the ancient burial chamber that she and Angus had used as a secret hideout as children. The entrance looked hardly bigger than a fox's hole but once you climbed in it opened into an earthen room big enough for a grown man to stand.

An oil lamp set into the wall, cast a weak glow. A man sprang up from the shadows; dark-featured and wearing a soldier's blue coat and torn breeches.

'Miss MacDonald?' he seized her hand and kissed it. '*Enchanté*. You are even prettier than MacEachen said.' His accent was strange.

Flora was quite overwhelmed. How should she address a royal prince?

'Sir – I'm honoured–'

'This is Captain O'Neill,' Lady Clan said quickly, guessing Flora's mistake. 'He's Irish Italian so has a double dose of the blarney,' she teased.

'But you must call me Felix,' the man grinned, still holding onto Flora's hand.

A bout of coughing came from the corner. A tall man got unsteadily to his feet. '*Mesdames*, welcome to my humble palace.'

Lady Clan curtsied; Flora followed. He bowed low which set off another coughing fit. Flora was aghast at the sight of his haggard face covered in sores where he had scratched midge bites till they bled. His dark red hair was matted and he wore the rough clothes of a drover. He looked ten years old than he should. She searched for any resemblance to the portrait of the dashing fresh-faced prince in wig and general's uniform that the Clanranalds had hanging in their priest's room.

'Please,' he croaked, speaking in Gaelic, 'you may sit.'

Neil gave them milking stools; his smile to Flora was encouraging. Lady Clan passed over the basket and the Prince at once insisted that they shared out the food and brandy.

'Please keep it for yourself, Your Highness.'

'Not at all, Lady Clanranald. You do us a great honour and we offer our Highland hospitality in return.' He grabbed the bottle and poured generously into a silver bowl brought from Nunton. 'Please drink; it will warm you inside and then being cold outside won't matter so much, yes?'

178

He turned to Flora and smiled. 'I feel most at home when I am surrounded by MacDonalds. But I never dreamt that such a bonny one would come to my aid. How is your baby nephew? Thriving I hope.'

Flora was astonished he should know. 'Very well, Sir.'

'That is good. It is heartening that new life comes to bring us joy in uncertain times. There is nothing to make the heart swell as much as a baby's smile, don't you think?'

Flora thought of Angie and nodded.

'Miss MacDonald,' he leaned towards her, the gaze from his big brown eyes unblinking, 'I know I am asking a lot – perhaps too much – of a young woman however brave. You may have come here out of a sense of obligation to your patron Lady Clanranald – or to your father Armadale who is risking his life to keep me from falling into enemy hands – this I know. If you feel the burden is too great then I will not let anyone press you into this. You look at me with doubtful eyes and who can blame you?' He gave a wry laugh. 'If the ladies of Edinburgh could see me now, they would not be queuing up to dance a minuet with quite so much enthusiasm as they did last autumn.'

'But look beyond my shabby clothes, Madam, and know that I *am* a Stuart.' His eyes shone with pride. 'It was my ancestors who reigned in Scotland for many glorious centuries, who gifted charters of land to your ancestors in a sacred bond under God. No Hanoverian can ever understand the ties that bind us Scots together.'

He reached for her hand and gripped it. 'You feel it, don't you? Every time you hear a pipe tune, or a slow air on the fiddle, or the wind blowing through the dunes. It's in your blood, Miss MacDonald, this bond with your people and the very land beneath your feet.' His look swept down. 'Pretty feet,' he smiled impishly.

Flora felt her hand tremble in his. She was suddenly overwhelmed with an emotion that rose up from the pit of her stomach.

'I felt the same,' the Prince continued in his strange lilting mix of Gaelic and English, 'as soon as I stepped off the boat at Eriskay. I knew I had come home.'

Flora's eyes stung with tears. His eyes were full of longing and vitality in a face lined with worry and fatigue.

'My enemies say I am finished – beaten – and you are probably thinking the same too. But we Stuarts will never be beaten. This is a setback. If I escape my persecutors I promise you that I will return. Scotland deserves so much better than foreign rule from faraway London by a rabble of greedy merchants and courtiers. Dear Miss MacDonald,' he said in concern, 'you are shaking. Take a sip of brandy.'

He reached for the silver bowl and pressed it to her lips. Flora took a gulp and at once felt the fiery liquor spread through her.

'Florrie,' Neil said urgently, 'two days ago a man-o'-war – the *Furnace* – was spotted in the bay off Wiay Island – within sight of here. Another one – the *Baltimore* – is anchored just to the south. Captain Ferguson is a vicious dog who doesn't think twice about kidnapping local men and

179

taking them on board for questioning. And I don't just mean a polite chat over a dram. He has an instrument of torture – a wheel – which he straps them to and stretches them out like deer skins until they're screaming for mercy and babbling what Ferguson wants to hear.'

Flora clapped a hand over her mouth, her throat filling with bile. The Prince raised a hand.

'Enough, my friend.'

Neil said something in French and the Prince replied. They began a rapid, heated argument that Flora could not follow. Abruptly, it finished. Neil put a hand on Flora's shoulder. 'Forgive me; I did not mean to upset you, dear Flora. It is just I am so concerned for the safety of our future king. The net is closing in by the hour. I'm asking for your help – pleading for it – not just because of who he is but because he is a man in need. He is being ruthlessly hunted – all that stands between him and execution are the compassion of us Highlanders. We never betray the man who comes to us seeking shelter and help. It is not our way – no matter how much money they throw at us, treating us like a race of Judases. Flora,' he squeezed her shoulder, 'your brother, your stepfather, Lady Clan – so many others – have gone out of their way to help the Prince. All we ask is that you do this one act of kindness and courage, as a MacDonald of Milton. Will you do it?'

There wasn't a sound in the chamber as they waited for her answer. Flora saw the fierce pleading in Neil's brown eyes. He had never asked her for anything before; it was always she who wanted something from him – friendship, love, a promise of marriage – but never had he needed her as he did in that moment.

'I shall do it because you ask it of me,' Flora answered. She glanced back at the Prince. 'And because I see a fine gentleman who is in great need. I will not go to my grave regretting that I did nothing to help when I had the chance.'

She saw the tears of gratitude well in the young prince's tired eyes. He reached for her hand and brought it swiftly to his lips. 'Thank you, Miss MacDonald. You will be well rewarded.'

'The only reward I seek,' Flora said, 'is to hear that you are safely escaped from those who would persecute you.'

'Brava!' cried Felix. 'You have charm as well as beauty and bravery, Miss Flora.'

They left soon afterwards, Lady Clan anxious to return home before complete darkness, fearful of being caught out at night by a passing patrol.

'I shall come with you and keep you ladies safe,' Felix insisted.

Flora threw a pleading look at Neil. 'Mr MacEachen knows the way better.'

'No,' said the Prince, 'I need Neil here. As a Gaelic speaker, he can pass himself off as a simple goatherd if raiders come looking.'

Neil gave her a shrug of apology. Outside, he leaned close to Flora and murmured, 'I will find a way of coming to you at Nunton. I want to repay your loyalty to the Prince and to me.'

His voice sent a delicious shiver through her. 'I shall wait with impatience,' Flora whispered. His bearded smile lifted her spirits.

***

Pre-dawn light was already leaking into the sky when they approached Nunton.

'Something's wrong,' Lady Clan stopped in her tracks. 'There's a light in my chamber.'

'Maybe your servant left it burning for you,' Felix suggested.

She shook her head. 'You must come no further, Captain O'Neill. I think we might have visitors. Stay back in the stables until I send word it's safe.'

The women hurried into the house. Sam, the cook's boy, rose from his post by the door. 'They came last night just after you'd gone,' he whispered, eyes round with fright.

'Who did?' hissed Lady Clan.

'A sea captain and two others. Captain's sleeping in your bed, Mistress.'

'He's what?' she cried. 'How dare–!'

Flora put a warning hand on her arm. 'Is his name Ferguson?'

'Aye,' the boy nodded. 'He made the master open up ten bottles of his best claret and smoked a dozen bowls of tobacco. Demanded to know where is Ranald Og – and you, Mistress.'

The women exchanged looks of horror.

'And the other men?'

'Passed out on the Master's study floor.'

Lady Clan said quickly, 'if anyone asks you, I've been away visiting a sick child, taking medicines. Is that clear?'

The boy nodded.

'Good Sam,' she smiled, 'you're a brave young MacDonald.'

Flora and Lady Clan bedded down in Penelope's old room, clinging together for comfort. Flora woke in full daylight, surprised that she had been able to sleep. The chief's wife was already up. Flora found her downstairs being polite to her unwanted guests at the breakfast table.

A man with grey receding hair and a jutting stubbled chin, scowled at her with bloodshot eyes. Her stomach lurched.

'This is Captain Ferguson,' said Lady Clan, her smile tense. 'I've just been explaining how we were absent last night on a mission of mercy. This is my young kinswoman, Flora MacDonald. She's staying with her brother in Milton – that's in South Uist–'

'I know where Milton is,' Ferguson interrupted. 'I've studied the bloody maps. I know every corner of this God forsaken chain of islands.' He looked Flora over. 'Can you speak English?' he shouted.

'Perfectly, sir,' Flora said.

'Then sit here and answer for yourself.'

Flora sat down, catching Lady Clan's encouraging look. It gave her pounding heart a moment of composure.

'Why are you at Nunton?' Ferguson began to question.

'Visiting my chief and Lady Clanranald. She is like a second mother to me. It would be rude to be staying at Milton and not pay a call.'

'You are travelling about unaccompanied. Why does your husband allow such a thing?'

Flora reddened. 'I'm not married, Captain. I live with my mother on Skye.'

'Skye?' he barked. 'What the devil are you doing out here? The place is hot with rebellion and crawling with Redcoats – and you choose now to go *visiting*? I find that hard to believe.'

Lady Clan said, 'my daughter has been blessed with her first child – an adorable baby and Flora's nephew – she could not wait any longer to see him.'

Ferguson snorted. 'I suppose a spinster without babies gets excited about such things.'

Flora curbed her annoyance by reaching for an oatcake. Methodically she spread it with crowdie, the salty white cheese she loved. While the suspicious captain plied her with questions about her mother, her family, her daily movements since coming to the Long Isle, Flora forced herself to swallow small mouthfuls between answers.

'So you were out all night attending this sick child too?'

Flora nodded.

'What was his name?'

Flora hesitated, trying to remember the story Lady Clan had concocted in the early hours of the morning. She had been tired and overwrought. Glancing at the older woman, she saw her look of alarm.

'Not a he, Captain Ferguson,' said Flora calmly. 'It was a wee girl, Mally. Her father's a stockman.'

She saw the flicker of irritation cross Ferguson's face.

'And where was this?'

'Over at Flodda. They'd taken cattle there for the pasture. Mally had eaten something poisonous and needed medicine – an antidote.'

'Flodda is only an hour's walk at the most. Why were you away so long?'

Flora took a sip of milk, searching her mind frantically for a plausible excuse. 'Flodda is tidal. We had to wait for low tide.'

Ferguson leaned closer. His breath reeked of stale tobacco and wine.

'The cook tells me that you went with a basketful of brandy and rich food. What would a sick child be needing with such things?'

Flora's stomach clenched. She saw the panic in Lady Clan's eyes. How much had the garrulous cook said?

'Not for the child,' Flora replied, 'but for the father. Lachlan may be a stockman but he is also a fine piper. Lady Clanranald was taking victuals

182

to one of the chief's favourite musicians. It's a way of paying the piper in kind. That's the custom in these islands, Captain Ferguson.'

His bleary eyes narrowed. 'If I find you're lying to me – if it turns out that you were helping feed and hide some treacherous rebel from His Majesty's forces – I will string you up by that slim pretty neck without a moment's hesitation. Do I make myself clear, *Miss* MacDonald?'

Flora swallowed hard. Her heart was racing; she could feel the prickle of sweat at her hairline. She forced a smile.

'I am a loyal subject, Sir. My mother's chief is Sir Alexander of Sleat – a man working with the Duke of Cumberland to restore order to our troubled lands. My stepfather's Hugh of Armadale – in charge of the militia here and actively seeking out the Pretender and his allies.'

She held his look; she would not be the first to look away.

Ferguson's thin mouth twisted in a sneer. 'Armadale? That one-eyed blackguard has sent General Campbell off to St Kilda to look for the foreigner. A wild goose chase, I'll warrant.' He scrutinised her. 'I think the Pretender is still on the Long Isle, close by, being protected by you heathens.'

Flora was suddenly riled. 'Are you accusing my stepfather of lying?'

'I wouldn't trust him as far as I could throw him,' Ferguson said, 'or any of his useless militia. But his days are numbered. Cumberland has lost patience. The Skye militia are to be disbanded and proper soldiers will take over the search.'

He gave a mirthless smile. 'I see from your look that this is news to you? I'm sure you and your Lady Clan here,' he said with disdain in his voice, 'will be heartened to know that it's just a matter of time before the foreign rebel and his savages are caught.'

Chapter 35

Shaken by the surprise visit of the arch-Hanoverian Captain Ferguson, Lady Clan was cautious about their preparations to aid the Prince. During the day, they carried on as normal; at night, she and Flora sat up late sewing petticoats and skirts out of coarse material until their fingers grew numb. They wanted no one to report anything unusual going on at Nunton. The Clanranalds did not believe any of their staff would betray them, but even the slightest whiff of gossip would be enough for Elijah Gunn to come calling or to send for the loathsome sea captain.

After a couple of days of Felix hiding in the stables, Lady Clan had sent the lively Irishman away. It was obvious to her how smitten he was with Flora, but an amorous admirer was the last complication that her young kinswoman needed and it would be dangerous for Felix to linger at Nunton too.

Flora was growing daily more nervous at the ordeal ahead. She was sleeping badly, jerking awake at the slightest sound. She worried for her stepfather. On a brief visit, Hugh had laughed off her concerns about what General Campbell would do to him when he discovered that the Prince was not hiding on St Kilda.

'I'll blame it on a rumour that came from the interfering Reverend Gunn,' he winked.

Before he left, he handed over a document. 'It authorises you to cross the Minch with your servant Betty Burke, as well as a kinsman to protect you both. I imagine the Prince will want MacEachen to go with him.'

Flora nodded. Only the thought that Neil would be there too, gave her the courage to face the task.

'It is also a letter to your mother explaining how you have recently employed the Irish spinner Burke. In it I tell Marion she can hire the woman to spin all her flax and any wool she might have.'

'Thank you Hugh,' Lady Clan said, clasping his hands, 'you are a good and brave man to put your name to this.'

'I shall do what I can in the short time I am still in command here,' he said with a wistful smile, 'but I'm being recalled to Skye in a matter of days. You must get the Prince away before the regular reinforcements arrive.'

After five days, Neil appeared late one evening. Flora thought how gaunt he looked under his fair beard.

'The Prince is growing impatient,' he told Flora and Lady Clan. 'I fear he might do something foolish like break his cover if we do not go soon. Surely his costume must be ready by now?'

'We have had much to deal with,' Lady Clan said defensively. 'We've had to stitch everything ourselves and we live in fear of snooping dragoons every day.'

'Madam, forgive me,' Neil said hastily, 'it's just difficult to wait in a hole in the ground with a caged lion.'

Lady Clan laughed. 'I imagine it is.'

'Are you ready Flora?' Neil fixed his look on her.

She nodded. 'I wish only to say goodbye to Angus and Pen.' She did not want to admit to him that she also longed to cuddle her baby nephew to her breast one more time. Neil might think it was a reproach for the children they did not yet have together.

'It will take another day or two for the boat to be made ready,' said Lady Clan. 'Why don't you spend a night at Milton and then make your way to Rossinish from there?'

Flora seized on the suggestion. Neil was less enthusiastic but agreed.

'I shall take you down to the ford,' he said, 'help find a way across that avoids the guards.'

'But they are my father's militia,' Flora pointed out.

'The situation is changing daily,' Neil said. 'I would feel better if I saw you safely over to South Uist.'

Flora thrilled to have Neil stepping through the heather by her side, under a new moon. It was midsummer and the sky was still half-lit by a sun which hardly set. She bombarded him with questions about his life in France and as a close confidant of the Prince. What had Edinburgh been like? Was England as flat and green as people said? Did Jacobites in the south sing the same songs and pass their goblets over a bowl of water when they made the loyal toast? Had he danced at the balls in Holyrood Palace?

Neil smiled and gave her evasive answers. When they drew close to the crossing, he pulled her close and kissed her on the lips – a long lingering kiss that made her legs go weak as a new-born calf's.

'Neil,' she gasped, 'I love you so–'

He put a finger to her lips and bade her be silent. She followed, trembling and frustrated by the one stolen kiss. They waded across the wet sand. Just as they reached the far side, a fox screamed close by. Flora cried out in fright. Moments later, the heads of two guards appeared over the hummock of heather. They had been lying hidden from view, perhaps out hunting. Redcoats.

'Halt!' one called out in English. They pointed their muskets straight at Flora and Neil. 'What are you doing out at this time?'

'Seeing the lady home,' Neil answered.

'Step closer, but don't try any tricks or you're a dead savage.' He prodded Neil with the end of his gun, pushing him forward. 'And you too wench. You look like bloody rebels to me.'

Flora stumbled after Neil, cursing herself for crying out. Why had she allowed him to go with her? Her selfishness could cost them dearly – and the Prince.

The soldier shoved them into a tiny byre stinking of manure and bolted the door. 'You can have your pleasure in their savages – tomorrow I'll hand you over to my superiors for questioning.'

In the dark, they stood in shock at how easily they had been captured.

'Neil I'm so sorry.'

'No, it's not your fault. I let down my guard in a moment of weakness. When they question us, you must deny that you know me. I'm just a gillie showing you across the bog.'

***

They dozed back to back. Raised voices got them scrambling to their feet.

'Get it open at once!'

'I don't take orders from you.'

'And I won't ask you again. Unlock the door or I'll hang you by your toenails till your eyes pop out.'

There was a scrambling at the door. It swung open. Flora nearly fell into her stepfather's arms.

'Florrie?' Hugh looked aghast as he pulled her out. 'This is my daughter, you *Sassenach* fool,' Hugh ranted. 'Can't you tell a gentlewoman when you see one? Or don't they exist in your part of the world?' He caught sight of Neil and for a moment was speechless. 'And – and this is a kinsman. A simple man who doesn't know his own name.'

'He didn't sound simple to me,' the soldier protested.

'I'm releasing them,' Hugh said.

'You can't do that. They're my prisoners.'

'And you'll be mine if you don't do as you're told. I'm in charge of this crossing and the head of the King's militia here.'

'You're not in charge any more. We're posted here now.'

'Until I receive orders to the contrary,' Hugh barked, 'I am the King's officer in charge. And you are in danger of being locked up in there if you don't obey my orders.'

The Redcoat looked uncertain. His fellow trooper pulled him out of the way.

'Let 'em go – it's just a maid and a simpleton. Not worth the bother.'

Hugh led Flora and Neil away from the byre and towards the ford.

'What on earth are you doing here?' Hugh growled.

'I wanted to say goodbye to Angus.'

'South Uist is no longer safe; it's crawling with dragoons. Take my horse and return to Nunton at once,' he said with quiet urgency, 'I can't risk you still being here when their officer turns out of bed.'

Flora clung to him. 'Will you be all right, Father?'

'Of course,' he smiled. 'Now go. God speed.'

Neil embraced him with thanks and helped Flora onto the horse, swinging himself up behind her.

Hugh clasped his arm. 'Look after my daughter, MacEachen, do you hear?'

'I promise on the Prince's life, sir.'

They avoided the main track and the villages, keeping away from Gunn's manse. At Nunton they parted.

'Come tomorrow to Rossinish,' Neil urged, 'we must wait no longer. The Prince's life depends on you Flora. We've had a lucky escape thanks to Armadale. He can't risk that again. Can I rely on you to be there?'

'Of course you can.' Flora felt hurt that he should doubt her.

'Thank you, dear Florrie,' he said, his drawn face breaking into a familiar smile.

She slipped into the stables with Hugh's horse. When she re-emerged, Neil was gone.

Chapter 36

Benbecula, 28th June, 1746

They gathered on the shore in the twilight; five oarsmen and the Prince's party. Flora was cheered to see Lachie from Balivanich and Katie's father, Ronald Oar among the crew. The sea was calm and visibility good.

'Too good,' Felix fretted. 'You will have to run the gauntlet of Government ships. I should be coming with you – you will need my protection.'

'Thank you but no,' Flora was firm. 'The pass is only for me, my kinsman and Betty Burke. If we are stopped, I cannot explain your presence.'

She was trying to stay calm yet her heart was jumping in her chest.

'I will pretend to be one of the boatmen.'

'Leave her be,' Neil said in irritation. 'Flora has made her decision.'

'I could go as the kinsman,' Felix said, 'instead of you, MacEachen. I would put up a better fight if we are caught.'

'No one is going to get caught,' Lady Clan intervened between the bickering men. 'Felix, you will stay and see me safely back to Nunton. But first we must get the Prince quickly away.'

Flora gave her a grateful look. The men were being more skittish than cattle in season. The Prince was struggling into his costume behind a rock, laughing and making bawdy asides. He was wild-eyed and exuberant; swigging from a flask that Neil had given him. Lady Clan was trying to supervise.

'It fastens up this way, Sir. And the cap should be the other way round – frill to the front.'

He strode from behind the rock almost tripping up in his petticoats. Flora, a bundle of nerves, clapped a hand over her mouth to mask a snort of amusement at the outlandish figure.

'You find me funny, Miss MacDonald?' Prince Charles pouted. 'I am pretty, yes? I have a nice smooth skin.'

Flora grinned. 'Very.'

'You boatmen will have to keep your hands off me,' the Prince teased them. 'Neil, pass me my pistol. I don't feel safe among all these men.'

Neil handed over his gun. The Prince lifted his skirts.

'No!' Flora blurted out. 'No maid would carry a weapon.'

'But I must,' the Prince snapped, 'and I will.' His smiles turned to glares, his mood volatile. Everyone fell silent.

Flora was about to relent but her fear of being caught was worse than her fear of upsetting this man.

'I'm sorry, Sir, but it's too great a risk. If you are searched they will suspect at once.'

The Prince looked thunderous. Abruptly, he threw back his head and laughed. 'Madam, if they search me that closely, they'll find out all too soon that I'm no woman.'

Flora and Lady Clan exchanged shocked looks, and then burst into laughter. Neil took back the gun and shoved it into his belt.

Minutes later, they were aboard the open boat; Neil helping Lachie and Ronald push it out from the shallows.

Four men took the oars; Flora sat in the bows next to her bulky maid while Neil sat in the stern with his helmsman from Howbeg, Ronald Oar. Flora watched until Lady Clan and Felix were dots on the shore, receding into the shadows. They scanned the rocky coastline; the ominous outline of a warship sat out at sea. The rowers kept up a steady rhythm. Flora clutched her military pass under her plaid; a talisman against capture. It seemed suddenly such flimsy protection. As they drew closer to the Navy ship she could see cannon on deck, the vast sails limp in the becalmed night air. Why did she ever think such a farcical plan would work? One look at their furtive boatload, setting out at night would bring sailors running on deck and a patrol boat sent to cut them off.

They rowed on. No shouts came from the ship as they slipped by. Flora let go a long breath as they inched away into open sea.

Within an hour, clouds blackened the sky completely and a westerly blew up. The crew hoist the sail and let the wind carry them. The weather deteriorated. Rain whipped in and the sea rose and dipped like a wild bull, tossing them up towards a pitch-black sky and down into foaming raging waves.

Flora grabbed the Prince and clung on, terrified they would be tipped overboard with every surge. He seemed undaunted – merry even – at the storm. He sang songs to keep up their spirits and cradled Flora in his lap.

***

She woke in daylight, embarrassed that she had fallen asleep in the royal Prince's hold. Sitting up, she saw him grinning at her from under a damp headdress.

'You were talking in your sleep, Miss MacDonald. Calling out a man's name.' He leaned close and whispered, 'it wasn't mine and it wasn't MacEachen's.'

Flora's stomach tightened. She had been dreaming about a patrol boat stopping them and men clambering on board. Allan Kingsburgh had been there and Flora had cried out to him, not knowing if he was going to arrest or save them. It left her anxious and aching inside. Was it possible that Allan would be one of the troops sent to guard Skye against any attempt of the Prince to escape the Outer Isles? Hugh had confirmed that the regular companies recruited by the Skye chiefs were taking over from Kingsburgh's militia. Cumberland had ordered it – he no longer trusted them – and the regular soldiers would have to be seen as more zealous in their work, no matter what their personal loyalties. If Allan were to apprehend their boatload he would have to turn them over to his military superiors.

She glanced down the boat at Neil. He was watching her, his look quizzical. What would happen if Neil and Allan came face to face; the one cornered by the other? Neil would not go willingly; there would be bloodshed. Please God, don't let Allan be on Skye, Flora prayed.

The rain had stopped and the men were rowing again. The wind had swung round and was blowing hard from the north-west. Huge cliffs loomed to their right.

'Where are we?' asked Flora.

'Off Dunvegan Head,' said Lachie. 'We drifted south in the storm.'

Flora looked in dismay; they were miles off course and the men were straining to make progress into the headwind. The Prince, still as jolly as the night before, began another singsong. She saw how it gladdened the sweating faces of the crew yet she scanned the cliffs for any sign of troops that might hear a snatch of Jacobite song on the morning breeze.

Two hours later, they came into the lee of the Waternish Peninsula. The rowers were exhausted. Neil decreed they should stop and rest.

'There's a cave below Ardmore,' he pointed, 'we'll shelter there.'

Flora was doubtful. 'Father said that Waternish will be well-manned with troops on the lookout. Should we be going so close?'

'It's Sunday morning,' Neil gave a wry smile, 'the pious Presbyterians should all be at kirk.'

They looked at the Prince for agreement. 'These men need a break from the oars – and I need to stretch my dainty legs,' he winked.

They clambered across slippery seaweed into the cave. Flora handed around chunks of oatmeal bannock and salty butter. The thirsty men licked the cool rocks where spring water trickled from above. The Prince shared the two bottles of milk and porter Lady Clan had provided. Outside the sky was clearing and the wind finally abating. The crew lay wrapped in their plaids and slept. The Prince watched over them like a mothering hen, taking sips from a flask that he kept to himself. Flora closed her eyes and dozed, aware of Neil and the Prince speaking quietly in French together. Making onward plans, she supposed. The less that she and the crew knew, the safer it would be for them, yet it niggled that she could not understand them and that Neil should be keeping secrets from her.

The afternoon was wearing on; Neil roused the rowers. The wind had died and the sail was useless. They set off across calm water, the oars dipping into the glassy shadows under the sheer cliffs. There wasn't a sign of humanity, the only sounds the distant bleat of a goat and the call of seabirds. They rounded Waternish Point, making good progress.

Flora spotted a flash of red above the stony beach. 'Up there!' she gasped.

A group of soldiers were strolling along the cliff edge in the sunshine; they stopped. It was too far to see their faces but close enough to know they were Redcoats. One of them pointed at the boat.

'*Merde!*' Neil swore.

'Ahoy there!' a be-hatted officer called down.

'Keep rowing,' Neil hissed.

The soldier cupped his hands and bellowed. 'Stop I say! Come closer.' He beckoned them to the shore. 'I order you to land.'

'Out to sea lads,' Neil urged, 'double quick time.'

Flora held her breath as the soldiers talked animatedly among themselves. The one who had challenged the boat was shouting and gesticulating. The next moment they were turning and running out of sight.

'They've gone,' she cried.

The Prince clapped in glee.

'Keep up the pace,' Neil commanded, 'they might have gone for reinforcements.'

Suddenly Flora saw them re-emerge, scrambling down a goat path towards the shore. 'There they are!'

'Stop!' their officer shouted, his voice ringing off the cliff walls. 'We'll shoot if you don't.'

'Row for your lives,' Neil ordered.

Moments later, the officer was down on the beach. He raised his pistol and fired. The noise cracked the air. Flora grabbed onto the Prince. Another shot came whizzing by and landed in the water beside them. She stifled a scream. The Prince seized her round the waist and pushed her to the floor. He stood over her, shaking his fists at their attackers.

'Come on my bonny men! Show them what we Highlanders are made of.' Musket-fire burst overhead. 'They won't get us without a fight.'

He cursed and mocked their attackers, rocking the boat dangerously as he tried to keep his footing in the tangle of skirts.

'Sit down, Sir,' Neil cried. 'You'll be hit.'

But the Prince stood facing the bullets and urging on his crew without a care for his own safety. Despite the deafening noise of fire and the shouts from the shore, the boat pulled away and was soon around the Point. They were out of sight of the troops but the rowers did not let up. Flora emerged, shaking and nauseous with fright, to see Neil peering through a spy glass at receding Waternish.

The Prince sat down, putting a comforting arm around Flora. 'We're safe. My boys saw them off. Here, have a sip to steady the nerves.'

He pressed his flask to her lips. She took a swig; it was strangely bitter. Calmness settled through her and she wondered what potion was mixed in with the whisky. Laudanum perhaps? Neil kept up a vigil at the stern, eyeing the coastline for any sign of the troops. But no boat came after them and no patrol rode the cliff tops.

'They must have given up,' Neil said at last. He gave Flora a smile of relief. 'Frightened off by your mad woman.'

The Prince chuckled. 'You see, Miss MacDonald, what a good disguise you have made for me.'

***

191

It was early evening before they grew close to the bulky Trotternish Peninsula and the green swards around Monkstadt House. The Sleats' lime-washed mansion glowed in the weakening sunlight, casting lengthening shadows. Flora's nervousness mounted once more. Neil instructed the oarsmen to row south to the secluded bay at Kilbride where they could hide the boat and more easily slip ashore. Neil helped her clamber from the vessel. She clutched her soft leather shoes in her hand and paddled through the shallows. The Prince followed, hitching high his skirts and wading after her, revealing hairy legs. The sight quite unnerved her.

'Sir, it's best that you stay here out of sight with the men while I get a message to Lady Margaret.'

'But I'm your servant,' he protested, 'and I must go with you.'

She gave Neil a beseeching look. 'Flora is right, Sir. There may be soldiers billeted at the house. Flora and I will go ahead – we need to make sure it is safe first.'

Flora added, 'I'm sure Lady Sleat will come for you as soon as she knows you are here. She is one of your greatest admirers.' She turned to Lachie. 'I know how hungry you all are but please don't move from here or draw attention to yourselves. We'll bring back food, I promise.'

They left a frustrated Prince pulling at his headdress and peering impatiently after them.

***

Lights already blazed in the upstairs dining-room. There were several horses in the courtyard. Lady Margaret was obviously entertaining. Flora wondered if Sir Alexander was back from Inverness having consorted with Cumberland. She had a sudden terrifying thought that the chief might be there with some of the high command from Cumberland's army – even the feared Duke himself.

She clutched Neil's arm. 'I don't think you should come any further. Let me go in and speak with Lady Margaret.'

'There is nothing but rumour to link me to the Prince,' Neil tried to reassure her. 'I am simply escorting you safely back to your mother in Armadale. Your ordeal is over, Florrie, as soon as we hand the Prince into Lady Margaret's care. There's nothing to be afraid of.'

But she was filled with unease.

'Please,' Flora insisted, 'wait in the walled garden just to be sure.'

Reluctantly, he melted into the shadows while she entered the kitchens. She recognised a maid who she remembered from her stay at the house and sent her to fetch Lady Margaret. Flora waited. No one came. The servants eyed her with curiosity. Her dress was salt-encrusted and her hair a mass of wavy curls like some mermaid washed up on the shore. She tried to smooth her appearance.

Finally, after an agonised waiting, the maid came back and summoned her upstairs. 'She'll see you in the parlour, Ma'am.'

'Did you say I wanted to speak with her in private?'

'Aye,' the girl looked agitated, 'but she's got guests.'

'Who?'

'Kingsburgh and some officers.'

Flora's stomach lurched. 'Old Kingsburgh or the Younger?'

'The older.'

Relief and disappointment rushed through her in equal measure as she hurried into the plush parlour.

'My dear, what a surprise,' Lady Margaret greeted her with a cautious smile. Thankfully, she was alone.

'I'm on my way back to Armadale,' Flora gushed, embracing her patron, 'we've had a nervous crossing. Neil MacEachen is waiting outside to hand over–' She hesitated, glancing behind her to make sure the maid had withdrawn. 'To deliver a certain precious person into your care. He is dressed as my spinning woman,' Flora grinned, knowing how Lady Sleat loved both dressing-up and intrigue.

The smile froze on the noblewoman's face. 'What are you saying?'

'Betty Burke, my Irish spinner,' Flora said eagerly, 'is really the royal-you-know-who. We've got him safely off the Long Isle. He is longing to meet you.'

'You've brought him here?' Lady Margaret gasped. 'To my *home*?'

'Aye, I have.'

She struck so quickly, that the stinging slap caught Flora off balance. She reeled backwards, knocking over a delicate table and sending a glass bowl splintered on the floorboards.

'You stupid girl! What were you thinking? This place is jumping with Redcoats and militia. If Sir Alexander were to find out–' She clutched her head in horror. 'My God, do you know what they're doing to people who harbour Jacobites – let alone that man?' she hissed. 'My husband will be done for treason. And you've put me in danger too. The whole world is looking for – for *him* – and you choose to bring him to my door. You'll have us all shot. Leave that!'

Flora was scrabbling on the floor trying to gather the broken shards of glass, pricking shaking fingers, reeling from the unexpected attack. She got up, sucking blood.

'I thought you'd want to help him,' Flora said bewildered. 'You sent me with those shirts.'

'Shut up! Don't speak of such things. My God, do you know who is under my roof tonight–?

Suddenly the door opened and Kingsburgh strode in.

'I heard a crash,' he stopped in surprise. 'Flora? What brings you here?'

Flora's heart plummeted. She had not seen him since her parents had taken over his house at Armadale; he might delight in seeing her arrested. After all he was in charge of the Skye militia and Sir Alexander's most trusted henchman. It was his job to capture the Prince. She couldn't speak.

'This foolish gypsy is putting all our lives at risk,' Lady Margaret trembled, almost in tears. She clutched her heart in a dramatic gesture. 'We're ruined.'

'Flora?' Kingsburgh frowned. 'What have you done?'

Flora swallowed. 'I'm on my way to Armadale, that's all.'

'Oh just tell him,' Lady Margaret cried, 'Tell him who you've brought with you. Go on, confess!'

Something in the man's look – a spark of compassion – made Flora trust him. She lifted her chin in defiance.

'I have Prince Charles down by the shore dressed as my Irish servant,' she said softly. 'I thought he would be safe if I brought him here, but I have misjudged the situation, and for that I am sorry.'

'And so you should be,' Lady Margaret said angrily.

Allan's father stared at Flora as if she had grown horns. 'How on earth did you manage that?'

'Neil MacEachen helped me. He's waiting in the garden to hand him over. You won't betray them will you?'

Kingsburgh flinched. 'Of course not.'

Lady Margaret began to sob. 'I won't have him here – you can't make me.'

He produced a handkerchief and held it out. 'You must try and calm yourself Madam.'

'Kingsburgh, you will have to deal with this,' she sniffed.

'Deal with what?' a voice came from round the door. 'I wondered where you'd all got to.'

Flora's insides crawled. She knew that pompous voice. Surely it was impossible? She turned to see a portly figure dressed in red uniform tread heavily into the room. MacLeod of Unish stared back at her in equal astonishment.

Chapter 37

Lady Margaret coughed into the handkerchief and recovered her poise with a supreme effort.

'Captain Unish,' she said, summoning a tense smile. 'We are just coming. You know Hugh *Cam*'s step-daughter, don't you? She's just called in unexpectedly.'

'Well, well, Miss Milton,' Unish said, stepping forward and taking her hand. 'How delightful.' He saw her cut finger and gave an enquiring look. 'You must be more careful.'

'It's nothing,' Flora said, snatching her hand back.

'How fortunate I am to have two special ladies dine with me tonight.'

'Oh, Miss MacDonald is not staying,' Lady Margaret gabbled. 'She has a long way to go.'

'And where is that?'

'She makes for Armadale and her mother.'

'Armadale tonight?' Unish exclaimed. 'Surely that is too far.'

The women were silent.

'You're right,' Kingsburgh intervened. 'I think Miss Milton should stay the night.'

Flora gave him a pleading look. Any questioning from Unish and her secret could be out. The urge to run from the house and warn Neil and the others was overwhelming. She clenched her hands fighting the desire to flee. How was it possible for Unish to be here? He had been exiled years ago after the scandal of the kidnapped islanders.

'Very well, you had better stay,' Lady Margaret said.

Kingsburgh poured out a large glass of claret and handed it to Unish. 'You'll need that after your long ride from Waternish. Where's your young kinsman, Alex?'

'Left him in the library with his nose in a book,' Unish snorted, unimpressed.

Flora's fear mounted. Was it Unish and his troop who had fired on them earlier?

'Come sit beside me and tell me what you have been doing since last I saw you, Miss Milton,' Unish ordered.

'Let us go and eat first,' Lady Margaret said, 'you travellers must be famished.'

Flora followed her to the dining-room with thumping heart; she felt the dread of the gallows weighing her down and dragging her footsteps. Unish's young ensign turned out to be Chief Norman's illegitimate son Alex whom Flora had last seen as a gangly boy. He had grown into a handsome youth with kind green eyes and a ready smile, his thick curly hair tied with black ribbon rather than hidden under a wig. She hoped they might be seated together, but Unish made sure he was sat next to her.

'Where have you come from today?' he began a relentless questioning.

'I crossed the Minch last night.'

'You've been in the Long Isle?'

195

'Aye, visiting my brother.'

'A strange time to be travelling with so much unrest in the islands, Miss Milton. I'm surprised your mother allowed it.'

'I was keen to see my new nephew.'

'Ah, the broody mother-hen, eh?' he leered at her. 'Not married yet?'

Flora did not answer.

'Don't leave it too late, else you'll soon be past childbearing age.'

Kingsburgh tried to divert him onto other topics, plying him with wine, but the officer kept on at Flora.

'And did you pick up any news of the Pretender in the Long Isle? It's common knowledge he's there.'

'There were rumours,' Flora shrugged.

'And what were they?'

She gave him a steady look. 'That the Prince was on St Kilda and also in Lewis and also in a hermit's cell on Pabbay. But no one really knows. It seems he's disappeared into thin air.'

Unish's eyes narrowed. 'Why are you here, Miss Milton? It's hardly a direct route home to Armadale. Quite the wrong direction in fact.'

'We got blown off course in last night's storm. I thought it best to come to Monkstadt and travel on by land. I am a terrible sailor.' She smiled.

'There was a boat passed close to Waternish Point earlier today. It wouldn't stop. I hope that was not you, Miss Milton. It would be a grave offence to disobey a military order. There was an excitable woman on board.'

Flora's palms began to sweat. 'It cannot have been me – I slept most of the way.'

'And do you travel alone?'

'So many questions,' Lady Margaret broke in. 'You are not to interrogate the poor girl any more.' She turned to the young MacLeod ensign. 'Alex, tell us what you were reading in my husband's library.'

While Alex talked readily about Greek mythology, Flora composed herself, gripping her hands in her lap to stop them shaking. When the conversation lapsed, she parried Unish's attempts to quiz her with questions of her own.

'When did you come back Scotland, Sir? You have been a long time away, have you not?'

He flushed crimson. 'I-I have been travelling on the Continent.'

'And what brought you back?'

'My chief needed me.'

'Ah, MacLeod of MacLeod gave you a commission?'

'He did indeed. I am honoured to serve him and King George.'

'And what does your father think of that?' Flora asked, getting pleasure from seeing him squirm. Unish's father, the Old Trojan, was one of the Prince's most staunch Jacobites.

'I haven't seen my father to speak to for some time,' Unish blustered. 'We do not hold the same views.'

'Flora,' Lady Margaret said abruptly, 'you look tired. Come with me – I'll have a bed made up. Let us leave the men to their tobacco and port wine.'

Lady Sleat did not make for the bedchambers but ordered Flora down the back stairs. Outside in the half-dark, her pleasant composure evaporated.

'Tell MacEachen I don't wish to see him. He must leave Monkstadt at once. I can't run the risk of the servants spotting him and gossiping to Unish's henchmen. I have half a dozen soldiers camped out in my granary.'

'But what of the Prince?' Flora asked in dismay. 'And the boatmen are famished too.'

Lady Margaret's resolve faltered. 'You can go to the kitchen and take some food and drink. Give them to MacEachen. But he must get *him* away from here tonight.'

'Where to, Mistress?'

'I'm not your mistress,' she snapped. She put a hand to her forehead and shuddered. 'I'll send for Kingsburgh. He'll know what to do. Go and wait in the garden.'

Flora found Neil pacing.

'What in the name of Saint Andrew has kept you?'

She quickly explained about Unish and his troops, and how Lady Sleat refused to shelter the Prince. Neil's face looked haunted in the moonlight. He did not like the thought of being beholden to Kingsburgh. 'He's too close to Sir Alexander and his son Allan is in the Government's pay,' Neil fretted. 'How can we trust he won't betray us?'

'He's an honourable Skye man,' Flora defended.

It seemed an age before Kingsburgh appeared alone.

'I've left Lady Margaret plying Unish with brandy,' he grunted. 'He thinks you've gone to bed, Flora.'

'What is to be done?' Neil asked warily.

'To hide the Prince where least expected – in the house of Sir Alexander's chamberlain.'

Flora gaped. 'Your house at Kingsburgh?'

Kingsburgh gave a grim smile and nodded. 'The Redcoats are on the lookout for a boat – every inch of coastline is being watched. So we'll take him overland.' He turned to Neil. 'Show me where Miss Milton's maid is hiding.'

'You would do this for the man you have been ordered to capture and handover to your superiors?' Neil questioned, still unsure.

Kingsburgh bristled. 'I will not go to my grave with the blood of a royal Stuart on my hands.'

Neil flashed a smile. 'Follow me Sir.'

'We must take food for the boatmen,' Flora reminded. The men hung back in the shadows as she slipped into the storeroom and grabbed a bottle of wine and wrapped bannocks in a cloth. She emerged and the three made their way quickly across the courtyard where Kingsburgh untied his horse. As they passed the stables a shout came from behind.

'Who goes there?'

Neil pushed Flora against the stable wall, flattening himself into the shadows.

'Go and see!' It was Unish's slurred command.

Kingsburgh turned, hand steadying his horse, as Alex ran up to him, pistol drawn.

His young face registered confusion at the sight of Kingsburgh leaving. Then he glanced to his right and saw Flora and Neil pressed against the stable wall, clutching provisions. He gasped.

'What are you–?'

Flora gave him a pleading look, pressing a finger to her lips to beg silence.

'Who is it?' Unish called again, swaying in the doorway. 'Who's out at this hour?'

Alex hesitated a moment. He held Flora's look. She couldn't breathe. The MacLeod chief's young son turned away.

'It's just Kingsburgh on his way,' he called across to his superior officer. With a nod at the chamberlain, he said in a loud voice, 'Good night sir, and ride safely.'

'Thank you, Alex,' Kingsburgh nodded.

From the house they could hear Lady Margaret beckoning Unish to come back inside. 'You let in the cold night air, Captain,' she chided. 'Let's have a whisky by the fire before you return to your billet.'

Kingsburgh walked his horse away from the light of the courtyard. Only when they heard the front door of Monkstadt close, did Flora and Neil follow.

***

They arrived at Kingsburgh late into the night, with the household all abed. Their host had insisted an exhausted Flora rode his horse while he and Neil guarded the Prince. The boatmen, after devouring the food, had been dispatched back to the Long Isle and pledged to keep silent on the daring escape. The Prince's skirts were tangled and ripped from ploughing through boggy ditches and under spiky hawthorn bushes to avoid the moonlit tracks. Flora wondered if Florence Kingsburgh would help her mend the disguise or if it was past repair.

Kingsburgh hurried to wake his wife and explain what had happened. Florence appeared flustered and agog, a plaid pulled hastily over her nightgown, jangling the keys to the larder.

'Heaven's above! Can it really be true, Your Highness?' She curtsied at the strange, bedraggled woman standing legs astride in her parlour.

'I am indeed your future King, Madam,' Prince Charles declared, throwing off his hated bonnet. He raised her to her feet and planted a kiss on her hand.

Florence nearly fainted with excitement. 'You must be hungry, Sir. When did you last have a proper meal? Sit yourself down and my husband will get you a drink while I fetch supper. I'll do it myself so I will. Flora, come and help me.'

Flora was so tired she could hardly stand but she went with Allan's mother and helped gather plates of cold meat, boiled eggs, and bread and butter.

'Who is at home just now?' she dared to ask in the kitchen.

'Ann and Macalister and the bairns.'

'So not Allan?'

Florence gave her a beady look. 'Allan is on the mainland with Sir Alexander's troops – Fort William I think. Why do you ask?'

Flora blushed. 'I wouldn't want to put him in the awkward position of having to arrest your guest.'

'My boy wouldn't do such a thing even if he had been here,' Florence said stoutly. 'He's had the Highland code of honour fed to him like mother's milk. No Kingsburgh would betray a fugitive who came to him for shelter.'

'Of course,' Flora said hastily. 'I didn't mean–'

'I know what you mean,' Florence gave a quick smile. 'You have a fondness for my son, don't you?'

Flora felt her cheeks burn. 'I – I don't know about that.'

'Well he cares for you. I've seen the miniature of you that he carries next to his chest in a leather pouch.'

Flora's eyes widened. Surely his mother was mistaken? The only miniature that had ever been painted of her, she had sent to Neil. She suddenly wondered if Neil kept it with him. He had never said.

'Are you sure it's of me?' Flora asked bashfully.

'Quite sure. Allan told me how he'd paid the painter for your sitting and asked him to do a copy. Perhaps I shouldn't be telling you. But I must say, dearie, you've got a lot of pluck. You've risen high in my estimation for your brave plan to get the Prince to safety. I'm quite surprised. I thought your head was too full of frivolity and frippery from living with Lady Sleat.' She passed a plate of duck for Flora to carry. Flora was speechless; her head spun to think that it was Allan after all who had paid for Thomas to do her portrait and not Neil.

Before Flora could question her further, Florence's conversation turned back to the matter in hand. 'Are the crew lying low for a few days? We could hide them in our boathouse. It won't be safe for them to travel for a while. Then they can slip back across the Minch separately so as not to raise suspicion.'

Flora's heart began to pound. 'We told them to go home. They're crossing back tonight.'

'What?' Florence cried.

'Surely it will be safer for them to get back home as soon as possible?'

'Safe?' Florence clasped a hand to her chest. 'They'll be questioned as soon as they set foot back on the Outer Isles. And then God help the poor lads!'

***

Flora was so exhausted she was beyond sleep. She tossed and turned in the truckle bed that Florence helped her make up in an alcove, curtained off in the guest chamber. The servants would be told that Flora was the guest and the truckle bed was for her spinning woman, Betty Burke. She couldn't stop thinking about Allan paying for her portrait and keeping a miniature for himself. Why had he never told her? He must have soon regretted doing so, for he had quickly given his own one to Amelia MacLeod. Yet did he still carry her picture as his mother believed he did? Flora lay in turmoil and waited for the Prince to come quietly to the guest bed.

But all pretence that the Prince was an Irish maid was abandoned by the early hours of the morning when he and Kingsburgh were still carousing over bowls of punch and goblets of claret, swapping tales and laughing raucously by the dying fire. Only when an anxious Florence signalled to her husband to come to bed and the Prince broke the punch bowl in his attempts to grab it and refill it, did the drinking and merriment stop. They helped their drunken, giggling guest into bed. Within minutes his loud snoring brought Flora fully awake. She wondered where Neil was and why he had not helped haul his royal friend upstairs.

Later, she heard muted arguing beyond the door between Ann and her husband. In the morning, Macalister had fled, fearful of being found under the same roof as the hunted royal. Ann was in a tearful and resentful mood.

'How could you be so irresponsible as to bring him here?' she rounded on a bleary-eyed Flora.

'It was your father's idea.'

'You put him in an impossible position.'

'I'm sorry,' Flora said, guilt gripping her insides.

'It's all very well for you,' Ann railed. 'You can just swan off home to your mother in Armadale where it's safe and comfortable. We're the ones who are left to face the consequences.'

'Leave her be,' Florence hushed her daughter. 'Tell me how he slept?' she was eager for details. 'Did he comment on my linen? Was he comfortable?'

Flora could not help a wry smile. 'I think he was too overcome with fatigue to notice what he slept on, Mistress Kingsburgh. But it sounded like he slept well – is still sleeping well.'

She escaped the parlour to seek out Neil. Eventually she found him deep in conversation with Kingsburgh under a rowan tree behind the stables. His eyes were dark-ringed as if he hadn't slept but he smiled when she approached.

'Your help is still needed, dearest Florrie. Can you be strong for another day or two?'

Her heart squeezed at his tenderness. 'If it will help you.'

'It will help the Prince.'

Kingsburgh broke in. 'I think that you have taken enough risks, Miss Milton. I would rather that you made straight for Armadale. We men can take care of things now.'

Flora looked between them. If she went home now, she didn't know when she would see Neil again.

'Will you be going with the Prince?' she asked Neil. He nodded. 'Then I will come too. Tell me what the plan is.'

He smiled in approval. 'Last night I spoke with Donald Roy.'

'Donald Roy is here?' Flora gasped.

'He's been resting nearby – Sir Alexander's doctor has been treating his foot. We are to meet him in Portree and hand over the Prince. Then others shall hide him.'

'Shall he continue as my spinning woman?'

'No,' Kingsburgh grunted. 'He doesn't make a very elegant lady. Portree is too populated and people might grow curious.'

'He will go as your manservant,' said Neil.

'He can have some of Macalister's tweeds,' Kingsburgh said, 'seeing as my brave son-in-law has scurried away like a frightened mouse.' He looked at her gravely. 'Are you sure you want to do this?'

Flora held his look. 'Aye, I do. The Prince has been kind and caring to me, so I shall do all that I can to protect him while I am able.'

He touched her lightly on the shoulder and smiled. For an instant she was reminded of Allan and she felt a stab of regret that it wasn't him standing before her. She smiled back, glad of the older man's approval.

Neil stood up. 'Kingsburgh; it's time to awaken your guest.'

***

'It seems a shame to disturb him,' Florence hovered outside the Prince's room. It was afternoon and yet still he slept. Flora was growing anxious, knowing she must get him to Portree that evening; Neil had gone to alert Donald Roy to the plan.

'We can't let him sleep any longer,' Flora insisted. 'You must go in.'

'I couldn't possibly do that,' Florence grew flustered. 'I'm a married woman not a maid.'

'You do it, Flora,' Ann pushed her forward. 'You've travelled with him like a gypsy – you can't hold your honour very highly.'

Flora flushed with indignation. 'My morals are every bit as strong as yours, Ann. And the Prince has acted as a gentleman towards me in every respect.'

'Of course he has,' Florence intervened. Steering Flora towards the door, she opened it a fraction and peered in. Hesitating, she whispered to Flora, 'Do you think I could have – do you think His Highness would mind–'

201

'Mind what?' Flora asked.

'If I could have a lock of his hair as a keepsake? You could just snip a wee piece while he's still sleeping.'

'Mother!' Ann was scandalised. 'You can't do that to a Prince.'

'Is that very bad of me?' Florence went pink.

Flora put a hand on her arm. 'I think it would be better if we asked him.'

'Will you do that?'

'If you want,' she smiled.

At once, Florence pulled a pair of sewing scissors from her gown pocket and handed them over.

'Flora,' Ann stopped her. She sucked in her cheeks, struggling to speak and then said, 'will you get me a curl too?'

Flora smothered a snort of laughter and nodded.

It took several shakes and hushed entreaties to rouse the Prince from deep slumber. He was groggy and disorientated, his hair tousled and his bleary brown eyes squinting in the light. Flora, standing back from the reek of stale liquor, reminded him where he was.

'Ah, how is my good Kingsburgh?' he rallied quickly. 'Have I missed him at breakfast?'

'And lunch too, Sir.'

He sat up with a wry grin. 'The Lady of Kingsburgh has made my bed too comfortable after months of sleeping on heather.'

She told him swiftly of the Portree plan and showed him the plain but warm clothes he was to wear.

'You'll be thankful to know you don't have to put on Betty's petticoats again,' she smiled.

With alarm, Flora saw tears well in his eyes. She had meant to amuse him.

'One day I will repay the debt I owe to you good people of the Isles,' his voice wavered. 'One day soon, I promise.'

'There is a way you could repay Mistress Kingsburgh now that would make her very happy.'

'Tell me!'

'She would like a strand of your hair to remind her of your stay in her home.'

Charles frowned and then started to chuckle. 'Come then, bring your scissors and sit beside me, Miss MacDonald.'

As Flora sat down on the bed, the Prince leaned over and put his head in her lap, circling her waist with his arms. Her heart lurched at the intimate gesture. This man – who might one day be King of all the British Isles – trusted her so completely that he would lay his head on her as if he were a boy having his hair trimmed. Suddenly she was overcome with shyness.

'Carry on, Miss MacDonald; else I shall fall asleep in your comfortable lap.'

She glanced at the door and saw the Kingsburgh women peering through the crack, hushed and expectant. Flora took a deep breath and ran her fingers through the Prince's tangled hair; it was soft and fine to the touch with coppery strands that gleamed in the light. She lifted the curls at the nape of his neck and snipped underneath where it would not show. As a man on the run, he had no gentleman's wig to cover his natural hair. Her fingers brushed his neck; it was slender and fair like a youth's, yet grimy from his weeks of living in caves and bothies. She felt a rush of affection and pity. His royal blood dictated his destiny – either a kingdom won or bloody execution – but he was also just a young man eager for friends and adventure. She shuddered to think of the cruel executioner's axe hacking at the head resting on her thighs.

Flora slipped two locks into her pocket. After a moment's hesitation, she snipped another curl for herself.

'Miss MacDonald; are you leaving me completely shorn?' the Prince teased.

'It's done, Sir.' She patted his head lightly. 'Thank you.'

For a few heartbeats he clung onto her as if he craved the touch of another human, and then let go and sat up.

She left him to dress and hurried from the room to where Allan's mother and sister stood wide-eyed with excitement.

***

Neil returned with alarming news. Troops were on the move on the road out of Portree and dragoons searching house to house. Kingsburgh was nervous. He had heard stories to make the blood run cold of the excesses of searching Redcoats raping women and murdering children and setting houses ablaze whether they harboured Jacobites or not. The MacLeod island of Raasay, close to Portree, had been torched twice over.

'I don't like the thought of Flora being caught with the Prince,' he told Neil. 'We must divide our party and draw less attention.'

It was agreed that Neil and Flora would travel ahead on horseback and secure a room at MacNab's inn where Donald Roy should be waiting. Kingsburgh would follow with the Prince.

Florence fretted. 'Husband, you are too well known in these parts and folk will remember seeing you with a stranger if the soldiers start to question them. I don't think you should go at all.'

'Is there someone else you could trust?' Flora asked.

'What about young Archie MacQueen?' Florence suggested. 'He's a sensible lad and could cross the moors blindfold, he knows them that well.'

'And can he be trusted with such a precious delivery?' Neil challenged.

'He'll do whatever I ask of him,' said Kingsburgh with a proud lift of his chin that made Flora think at once of Allan.

It was agreed to share the secret plan with the young drover, Archie.

***

The ride to Portree was so tense with worry at being challenged by patrols of Redcoats, that Flora could hardly enjoy the couple of hours alone with Neil. They stopped once for the horses to drink at a secluded burn, hidden by hazel trees, but although the rain came on, he would not allow them to linger in the shelter of the trees. By the time they reached the village of Portree, nestled above its sheltered bay, they were drenched and disorientated in the mist.

Neil put on a Skye accent and asked in Gaelic for MacNab's. To Flora's delight, Donald Roy was there to greet them and the friendly MacNab stoked up the peat fire, gave them dry plaids and bowls of hot punch then left them alone.

'You are taking a great risk being here,' Flora murmured, clasping her Benbecula neighbour by the hands. 'But my heart is gladdened to see you.'

'Mine too,' the beaky-nosed soldier grinned with affection. 'Your courage outshines us all, Miss Flora. Where is the Prince?'

Flora explained how the party had had to split up. 'He is dressed as my manservant – Kingsburgh's young drover is guiding him – they can't be far behind.'

But as time dragged on and the storm outside grew worse, concern for the Prince mounted. Donald Roy could not settle by the fire and kept limping outside to peer through the mist but there was no sign of either the Prince or Archie MacQueen.

'Try and stay calm,' Neil warned. 'Going to the door every quarter hour won't make them come any quicker. It will just draw attention.'

Flora knew he was right but she sympathised with the Baleshare MacDonald; he was a man used to action and was driven distracted by this endless waiting.

At last, a youth appeared dripping at the door and asked for Donald Roy.

'What's your name?' Neil was cautious.

'Archie MacQueen, Sir. There's a gentleman waiting by the rock wants to meet a MacDonald.'

Donald Roy leapt onto his good foot. 'Take me to him laddie.'

Minutes later, he was back with a figure wrapped in a sodden herdsman's blanket. The Prince looked ashen, shaking and numb with cold, water running from his rough tweed jerkin and breeks into pools on the floor. MacNab fetched a dry set of clothes and revived his mute guest with a hunk of goose meat, barley cakes and whisky. The innkeeper did not question who the stranger was.

When MacNab withdrew, Archie reported how they had almost run into a patrol at Borve. Quick-thinking Kingsburgh had ordered Archie behind a gorse bush with the Prince – telling them to carry on alone – while he went ahead and engaged the soldiers in conversation. They had stayed hidden until the rain came on so strongly that they could carry on by a goat track under cover of driving rain and mist.

'The Master turned for home so as to draw the soldiers further away from us,' Archie said.

'I hope he's safe,' Flora worried.

The Prince, now fortified with whisky and food, drew out a silver coin and slammed it on the table. 'Take this, brave young MacQueen, for all your trouble – and hasten back to Kingsburgh. Thank my loyal friend for sending you as my guide.'

Neil grabbed the coin. 'Sir, you mustn't throw down coins like a man of means – you are supposed to be a servant.'

'Young Archie won't breathe a word,' the Prince protested.

'And how will he explain how he came upon a silver coin? You endanger his life with your generosity, Sir.'

Archie spoke up. 'It is little that I have done and I want no payment for it.'

'Well spoken,' Donald Roy said, clapping the youth on the back.

He would not wait for the rain to ease, so Flora put barley cakes in his pocket and he slipped out as quietly as he had come.

The Prince settled himself by the cosy fire once more, but Donald Roy grew anxious. After news of Kingsburgh's brush with the military, he was keen to get the Prince away from Portree.

'We must not stay the night here, Sir. There is a friend who is bringing a boat. It will be dangerous for him to come ashore so we must meet him down in the bay.'

'Who is it?' asked the Prince.

Donald Roy glanced at Flora. 'It's best if we don't talk names and places. I don't want to put Miss Flora in any greater risk.'

'Of course not,' Prince Charles jumped to his feet. 'We will take our leave at once.'

In the dim room that reeked of peat smoke and damp woollens, the Stuart prince took Flora's hands in his – chapped and roughened by living outdoors – and raised them to his lips. Brushing them with a butterfly touch, he gave her a wistful smile.

'Madam, for all your great kindness and courage, I thank you from the depths of my heart.' His eyes shone with a fierce light as he squeezed her hands. 'One day, when I am king, I trust that we will meet again – not skulking in bothies – but with you as my guest of honour at St James's Palace in London.'

Flora's chest swelled with emotion; she was in awe of his conviction. Despite all the setbacks and dangers, this man believed utterly in his destiny as king. She swallowed down tears.

'I hope for that day too, Your Highness, for it would give me the greatest of pleasures.'

They smiled at each other. Twelve days ago, she had not known him. But these past three days with the Prince had been the most intense of her life; frightening and exhilarating in equal measure. Would he remember her as vividly as she was certain she would remember him?

He let go her hands and pulled on the rough plaid that Donald Roy gave him. Flora watched as Neil bade them farewell and exchanged quick words in French with the Prince, and then the Prince and young Baleshare were battling out into the rain once more.

Chapter 38

Flora and Neil sat by the dying peat fire in the smoky room at MacNab's until late into the night. They reminisced about their childhood – the trips to the summer shielings with her father's cattle and learning to ride with her brother and Ranald Og – anything except talk about the events of the past few days. They dared not mention the Prince or any of the friends who had helped him escape this far.

'You should get some sleep,' Neil said when they ran out of things to say. 'We'll leave as soon as it's light. I'll come with you to Armadale.'

'And then what?' Flora asked, hardly daring to hope he might stay with her.

'One day at a time,' Neil advised.

Flora lay on a pile of hay in the corner of the room, wrapped in one of MacNab's blankets. She watched Neil as he sat dozing in a chair, never allowing himself to completely nod off. She tried to see him as a stranger would; he was hollow-cheeked and weather-beaten, his wavy hair receding from a high brow marked with frown lines. His brown eyes were his most arresting feature; his look was keen and full of interest, and when he focused on her she felt that only she was important. Yet they were hooded eyes; ones that kept secrets so that she never really knew what he was thinking.

***

It seemed she had hardly fallen asleep when Neil was gently waking her and handing her an oatcake and cup of warm milk. A quarter hour later, they were paying MacNab for his hospitality and taking Kingsburgh's ponies from the stable.

They rode south down Glen Varragill then followed the passes through the Cuillin Hills, avoiding the busier east coast route patrolled by naval boats. Reaching Strath in the late afternoon, they found Mistress Catherine MacKinnon – a sister of Captain Malcolm MacLeod's who had married the genial and pro-Jacobite Laird of Strath – at home. She remembered Flora from dances at Dunvegan and as she plied them with refreshment, she asked for news; Flora liked the plumply pretty Catherine, who showed her such concern, and confided about aiding the Prince.

Neil would not let them stay the night, eager to put distance between Portree and themselves, and to get Flora safely home. They left Kingsburgh's exhausted ponies with Catherine and she arranged for her boatmen to ferry them from Loch Eishort around the Sleat peninsula to Armadale.

'You were unwise to tell Mistress MacKinnon so much,' Neil chided, as a brisk wind carried them swiftly around the Point of Sleat.

'She's hardly going to betray us when her own brother and family are at risk,' Flora retorted. 'Captain Malcolm fought at Culloden for the Prince.'

A flash of impatience crossed his face. 'That depends on how much pressure the searching parties apply. Ferguson and men of his kind are ruthless when it comes to extracting information or confessions. They can tell all too easily if their victim has something to hide.'

'Victim?' Flora shivered at his words, appalled that she might have put Catherine in danger.

She searched his face for reassurance but Neil looked away.

They arrived just before midnight. Flora clambered ashore on wobbly legs, completely drained. Her mother was roused from her bed by their knocking.

'Florrie?' she gasped in bewilderment and then snatched her to her breast in a hug of relief. 'You're safe!'

Over bowls of barley broth and a jug of beer, Marion listened open-mouthed to her daughter's story. At first Flora was reticent – Neil's warning over telling too much still rankled – but her mother demanded to hear everything. Neil too was persuaded to talk about his time in hiding with the Prince.

'Father gave me this to give to you,' Flora produced the pass and letter about Betty Burke. It was wrinkled and the ink smudged from the previous day's rain. 'It was to give us protection if we were stopped on the way.'

'Oh Hugh,' Marion exclaimed with exasperated affection, 'what risks he takes. I don't think that man will ever be content with a settled life.'

'He was heroic in what he did,' Neil said, 'you should be very proud of him.'

She gave him a sharp blue-eyed stare. 'I'll be prouder if he comes home to me and the family in one piece, Neil MacEachen.'

'If who comes home?' a sleepy Annabella stood in the doorway in bare feet.

Flora rose to greet her. Annabella ran to her and flung her arms about her adored older sister.

'You came back! I thought you'd stay with Baby Angie and not want to come home.'

'Of course not.' Flora kissed her forehead. Tears stung her tired eyes. Right then, she didn't want to be anywhere else but in the safety of her mother's home in Armadale.

***

Hugh *Cam* appeared home three days later, breezing into the farmhouse as if he had just returned from a day's hunting. His wife and daughters fell on him with squeals of delight, kisses and questions.

'Let a man get his boots off first,' Hugh laughed.

Later, as the adults sat around the dinner table, they learned that the Skye militia Hugh had been commanding had been ordered back from the Long Isle the day after the Prince's escape. He had waited at Kylerhea for

Kingsburgh to disband them but his superior had not turned up for several days.

'He was able to tell me why he was delayed,' Hugh said with a look of admiration at his step-daughter.

'Is he in good spirits?' Flora asked. 'Is everything quiet at Kingsburgh?'

Hugh nodded. 'Quiet aye, but Kingsburgh advises us all to stay at home and be watchful.'

'What troubles you, Armadale?' Neil asked unexpectedly.

The men exchanged looks. Hugh lowered his voice so that Flora and Marion had to lean forward to catch it.

'I saw more troops coming across from the mainland at Kyle making for Portree. Kingsburgh said that Raasay had been raided yet again.'

Neil flinched.

'Is that where Donald Roy was going?' Flora whispered.

Neil did not answer her question but asked one of his own. 'Where could they have got their intelligence?'

Hugh's look was grim. 'If they are stepping up the search on Skye then they must know the Prince is no longer on the Long Isle.'

'The boatmen,' Flora gasped, 'Lachie and Ronald Oar.' She felt a sick churn in the pit of her stomach. 'Mistress Kingsburgh was worried about them returning so quickly in case they were questioned–'

Her mind filled with the menacing, hate-filled sneer of Captain Ferguson and his dire threats.

'The Redcoats must have extracted confessions,' Neil said, his teeth clenching.

'What will that mean for Florrie – for all of us?' Marion asked fearfully.

No one voiced an answer; their troubled looks said it all.

***

A week went by after Hugh's return but all remained calm at Armadale. Flora began to hope that they had got away with their daring escapade. Perhaps the boatmen had said nothing of consequence – at least not named any names – and the troop activity on eastern Skye was just to keep Cumberland happy. Her spirits were further raised by Neil's continuing presence, though his mood was distracted and he disappeared each day with his spyglass to keep a watch on ships in the Sound. She suspected he was awaiting someone's arrival with news of the Prince, but he brushed off her questions with vague answers and a disarming smile.

Then one still evening, when the midges were dancing over a glass-like sea, Donald Roy came limping out of the trees.

His normally jovial face was grim, his clothes dishevelled and his bonnet gone. Marion revived him with food and Hugh poured out a large dram.

'We were nearly caught on Raasay,' he told them. 'Captain Malcolm had thought the Prince would be safer there because it had so recently been raided – but they came back yet again – my God, the punishment those

209

evil devils have inflicted on the Raasay MacLeods is beyond belief. We only just got Prince Charlie away to Skye – hid in a cave until nightfall. We planned to take him through the Cuillins but Captain Malcolm said I'd hold them up with my bad foot, so they went on ahead.'

'Where were they making for?' Neil asked.

'MacKinnon of Strath and Malcolm's sister – then possibly a boat to Eigg and down to Arisaig. The Redcoats are everywhere and the sea is just as dangerous. His only hope now is to get to the mainland and lie low in the mountains – and to try and get a message to the French to rescue him.'

'He needs me,' Neil said at once, 'I'm the one who can make contact with the French.'

'How will you do that?' Flora asked anxiously.

'Don't ask such things, Florrie,' Marion said, her hands twisting in her lap.

'I'll go tomorrow,' Neil said, 'my being here is making it more unsafe for you all. I was hoping to hear that the Prince was long gone and the trail we had left had gone cold.' He gave Flora a look of regret. 'I'd like to have stayed much longer.'

'We still don't know that our plan has been uncovered,' Flora said.

'It's a matter of time,' Neil replied. 'Donald Roy, you should be taking to the hills too. The Redcoats are thirsting for the blood of men who fought at Culloden – let alone helped the Prince to escape.'

'Oh Hugh,' Marion cried. 'Will you have to go skulking like a criminal too?'

'Certainly not,' Hugh was bullish. 'I've been in the King's militia; they can't touch me.'

***

They were roused in the early morning by hammering on the door. To Hugh's alarm, he found Alex MacLeod, Unish's tall young ensign filling his doorway.

'Come away,' Hugh blustered. 'How is your father, Chief Norman? I'm not long back from militia duties in the Long Isle. What can we do for you?'

He hurried him into his study where the soldier, looking embarrassed, handed over a message from Unish.

'Miss Milton is requested to make her way to Castleton to meet with my superior.'

'And is this a friendly visit – a social call over the tea table?'

Alex held his look. 'Captain Unish has certain questions about Miss Milton's trip to South Uist.'

'Well my step-daughter is very fatigued after her journeying. I'm sure in a day or two she would be happy to call on Unish. I will bring her there myself.'

'I've been asked to escort her today, sir.'

210

'She certainly is going nowhere until she has eaten a good breakfast,' Hugh protested. 'You can return to your billet and I will make sure Flora comes later in the day.'

Alex hesitated and then nodded agreement. He took a breakfast dram with Hugh and then made to leave. At the door he said, 'it might be wise not to come yourself, Armadale.'

Hugh flinched under the youth's steady gaze. He was warning him. Could Unish possibly know everything already?

'Thank you, Alex,' Hugh grasped his hand and sent him on his way.

The summons threw the household into a panic.

'They know about you Florrie,' Marion cried. 'Don't go. They'll take you away and I'll never see you again. I'll never forgive that wretched Lady Margaret for sending you off in the first place – and then she has the gall not to help you with the Prince.'

'I can bluff,' Flora said, 'and deny the accusations.' She was trying to be brave but felt as if she would vomit with fear.

While the wrangling went on, Neil went out to survey the sea and came back with bad news. 'There's a sloop-of-war dropped anchor in the night off Castleton. The *Furnace*.'

'Captain Ferguson,' Flora gasped.

Marion put a hand to her mouth to stifle a wail.

Hugh, seeing her distress, was galvanised into action.

'Neil you must leave at once. You can take my militia jacket and I'll get one of my men to row you across to the mainland.' He turned to Donald Roy. 'You, my friend, must go to the hills and fend as best you can. Marion will send you with provisions. I will take Flora to a cave I know across the Sgurr at Inver Dalavil where she will be safe until the hunt dies down.'

They all turned to Flora. She saw their faces full of anguish. She knew in that moment how much she was loved – how much she loved them back – and what she must do.

'No Father,' she said quietly, 'it's me that Unish wants. If I disappear they will take you instead. Mother and the family need you here.' She tried to control the shake in her voice. 'I will go and keep them occupied with their questioning – it will give Neil and Donald Roy more time to get away. Besides,' she forced a smile, 'Unish may just be going through the formalities. He cannot prove anything. No doubt I'll be home before nightfall or by tomorrow at the latest.'

'I can't let you do that,' said Hugh.

'Please don't, Florrie,' pleaded Marion.

'I'll give myself up instead,' Donald Roy declared.

'If you do that you will be going to certain death,' Neil spoke up. He fixed Flora with an intense look. 'Flora is right; she is the only one can sweet-talk Unish into dropping the matter. Deny and delay is the tactic. The more of their time she can waste, the more time the Prince has to escape.'

211

'Then it is decided,' Flora said, meeting his look. Above all, she was doing this for Neil.

Neil's eyes glistened as if he understood that. He stepped towards her. She longed to be alone with him so she could say what was in her heart.

'Flora, do you still have the pass that was signed by your father?'

She was momentarily thrown, thinking he was going to take her aside.

'Aye, I do.'

'You must destroy it before you go. It will get Armadale into trouble if Unish gets his hands on it. He will never believe that your father did not know the identity of Betty Burke.'

Flora went at once to fetch the document; Neil lit a taper from the embers of last night's fire and they watched it burn in the grate. Neil stabbed the ashes with the fire poker until there was nothing to see.

But Marion still fretted for her daughter. 'What can she tell Unish that won't get her arrested for treason? She must have a story that can be believed.'

The men began to concoct one. 'Betty Burke was a lusty Irishwoman who asked you a favour.' Hugh said. 'She needed to get to Skye.'

'Why?' asked Flora.

'Because her husband was a soldier,' said Donald Roy, 'and she heard he was on Skye and begged you to give her passage in your boat.'

'What was an Irishwoman doing on South Uist?' Marion questioned.

'She'd escaped a transport ship taking indentured servants to America,' Neil suggested.

'But what about you Father?' Flora worried. 'You listed her as a spinning woman and my maid in my pass as if you knew about her – even recommended her to Mother. Even though the pass is destroyed, they will ask me how I got permission to travel back to Skye.'

'That's a risk I'll have to take,' Hugh was fatalistic.

'Did anyone else see the pass?' Neil asked.

'No one asked me for it,' Flora shook her head.

Hugh shrugged, 'there was a Redcoat officer at the checkpoint – he glanced at it as I was writing but made no comment.'

'Then,' said Neil, eyeing Flora, 'you can say you don't remember the details of the pass; you just asked for a permit for yourself and an Irish woman in distress.'

After that, there were frantic preparations for flight. Hugh left with a reluctant Donald Roy in the direction of the remote cave he had mentioned. Before setting out in Hugh's military uniform for a boat that was waiting for him in a rocky cove south of Armadale, at a distance from the *Furnace*, Neil took his farewell of Flora. They stood in the lee of the house.

'You are the bravest lassie I know,' he said, his smile wistful. 'It is a great thing you have done for our Prince.'

'For you, Neil,' Flora said, her heart leaden at their parting. 'You know I did all this because you asked me.'

He raised her hands and kissed them fondly.

212

'Will we ever see each other again?' she croaked, her eyes welling with tears.

'I will come back, I promise. One day we will be together forever – you will be my lady at the court of King James and your friend Prince Charles shall shower you with honours and riches beyond imagination.'

Flora desperately wanted to believe in his dream but the enormity of what she was about to do – hand herself over to Unish – was suddenly terrifying and far more real.

'What if I came with you now?' She tried to keep the panic out of her voice. 'You could take me with you and the Prince back to France. We could live in exile – I wouldn't mind – as long as we were together.'

She saw his hesitation and how he struggled with mixed emotions. She held her breath as her fate weighed in his hands.

'Florrie, I would like nothing better but you know they would come after you at once. Us two running off together would only endanger the Prince further; you must see that.'

Flora swallowed down bitter disappointment. 'Aye, of course.'

Briefly, Neil pulled her into his arms and gave her a hasty kiss on the lips.

'Courage my dearest Florrie,' he said as he let go, 'I will think of you always.'

Numbly, she watched him skirt along the shore and disappear from view. Not once did he look back or wave; but then to have done so would only have drawn attention to himself or to her.

Flora took her time getting ready to set out for Castleton which lay four miles north of Armadale. The longer she delayed, the better it was for the fugitive men. Marion fussed around her, trying to stay strong and not break down in front of the younger children. Annabella showed a plucky spirit by helping Flora tie up her hair and decorate it with a scented briar rose, chattering constantly to fill the tense silence, as if her sister was merely going out to take tea with a friend.

'Why don't you wait here,' Marion said, 'and let them come asking. I'll worry about you going on your own.'

'I'll take Katie,' Flora reassured, 'then she can return and tell you I am safely arrived.

'I'll go too,' Annabella volunteered, 'at least for the first mile or so.'

'Thank you,' Flora smiled.

The three young women set out together that afternoon. Half way to Castleton they were met by Ensign Alex and two other soldiers on their way to fetch her.

'Captain Unish grows impatient,' he explained, 'I'm sorry but you can't delay any longer.'

Flora hugged her sister and maid. Her courage almost failed her at their sobbing.

'I'll be back soon,' she said, gently pushing them away. The sound of their weeping tugged at her heart until she was over the next hillock and out of sight.

Chapter 39

'You can save us all a lot of bother, Miss Milton, if you tell me everything,' Unish drawled. 'Then you can go home and I will get a pat on the back for doing my job.'

He kept Flora standing, not offering her a seat in the dining-room he had commandeered at Castleton.

'Tell what, Captain Unish?'

'You know perfectly well. I want to know what you were doing at Monkstadt and who you were with.'

'I seem to remember I was with you, sir,' Flora said with an innocent smile.

'This isn't a game, damn it!' he went puce as he thumped the table, making her jump. 'You're in serious trouble. Now answer my questions. Who travelled with you from the Long Isle?'

'I wish I could remember – but I have such a headache. Perhaps I could sit down.'

'Very well.' Unish waved at her to sit.

Flora took her time pulling out a chair and sitting down, fanning herself and sighing. 'It's very stuffy in here. Could I please have a drink? The walk has made me thirsty.'

'Not until I get some answers,' Unish snapped. 'Where did you sneak off to the night you visited Monkstadt?'

'I didn't sneak off. I retired early to bed and left early the next morning before you arose. I wanted to get a good start for Armadale.'

Unish pushed himself to his feet and leaned across the table, eyes bulging.

'I'm the only who one can save you from being handed to Cumberland's men, Flora. And by God, I wouldn't wish that on anyone, not even an infuriating girl like you. You look down your arrogant MacDonald nose and think you can fool me. Well, I'm not the one you have to fear. Ferguson and his pack of dogs will show no mercy.'

The look he gave her was almost beseeching and for a brief moment, Flora felt a twinge of pity. Even Unish did not want to hand one of his fellow island gentry over to the men from the south.

'Stop protecting people who have done nothing to protect you from all this,' Unish urged. 'Your loyalty is misplaced.'

Flora gave him a cool look. 'And where, Captain Unish, does your loyalty lie? With your people or with the likes of butcher Cumberland and his Lowland lackeys?'

Unish glared at her in fury. 'If you won't let me help you, then I won't be responsible for what happens to you.' He pushed back his chair and stormed from the room.

Within the hour, Flora was being bundled into a boat and rowed out to the *Furnace*.

***

214

Flora was taken below deck by two English marines and then man-handled down a hatchway into a stinking dark hold. She stumbled on the bottom steps as the hatch was slammed shut above, plunging her into the pitch black. She clung to the ladder, heart pounding and struggling to breathe in the fetid air.

'Is anyone else in here?' she called out in Gaelic.

'Aye,' a man's voice croaked back, 'there's the two of us.'

Flora recognised the accent. 'You're an Outer Islesman. South Uist?'

She heard a movement in the dark; a chain rattling. 'Is that you Miss Flora?'

'Yes.' Her heart lurched. 'Do I know you?'

'I'm Ronald Oar, Mistress. And Lachie's with me.'

'Ronald Oar!' Flora groped towards the voice, banging into a barrel and her feet splashing through effluent. Her eyes were growing used to the dark and she could make out two figures propped against the hold, their feet and hands shackled. 'I'm so sorry to see you like this. How long have you been here?'

'A week perhaps. You lose count of the days down here. But you, Mistress, it's a terrible thing to see a lady of Milton brought to such a place.' His voice grew choked. 'I'm ashamed to think we had a part in it.'

'It's not your fault,' Flora said. 'We should not have put you in danger by sending you back home so soon. Has – has Ferguson treated you very badly?'

'He's a cruel devil,' Ronald muttered. 'Put Lachie on the rack – tore his arm out of its socket.'

'Lachie!' Flora cried, nausea rising to think how her brother's childhood friend had been tortured. 'Are you still in great pain?'

'He doesn't speak,' Ronald answered. 'Hasn't said a word since they took us off the Long Isle.'

Suddenly, there was distant shouting and running overhead, and strange creaking and groaning. The boat began to rock.

'What's happening?' Flora gasped.

'They're lifting anchor,' said Ronald, 'we're sailing on.'

Flora panicked. She scrambled back to the ladder and climbed, tearing her skirt and knocking her shins. She hammered on the hatch.

'Let me out! I haven't said goodbye. They don't know where I am. I must see my mother. Please!' She pounded her fists until her knuckles were bleeding. 'Don't take me away. I want my Mammy!'

As the sails caught in the wind, the shifting ship threw her off the ladder. Flora tumbled into stinking bilge water and lay sobbing and shaking with terror.

***

Late that night, Flora was hauled out and taken to Ferguson's cabin with her hands bound behind with rope. He sat swigging from a bottle of brandy, the lamp above the table swaying and casting shadows.

'Clanranald's brandy,' Ferguson slurred, 'is the only palatable thing to come out of these God forsaken Erse-speaking islands.'

Flora's fear at being brought before him eased a fraction. He was a thief – contemptible – and she would not be intimidated.

'I don't see the point in asking you questions,' he continued, 'you're as guilty as sin. We have enough witnesses to say it was you who helped the foreign Pretender escape to Skye. Including those savages down in the hold. But General Campbell wants to go through the motions.'

'Then I shall answer to the General,' Flora said. 'Where is he?'

'He won't be on board until the morrow, so we can have some sport before then.'

He got unsteadily to his feet and lurched towards her round the table. The knot in her stomach tightened.

'Have they kept you satisfied – those peasants down below?' he leered. 'One of them's not as able since he's been on my wheel – but the other one can still pleasure you.'

He thrust his face in hers. Flora froze.

'That's what you like, isn't it, you savages? To fornicate and dance to the Devil's music on those blasted pipes,' He sneered. 'Or do you prefer your men with more refinement? Will you only open your legs for gentry like MacEachen or jumped-up royals like pretty-boy Charlie?'

She gave him a look of utter disdain. Suddenly, he grabbed her round the throat and thrust her against the door. She gasped for air. His other hand lifted her skirts. She struggled and tried to push him off, twisting her body away.

'Get your hands off me,' she said in a strangled voice.

He laughed and forced his mouth onto hers. Flora clamped her eyes and mouth shut. The ship listed and he stepped back to balance himself. She spat in his face. He slapped her hard across the cheek.

'Who's the savage now?' she hissed.

He grabbed her by the hair and shoved her against the table, bending her backwards, forcing his weight on her. Her arms, pinned underneath, went numb. Flora screamed.

'Do you think anyone's going to come running to help you, you heathen slut?' Ferguson taunted. 'I could take my pleasure and chuck you overboard. No one cares a fig about Erse-speaking traitors like you!'

Flora saw the crazed look in his drunken eyes. She was going to die a horrible death at the hands of this fiend. She was too terrified to weep.

'Plead for your life then,' he commanded, 'like the other Highland trollops who've protected Jacobite savages.'

Flora gritted her teeth and said nothing. She would rather die than beg to this monster. His rank breath and the weight of him made her feel faint.

'Admit that you ferried the Foreigner across to Skye dressed up as a maid,' he demanded. 'Say it!'

'I took a poor Irishwoman in great distress in my boat,' Flora panted. 'She wanted to find her soldier husband on Skye.'

'Liar!'

'She'd escaped off a ship taking her to the colonies – to America. She was Irish. I don't know where she went after we landed.' Flora clung to her story. 'I never did meet any Pretender.'

'I don't believe a word–'

There was an abrupt knock at the door. Ferguson looked annoyed but pushed himself off Flora. 'What is it?'

A sailor put his head round the cabin door, stooping. 'Captain; there's a boat on its way out – looks like the General's arriving early.'

'Get her out of here,' Ferguson growled. 'Throw her back in the hold.'

Never had Flora imagined how glad she would be to find herself back in the dank, fetid bowels of the cramped ship. At the hatch, the sailor untied her hands so that she could descend the ladder. She collapsed at the foot, shaking and gulping back tears of relief.

***

The next day, Flora was brought before General Campbell. He had a broad face and shrewd eyes. When he took off his wig to scratch at midge bites, his head was completely shaven.

'I'm sorry you have been roughly treated and lodged with common criminals,' he said. 'You will be given a cabin from now on.'

'The men in the hold are no criminals, General,' said Flora. 'They are my clansmen. The bruising on my face was a present from Captain Ferguson.'

He frowned. 'I'm dismayed to hear that. You shall not be ill-treated by me, Miss MacDonald. But I expect your co-operation in return.'

Flora kept doggedly to her story of the distressed Irishwoman, making no mention of Neil or her stepfather's part in providing a pass.

'I then stayed at Monkstadt with my former patron, Lady Margaret, before returning to Armadale.'

The General unnerved her with his unblinking stare while she gave her story.

'A pretty tale, Miss MacDonald,' he said brusquely, 'but you have wasted your breath. What irritates me more is that you are wasting my time.'

'What do you mean, Sir?'

'We have Lady Clanranald under arrest at her house. We also have her cook who is willing to testify that you and his mistress spent many hours making up dresses to disguise some man as a common spinning woman. We have several boatmen who have admitted to rowing you, the Papist Neil MacEachen and this so-called spinning woman across to Skye. One of them was persuaded to tell us that the woman was in fact the Pretender himself.'

217

He leaned his elbows on the desk between them and pressed the tips of his fingers together, scrutinising her. Flora tried to hide her shock at his words. Lady Clan arrested and MacEachen identified?

Pursing his lips, he continued. 'Kingsburgh has given a statement confessing that he brought you and your so-called maid to his own house from Monkstadt then sent you on your way to Portree. What do you have to say to that?'

Flora thought rapidly. Unish had seen Kingsburgh at Monkstadt but did not know that she had taken refuge at the Kingsburghs' with the Prince. That must have come from Lady Margaret. Kingsburgh had had to admit to Flora being there but was still protecting the Prince by keeping up the pretence of not knowing who Betty Burke was.

'It's true,' Flora licked dry lips, 'I did stay at Kingsburgh on my way home. I was taken ill, you see; and threw myself at the mercy of the kind Kingsburghs. But I recovered quickly and went on my way.'

'With your Irish maid?'

'Aye, with my maid.'

'And Neil MacEachen?'

'Flora frowned. 'MacEachen?'

'MacNab the inn-keeper where you stayed told us clearly that you were there with a man called MacEachen and two other men – one he gave a set of dry clothes to. But there was no mention of a maid, Miss MacDonald.'

'He – he must have been mistaken.'

He looked about to argue but changed tack. 'Why did you sail to Monkstadt? It was not the direct route to Armadale by any means.'

'We were blown off course.'

'Did you think that Lady MacDonald of Sleat would help you in your desperate attempt to hide the Pretender?'

'I helped a wretched Irishwoman,' Flora persisted, 'not the Pretender. Lady Margaret merely gave me shelter as an old friend. I was her lady-in-waiting–'

'She claims to have hardly met you,' interrupted the General.

'What do you mean?' Flora faltered.

'Lady Sleat says she's only met you once or twice before and was astonished when you turned up at her house. She appears to know nothing of you bringing the Pretender close to Monkstadt. She was shocked to hear this when we questioned her three days ago. In fact she was very indignant that you would even think of trying to incriminate her or Sir Alexander by such a treacherous action. She called you a troublesome Long Isle gypsy. What do you say to this?'

Flora flushed. 'Of course she knew nothing, because the Pretender was never there.'

'Do you know what I think?' the General said, losing patience. 'I think the whole idea of dressing the Pretender up as an Irish maid and getting you to take him across to Skye was the scheming of that Jacobite-loving Peggi MacLeod – your precious Lady Clan. She bullied her husband and

218

son into supporting the Pretender; she coerced you into the escapade. She and your treacherous stepfather, Armadale.'

'No, you're quite wrong.'

'We know that Armadale supplied you with a military pass. Oh, he thought he was running rings round me,' General Campbell said with a mirthless smile, 'sending me off to St Kilda on a wild goose-chase. By God, I'd like to get my hands on that smirking one-eyed villain.'

'My father was searching high and low for the Pretender,' Flora defended. 'I went to him for a pass because I was growing fearful of all the troops arriving on the Long Isle and wished to go home. I asked for him to put Betty Burke on the pass too – which he did out of compassion for the woman.'

Abruptly, General Campbell pushed back his chair. 'I've heard enough of your fanciful tales, Miss MacDonald. We have Felix O'Neill on board. He's told us all we need to know about the escape plan on the Outer Isles. Now all I need is to get to the truth of what you did with the Pretender on Skye.'

His look was grim. 'That shouldn't take long. Kingsburgh is being interviewed again – this time by Captain Ferguson. I don't doubt that the threat of having his home and farm put to the torch, and his family threatened, will have the desired effect.'

***

Flora's tiny cabin had no porthole; it was little more than a cupboard in which a cabin boy would sleep on a shelf. She listened out for any sounds of footsteps or voices that might give her an inkling of what was happening to the other prisoners. Was Kingsburgh really on board being questioned for a second time, and had they captured Felix? Or was it all a bluff by the General to catch her out and make her confess.

She paced the cramped room, knowing the torture of a caged animal. Unexpectedly, the door was unlocked and a sailor beckoned her to follow him up on deck. Flora gulped at the fresh sea air that whipped at her face. As she pulled hair from her eyes, she saw a familiar burly figure dressed in MacDonald kilt and plaid being led across the deck.

'Kingsburgh,' Flora gasped.

He turned, startled and stopped in his tracks. His face broke into a worried smile. 'Flora. Are you all right?'

The marines either side, pushed him forward. 'Keep going,' one ordered, 'and say nothing.'

Kingsburgh struggled against them, but they dragged him towards the stern. He shouted back in Gaelic. 'Courage, daughter of Milton! I'm sorry I couldn't protect you for longer. God be with you, lassie!'

She watched as they bundled him over the side and away on a rowing boat back to shore. Flora noticed numbly from the shape of the hills that they were anchored off Portree.

Back in the claustrophobic cabin, she realised that she had been deliberately brought on deck to witness Kingsburgh being humiliated, so that she would know he had confessed all that he knew. She was left to stew in her fearful thoughts for another sleepless night.

The next day, she was summoned once more in front of General Campbell. With a heavy heart, Flora confessed to her part in helping the Prince, gulping back bitter tears as her captor made her repeat her words as he laboriously wrote them down.

'I'm sorry that you were so easily mislead into this foolishness,' sighed the General, finally putting down his pen. 'I'm impressed with your dignified manner, Miss MacDonald, and your loyalty – however misplaced.'

'No one misled me, General,' said Flora, meeting his gaze. 'I saw a man in a wretched state and in great need. I did not hesitate to help him. As a fellow Gael, I'm sure you understand that.'

Chapter 40

Fort Augustus, Invernesshire, late July, 1746

Allan and his Skye comrades picked up the rumour that Sir Alexander was on his way to Fort Augustus with prisoners. They were sickened at the wanton destruction and brutality they had witnessed all summer across the Western Highlands. Cumberland had confined their company to barrack duties, not trusting them to carry out his reign of terror – the burnings and killings – that he ordered daily.

'He hates us Skye men the most,' Allan had discussed it with James, Hugh *Cam*'s young son. The boy's enthusiasm for soldiering had been blunted by the carnage he had witnessed.

'But why? We are better swordsmen than the *Sassenachs* he keeps around him,' James complained.

'He never trusted us to begin with – the Skye clans have fought for the Jacobites too often in his opinion – but now that the rumours are saying the Prince has got away from Skye to the mainland, he loathes the lot of us. I've heard he's itching to get back to London – would have been long gone if the Prince had been caught.'

'Do you think Sir Alexander has captured the Prince?' James was wide-eyed.

'It must be someone important if he's bringing him in person to the Duke,' Allan said gravely.

***

The bellowing in the courtyard was nothing new. The men were used to Cumberland flying into a rage and ranting abuse at the slightest thing. Tardy reports, summer flies, runny milk puddings and men joking in Gaelic were enough to provoke his temper and a whipping for anyone who got in his way.

The MacDonald men were emerging from the guardroom to greet their chief when James put a hand on Allan's arm.

'There – in the middle – isn't that your father?'

The barrel-chested Duke, puce in the face, was shouting at Sir Alexander as if he were an errant schoolboy.

'You let the traitor ride in here on his *own* horse? He should have been chained up and running along behind, you bloody idiot!' Cumberland lunged at the man behind and tried to drag him from his horse.

Allan's disbelief turned to fury. Butcher Cumberland was manhandling his father! He sprang forward but James and two others grabbed him and blocked his way.

'He'll have you hanged in a trice,' James hissed. 'Stay back and be quiet.'

They were too far away to hear what Sir Alexander said, but he appeared to be pleading on behalf of Kingsburgh. The Duke was having none of it.

221

'Take him away and shackle the blighter!' Cumberland bawled. 'Throw him in gaol where he belongs.'

Allan watched in helpless fury as his father stumbled on wobbly legs and was dragged off by two dragoons.

***

It was not until two days later, when Cumberland had departed swiftly for London, that Allan bribed a guard with whisky to let him see his father. He was chained to the wall in the common gaol-house alongside others awaiting trial for murder and theft.

They embraced with difficulty. Allan could hardly contain his anger.

'What are you doing here? You're the head of that bloody man's militia, for heaven's sake!'

'Do you have anything for an old man's thirst?' Kingsburgh's voice was a dry whisper.

At once, Allan produced a flask of brandy and held it to his father's lips. After that, his father revived enough to tell him all that had happened since the fateful night when Flora had turned up at Monkstadt. Allan listened first in disbelief and then utter amazement to the tale of the audacious escape plan – with Flora at its heart – that had reeled in his own family.

'The Prince stayed the night in our home?' Allan was dumbfounded.

'And most of the next day,' Kingsburgh grunted. 'We supped long and late. Flora had the devil of a business trying to rouse him. And then your mother and sister delayed matters by wanting locks of his hair cut off.'

'Did Flora do that too?' Allan felt a surge of jealousy.

'Aye, the lass had grown close to Prince Charles in a short time. If you ask me, he was quite taken with her.'

'That wouldn't please MacEachen,' Allan snorted.

'Why do you say that? MacEachen is devoted to the Prince – he seemed to be the driving force behind the madcap plan.'

'That's as maybe, but he and Flora have some sort of understanding.' Allan was glad that the gloom of the cell hid his blushing.

'Then I'm sorry for the poor girl,' sighed Kingsburgh. 'MacEachen's fled and the Redcoats are after him. Just as they came after us all. Donald Roy, Armadale, Captain Malcolm – it's just a matter of time before they are captured too.'

'And Flora?' Allan's heart thumped as he peered at his father. Kingsburgh's look was full of sorrow.

'Aye, Flora too. She's General Campbell's prisoner. I saw her on board the *Furnace*.'

'*Furnace*?' Allan gasped. 'Isn't that captained by the notorious Ferguson?'

This seemed to agitate his father. 'I had no choice – I had to tell him everything – he threatened to burn down Kingsburgh House and butcher our cattle. I couldn't see your mother turned out like a tinker, could I?'

'Of course not,' Allan assured. He knew all too well that the Redcoats' threats of reprisals were not mere words of terror. 'You were put in an impossible position.'

'It's me who has put Sir Alexander in an impossible position,' said Kingsburgh, his voice wretched. 'I was supposed to be helping him capture the Prince and hand him over to Cumberland – now my chief has to come up with reasons why I shouldn't be hanged at once.'

'I'll speak with Sir Alexander,' Allan said, 'and do all I can to help.' He gripped his father's shoulders. 'I will not let you rot in here – and I'll not see you hanged. They'll have to deal with me first.'

Kingsburgh's eyes glistened. 'Every day of your life you've made me proud, Allan Og. I know you will take good care of the family now that I can't.'

'You will be home soon,' Allan encouraged. 'Sir Alexander will see to that.'

'What can one man do against a government intent on laying waste to our people and our ways? I saw the devastation as we rode from Skye. It matters not if we supported the Prince or the Hanoverians – our treatment is the same.'

Allan was chilled by his father's bleak words; he had never heard him so pessimistic. He tried to reassure him that now Cumberland had gone south, the military would quietly release him.

The gaoler warned him there was a change of guard due. As he made to leave, Allan asked, 'what is to become of General Campbell's prisoners?'

Kingsburgh said in a leaden voice, 'if Ferguson is to be believed, they are all to be shipped to England – to the Tower of London – and put on trial.'

Chapter 41

On board the Furnace, off Skye

Foul weather and north-westerly gales kept Flora confined to her tiny cabin feeling sick and wretched. There was far too much time to dwell on her imprisonment and her fears for the future. Ferguson had kept his distance since the General had come aboard but he still took delight in needling her with cruel comments when they passed on deck.

'Enjoy the fresh air while you can – they say the air in the Tower of London can be cut with a knife. Still you won't be worried by that for long. I wonder if they'll hang you like a commoner or treat you like gentry – seeing as how you all think you're so royal. Yes, they might decide on the axe. Quicker death and it won't take long to cut through that pretty, slender neck of yours.'

Flora tried to ignore his jibes, feigning indifference, but during the long hours of the night his words came back and her mind filled with bloody horrors.

When the weather cleared, she found that they were at Glenelg and taking on more prisoners. The sailor who brought her meals told her the newly captured were from South Uist.

'Some of your lot,' he gave a toothless smile.

Flora worried about who they might be and was Neil one of them? Two days later, the General summoned Flora into his cabin. Her legs nearly gave way as she recognised a second man.

'Angus?' She stumbled towards her brother and he caught her in his arms.

'Florrie,' he hugged her tight.

She burst into tears. 'Not you too?'

Gently he held her away and steered her into a chair.

'Milton is to be released,' said General Campbell. 'He has satisfied me that he never did intend to take up arms to fight for the rebels – even though put under pressure by the Pretender and by young Clanranald to do so.'

Flora felt faint with relief. 'I'm thankful to hear it.'

'He has also persuaded me to let you visit your mother one last time. We are anchored off Armadale.'

Flora's eyes widened. Angus nodded that it was true. 'I'm to accompany you.'

'That's wonderful–'

'But,' warned the General, 'you are to be under armed guard and must promise not to speak Gaelic to your family. It appears that your stepfather is not at home so you'll be saved from his scheming. However, if you break my trust and attempt escape, your brother will be re-arrested and I will show no mercy on the rest of your family. Do I make myself clear, Miss MacDonald?'

'Perfectly,' said Flora, meeting his assessing gaze.

'Florrie!' her mother screamed at sight of her daughter running into Armadale farmhouse. They flung their arms around each other. When Angus followed, Marion had to be helped to a chair to recover from the shock. The appearance of four marines dispelled Marion's first wild excitement that Flora had been released.

Flora's half-siblings rushed around her and demanded to know what life on the ship was like, but the officer in charge shouted at them.

'No speaking in Erse – English only or I take her back now.'

The conversation was stilted, each frustrated that they could not really say what they wanted or exchange real news. Angus talked about Pen and baby Angie, until the officer grew bored with their conversation and wandered to the door. Flora saw her chance to ask about her stepfather.

'Is the one-eyed herdsman well?' she asked cautiously.

'Yes. He is off to the shieling to see to the lame bull,' Marion said, 'the one with the injured hoof.'

Flora nodded, knowing this was code for saying that Hugh was looking after Donald Roy – perhaps had joined him in hiding.

'I'm sorry to miss him,' said Flora, 'but it's more healthy for the bull to keep in the high pastures at this time of year.' She kept her voice light. 'Have you heard from the drover who passed this way last month? The one with the red bullock that would fetch a good price at market.'

Marion, knowing that she referred to Neil and the Prince, glanced at the officer's back and shook her head with a smile. 'Nothing. They must be far from here by now.'

Her mother delayed the soldiers by inviting them to eat. Janet appeared from the kitchen with freshly toasted oatcakes and bowls of creamy flummery, thick wedges of cheese and crowdie. Flora was touched by the old cook's hurried attempts to give her the food that she loved, yet the desolation that she was soon to be returned to captivity on board the *Furnace* made it hard to eat a mouthful.

When the officer ordered that it was time to leave, Marion insisted on looking out fresh clothes for her daughter.

'And you must have a maid with you. You cannot be expected to fend for yourself or have sailors do your washing.'

'I'd like to take Katie if she'd come,' said Flora. As her maid spoke no English she could not warn her that her father Ronald Oar was a prisoner on board but Flora thought it would do his morale good if he caught a glimpse of his daughter. Flora also suspected that Katie was the only maid who would have the courage to go with her.

At once, loyal Katie agreed to go with her mistress.

The officer grumbled. 'I'm not authorised to take anyone else on board.'

Marion berated him. 'Look at the state of my daughter's clothes! She's a descendent of the Lord of the Isles. The very least General Campbell can do is to see that she is looked after like one of his own class and the very least she needs is her own maid. I'll come and tell him myself.'

'There's no need for that,' the officer relented. 'We'll take the girl. But it's up to the General if she stays on board or not.'

Marion and her children followed Flora and Katie down to the shore, Angus carrying a bag of clothing. Flora steeled herself to be brave and not show how much her heart ached at leaving them. She tenderly kissed her sisters, Annabella and Tibby, and hugged her brothers. Sorley clung on to her and Magnus burst into tears. Flora squeezed them to her and kissed their heads.

'Take care of each other, won't you?' she smiled at them tenderly. 'No fighting.'

At the moment of parting, Marion broke down sobbing. 'May God go with you, my beloved daughter! I will pray for you always.'

There were so many things they wanted to say to each other but did not have the time or the words.

'You must not worry about me, dearest Mother,' Flora said through a blur of tears, 'I have done nothing wrong in the eyes of God so perhaps my captors will be merciful. But I will bear whatever I must. I will always be proud to be a MacDonald of Balivanich and Milton – and to be your daughter.'

They clung to each other until Angus stepped forward and gently pulled his mother away.

'It's time to let Florrie go.' He helped his sister into the rowing boat and gave her hands a squeeze of encouragement before letting go.

Flora thought her heart would break at the sight of her family on the shingle weeping and huddled together around Marion, comforting each other. She stood in the boat as it pulled away, gazing back at the rocky beach, the green pastures and the farmhouse beyond. In the distance she could see the slated roof of Armadale House peeping out of its cloak of tall ash and birch trees. The tang of peat smoke and the bellow of cattle carried on the breeze. It all seemed so normal – this last sight of Armadale – apart from the forlorn group on the shore watching her go.

***

Within hours, the ship was pulling anchor and sailing south to join a convoy of other naval ships collecting prisoners. Flora was numbed to it all; completely overwhelmed by the enormity of leaving Skye and her family without any real hope of seeing them again. She could not even find words to speak to Katie.

Then, as they pushed out into open sea they heard a familiar sound; the rhythmic singing of rowers. It was muffled and indistinct but Flora knew it was coming from the prisoners in the hold; they were keeping up their spirits with their ancient Gaelic songs.

A sob rose up in her throat. Instinctively, Flora and Katie reached out and clung together.

'Sing, Katie!' Flora said in defiance. 'Sing at the top of your voice.'

In the confines of the cabin, they stamped their feet in time and sang along until they were hoarse. Even the ship itself seemed to rise and dip to their Gaelic chanting, as it took them away from the world that they knew towards a fearful future.

Chapter 42

Leith, Edinburgh, November 1746

Flora knew from the activity on board that the crew were preparing for something. Rigging was being tested and supplies brought on board; a series of rowing boats was to-ing and fro-ing across the choppy grey water to Leith harbour.

She peered through the porthole from her cabin at the distant warehouses and seamen's cottages, as the ship rocked from side to side. After four months of living on the sea, she hardly noticed the listing or creaking, though Katie had never got used to it and was often seasick even in the shelter of the bay.

It was four months since they had last stood on land. Even though they had been transferred to a larger frigate, the *Eltham*, and then to the *Bridgewater* with its kindly naval commander, Commodore Smith, Flora and Katie had longed to feel the earth beneath their feet. It had taken two months of sailing – stopping at length at Orkney to pick up more prisoners and witnesses – to reach Edinburgh.

Here they had been anchored for nearly two months, confined to the ship, with tantalising glimpses of the ancient city in the distance; impossibly tall houses wreathed in smoke and a stark castle clinging to a rocky crag. Flora had given up asking what was to become of her. No one – least of all the fatherly Commodore – seemed to know what to do with their notorious female prisoner who had rapidly become a source of curiosity.

Flora knew her captor must now regret his weakness in allowing her to have contact with the world beyond. Lady Bruce, a powerful grand dame of Scottish society who lived in Leith Citadel, a converted mill, had begged permission to come aboard with warm clothes along with needles, thread and material to make more.

'The poor girl must have something industrious to keep her occupied,' she had insisted.

Flora had been deeply touched and grateful. 'The days drag terribly and I hate being idle – this is the best present I've ever had.' At once, she set to sewing clothes for herself and Katie.

Lady Bruce returned with a Bible to read and writing paper and pen. Flora was delighted with her company, though embarrassed at her lack of letter writing skills when she attempted to sit and write to her mother.

Her important visitor was soon bringing her well-to-do friends who made little secret of their admiration for the Prince, and pressed Flora for details about him.

'What a brave lassie you are,' Lady Cochrane cried, as Flora retold her story for the umpteenth time. 'It would be a stain on the nation if they were to carry out your ...' She waved her hands in the air, unable to speak the word execution.

Her friends tutted and shook their fans with vigorous disapproval.

It was from Lady Bruce that Flora first learned that the Prince had got away safely to France. He had slipped Cumberland's net, and been rescued by a French vessel at the end of September, although news did not filter back to Edinburgh until October. Flora was gladdened by the news – she and Katie did a jig in celebration – and she hoped that Neil had got safely away too. Later however, she had time to ponder that Cumberland and the Government might be all the more vindictive to the other Jacobite prisoners for being outwitted by the Prince.

As October wore on, the number grew of visitors rowing out to see her.

'You have more admirers among the ladies of Edinburgh,' teased Commodore Smith, 'than the Pretender ever did.'

Articles about Flora appeared in the broadsheets. She was hailed as a tragic heroine, affectionately named 'that Jacobite lass' and every detail of her appearance and manners were scrutinised. The sophisticated ladies of the Lowlands were astonished at her genteel manners.

'She speaks English without an Erse accent,' they reported, 'and reads books.'

'She dances with such ladylike steps.'

'Miss MacDonald's singing would grace any Edinburgh salon – and they say she plays the spinet too. Such accomplishments for a girl from the far islands.'

'Quite astonishing!'

'And she knows how to behave at the tea table.'

'Well they say that Lord Eglinton's daughter – the one who married that MacDonald chief – taught her tea table etiquette.'

Flora was baffled and overwhelmed at the attention she attracted but accepted their patronising comments and curiosity with good grace – even welcomed them for keeping fearful thoughts at bay – but knew that they could not prevent the inevitable.

As she watched the preparations for sailing, Flora grew tense. When Commodore Smith sent for her later that day, his news came as no surprise.

'We sail for London on tomorrow's tide. We'll be at sea a couple of weeks. I'll try to make your voyage as comfortable as possible,' he said, 'but I have no authority over the weather, I'm afraid.'

Flora swallowed down panic. There would be no more visitors bearing gifts and gossip. Soon she would be saying goodbye to Scotland for good.

'You and your men have been very kind to me, Sir,' Flora said, 'and for that I am truly grateful. I wonder if I could ask one more favour.'

'Ask away,' he nodded.

'My maid Katie is not up to such a voyage – she gets sick at sea and, worse, she is sick at heart. She pines for the islands. I would be indebted to you, sir, if you would send her safely back to Skye.' Flora fished in her pocket and drew out a velvet purse.

'Lady Bruce kindly gave me some money to buy some comforts should I need them. I'd like you to buy Katie protection on the road north.'

229

He hesitated. 'But you will have need of her in London too,' the Commodore blustered. 'You must not give up hope that things will turn out well for you.'

'I will miss her company,' Flora said, 'but I would be happier thinking of her back at Armadale being a comfort to my mother.'

He gave her a sorrowful look. 'Of course, I will arrange it, if that is what you wish, Miss MacDonald.'

'It is,' said Flora, 'and thank you.'

They exchanged smiles. Flora went back to her cabin and steeled herself to part with her faithful maid – the last physical link she had with home.

Chapter 43

London, December 1746

The ship sat lolling in the estuary for days while messages were sent back and forth about the fate of the prisoners. The Commodore, via the Admiralty, petitioned the Secretary of State to have Flora treated with respect and housed quickly in London and not transferred to another prison ship or any of the common prisons.

On a bitingly cold day of raw winds and sleet, Flora was taken off the *Bridgewater* and rowed up a wide river. Despite her fear, she was awe-struck at the buildings crowded on the riverbanks; church spires, palace roofs and labyrinths of streets in every direction. On unsteady legs, that had walked no further than a cramped deck in months, Flora was taken under armed guard towards a vast fortress. Her heart pounded. She didn't need telling that this was the notorious Tower.

Suddenly, a huge black bird swooped in front, cawing noisily. Flora lost her balance and fell onto frozen mud. Looking up, she gasped in horror. Above her, two human heads were impaled on spikes; the raven flapped around one and pecked its eyes. Flora retched.

One of the guards hauled her up and brusquely pushed her forward. 'That's them rebel lords – bloody Scotch traitors – chopping their heads off was too good for them, if you ask me.'

Flora stumbled on, unable to rid her mind of the grisly sight. As the gate clanged behind her, she fought down her panic and forced down the scream of terror in her throat.

***

Flora was shoved into a low-ceilinged room and the door locked behind her.

'Florrie!' a voice croaked in the gloom.

As she peered, a woman rose and threw out her arms.

'Lady Clan?' Flora gasped. 'Can it be you?'

'Aye, dearie, it is.'

The two women fell into each other's arms and wept. Huddled together on a hard bench, shivering with cold, they told each other all that had happened since they had parted on the shore at Benbecula that fateful June evening.

'Flora, I am so sorry that I agreed to you being a part of the plan. That it should have come to this …'

'Don't be,' Flora insisted, 'I would do it again if asked. I draw comfort from knowing that we got the Prince safely away to France.'

Lady Clan hugged her gratefully. 'I could not be more proud of you if you were my own daughter.' Then Peggi MacLeod wept loudly to think how she might never see her own children again.

231

After a while, Flora whispered, 'What will happen to us now? I saw those terrible heads hung out for all to see.'

'The poor Dukes Balmerino and Kilmarnock,' shuddered Lady Clan. 'I met them both in Edinburgh as a young woman. And they accuse us Gaels of barbarism!'

'Is that what they intend doing with us all?'

'I cannot say,' Lady Clan fretted. 'I just wish I could see my husband – and I worry so for my darling Ranald Og. He didn't get away with the Prince – Ferguson took great pleasure in telling me how he was intent on hunting him down.'

'Then he is still free,' Flora comforted, 'else you would have heard. Now winter's set in, they'll not go searching till the spring.'

Lady Clan squeezed her hand. 'You're a kind lassie. I thank the saints that you have been sent to keep me company.'

***

Tense days followed. Their gaolers told them gleefully that Lord Derwentwater's head had joined the other traitors on the walls of the Tower.

One morning, they were abruptly awoken and herded out of the room. The women clung to each other, fearful of what would be done to them. But out in the freezing, dank courtyard they were wrenched apart.

'Please let us stay together!' Flora pleaded. But the guards ignored her and refused to tell her anything.

As she was bundled onto the back of a cart, she heard Lady Clan cry out, 'stay strong Flora of Milton and remember you are a proud MacDonald!'

Numbly, Flora was taken from the stark fortress in a cart that bumped across cobbles. Was she being taken to court? Tightly packed houses loomed over her. Even in the cold, a rank stench rose from open drains. As she was led through a maze of streets – how could people bear to live so crowded together? – Flora craned for a glimpse of the sky beyond. If she were to die soon, she wanted to see the sky and imagine her beloved family existing under it far away to the north. But a blanket of wood smoke hung over the city as thick as that inside a Hebridean thatched cottage and hid the heavens from her.

The cart stopped outside a narrow house. Perplexed, Flora was hauled out and handed over to a small wiry man in a Redcoat army jacket who introduced himself as Mr Dick. He was an army messenger who was now making money by housing prisoners.

'You've made quite a name for yourself,' he told Flora with a smirk of admiration. 'London newspapers are already full of your exploits. I can charge quite a bit for keeping you locked up here; six shillings and eight pence a day. Not ideal for you, maybe, but a mile better than the Tower, eh?'

'B-but I can't afford to pay you anything like that,' Flora stuttered.

232

'Well it appears your supporters can,' Dick snorted.

'My supporters?'

'The ladies of London who have more money than sense. Lady Primrose, the Viscount's widow, has guaranteed payment. Come on, there are others here you'll no doubt know – all jabbering away in Erse.' He led the way in, chattering non-stop as he ushered her up three flights of stairs. 'Can't let you go out but you can keep each other company. I was up your way during the rebellion – took messages from the Duke of Newcastle to Cumberland – 'Sweet William' they nicknamed him – nothing sweet about his temper I say. Fort Augustus – that's where he was. Saw your MacDonald chief ride in.'

'Sir Alexander?' Flora asked in astonishment.

'Yes, seemed a dignified sort. Rode in with a special prisoner – set the Duke off like a firework. Shame about that gent, I must say. On his way to London too.'

'Who was?'

'Here we are then.' He opened a tiny door into the eaves of the roof. 'You've got the garret room being the only woman but you can join the gentlemen in the parlour downstairs for meals.'

'Which gentlemen?'

'Ones that can afford to pay, that's who.'

Even Flora had to stoop to enter the attic room and could not stand upright. There was a straw mattress with a grubby blanket in the middle of the room, a chair under a tiny window and a pail in the corner. Flora's spirits plunged. She almost wished herself back in the Tower; at least there she had Lady Clan.

'Can I join the others now?' she asked before Mr Dick retreated.

He shrugged. 'If you want. Follow me.'

The murmur of male voices ceased as Mr Dick opened the door to the parlour and ushered her in. A group of men sat around a tiny table playing cards by a smoky fire.

The first face she recognised was that of the handsome cheerful Captain Malcolm MacLeod.

'Miss Flora?' he cried, leaping to his feet. 'What a sight to gladden the heart!'

He came forward to greet her. The others crowded around; her chief Clanranald looked gaunt but pleased to see her, while bearded Aeneas – a cousin on her father's side whom she hadn't seen since she was a child – kissed her hand. They introduced her to a Dr John Burton, an older man with a shock of grey hair who came from York.

'The good doctor is a worthy companion of your chief,' Malcolm teased in English, 'for all he's a *Sassenach*.'

They brought her to the table, sat her down and poured her a glass of tepid stewed tea. Clanranald was eager for news of his wife.

'They've told me we aren't allowed to be together,' he said with a harrowed look. 'I miss her more than anything.'

'She's in great good heart,' Flora said, 'shouting encouragement when we parted.'

'Sounds like my Peggi,' he said tearfully.

They swapped stories of their capture and their prison ships. Malcolm told her in hushed tones about ferrying the Prince from Raasay and getting him across Skye to the Mackinnons.

'The Laird has been taken too – as has Kingsburgh.'

'I know,' said Flora, 'I saw him briefly on board the *Furnace*.'

'It's thanks to Sir Alexander that his chamberlain is imprisoned in Edinburgh and not brought to London,' said her cousin Aeneas, 'he'll have a better chance of escaping execution there away from the Hanoverian persecutors.'

Malcolm threw him an angry look.

'I'm sorry, I didn't mean to make you anxious Flora,' Aeneas said quickly. 'As a woman, I'm sure your case will be different.'

'Perhaps,' Flora said, her stomach knotting once more. 'But I doubt Sir Alexander will be able to speak up for me – Lady Margaret has already painted me as the villain in the escape plot.'

The men exchanged uncomfortable looks.

'What is it? Has something else happened?'

No one spoke. Malcolm nodded at Clanranald.

'You should be the one to tell her, sir.'

Clanranald cleared his throat. Tears brimmed in his eyes. 'We got news a few days ago. Sir Alexander is dead.'

Flora was stunned.

'He took ill suddenly at Glenelg three weeks ago – pleurisy took him in a day – or so young Kingsburgh reported.'

'Allan?' Flora whispered.

'He was travelling with him. By all accounts he is in black mourning for his chief. They were practically like brothers – brought up together.'

'Yes,' Flora said, her heart twisting, 'Allan was devoted to him.' She could not believe that the youthful vigorous chief could be taken so cruelly. 'Lady Margaret will be devastated.'

She looked at their unhappy faces; the tears trickling down Clanranald's leathery cheeks.

'We hear,' said Malcolm, 'that Lady Sleat is inconsolable.'

'And bitter at Kingsburgh,' said Aeneas.

'Why?' Flora was baffled. 'She holds him in high regard.'

'Not since he got embroiled in the Prince's escape and got arrested,' said Malcolm. 'She blames him for her husband's death – for Sir Alexander riding all over the Highlands in terrible weather trying to secure Kingsburgh's release.'

'Sir Alexander and Allan were on their way to London to plead again for Kingsburgh's life,' said Aeneas.

'Allan was coming to London too?' Flora felt her heart lurch. How it would have comforted her to see him – to hear his teasing Highland voice

234

– and tell him how sorry she was to have brought such trouble to Kingsburgh's door.

The sudden aching void she felt inside took her quite by surprise. Was it just the shock of hearing of the chief's death? Flora knew it wasn't. During the long months of worry and loneliness at sea she had buried her feelings for Allan. Now the thought of him so bereft – his father under sentence of death and his beloved chief dead – made Flora desolate.

She bowed her head as emotion convulsed her body and she broke down weeping. Strong arms came around her shoulders and hands patted her back in comfort.

Chapter 44

London, 1747

Flora and her imprisoned companions existed in a state of limbo all winter. Tense weeks of inactivity and being confined together at close quarters frayed their nerves. Aeneas and Malcolm argued over old clan squabbles; Clanranald grew silent and morose, suffering from chest infections and pining for Lady Clan who was housed with a different messenger. Even the mild-tempered Dr Burton lashed out angrily when teased about his being too English and not joining in their singsongs and drinking.

'Why should I join in when you're always speaking in Erse? I know you just do it so that you can talk about me and say unkind things!'

It was Flora who always intervened and calmed tempers.

'We never talk about you in Gaelic,' she assured him, 'but it comforts us to speak in our native tongue – it makes us feel nearer to home. If you would rather we didn't then we shan't.'

Dr Burton was mollified. 'Of course you mustn't just speak English on my account. Forgive me. I can understand how much you are missing home and your families. I long for my dear wife Lucinda.'

'Tell me about her,' Flora encouraged.

Over the months in captivity she grew fond of the gentle doctor, his love of learning and his quiet sense of justice. He talked wistfully of his home city of York with its ancient walls surrounded by green meadows, proud of its beautiful minster which, he explained to a curious Flora, was a vast church.

Yet Flora felt closest to Malcolm, not only because they had been friends in an earlier happier time, but because they shared a special bond of comradeship; both of them had been crucial to the Prince's escape.

As spring came, they found their incarceration all the more intolerable. They were used to a life lived outdoors, to open skies, to walking and riding for miles. Even Aeneas, the Prince's banker, who had known city life in Paris, railed against their endless captivity.

'I wish they'd just come and take me and be done with it,' he cried. 'Losing my head can't be greater torture than losing my mind in this hovel of a place!'

The court trials of the rebels dragged on into the spring. The mood in London grew ugly against both Jacobites and Scots in general. Anyone with a Scottish accent was spat at in the street as a traitor. From newspapers Mr Dick's prisoners learned that Highland dress and tartan were banned, along with the playing of bagpipes and the carrying of weapons. Chiefs were being stripped of their powers to hold courts of law and dispense justice over their people.

In the fuggy parlour the men debated angrily over the measures.

'They want to destroy our way of life altogether,' Malcolm fumed.

'The Hanoverians are the traitors not us,' said Aeneas, 'they are punishing all Highlanders.'

'They'll not be happy till they've wiped Gaeldom from the face of the earth,' wheezed Clanranald.

In early April, Mr Dick told them that Lord Lovat, one of the leading Highland Jacobites, had finally been caught and swiftly executed.

The friends were stunned. Malcolm stood up, tears in his eyes.

'His mother was a MacLeod,' he said, 'a kinswoman of mine.'

He left the room to be alone. The capture of Lovat, after months of evading government troops, set them all worrying anew about their kinsmen and friends still in hiding.

A week later, London erupted in an orgy of anti-Jacobite outpouring. From the attic, Flora heard the sound of gunfire and looked out of the tiny window to see flames leaping on a pyre in the distance. Unjamming the window she heard a mob below shouting, 'Down with the Scotch!' and 'Long live the King!'

She ran down to the parlour.

'London's on fire! Are we under attack?'

Mr Dick hurried in and lit a lamp in the window. 'Don't be alarmed but best if you go to your beds and stay there quietly.'

'What's happening, man?' Malcolm demanded. 'Can't you see how you frighten Miss MacDonald?'

'They're celebrating the anniversary of Culloden, sir. I'm taking my girls out to see the bonfires and fireworks. But I'd thank you to stay away from the window – it's getting lively out there and I don't want my windows putting in. A lamp shows that we're loyal supporters of the King.'

When he'd gone, locking the house and leaving the door guarded, they sat in silence listening to the frenzied shouting and singing going on in the street.

'A year to the day,' sighed Dr Burton.

'They'll hate us even more after this,' Clanranald said bleakly.

Flora saw that Malcolm was too overcome to speak, haunted by memories of defeat and slaughter. She began to sing a Gaelic lullaby; so quietly at first that it could hardly be heard over the noise from outside. Then it grew in strength until her voice filled the room; a song not of war but of cows being milked and a father returning from the mountain and a mother keeping watch over her sleeping baby. The words seemed to wrap around the men like a comforting plaid, soothing and calming.

When it came to an end, Flora sat with her hands in her lap thinking of home and felt strangely at peace. She would accept whatever was her fate without complaint. They might keep her locked up for years or take her life, but they would never be able to destroy her thoughts, her love of her people and homeland, her spirit that kept her connected to them no matter how great their separation.

Malcolm stood and saluted her. Then he turned to the others and began to sing a rousing Jacobite song that Flora had last heard when the Prince sang it on the boat to Skye.

Soon they were all joining in, raising the roof with their singing, and not caring who heard them. They were still singing when Mr Dick returned, rebuking them for their defiance and chasing them all to bed.

***

Shortly after this, Mr Dick came seeking Flora in a panic.

You're to receive a royal visitor,' he gabbled, chasing the men from the parlour.

'Not Cumberland?' Malcolm cried. 'If it's that devil, I'm staying to defend her.'

'Not the Duke,' said Dick, his eyes feverish with excitement, 'but Prince Frederick himself. Just think of it; the Prince of Wales coming to my humble home!'

Flora hardly had time to take in what was happening before a carriage drew up in front of the house and there was a frantic scrambling of servants and equerries in the hallway.

In swept Prince Frederick, a tall man with a fashionably short wig and expensive clothes. For a heartbeat, he reminded Flora of his distant cousin Prince Charles; the high forehead, the lively eyes and the interested smile. But then he spoke her name and the likeness was gone. Flora curtsied politely, trying to hide her alarm. What could he possibly want with her?

A servant brought a chair for him to sit on.

'Please, Miss MacDonald, sit with me,' said Prince Frederick, gesturing for her to join him.

Flora sat straight-backed, hands clasped in her lap, waiting. He stared at her.

'You're very small for someone who's made such a stir. I half expected some tall goddess of the hunt with golden bow and arrows – a pagan princess.'

Flora was nonplussed. 'I believe, Your Highness, that we pagans are no longer allowed to bear arms.'

His prominent eyes bulged. Suddenly he laughed. 'An impudent remark, Madam, but I like a woman with spirit. Tell me about your adventures. I have read pamphlets about you – the ladies of the court talk of little else.'

Flora hesitated. Was this some trick of the government to get her to talk unguardedly about those who were still at large; her stepfather or Donald Roy or Neil? She did not want unwittingly to be a witness against her own kind.

'I think the words they write about me are exaggerated, Sir. I have always led a quiet life and done little that is out of the ordinary.'

'Come, come,' he looked irritated. 'Dressing a foreign prince in women's clothing and spiriting him across the sea under the noses of my father's military, is hardly ordinary. It is a feat of great daring – and a treasonable one. Do you deny that you did such a thing?'

'I cannot deny it, Your Highness. I have already confessed my part in Prince Charles's rescue.'

'You don't seem in the least contrite,' he scrutinised her. 'This is your chance to throw yourself at my feet, begging for mercy and forgiveness for your actions. Do you not understand you are in the presence of the second most powerful man in England?'

'I seek no forgiveness, Sir,' Flora said quietly, meeting his look. 'I am prepared to pay the price for what I did.'

'Why risk your life with these other rebels? I can see you are not like them. You are a gentlewoman of some breeding and you speak English well. What possessed you to assist this Pretender? He's a wicked rebellious man who wished to take my father's throne by force – and rob me of my right to be king too.'

Flora saw the flush of indignation in his florid face. Yet she sensed that his protesting was play-acting. She had heard how King George and Prince Frederick were estranged and could barely speak to each other. He was here out of curiosity not to berate her for disloyalty to the King.

'I had no wish to be involved in any rebellion, Your Highness. I didn't see it as taking sides. When I was brought to the man you call the Pretender, I found a poor wretched soul living in great hardship – ill and desperate. My heart went out to him – not as a prince but as a fellow being.' She fixed him with a steady gaze. 'Sir, I would have done the same for any man in such a condition. I would have done the same for you had you been in that cold wet bothy.'

He gave her a long hard look. Flora was astonished to see his eyes glint with unexpected tears. Prince Frederick nodded and cleared his throat.

'Tell me more about him. What is he like?'

They talked for half an hour. He seemed eager to know all about her and life in the remotest part of the kingdom. Flora warmed to him, once he had forgotten to be regal and pompous. She felt he was genuinely interested in life beyond London and the gossip of the court. Perhaps one day he would make a good king.

Before he left, he asked, 'Tell me, Miss MacDonald; are you well treated here?'

'Mr Dick is a fair man,' she replied, 'and the conditions tolerable.'

'You must say if there is anything you would like to make your stay here more comfortable. You will tell Mr Dick and it shall be yours. I will personally enquire after your wellbeing. You have impressed me very much with your honesty and courage, Madam.'

'There is one thing, Your Highness,' Flora said, 'that would make such a difference to our spirits here.'

'Go on.'

'To be allowed to take the air. We island people crave the feel of the earth beneath our feet. Would it be possible to be taken to one of your parks? Or if not, then to Lady Primrose's house where we could sit a while in her garden?' She could not keep the yearning out of her voice. 'I ask this for my fellow prisoners too – and for Lady Clanranald who I hear has been poorly with the ague in confinement. It would be better than any material comforts to be allowed to see my dear friend.'

'For your own safety,' warned Prince Frederick, 'it would be better that you stay here and do not excite the crowd. There is still bad feeling against you Erse-speakers.'

'We would risk that for a lungful of fresh air,' Flora smiled.

He grunted. 'Fresh it may not be, Madam, but I don't doubt that you are brave enough to risk it.'

***

Word soon spread about the Prince of Wales's daring visit to the most celebrated of the Jacobite rebels. As Flora's fame grew, there was a subtle change in public opinion; a shifting away from criticism of the Scots prisoners to condemnation of Cumberland's bloodthirsty revenge and barbarity towards innocent Highland families. After a year of persecution and blood-letting, the country was sickened by stories of brutality and wanted no more.

Flora and her friends were allowed to make visits under guard to the house of sympathisers such as Lady Primrose who had taken it upon herself to champion Flora's case. It was as much the attention of this young and spirited widow as that of Prince Frederick, that brought the members of London society flocking to meet Flora whenever she was allowed a few hours beyond the confines of Mr Dick's.

Flora took along Mr Dick's two daughters whom she had befriended over the winter – they reminded her of Annabella and Tibby – knowing that they would enjoy an outing to grand Essex Street too. She was overjoyed to find Lady Clan also being entertained by Lady Primrose. The women embraced, tearful at seeing each other again. Flora was shocked to see how thin her chief's wife had become, yet Lady Clan was just as vivacious as ever.

'Long may we continue to meet at the Primrose tea table rather than the scaffold, dear lassie,' Peggi MacLeod joked.

***

The announcement came abruptly at the beginning of July. Mr Dick came tearing in waving a newspaper.

'He's gone and done it. It's here in print.'

'What is?' Malcolm stood up in alarm. 'Who has done what?'

'The King – he's signed an amnesty for all you rebels.'

'An Amnesty?' Aeneas repeated, snatching the paper from their gaoler.

They all stared at him, holding their breath. He frowned. 'We have to petition the King for our freedom.'

240

'Give it to me,' Malcolm said, reading it quickly. 'It's a formality.' His face broke into a grin as he punched the air. 'We're not going to be hanged. By God, we're going home with our heads intact!'

The room erupted in shrieks of delight as they hugged each other in disbelief. Clanranald stood shaking and weeping. Flora put her arms around him. She didn't have to say anything; they both knew he was overcome with relief at the thought of being reunited with his beloved Lady Clan.

***

After the initial euphoria died down, they waited impatiently for their applications to be considered. Dr Burton was the first of them to go.

'Come and stay with me and Lucinda on your way north,' he urged Flora. 'I would be honoured to have you as my guest.'

As Flora's case appeared to be taking such a long time to consider, Lady Primrose secured agreement that she could take her to Essex Street and be her guardian in the meantime. Mr Dick grumbled at the loss of earnings but when Flora insisted on still inviting his daughters round to tea, he was quick to wish her well.

To Flora's embarrassment, Lady Primrose revealed how she had been raising a subscription to pay for Flora's return to the Highlands and her future advancement.

'You are a young woman of talent,' her hostess declared, 'I recognise myself in you. I want you to have the chance to improve yourself, Flora, without being dependent on a man for every penny you need. I'm a woman of means and I relish my freedom to spend it how I see fit.'

Flora was astonished at the woman's frankness. She thought how her own mother had railed at her widowed state when Milton had died and all his male kin had gathered to sell off his cattle and possessions, leaving her at the mercy of her brother Archibald and his penny-pinching wife Agnes. It intrigued Flora that not all women depended on husbands for their livelihood and not all widows were sent back to their families to live on charity.

As July wore on, she enjoyed trips to Windsor park with Malcolm and Aeneas, parties at Lady Primrose's and visits to the parlours of other Jacobite sympathisers who were once again feeling safe to socialise together. Flora felt her apprehension grow at leaving London.

She yearned to be free to go north again and be reunited with her family, yet a small part of her was fearful of leaving the close-knit circle of fellow prisoners and supporters with whom she had spent so much time in the past fraught but intense months. She could not pinpoint what it was that caused her unease, yet she knew that nothing would be the same again after the terrible upheavals of the past two years.

Infrequent letters from her mother told her little of consequence; they were cautious notes about her sisters and brothers and life at Armadale, telling her nothing of her stepfather, or Donald Roy or the Kingsburghs.

The main news she had learned was that her half-brother James had got a commission in the Dutch army and gone to Holland, and that Lady Margaret had left Skye and taken her young boys, James and Alexander, with her to Edinburgh, declaring seven year old James too young to be chief.

She listened to the hushed conversations in London salons about the possibility of a return of their Bonnie Prince Charlie.

'He's still the most eligible royal in Europe. They say if he would just renounce his Catholicism, the country would rise up again for him in a trice.'

Flora thought of the hardships being endured in the Highlands and doubted if there was any appetite for further conflict.

Finally, at the beginning of August, Flora was granted her freedom. Lady Primrose insisted she would pay for her young protégé to be transported as far as Edinburgh in a post chaise.

'Can't have you jostled around in a coach for three weeks,' she declared, 'most uncomfortable. And you'll want to get to Edinburgh and your supporters there as quickly as possible. Tell me who you would like as your travelling companion. You can choose any of your fine Highland gentlemen to protect you and I will pay for him too.'

'You are so kind, my lady,' Flora was overcome. She asked Malcolm if he would accompany her north and he seized the chance with delight.

'I would like nothing better than to go north in triumph with you, dear Miss Flora,' he beamed.

Lady Primrose urged them to be cautious on the road. 'I have booked the chaise in the name of Mr Robertson and his young sister. There are still those who would set upon you if they knew you were Jacobites.'

She bade a tender farewell to Flora. 'I will so miss your company, my dear. Life in London will be the duller for your going.'

'You have been like a mother to me,' Flora said tearfully, 'and I can't thank you enough for all you have done – continue to do for me. I could not have endured these past months without your friendship and help.'

'I was pleased and honoured to give it. You are the most noble and courageous young woman I am ever likely to meet – the saviour of our dear Prince.' Lady Primrose smiled. 'I hope you will return to London and visit me some day. Please don't forget you have loyal friends here.'

'I will never forget you,' Flora insisted. 'I thank you with all my heart.'

***

Breaking their journey to Scotland, they rested for two days in York with Dr Burton and his wife who were charming and attentive hosts. For Flora it was like visiting long lost friends; she knew so much about this couple from daily conversations with the doctor when in captivity.

'My husband is keen to record the experiences of those involved in the recent – er – troubles,' confided Lucinda, 'and would very much like to interview you for his journal. Would you consent to having your story written down? He quite understands if you prefer to put it all behind you.'

At first Flora was reluctant; she had grown tired of having to repeat her story endlessly for the entertainment of London society. She had told it so many times that it had become just a form of words as if she had been telling someone else's tale. But it was different with Dr Burton who had shared some of the same hardships and knew what it was like to live with the threat of execution hanging over them.

They spent an afternoon in his study while she re-lived the events of the previous summer – almost a year to the day of her being taken prisoner on Skye – and he patiently wrote it all down. At the end, Flora sat in silence exhausted at the effort but feeling a strange sense of release at having committed the memories to paper.

She would have happily stayed on with the Burtons but Malcolm was restless. He felt an uneasy atmosphere in the city – under the new anti-Scottish laws a piper had recently been hanged for playing his bagpipes – and Malcolm was keen to get north of the border.

Two days later, with a stiff south-easterly breeze at their backs, they were trotting into Edinburgh.

Chapter 45

Edinburgh, January 1748

Flora brought in the New Year with her new friends the Callanders in their cosy apartment off a narrow tenement close next to the High Street. From the parlour window to the north of the ancient city they could see the clearing and drainage work being done to prepare for the new town. Josiah Callander was a merchant and a quiet bookish man; Flora had been companion to his daughter Maggie since taking lodgings there the previous August.

It was the practical Mrs Callander who had recommended the teacher David Beatt to Flora.

'He's a cousin of mine, and if you're serious about taking writing lessons, then you won't find a more patient and diligent teacher of letters. But he's out of the city until the end of September, so if you're in a hurry to travel home, perhaps you should find someone else?'

'No,' Flora had been quick to seize on the delay, 'I won't leave Edinburgh until I've acquired better writing skills – I feel quite inadequate writing to my friends in London – their letters are works of art. I'll wait for Mr Beatt to return from the country.'

She had not meant to stay this long away from the Highlands but her nerve had failed her. To no one – not even her new confidante Maggie – could she say that the main reason was the attitude of the Kingsburghs.

When Allan's father had been released from prison he had not waited in Edinburgh to greet her and Malcolm, although he had known they were on their way there. He had avoided them and instead gone hastily to Skye with Mistress Kingsburgh as soon as he was released. Flora had hidden her hurt at this; at the time she still longed to see people who had lived through the same danger as her with the Prince. And then the hurtful letter from Allan's sister Ann had arrived.

So when Malcolm had made ready to return to the islands in October, Flora had used the writing lessons as an excuse not to go with him.

He sought her out before returning to Raasay. He'd been staying at Leith Citadel with Lady Bruce, basking in the admiration of her Jacobite friends.

'So this is where you've been hiding away. Too good for your old friends, eh?' His rebuke was tempered with a smile.

'Not too good,' Flora had avoided his look, 'just busy. I'm taking lessons in writing and improving my spinet playing and learning French.'

'French? Do you have plans to emigrate?'

'No plans.'

'That's it! You are going to run away and join Prince Charles's court.'

'I'm not,' she had laughed.

'I hear that a certain French-speaking gentleman who now goes by the name of MacDonald is back in Scotland. Have you heard from MacEachen?'

Flora had felt the blood rushing to her cheeks. 'I've had a letter. I believe he is somewhere in the Highlands but coming to Edinburgh soon.'

'Is that why you want to stay here?'

When she did not answer, Malcolm had sat down and taken her hand. 'Flora, come home. Your mother will be anxious to see you. What is stopping you? I can tell there is something the matter. It's not like you to avoid your friends – Lady Bruce and her ladies long to make a fuss of you – and the priest Robert Forbes keeps pressing me to gain an interview with you for his book. He's much piqued that you gave such a long account to Dr Burton yet won't speak to him.'

'I'm so tired of all that,' Flora had protested, withdrawing her hand. 'I don't want their adulation – I'm not the heroine they all want me to be – I never looked for fame.' She'd given a despairing look. How could she make him understand how adrift she felt, belonging nowhere? 'Don't you ever wish that none of this had ever happened – that we could wind back time and be the people we were before the Rising? I don't know who to trust any more. I've heard that Lady Bruce's circle has been infiltrated by a government spy. If I talk to this Forbes, something I say may be used against others. I still have people to protect like my stepfather.'

'And Neil MacEachen?'

'Aye, and Neil. He's the one who warned me.'

Malcolm's gaze had been sorrowful. 'Has he also warned you not to go home? Are you frightened of the reception you might get?'

Flora had nodded and gone to retrieve two letters. One was from Lady Margaret and the other from Kingsburgh's daughter Ann.

'They both blame me for the ills that have befallen their families. I tried to visit Lady Margaret to give my condolences about Sir Alexander but she refused to see me. She said if I hadn't brought the Prince to Monkstadt, Kingsburgh would never have suffered a year in prison and her husband wouldn't have died trying to have him freed. Ann says much the same – how all the Kingsburghs have suffered with her father in prison – how the estates have gone into debt without his stewardship and Allan has had to give up ideas of getting an army commission and going abroad. He resents me for it. I'm to blame for it all, it seems.'

Flora had not said how the criticism from Allan had cut her to the core. She had dreamed of an emotional reunion with him – spent long nights in the dismal prison garret imagining him welcoming her back to the island – telling her how he had missed her and waited for her, rejecting all others. How could she face him now?

'Poor Flora,' Malcolm had swung an arm about her shoulders, 'always taking the cares of the world on your slim shoulders. But they are wrong to add to your burden. You mustn't feel guilty. Kingsburgh had a choice in the matter and he didn't hesitate to do the right thing. Just as you did. You have nothing to be ashamed of. Things will settle down again.'

'Thank you,' she had kissed his cheek with affection.

'And if the MacDonalds insist on turning their backs on you, come and live with us MacLeods,' he had winked. 'So will you travel home with me?'

Flora had shaken her head. 'I'm not ready and I'm not sure where home is any more. When we were in London I longed to be back on Skye. Now that I'm here, I think of going back to London.'

'You can't run away forever, Flora.' Malcolm had saluted her and left.

After that, Flora had thrown herself into her new activities and written to her mother explaining how she was making the most of this opportunity of being in the city and improving herself. Marion had written back giving her blessing. Hugh was once more at home and so her mother was happy again. Flora's guilt at not going home eased a fraction.

She had waited tensely for Neil to appear in Edinburgh but a letter had come in December saying he had been called back to France to take up a commission as lieutenant in the Albany Regiment, a cohort of Scots in the French army. He had sounded as excited and optimistic as ever for the Cause and assured her he would be back in Scotland within the year.

'So what is your New Year's resolution?' Josiah asked, dragging Flora's thoughts back to the present.

'Not to look too far ahead,' Flora answered, 'and to live each day as it comes.'

'That's a bit boring, Flora,' Maggie protested. 'You sound like an old maid.'

'Flora snorted. 'In my twenty-sixth year, many would consider me just that.'

'Well you don't look a day above twenty,' Maggie said. 'We could be twins, couldn't we, Father?'

Her father puffed on his pipe. 'If twins can be both fair and dark,' he pointed out. 'And what do you wish for, daughter?'

'To travel with Flora,' she said eagerly, 'and go west and meet real Highland gentlemen and see the places where Bonny Prince Charlie hid.'

Flora's heart sank. Would she ever be free of her infamous connection?

***

A week later, a surprise visitor, stamped up the stairs to the Callanders' apartment and called out in Gaelic for the daughter of Milton. Flora nearly fainted at the sight of her old friend and neighbour.

'Donald Roy?' she gasped.

'It's me and not my ghost,' he grinned.

She threw her arms around him and burst into tears. Laughing and crying, Flora pulled him inside and while Maggie and Mrs Callander fussed around and plied him with food, Donald Roy told how he had walked from Skye to Edinburgh.

'Testing out my foot,' he claimed, 'and it appears to be in full working order again.'

'But why Edinburgh?' Flora puzzled.

'To give my version of events to Robert Forbes. We've been exchanging letters and he's very keen to have my story.'

Flora sat back and folded her arms. 'I don't see why this Episcopalian priest needs to keep digging up the past. Why can't we just be allowed to get on with our lives in peace?'

'So you haven't been persuaded to talk to him yet?' Donald Roy eyed her.

'Why should I? He's just another of these seekers after notoriety who wants to make money out of others. London was full of such pamphleteers making up stories about me that hardly had a grain of truth in them.'

He raised an eyebrow. 'He's a cultured man and well on the way to being a bishop, so I'm told. Hardly the type to be writing salacious pamphlets. Forbes is a chronicler – he's not interested in publishing – he wants to talk to those who were there and record their history, to give a voice to the side that lost. He was a supporter of the Prince and suffered imprisonment in Stirling Castle and then Edinburgh.'

Flora's interest flickered. 'I didn't know he had been a prisoner.'

'Aye,' Donald Roy said, 'that's where he met Kingsburgh and decided to write things down while still fresh in the mind.'

Flora's stomach churned. What bitter things might Kingsburgh have said about her to Forbes?

'Why don't you come and meet him?' Donald Roy encouraged. 'You don't have to tell him anything, just pay him the courtesy of hearing what he has to say.'

'I would come with you, Flora,' Maggie said at once.

'I will be staying at the Citadel too,' said Donald Roy, 'so if you want to see me again, you must venture to Leith.' He smiled. 'And there is another staying there who would gladly see you.'

'Who is that?'

'Your half-brother James.'

'James is in Leith?' Flora cried. 'I thought he was on the Continent with the Dutch army.'

'He's been sent to Scotland to recruit some more men for the Scots Hollanders. And in the present state of the Highlands,' Donald Roy grunted, 'he shouldn't find any difficulty. The young lads are desperate for commissions.'

Flora was filled with a sudden urge to be with her young brother. They hadn't seen each other since he had marched away as an ensign in the same MacDonald Company as Allan.

'Very well,' said Flora, 'I'll come with you to the Citadel.'

***

Flora's visit to Leith was a turning point. She had an emotional reunion with Lady Bruce – they had not seen each other since her captivity on the *Bridgewater* – who welcomed her like a long lost daughter. The

247

formidable grand dame of the Jacobite ladies would allow no reproof from the others for Flora staying away so long.

She was soon won over by the warmth and sincerity of Robert Forbes and renewed her friendship with Rachel Houston, a young unmarried protégé of Lady Bruce's who had visited and befriended Flora on the prison ship. Above all, she was reunited with her affectionate brother James. They grinned at each other. His fair face had the beginnings of a beard and his boyish figure had broadened at the shoulders. He had grown six inches.

'How grown up you look, Jamie,' she cried.

'And you've turned into a sophisticated Lowland lady in your fancy clothes,' he teased.

'I like living here,' Flora said.

'She's just the same Long Isle lassie under the satin and frills,' Donald Roy declared.

Flora smiled at her friend even though she no longer felt like that person he described at all.

After that evening, she came frequently to the Citadel to see her old friends and to meet with Robert Forbes. She noticed with approval how attentive the priest was to her friend Rachel and hoped something would come of the pair's growing fondness for each other. Not only did Flora answer Robert's many questions on the details of the Prince's escape but she probed him for information on his incarceration in Edinburgh Castle.

'Did Kingsburgh say much about me?' Flora forced herself to ask.

Robert gave his earnest look. 'He didn't say much about any of it – he much preferred to talk about the old days and clan tales. But I've been in correspondence with him and he's agreed to write it down now he's had time to reflect.'

Flora's insides churned. She dreaded what he might record. Would Kingsburgh reinforce Lady Margaret's story that it was all Flora's fault for bringing the Prince to Monkstadt and putting the chief's family and their chamberlain in an impossible position? How easy it would be to take her revenge on them by telling Robert how Lady Margaret had been the one to send her to the Long Isle in the first place; Sleat's wife had almost commanded her to help the Prince and take him supplies. She could say how Lady Sleat had aided the Prince behind her husband's back – she was the one who had put her husband's position in jeopardy – so it was only natural that Flora would bring the Prince to her for safekeeping.

Yet she did not say a word against Lady Margaret; the woman was grieving for her husband and Flora knew how lonely and frightened her former patron must be without him. Lady Sleat's bitter recriminations were the sign of a deeply unhappy woman. As for the Kingsburghs, Flora could not bring herself to say an unkind word against them; they had shown her great kindness and generosity, even if they had later regretted it, and so that is what she told Robert.

As spring came, Flora's spirits revived. She came to terms with her unlooked for status as the country's foremost Jacobite heroine, and grew to enjoy the convivial company at Lady Bruce's home. So many interesting people came and went; she made new friends such as the Maxwells from Dumfriesshire in south-west Scotland, a kindly elderly couple who had lost their daughter to smallpox.

'You are welcome to come and stay with us for as long as you like,' enthused Lady Maxwell. 'If you tire of the town and Edinburgh's east winds – our place is the perfect cure.'

Flora's thoughts turned more and more to returning to the west and the Highlands. As Maggie continued to badger her about a visit to Skye and Flora's own longing to see her family again grew overwhelming, she knew she would have to go sometime that summer. She began to lay plans to go west; first to her cousin Elizabeth in Argyllshire and then to Skye. The idea filled her with equal amounts of excitement and dread.

She decided on a secondary plan to go south in the autumn – York and then London – and wrote to the Burtons and to Lady Primrose to suggest such a visit. She needed to know she had a place of refuge if her visit home proved a disaster and Lady Primrose had kept urging her to return to the capital to see her friends there.

'That's thrilling!' Maggie was full of glee when Flora asked her to be companion to all these visits, and secured the permission of the indulgent Callanders for their daughter to accompany her.

Hearing that her brother James was returning from Skye to Edinburgh at the end of April on his way back to Holland from his recruitment drive, Flora delayed the start of their journey so that she could see him and hear at first-hand how her family and the island were faring.

She and the Callanders were invited to the Citadel for a farewell dinner.

'We shall celebrate your return to the Highlands, my dear,' said Lady Bruce, 'and James's future career in Holland.'

As they arrived at the old windmill and climbed the spiral stairs to the homely circular dining-room, Flora heard the bellow of men's laughter. She hastened her step, picking up her skirts and rushed into the room, breathless to see her half-brother.

'James!' She saw him across the room. Then the broad-set man her brother was speaking to turned around. Flora stopped in her tracks. The jet-black hair, the piercing blue eyes. He stared back at her. She was so shocked to see him that she could not even speak his name. She could not speak at all.

'Miss Milton,' Allan said, with a curt bow.

It was James who came to the rescue and introduced Allan to the Callanders.

'My good friend, Young Kingsburgh, has come in person to the Reverend Forbes to deliver his father's account of Prince Charles's escape.'

Chapter 46

Allan sat across the table from Flora, in a place of honour beside Lady Bruce and with the chattering, flirtatious Maggie Callander on his other side. Allan kept glancing across at Flora but she avoided his look, deep in conversation with James to her left and the priest Forbes to her right.

He was in awe of her beauty, the chestnut hair styled into ringlets with a white Jacobite rose at her creamy brow. Her face was slimmer – the fine-boned features more pronounced – and her pink lips curved into wry smiles as she talked animatedly to all but him. She was dressed in a low-cut blue silk gown which showed off her bosom and kept distracting him from his conversation with Lady Bruce. Only the eyes – a pensive blue-grey under the dark lashes – betrayed any hint of her year in captivity.

He marvelled at her poise and elegance; she was a sophisticated mature young woman in fine clothes and of polished manners, conversing easily with some of Edinburgh's social elite. He struggled to see anything of the old Flora – the easily-blushing, saucy girl with the quick remarks and teasing put-downs – who would have quipped across the table that Maggie oughtn't to believe a word he said and would have demanded to know why he wasn't being brave like her brother and going to join the Scots Hollanders.

His impatience to see Flora again – baffled by her decision not to return to Skye when his father had – was the reason he had volunteered to travel with James to Edinburgh and hand over his father's manuscript in person. But Flora's glittering beauty and air of disdain for him the minute she had swept into the room with a rustle of fine petticoats had rendered him tongue-tied. His stomach was in knots just looking at her, but he could think of nothing that would amuse or entice her into conversation with him. So he drank more claret and forced himself to concentrate on Flora's pretty flaxen-haired friend Maggie, the merchant's daughter, who gazed at him as if her were some god fallen from Mount Olympus.

'I hear you are coming to the Hebrides, Miss Callander,' he smiled. 'Will it be your first visit to those parts?'

'Indeed it will, sir.' Maggie was breathless with excitement. 'I cannot wait to visit your Isle of Skye.'

'I fear you will find it dull compared to the city,' Allan replied.

'Oh but Flora assures me that the entertainment of the chiefs and the Skye nobility are second to none – you have feasts and dancing and sport that last for days at a time.'

'Does she?' Allan flicked a look at Flora but she was studiously ignoring him.

'Flora!' Maggie called for her attention. 'Haven't you told me all about Highland hospitality and how much you eat and drink and make merry?'

Allan saw the colour rise in Flora's cheeks. He had her attention at last.

'Well, yes,' Flora said, 'I've talked of my time in the Sleat household and the parties we had.'

'See!' Maggie grinned.

'That is not the case now,' Allan said. 'Not since our great chief died. We are all still in mourning.' He felt again the pang of loss for Sir Alexander; he had idolised him as a boy and would have gone to the ends of the earth to serve him. He had been a gentle but brave nobleman who loved his people deeply. Allan still felt guilt at having encouraged his chief to make the arduous winter journey to London to plead for his father's life, not realising how exhausted and ill his master was.

He frowned at Flora. 'You will not find much to celebrate when you return.'

'I will be happy just to see my family and friends,' she said with a cool look.

'You've taken your time about it,' he chided.

'I've had my reasons.'

'Flora has been improving herself,' Maggie said. 'And she's the most wonderful companion I could wish for.'

Allan smothered his annoyance at this remark. Why should it matter to him that Flora chose to live among these Lowlanders rather than her own people? His jaw clenched as he strove to be civil.

'So what do you plan to do when you visit Skye, Miss Callander?'

'I've told Flora I want to see all the places that Bonny Prince Charlie went to – the places he hid and where he stayed and nearly got caught and the caves and things – I want to see absolutely everywhere that he skulked – isn't that the word you Highlanders use?'

Allan hid his impatience. Why were these Edinburgh women so obsessed about the Prince who had brought nothing but chaos and destruction to their homeland? But Maggie persisted.

'If I ask really nicely, will you show me where the Prince slept at Kingsburgh?'

'I wasn't there; your special friend knows far more about the royal sleeping arrangements than I do.' Allan drained off his wine and poured more. 'But I can show you the parlour where my mother and sister were threatened with eviction by Captain Ferguson if they didn't say where my father was *skulking*, as we Highlanders say.'

'Oh dear, how terrible.'

'He's teasing you,' Flora said, flashing a warning look at Allan.

'Are you teasing me?' Maggie gave a nervous giggle.

'Of course,' Allan said with a tight smile. 'So Miss Milton, are you going to make a living giving tours of the Prince's escape route?' Allan shot her a look. She didn't reply.

'Flora doesn't need to earn money being a guide,' said Maggie, 'she's a woman of fortune now. Aren't you, Flora? Tell Mr Kingsburgh how your admirers have raised a subscription on your behalf.'

Allan raised his eyebrows.

'That is my business,' Flora said, flushing deeper.

'Quite so,' he said. 'Best not to boast of how you have profited from the rebellion while so many on the island have been ruined by it.'

'That is unkind,' Robert intervened. 'Miss Flora has suffered a terrible year of imprisonment and the threat of the scaffold. It is her courage and good nature that have led to funds being raised on her behalf, not any profiteering on her part.'

Allan felt ashamed at his words and yet riled at the young priest's lecturing him in front of the others.

'I apologise for the slur,' he said, 'but there is great suffering in the islands and it's hard not to be bitter when those of us who did not fight for the Prince are persecuted as if we did.'

'Perhaps if more of you had fought for him,' said Robert, 'then we would all be feasting at Holyrood Palace and the Highlands would not be a wasteland of burnt out ruins.'

Allan thumped the table. 'Don't you dare blame that on us Highlanders!'

'Gentlemen,' Lady Bruce interrupted, 'let us not argue over politics. We are here to honour Flora and wish her well on her journey.'

James stood and proposed a toast to his half-sister. Allan could see that his friend was embarrassed by the wrangling; he cursed himself for drinking too much and being so easily upset. He had not meant to spoil this brief reunion between his former comrade and Flora; to James she was just his adored older sister and her fame counted for little.

Allan joined the men in the toast. Afterwards, he made an effort to be friendly.

'Perhaps I could join you ladies on your journey north? You will need male protection and someone like myself who knows the routes through the Highlands well.'

'That's very kind,' beamed Maggie, 'isn't it Flora?'

'Very,' Flora said. 'But we are not going directly to Skye. I'm taking Miss Callander to visit my cousins at Largie in Argyllshire for a couple of months first. Cousin Aeneas is to accompany us.'

'The banker?' Allan asked.

'Yes, the one who was imprisoned with Flora in London,' said Maggie. 'I'm dying to hear his stories about the Prince – Aeneas MacDonald travelled with Prince Charles and looked after his fighting fund.'

'Well I hope he takes better care of you than he did of the Prince's gold,' Allan grunted.

'Aeneas is an honourable man,' Flora sparked, 'and I resent your insinuation.'

'I'm sure he is,' said Allan. 'I merely meant that the Prince came with such little backing that every penny counted. I hear a lot of it went on feasting and by the end there wasn't enough to pay the men.'

'Whereas those of you in government regiments got well paid for your work,' Robert needled him.

'It was my chief's regiment,' Allan scowled. 'Our loyalty was to him. Isn't that right, James?'

'Allan speaks the truth,' James nodded. 'We would have followed Sir Alexander whichever side he chose to support.'

Lady Bruce rose. 'Ladies, we will leave the gentlemen to their discussion and retire to my chamber for tea and a glass of Madeira. Flora and Maggie have a long journey ahead of them and will not want to be late to bed.'

The men stood. Maggie put a hand on Allan's arm to help her up from her chair.

'I do hope we can come and see you at Kingsburgh,' she smiled.

'You will be very welcome. How long do you intend staying, Miss Callander?'

'A month or so. Flora is keen to get back to London in the autumn while travel is still easy. We're going to go via her friend Dr Burton in York. It'll be my first trip to England and I'm so excited.'

Allan felt winded. 'So you do not intend to stay in Skye?' he frowned at Flora.

She seemed flustered. 'Our plans have not been finalised.'

'But we are going to London, aren't we, Flora?' Maggie looked expectant.

'Probably. We'll see how things go.'

'Of course,' Allan's look was scathing, 'it's always good to have an escape plan. But then, Miss Milton, you are the mistress of such things.'

He felt numb as Flora swept out of the room behind Lady Bruce with no more than a disinterested glance in his direction. Let her go! With her haughty airs and English speech, she was no longer the girl that he had hungered for all these years. He turned to James and clapped an arm around his shoulder.

'Let's fill ourselves full of Jacobite brandy and drink to the Hollanders. I might even change my mind and come with you.' He gave Robert a wary smile. 'Come on Forbes; let's see how well a Jacobite priest can hold his drink against a damned Hanoverian Highlander.'

***

Flora fought back tears as they sat in Lady Bruce's cosy round chamber with a wood fire burning in the grate, keeping the late spring chill at bay. She let Maggie chatter on about their trip to the other women while she tried to bring her emotions under control.

The shock of finding Allan in the Citadel – of seeing his handsome face and his manly figure dressed in best doublet and trews – had completely felled her. How often had she daydreamed about the moment she would see him again, and rehearsed the words of apology she would say to him about his father's imprisonment? He would be understanding and forgiving and full of sympathy for the ordeal she too had endured; he would press her for details and take her cold hands – they were always cold since imprisonment – in his large warm ones and kiss life back into her fingers, into her frozen heart.

But the reality had been quite different. Right from the moment he had called her Miss Milton with that grudging little bow, she knew that the words Ann had written were true; Allan blamed her for his family's ills. Throughout the tortuous dinner his look had been bitter and brooding; it was obvious how much he resented her being the centre of attention. He had likewise been maddened by Maggie letting slip that Flora now had her own money, as if a woman shouldn't have security independent from a man.

Well it wasn't her fault that people had generously provided for her future, and from what James had told her about the stagnating economy on the islands, she would need to be a woman of independent means. She couldn't expect to be kept by her parents when they had to provide for her younger sisters and brothers, or by her brother Angus who now had his own family to look after. It was she who would be able to help them. But she would not be held responsible for all the poor of Skye. Allan and the Kingsburghs had a greater responsibility; they were the family who ran the affairs of the MacDonald lands so if there was hardship on the island then it was their bad management.

The feeling of guilt that Allan had provoked in her, eased with this bleak thought. Let him stew in his own bitterness; she was going to live her life how she pleased. When she had been shipped to London, Flora had been convinced that she would die. She hadn't gone looking for notoriety or thought that what she had done was noble or spectacular, but she had been prepared to take the consequences. She would have died for the Prince and for friends in danger such as Donald Roy and Malcolm MacLeod. Now it was only just sinking in, after all these months, that she was not going to die. She gulped down tears. She was going to live. And by heavens, she was going to enjoy her life!

***

James came to bid her farewell the following morning.

'You look like you've been up all night,' Flora said with a wry smile. 'Head like a bear, I bet?'

'Never try and out-drink a Kingsburgh,' he groaned. 'Allan and Robert were still sharing a punchbowl and arm-wrestling at four in the morning.'

'Boys!' Flora rolled her eyes. She put her arms around him and hugged him. 'Take good care of yourself, Jamie. May God go with you.'

'And with you, dearest Florrie,' he squeezed her tight. 'You will get a warm welcome at Armadale. Mother pretends she's happy that you are being feted around the country but she can't wait to see you.'

'Thank you,' Flora smiled, her eyes prickling.

As he left, he turned on the stair. 'Oh, I nearly forgot. Allan asked me to give you this.' He pulled out a small leather pouch and handed it over.

Flora took it, her heartbeat quickening. Perhaps she had misjudged Allan and this was a peace offering? Hope leapt inside.

'He wasn't making much sense with all the drink,' said James, 'but he said something about you needing this in London. To give it to one of your suitors – the man you wish to marry. Do you have a suitor in London, Florrie?' James smirked.

'No.'

'Oh well,' James shrugged, 'just one of Allan's jokes.'

She watched him clatter down the stairs, wave at the bottom and disappear into the close. Flora felt sick; bereft at his going and at what she held in her hand. She knew what was in the pouch; Allan's mother had told her how Allan had kept it next to his breast.

With fumbling fingers she pulled it from its leather casing. He'd had it mounted in a silver frame; the miniature of her eighteen-year old self painted by Thomas.

Flora felt a sob rise up in her chest. This was no joke. This was Allan rejecting her for good.

Chapter 47

Armadale, Skye, July 1748

Flora ran into her mother's arms like a child, squealing her delight. Marion kissed her and put her hands around Flora's face, as tears streamed down her own.

'Let me look at you, lassie. Your face is too thin. Has Cousin Elizabeth not been feeding you properly? And what's this old plaid you're wearing? Have you not being spending your new money on yourself?'

'Don't fuss,' Flora grinned and introduced her to Maggie.

Annabella, Tibby and their brothers crowded around – shyly at first – worried that Flora might have changed.

'Was it very horrible in prison?' Sorley asked.

'Did they chain you upside down and make you eat rats?' asked Magnus.

'Only on Thursdays,' Flora winked.

Soon they were chattering as normal and pulling her into the house. Annabella and Maggie were instant friends; it did not surprise Flora that her boisterous family took her sociable friend straight to their hearts. Marion and Janet brought out flummery, oatcakes and crowdie to celebrate.

When Hugh came home, he insisted on a lamb being slaughtered and claret brought up from the cellar. Flora marvelled at how his year of living wild on the mountains avoiding arrest, did not seem to have aged him a bit. He was just as vigorous and full of life, his good eye flashing wickedly as he recounted tales of skulking to a wide-eyed, impressionable Maggie.

For days, neighbours and kin from far and wide came calling at Armadale to welcome back Flora and press her to tell of her adventures. Marion and Hugh seemed to enjoy the fuss, prompting their daughter on details of the well-worn tale.

'Tell them what Commodore Smith said to you on board the *Bridgewater*,' beamed Marion, 'about you having the breeding of a royal princess.'

'Flora met Prince Frederick, you know,' Hugh boasted. 'Had him eating out of her hand. Changed public opinion, I'm sure of it. Government didn't dare mistreat the prisoners after the heir to the throne championed her cause.'

Flora was pleased to see them so happy and enjoying the attention, but began to tire of it and longed just for time alone with the immediate family.

'I don't know half these people,' she said in bewilderment.

'Well they know you,' Marion replied. 'Everyone on Skye knows you now.'

Yet Flora was most content when she was able to slip away from the house and walk along the shore or up on the hill, enjoying the sound of the curlews that she had missed. One day, when a sudden shower came on she took shelter at the cottage of her former maid Katie. The girl still worked for Marion in the dairy but had swiftly married a farm labourer on her return from Leith. Flora had been looking for an opportunity to talk to her alone and was glad to find her at home, yet was shocked at the dilapidated state of the bothy. Its roof leaked and the fire was out. Katie seemed alarmed by her appearance.

'I'm sorry, mistress, but I wasn't expecting you. I-I have nothing to offer …'

'I don't ask for anything,' Flora smiled, 'just your company. I think often of our time together on the ship – I couldn't have got through those months at sea without you. Do you think of those dark days too, Katie?'

'Not so dark,' Katie said ruefully. 'At least we ate and went to bed with a full stomach – even if I often brought it all back up.'

Flora peered at her in the gloom. 'Is your life hard Katie? Harder than it was?'

'We've had two bad harvests since you've been away, Mistress. My Seamus finds it hard to get work and we can't afford to buy our own cow. If it wasn't for your mother keeping me on at the dairy out of charity, we'd have starved. I thank God every day for her kindness.'

Her voice sounded flat, not bitter; just stating how it was. Flora was filled with pity. 'Let me help you. I could buy you a cow.'

'No,' Katie gasped, 'we're not beggars. Seamus would be ashamed of you helping us.'

Flora let the matter go for the moment. 'Tell me how your father Ronald Oar is. Is he back on the Long Isle now, like the Clanranalds? Lady Clan wrote and told me how glad she is to be back with her children – though they are driving her to distraction again. She was joyful to hear that Ranald Og had escaped capture and gone abroad.'

Katie hung her head.

'What is it?' Flora asked.

'My father never came home after prison. The last we heard, he'd gone on a boat from London to work his passage to Ireland and then to the Isles. He told Lachie it would be quicker than walking. Lachie was home before last winter. He thinks my Da's boat went down. Ma still hopes …'

Flora went to comfort the girl. 'I'm so sorry.' She rocked her in her arms. How could she possibly have foreseen that agreeing to help the Prince would have led to tragedy for Katie's family? Yet she felt the burden of it. For a moment, Katie leaned into her hold and then she stiffened and pulled away.

'Don't be sorry,' she sniffed. 'Others have greater troubles to bear than I do. I have my Seamus and a roof over my head.'

Flora left, deeply upset at her friend's plight. After that, she took to riding daily and roaming further, growing more and more upset at the suffering of many islanders that she witnessed; gaunt men taking an age to cut their peats for the fire, women struggling to squeeze milk from scrawny cows, half-naked children with hacking coughs, running after her for food.

Hugh tried to answer her questions. 'The estates are in debt – the Rising cost both sides dearly in money and men. Lady Margaret insists the rents must go up to pay for her family's needs but the farmers can't afford it – the price of cattle has fallen so the only way they can pay the new rents is to ask more of the labourers.' He sighed. 'But if you think it's bad here, you should see what it's like where they supported the Prince – Raasay still smells of burning and some folk are living on the shore in caves. Even their boats were destroyed, so they fish off the rocks.'

'What can be done?' Flora asked in anguish.

Hugh said grimly. 'We need strong leaders who don't live beyond their means in the south. Kingsburgh is battling to get the young chieftain James back to Skye to live and be fostered in the old way by his family. Lady Margaret has other ideas.'

Flora's heart twisted at the mention of the Kingsburghs. They had stayed away from Armadale and Flora had resisted Maggie's badgering to go and visit Allan. She could not bear to face him. He had warned her of the suffering yet she had thought him just bitter at her good fortune. Now she had seen for herself the poverty and sickness among the people; it was overwhelming. She knew she could not stay. What use was she here; just one more mouth to feed? The problems were insurmountable.

When Maggie grew bored of the restricted social life and the weather of early autumn worsened, Flora made her friend the excuse to leave Skye. She left money with Hugh to buy a cow for Katie and Seamus. On a calm morning, the sea like a looking-glass and the trees tinged with russet and gold in the sunlight, the young women left.

'Skye does this to you,' Flora said as she parted with her family, 'puts on her best dress so you don't want to go.'

But her parents did not urge her to stay – not even her emotional mother – as if they thought she had become too famous to live contentedly among them and belonged elsewhere. Flora kissed them goodbye and climbed into the boat after Maggie. Her heart ached with sadness, yet as they pulled away from the shore and her home receded, she felt guilty at her pang of relief. She doubted she would ever live here again; she had resolved to make a life for herself in the south.

Chapter 48

Back in Edinburgh, Flora threw herself into city life, filling her hours with visiting friends, riding out to view the new town being built, attending recitals and lectures, dances and dinners. She continued to live with the Callanders but Maggie was being courted by a young lawyer and had soon dropped the idea of travelling to London for the winter.

In October, the Jacobites meeting at the Citadel in Leith were plunged into gloom at the news that the Hanoverians had forced a truce with France. As part of the treaty, the government in London was insisting that the French expel the Stuarts and their supporters from France; there was to be no more French backing for Jacobite rebellion.

Quite unexpectedly, Neil appeared in their midst.

'You mustn't lose heart,' he encouraged, 'the French may sign up to the treaty but they will pay lip-service to its content. King Louis is just as keen as ever to see the Stuarts on the throne here. And he won't dare throw the Prince out of Paris – he is the darling of the people – it would cause a riot.'

Flora was gladdened to see him again, yet they had little time to speak alone. He steered her into a corner seat.

'I'm enjoying the life of a French officer,' he admitted, 'but my work in Scotland is just as important.'

'What work?' she puzzled. 'Isn't it dangerous for you being here?'

'I will do whatever advances the cause of the Prince. He asked me to come and make contact with his friends. I think nothing of danger.' He lowered his voice. 'But how are you Florrie? You look well. You are happy here among like-minded people, no doubt?'

'I am content.' She searched his face, waiting for him to speak what was in his heart.

'*Très bon*!' he smiled and patted her hand. 'I'm happy to hear of your good fortune.'

'So you aren't staying?'

'I must return to France until things are more certain and be there for the Prince at this testing time.'

'Is Ranald Og with you too?'

'Aye, he is. He was on the run for over a year then disguised himself as a Mr Black and sailed straight out of London under the nose of the Hanoverians,' Neil grinned. His hand lingered on hers for a moment. 'Will you come to Paris when I send for you, Flora?'

She was quite taken aback by the abrupt suggestion; she had thought Neil would never go through with his pledge. Was this finally a serious proposal of marriage? It didn't quite sound like it. Yet her heart thumped at the thought of a new life at the exiled court among the elite Scots and sophisticated French, far from the poverty of the Highlands. Wasn't this what she had always wanted; to be with Neil wherever he was?

'When would that be?' she whispered, finding it hard to breathe.

'Soon,' he promised, 'when things become clearer.'

Flora withdrew her hand, her hopes deflating. Even now, after all these years of waiting just for him, he wouldn't commit himself to giving her a firm proposal. 'Ask me when you know,' she said, 'and then I'll give you my answer.'

***

Neil's sudden visit left Flora restless and discontented with Edinburgh. She tried to imagine what life in exile with the handsome but elusive man would be like; exciting and glamorous no doubt, settled and content probably never.

In December, still undecided what she would say in reply to Neil's veiled proposal, Flora travelled back to London to spend the winter with Lady Primrose. She was greeted with the news that Prince Charles had been arrested in Paris on his way to the Opera. He had been released after agreeing to leave France.

'They say he's in the papal lands at Avignon,' Lady Primrose said unhappily.

'What of the others?' Flora asked in dismay. 'His supporters in France?'

'What indeed.'

***

It was not until February of 1749 that a long letter came from Neil – the first Flora had had from him since their short intimate conversation at the Citadel – telling her in detail of the Prince's arrest. She recounted bits to Lady Primrose.

'He and Ranald Og had been dining with the Prince just moments before his arrest; imagine that! *The Prince was in high spirits and felt no alarm so we did not accompany him to the Opera.*' Flora read out. '*As soon as we learned of his unjust arrest we went at once to the prison. The Prince asked for me in particular to be allowed to stay with him and this I did with no hesitation. We were there four days and then the Prince was taken in a post chaise out of the country and I went back to my barracks.*'

Lady Primrose gasped. 'What a brave man your MacEachen is.'

'He goes by the name of MacDonald now,' Flora said. 'The Prince likes to call him that.'

She kept to herself how Neil had confided in her that he was convinced Clanranald was his natural father. Even though Clanranald had always shown Neil affection and tutored him in Classics, she was sceptical; but Neil liked to think himself more special than his MacEachen brothers. It suddenly struck her how Neil was enjoying this latest drama and intrigue; his boyish eagerness shone through his words. Even with the Prince in danger, Neil was at the centre of it all having the time of his life – or had been until the Prince was banished.

'So will he follow his master?' asked Lady Primrose. 'Where he is writing from?'

'Neil is still in France,' Flora gave an anxious shake of the head, 'he must stay and serve the French Army in the Albany Regiment with other Scots. He says that it will keep them fighting fit for when the Prince or King James calls on them in the future.'

'Well at least it pays them a living in the meantime,' sighed Lady Primrose.

Flora kept to herself the request at the end of the letter for a small loan of money; the French had reduced them to half-pay now that peace with Britain had been declared. There was no mention about her going to join him in Paris; future plans were once again in limbo.

Chapter 49

London, 1749

Flora spent the winter and spring in London with Lady Primrose and grew close to her benefactor. Only ten years Flora's senior, she became more like a sister to her, sharing thoughts and confidences. Flora began to devour books and learned the ways of the salon and how to talk to men of letters about culture and topics of the day. Several bachelors made proposals of marriage which Flora turned down politely but firmly. In her own mind she was still promised to Neil, although marriage to him seemed as hard to grasp as Skye mist. But it made it easier to reject these other suitors; she was not attracted to the ones who had money and Lady Primrose cautioned her against fortune-seekers who had heard of her wealth. Flora was happy to live the life of lady's companion.

Lady Primrose insisted that she sit for the famous court artist, Allan Ramsay. She was dressed in finest silks with Jacobite roses in her hair and at her breast, and (in defiance of the ban on tartan) wore a red and green plaid pinned to her shoulders to trumpet to the world that she was a proud MacDonald.

She talked to the Scottish artist about his home town of Edinburgh and people they knew in common, warming to Ramsay's open friendly nature and pithy remarks. For the first time in months, Flora felt a stab of homesickness for Scotland.

'I painted Bonny Prince Charlie too, you know,' he smiled, 'and he *was* bonny – compared to some of our Hanoverian royals with their big noses and jowls. Too much beer and fatty English beef if you ask me.'

Flora spluttered at his daring remarks. 'Well I hope you don't show me with a fat chin – I never get the chance to walk off rich food here.'

'You are a perfect shape,' he winked. 'The very personification of a beautiful Highland lady.'

It was Lady Primrose who diagnosed Flora's increasing lethargy and pensiveness.

'It's the hot weather and being in the town – it doesn't suit your northern constitution – you need a change of air. Why don't you go and stay with your friends the Maxwells in Dumfries? Lady Maxwell has written several times asking and June would be a glorious time to go, so I've heard.'

'Would you come too?' Flora brightened at the suggestion.

Her friend touched her cheek. 'I'm not like you – I don't flourish in the country – but I can't deny how I will sorely miss your company. You know you always have a home here whenever you want.'

'Thank you,' Flora smiled, deeply grateful. 'I'm sure I'll be back come the autumn.'

Before she left, Lady Primrose made sure that all the money raised on her behalf was lodged with merchants Innes and Clark. Flora was speechless to discover that it amounted to almost one thousand and five

262

hundred pounds sterling. She had no inkling she was such a rich woman. A normal dowry among the Highland nobility would be nearer to one hundred pounds.

'I-I can't accept so much,' she gulped.

'You can and you must,' her benefactor was brisk. 'When you need to draw on the sum – and if you are still in Scotland – they can arrange for a bond to be sent to a lawyer in Edinburgh.'

***

Travelling north, Flora rested a few days with her friends the Burtons in York, Dr Burton presenting her with a copy of his newly published pamphlet: *Narrative of the Several Passages of the young Chevalier.* Flora found it strange to read about herself and the Prince's escape as if she were some character in a story. Would these words still be read long after she had died? The idea troubled her. She felt pinned in time to this one event, unable to move on.

Soon Flora was moving on to Carlisle in the west and then into Scotland to stay with the welcoming Sir William Maxwell and his wife at Springkell, their modern mansion near Gretna. Here, in lush and temperate Dumfriesshire, Flora found herself able to relax and draw breath after nearly a year of living in cities and filling every waking moment with activity and socialising.

The Maxwells spoiled and cosseted her like a daughter but allowed her the freedom to wander the grounds or ride around the countryside if she wanted solitude. Flora rediscovered her love of simple homely pursuits; the picking of berries and making preserves, spinning flax for linen and churning butter. She was just as happy spending a morning in the dairy chatting to and helping the maids as she was sitting in the grand parlour on a Chippendale sofa with Lady Maxwell talking politics over their embroidery.

The year turned again and Flora wondered what 1750 would bring. Neil continued to write to her from France. His letters were circumspect about the Prince. He never displayed the same pessimism over future Jacobite hopes as her hosts did, who were all too aware that the unlucky royal was wandering Europe looking for support and a place to call home.

'*I will be returning soon,*' Neil promised. '*Be in London in the autumn and I will meet you and we will make plans to be together. I very much hope that the person who you once had the honour to conduct to safety will be with me. I know you will be as willing as I to help our special friend in any way you can in raising funds and furthering his just cause.*'

Flora had plenty of time to ponder his words and think about the past and her future. Was Neil really serious about making plans to be with her? Or did he just enjoy the romantic idea of his childhood sweetheart waiting steadfastly for his return until he could sweep back into Scotland as Prince Charles's most loyal henchman? Did he truly love her – or just the idea of her? Was he simply after her money?

263

She dismissed at once this last unkind thought; Neil was an idealist not a heartless manipulator. Yet he was a spy for the Jacobites and possibly the French too; he would have had to make hard choices in the past and act ruthlessly if he thought it furthered the Cause. It had been Neil's idea, after all, to involve her in the Prince's daring escape; he knew she would have done anything to please him. Had she been foolish in her stubborn attachment to Neil – her idealised love of him – forsaking all others in the hope of being his wife?

As the weeks slipped by, Flora's doubts about Neil mounted. It had always been her who had pushed for them to be together and pressed him to declare his love for her, yet when had he ever done more than offer vague promises of a future life as husband and wife? His pledges to her had always been tempered by his commitment to the exiled Stuarts; first and foremost, she realised with a sore heart, his loyalty was to the Prince.

She forced herself to examine her own heart and her motives for clinging to the idea of marrying Neil. Did she really love him, beyond the calf love and adoration of a young girl for her brother's good friend? Or was it to protect herself from admitting that another man had long ago stolen her heart? A man of passion whose good looks and physical presence left her winded with desire. A man who plagued her in dreams and would not let her live completely at peace no matter how far she travelled away from him. A man who had made no secret of his wish to make love to her, yet her last anguished sight of him had been his stormy face and blue eyes glaring his anger and disappointment in her. Allan of Kingsburgh.

***

March came and she accompanied the Maxwells to their house in Edinburgh. Her friend Maggie was to marry her lawyer that summer and Flora joined in the excited preparations. For the first time, she felt a wave of envy for one of her friends being on the verge of marriage. It was a match nurtured and approved by the parents of bride and groom, yet Maggie was obviously in love with her future husband too.

Flora delayed sending her letter to Neil telling him that she was unlikely to be in London in the autumn and would not be going with him to France because she did not love him enough. She couldn't quite bring herself to cut her ties with the man she had spent so long waiting for. And at her age, what was the alternative? Perhaps a lukewarm marriage was better than none? Still unsure, she tore it up.

In July, on the eve of Maggie's wedding, a messenger arrived with a letter from Skye. Flora saw with alarm that it was her stepfather's writing and not Marion's. Surely nothing had happened to her mother? She tore it open.

White-faced, Flora sank into a chair, gripping the letter in disbelief.

'Whatever is the matter, dear girl?' Lady Maxwell went straight to her. 'Is it bad news?'

264

Flora nodded. 'Terrible,' she whispered. Her throat filled with bile. She swallowed. 'My brother James – he's died of fever in Holland.' Her eyes stung with tears.

'Oh my dear, I'm so very sorry.'

'And my wee brother Sorley is gone too,' Flora croaked. 'Fell from a boat and drowned.' She bent double as the pain of realisation hit her like a fist in the stomach. 'Oh Mother! Oh my poor, poor mother!'

Chapter 50

Skye, autumn, 1750

Flora kept Marion company day and night. Her mother's 'black storm' had returned with a vengeance; she was beyond distraught at the loss of two sons in a matter of weeks. Marion was rendered speechless for much of the time, at others she fretted and muttered about being cursed and how she knew it was all going to happen one day.

'I wish I'd never given birth to them! Better to be childless than to love them and lose them. You are blessed to be unmarried and a spinster without bairns, Florrie. They break your heart.' She would sit and rock back and forth on the floor and not be soothed. 'It's all my fault. I made that witch angry – she cursed me and said my boys would drown. Oh, how can I bear it?'

Hugh was at a loss what to do with his broken-hearted wife. He coped with his grief by working every daylight hour, riding long distances around the Sleat lands on business and helping out with the harvest, stripping off and grafting with the labourers. Flora understood his need to keep busy and would not have him criticised. She gently chided her mother when Marion complained that her husband shared none of her grief.

'He feels it like a solider feels a raw wound,' Flora told her. 'The only way to bear the pain is to bind it up and carry on fighting. He does so through gritted teeth.'

Marion showed a glimmer of her old spark at this. 'Raw wounds and gritted teeth? You can tell you've been swallowing poetry and books with your London friends.'

Flora took encouragement from these rare breaks in her mother's grief. She was thankful that Annabella showed great courage in taking care of her bereft sister Tibby and brother Magnus. Magnus wandered like a boy looking for his shadow, not knowing what to do without his constant companion. He had learnt his lessons, fought and played with Sorley every day of his life.

To add to the family's distress, Sorley's body had never been recovered from the sea while James had been buried swiftly in a foreign grave, and his possessions burnt for fear of spreading the fever. It was Flora who encouraged her mother to go to the long overgrown grave of Marion's eldest son, Ranald, who had died at Armadale in an accident just before Flora was born.

'Perhaps the spirits of my other brothers will gather there,' Flora suggested, grasping at anything to ease her mother's agony.

Marion seized on this idea and went daily to the grave, tending it and laying flowers and whispering under her breath to her lost sons. Gradually, the pilgrimage to the grave became less frequent – two or three times a week –and Marion could bear to let her other children out of her sight for long hours at a time.

Flora coped with her own grief by slipping off to the dairy, sitting down on the milking stool and pressing her cheek to the warm flank of her favourite cow, Bracken. She found comfort in the rhythmic pulling and squeezing of milking the cow, the pungent smell of the cowshed and the gentle snuffling of the animal that did not seem to mind Flora's tears wetting her rump.

To Bracken she told her sorrow and whispered her hopes that life and laughter would one day return to their grieving home.

***

Hugh came home one day that autumn talking of the drovers returning from the tryst at Falkirk. Flora could not stop her heart beating uncomfortably as the vivid memory resurfaced of Allan Kingsburgh bringing the cattle across at Glenelg, plunging naked into the sea to save one of the struggling beasts.

She knew Allan was one of the drovers who had been away to sell the MacDonald cattle at the Lowland fair, for old Kingsburgh and Florence had come to offer their condolences on behalf of the family and told how their son was absent or he would have come too. Ann was heavily pregnant with her fifth baby and not travelling. It had been a strange meeting for Flora; awkward and yet emotional with the couple who she had not seen since that fateful night when they had harboured her and the Prince. Few words had been said but they had embraced her with warmth and pity.

'Come and visit us when you feel up to it,' Florence had said, 'you mustn't stay away like before.'

Flora had puzzled over these words. Had Mistress Kingsburgh merely been polite or was this a sign that Flora had been forgiven for embroiling Kingsburgh in the Jacobite plot to save the Prince? She found herself dwelling more and more on the Kingsburghs and whether she should take her courage in her hands and let Allan know how she felt.

That night, brushing out her mother's hair, she asked, 'Is it true that young Kingsburgh is yet to take a wife?'

'It would seem so,' said Marion. She eyed her daughter in the looking-glass, noticing the flush to her cheeks. 'Perhaps he has yet to find a woman who will match him in spirit as well as breeding.'

They talked of other things for a while and then Marion asked, 'how long will you stay here Florrie? I have been selfish keeping you away from your friends in the south. You don't have to remain for the full period of mourning. I can bear it a little bit more each day. Don't stay just for me – let it be for a better reason.'

'I don't know how long,' Flora put down the brush, 'but I don't want to be anywhere else at this time.' She kissed the top of her mother's head. 'Janet once told me about Mairi MacVurich and her curse.' She felt her mother stiffen. 'Mairi is no witch,' Flora said gently, 'she is just someone

267

with too much imagination who speaks before she thinks. You mustn't let her continue to hold you in her power.'

'But her curse came true – I lost my boys,' Marion trembled.

'She said that two would drown but James didn't,' Flora pointed out. 'And neither did your first born, Ranald.'

Marion grabbed her hand. 'She said I would have a daughter who would be famous throughout the land and beyond. That came true, didn't it? She saw into the future and there you were.'

Flora felt a shiver go down her back. 'Just a fanciful guess, not a prophecy.' Flora dismissed it.

'You're probably right.' Marion let go a long sigh. 'The strange thing is that now the worst has happened, I don't feel frightened of her any more. For years I have lived in dread; now it's over. Perhaps one day I'll stop hating her too.'

'She once told me that she was jealous of you,' Flora said, 'she wanted what you had – that's why she said those hurtful things. She's more to be pitied than hated.'

As Flora stood up, Marion said. 'Don't let anyone in your life keep a hold over you. Stand up to them, Florrie, and say what's in your heart.'

The next day, Flora sat down and wrote two letters. For the next few days she paced the house and could not settle. She rubbed the green stone that she hung around her neck for good luck; the one that Angus had given her as a baby to keep her safe and which she had kept with her all through her trials in captivity. Her future hung in the balance. If she had misjudged the situation then she would have to leave Skye for good. It was only as she contemplated this that she realised how much she wanted to stay; to return to the south would be like going into exile.

***

She was in the dairy milking Bracken and humming a Gaelic lullaby when she heard heavy footsteps at the door. Turning, and pushing back a stray lock of hair from her eyes, she saw Allan standing staring. Flora stood up startled, knocking over the stool. The cow bellowed and shuffled back in protest. Flora, trying not to get kicked, tripped and almost fell.

Allan sprang forward and caught her. Flora gasped and he let go. She hastily unhitched her woollen skirt which she'd tucked into her belt and smoothed it down over her legs with trembling fingers.

'Well I came looking for Miss Milton, the darling of London society, and found the dairymaid,' Allan said, his mouth twitching.

'I'm sorry if you're disappointed,' said Flora.

'Not in the least. A charming sight. No doubt such skills have grown rusty in the city?'

She snorted. 'Not at all. It's true most Londoners think milk grows in the churn but I have not lost my touch.'

'I'm glad to hear it.'

268

They stood eyeing each other, wary. Flora thought her heart would burst out of her chest it was banging so hard. If she said the wrong thing now she would never get another chance.

'I'm very sorry about your brothers,' Allan spoke before she could. 'James was a dear friend and a fine man. A great loss to the whole clan.'

'Thank you.' Flora's eyes welled with tears. She fought to control her emotions knowing that if she didn't speak swiftly she would never be able to say what was in her heart. Yet she felt struck dumb. He frowned at her in confusion.

'Why did you send me back your miniature, Flora? Your note did not explain. Is it some sort of joke? A tale to amuse your London friends.' Flora felt panic at the hardening of his tone and his look of irritation. 'I hope I haven't ridden over here just to be made a fool of?'

He stepped back.

'No,' Flora said, her mouth dry with nerves. 'It's no joke. I thought you would understand. You told me to send it to the suitor I wished to marry.' She saw by his baffled look that he had no recollection of this. 'James told me that's what you'd said when you had him return it to me. Don't you remember?'

'I was very drunk that night,' Allan said, his jaw reddening. He scrutinised her. 'So what are you saying? That you want me for a suitor now?'

'Aye, I do.' Flora felt her cheeks were on fire.

Allan gave a snort of disbelief. 'Run out of options have you? Do the gentlemen of London think you too old?'

'I've had several proposals of marriage,' Flora sparked back, 'all of which I've turned down – some of them from men younger than you.'

Allan folded her arms. 'And what about Neil MacEachen? You claim to have been promised to him practically from birth.'

'I've written to Neil releasing him from his pledge. I realise now that I don't wish to marry him. I want to marry you.' Flora ploughed on. 'I can bring you a dowry of nearly a thousand pounds – enough to set you up with your own cattle farm and live in comfort – but I want it written into the marriage contract that I must have my own stipend so that I have private means even if the marriage doesn't work out and we part – at some time in the future – or you die. I don't want our children – if we have children – to be left without means and for your family to take it all – as happened to my mother. The law is cruel to widows.'

He gazed at her as if she had grown a second head. 'I suppose I should be flattered,' he frowned, 'but you make it sound more like bargaining at the mart.'

'I just wanted to speak plainly so there was no misunderstanding.'

'Good God!' Allan cried, grabbing her suddenly by the arms. 'Do you think I'm interested in your wealth? I don't care two figs for your gold and I won't be bought for any amount of money. I'm insulted that you think you could buy me like some prize bull. Well I'm not like your *Sassenach* friends who think friendship and love of so little consequence.

The woman I marry will want me for who I am – and I for her – even if it's a life of poverty and hardship we have to share. All that matters will be that we love each other!'

He pushed her away from him and strode to the door.

'I do love you!' Flora cried, going after him. 'I thought that it didn't need to be spelled out. You must know how I feel about you. Why would I have sent back my picture otherwise?' She held onto his arm and pulled him round. 'I've loved you for years – tried not to – but I can't help it. You are in my thoughts every day – I dream about you at night. I cannot imagine being with any other man. I want you as my husband – my lover – I want you to be the father of my children. I love you, Allan Kingsburgh, *you* and no other man.'

He searched her face. 'Do you mean it, Florrie? Or am I caught in some strange dream?'

She put her hands around his face, leaned up and kissed him on the mouth. 'Now do you believe I mean it?'

His arms came about her and he pulled her to him. Allan bent and fastened his lips on hers and kissed her with such passion she thought he would devour her. His hands went into her hair and he groaned with joy and relief.

'Oh, Florrie,' he gasped, 'I've yearned to kiss you like that for so long.'

'And I you,' she smiled.

'I thought I'd lost you to the *Sassenachs* – seeing you in all your finery at the Citadel surrounded by your grand friends – I was sick with jealousy. You seemed so changed.'

'I thought you hated me for my part in your father going to prison – and for your disappointment in not getting a commission and going abroad.'

'I could never hate you. And I never blamed you for such things. The only reason I wanted to go with Sir Alexander to London was to see if I could help you – I was in hell thinking of you in prison – I never wanted to join the Hollanders. And as for my father, his capture was not your fault. Like you, he is proud of what he did for the Prince.'

'But Ann wrote and told me–'

'My sister was very upset for a long time,' Allan admitted, 'but she holds no grudge against you now. Father has made her see sense.'

Flora was doubtful.

'If she had not forgiven you, she would not be calling her new baby daughter Flora, would she?'

Flora gaped. 'She has?'

Allan laughed and squeezed her close. 'You are the most celebrated woman in Scotland – why would she not want a touch of that glory?'

'But you as a proud man do not?' Flora teased him.

Allan's mouth twisted wryly. 'I wanted you long before you were famous, remember? When you were a young lass hopping about in the dawn in your nightclothes like a water nymph. It was the wild Long Isle girl from Benbecula who I fell for.'

270

'That's good,' Flora grinned, 'because that's the girl whose heart was lost to the handsome dark-haired lad who skimmed stones on the shore at Armadale – and thought he could outrun me.'

Allan laughed.

'Let's marry at once, Florrie,' he said eagerly. Then his face clouded. 'Sorry, I know your family are in mourning – I should not have suggested it. I just cannot contain my impatience.'

'Neither can I,' said Flora, clinging to him, 'and I think it would give my poor mother something to ease her sorrow to see me happily wed. I think she thought the day would never come.'

'Then we will go to our parents with our plan and ask their blessing. The day cannot come soon enough.'

Flora thrilled at his words. She could hardly contain her joy at being in Allan's arms at last, knowing that he still loved her as passionately as she loved him. Whatever uncertainty lay ahead for their people and their islands, they would face it together, united.

'Let's seal our love with another kiss,' Flora smiled into his loving face.

Allan smiled back and did so with an embrace both passionate and tender.

The End

If you have enjoyed THE JACOBITE LASS, you might like to read another of The Highland Romance Collection.
HIGHLANDER IN MUSCOVY: a tale of treachery, secrets and undying love (publication due end of 2014)

1700s: Beautiful and impulsive Katherine Putulo, daughter to a Scots doctor, is raised in the foreign quarter of Muscovy (Moscow) among European émigrés. On her sister's wedding day, Katherine rashly disguises herself as a peasant girl and joins in the revelry of Tsar Peter's victorious returning army, dancing with other Russians in a forbidden part of the city. There she captures the interest of hardened mercenary and handsome Scottish Highlander, Major Alexander Ballantyne, one of the Tsar's most popular soldiers who has caused scandal by taking a Russian princess as his mistress. Smothering her attraction to Alexander, Katherine finds herself the target of unwanted attention from selfish and scheming, Hector Maitland, her godfather's nephew. Under the thin veneer of civility in the foreign enclave lies tension and betrayal; a shocking murder leads to Alexander's arrest and Katherine is forced to make the hazardous journey back to Scotland – the land of her father yet a foreign country to her. Yet it is not the safe haven for which she longs. Who can she trust and will she ever see Alexander alive again?
From the glittering Russian court of Peter the Great to the wild Scottish Highlands, HIGHLANDER IN MUSCOVY is a fast-paced tale of ambition, betrayal and unbreakable bonds of love.

***

Extract from the beginning of HIGHLANDER IN MUSCOVY

PROLOGUE

Moscow, May 1682

Dr Ewen Putulo gazed uneasily from the large first storey window of his home, across the deserted square and the elegant brick mansions of the Foreign Quarter.
The only noise in the deathly calm was the listless splash of the fountain. No children played, no merchants called to each other down the leafy avenues, no ladies took the air. All were barricaded behind locked doors, waiting and fearful.
At any moment the bloodbath gushing through the streets and palaces of the royal Kremlin fortress could boil over and swamp the fragile safety of Moscow's foreign enclave. Was it only two days ago that his beloved Sybil had given birth to their second daughter and they had rejoiced at the happy event? Away across to the west, the golden domes of the city flashed in the harsh fiery sunset, bold and ominous.

'Sir,' an urgent voice broke through the doctor's thoughts. He turned to see Fiona the housemaid hurriedly entering the drawing-room, her pale thin face anxious under the severe white cap. 'Sir, there is someone beating at the back entrance,' she gasped, 'I'm afraid to open up–'

'I'll go,' Ewen Putulo said at once, glad of the diversion from fearful imaginings. 'Does your mistress sleep?'

Fiona nodded. 'And the bairns too, the Lord be thanked.'

'Good,' he smiled tenderly as he thought of them. 'Now go upstairs and lock yourself in with them,' he ordered more briskly. 'I may be needed somewhere in the Quarter and I don't want you to move, do you hear?'

'But master,' Fiona protested, 'it's too dangerous–'

The doctor recognised the beginnings of a Presbyterian sermon and cut her short.

'Don't be afraid,' his deepset eyes filled with kindness in the tired lined face, 'I will be careful for all our sakes.'

The pounding grew louder as Ewen Putulo headed down the back stairs, anxiety gripping him once more. 'I'm coming,' he shouted and pulled back the iron bolts.

A tall peasant dressed in a rough cloth shirt tied at the waist with string and baggy trousers stuffed into cloth leggings, stood before him. The doctor stared in surprise; the man appeared to be alone, his bearded face shadowed by a worn fur cap in spite of the warm evening.

'Putulo, please in God's name let us in!' The man gripped the physician's arm with iron strength. This forceful man was no peasant; Ewen Putulo recognised his lilting voice and raised the lamp to search his face.

'James MacQueen!' he gasped in disbelief at his old friend. 'What is one of the Tsar's officers doing dressed like a Russian woodsman?' For a moment he wanted to laugh out loud at the comical appearance of this proud Highland chieftain, but the grim shocked face dispelled his mirth. Sweat ran down his dust-stained cheeks and brow. He seemed on the point of fainting; the doctor steered him onto a rough kitchen chair.

'Ewen, it is my wife,' James MacQueen fretted, eyes glazed with pain. 'You must help Katya. She's outside ...'

Ewen Putulo turned and strode quickly back across the courtyard to a cart half hidden by overhanging trees heavy with blossom. A small delicate woman lay enveloped in a coarse loose gown and as he gently coaxed her down, he felt the largeness of her belly. The poor woman was heavy with her unborn child.

'Come my dear,' he spoke to her soothingly, concerned by the feverish flush of her dark handsome face and the huge slanting eyes filled with terror, 'you will be safe here with us, you and the child.'

She did not answer, staring fixedly ahead as he helped her indoors. The doctor remembered James MacQueen had caused a scandal in both the Russian and foreign communities by marrying a lower-ranking Russian princess, but his military skills were so sought after that Tsar Fedor had smothered the criticism of his xenophobic Muscovite nobles. Ewen Putulo had often wondered what James' father, the old Chief of Mac-

Queen, had thought of the match. This was the first time he had ever set eyes on the beautiful princess, for she had remained a recluse in the Russian manner despite her marriage to an 'infidel'. He understood why the forthright James had ignored opposition to the match.

'She does not understand what you say,' MacQueen said wearily as the doctor helped her inside. 'And the sights of these past two days have left her speechless ...' His voice trailed off as the vivid nightmare of the carnage in the Kremlin squares and palaces overwhelmed him anew.

He had dragged Katya from the tiny windows of the *terem*, the women's quarter, as the rampaging Streltsy guards skewered her relations onto their pikes and trampled them underfoot in an hate-fuelled orgy of bloodletting. MacQueen retched now at the memory of the soldiers' blood-spattered green and blue coats, their yellow boots stained dark red as they guarded the piles of dismembered bodies in front of St Basil's Cathedral.

Ewen Putulo asked no questions, but called for Fiona and set about making them comfortable in an upstairs room, bidding his nervous maid boil water for washing and prepare glasses of vodka and a plate of smoked fish with which to revive them.

Later, while Katya slept fitfully upstairs the doctor joined the chieftain in the drawing-room. MacQueen sat in the shadows below a gilded mirror, the room lit pink by an eerie summer's night sky. Behind him a clock chimed prettily inside an inlaid cabinet and he found it unbelievable that so much horror could be going on so close to this quiet civilised home.

The doctor regarded his friend. It was some time since he had seen him, for MacQueen's profession as mercenary soldier kept him away from the Quarter for long periods. The aquiline nose and strong square face – bearded in the Russian fashion – was the same, proud and regal. But the grey eyes were dark-ringed and new lines around his mouth scored the handsome face and spoke of his harrowing escape. MacQueen threw back his vodka and began.

'It was terrible,' he whispered, 'even the Tartar hordes are not so barbarous. They could not hack the boyars and princes into small enough pieces, these devils that call themselves the Kremlin's guards! Even Tsar Peter is threatened and he a boy of ten. They think his family poisoned Tsar Fedor, but it is just an excuse to take revenge on some of the nobles.' MacQueen shook with anger and his friend filled up his glass and let him continue.

'I tell you none of us are safe Ewen, they are hounding out foreigners as well as the Naryshkin royals. They think we are about to take over the army,' he laughed harshly. 'Would that I had never set foot in this barbarous country,' his look was bleak.

'You would never have met your beautiful wife then,' Ewen Putulo added gently. James MacQueen met his steady compassionate look, feeling unaccustomed tears of exhaustion and sadness sting his eyes.

'Oh, my dearest Katya,' he shuddered, 'she will never be the same after this insanity. She has not spoken one word since witnessing the murders from the Kremlin palace windows. I tried to cover her eyes as we escaped through the bloody streets, but I could not protect her from the screams and the murderous shouts of the crowd.' The chieftain grew agitated again and leaning forward, gripped the doctor's arm. 'You are a good physician, Ewen, tell me what you think. I fear she does not even recognise me anymore.'

For a moment Ewen Putulo hesitated, and then he gently removed his friend's hand and stood up, walking to the un-shuttered window. He thought of the silent woman upstairs, too deep in shock to respond to Fiona's kindly ministering. Such a traumatic episode might well bring on her labour and he feared she might not be strong enough to go through with it.

'She must stay here until she has had the child,' the doctor spoke matter of factly, 'for her to travel now in such a state of shock would be folly. She would almost undoubtedly lose the baby and her own life would be in danger too, James.'

'No!' the other man got to his feet and clattered his glass onto the delicate table. 'We have placed you in enough danger by coming here tonight, I must get Katya safely away from Moscow. We will find a passage back to Scotland with one of our merchants. Besides Katya is a strong woman.'

'I won't hear of her travelling in such a condition,' Ewen Putulo was firm. He turned to confront the black bearded chieftain and spoke more gently. 'Do you have any idea how long it might take you to reach Archangel? Weeks on those rough roads in the summer dust and heat would tire the fittest of women. Your wife is about to give birth and she has suffered too much already.'

The doctor's gaunt face and kind dark eyes shone in the glow of the lamplight. He pitied his friend and the decision he must make, but he was not going to risk the life of the woman upstairs whom Ewen Putulo now thought of as his patient.

'You must leave tomorrow alone,' he continued with quiet authority. 'If they want you as a scapegoat for the many foreigners who make their living here in Muscovy, then you only endanger all our lives by remaining here.'

'But how can I leave Katya?' James MacQueen almost sobbed in his frustration.

'Because it is the safest thing you can do,' the doctor steeled himself against his friend's obvious anguish. 'My wife Sybil has just given birth to a girl. If necessary we can pass Princess Katya off as her wet-nurse when her baby is born. It is unlikely that anyone will come asking questions and the bloodletting will stop like a staunched wound soon enough.'

James MacQueen bit on his knuckles but did not argue, so the doctor went on. 'You must make your own way to Archangel. Arrange a ship and wait until I get word to you that your wife and child are strong enough to travel,' Ewen Putulo instructed. 'If all goes well you should be able to leave Muscovy with your family before the port freezes over at the summer's end.'

James MacQueen sank back into his chair with sudden exhaustion. He did not have the will to fight his friend's logic although he was grief-struck at the thought of leaving Katya so abruptly and in such a tortured state of mind. But perhaps if they could get back to Scotland safely, the wild beauty of his lochside fortress at Penstroun would be a place where she could heal her wounds. He tried to imagine his quiet, proud Russian wife running affairs in his ancestral home, yet the picture would not come. She had never been out of Moscow before, hardly out of the maze of palaces and churches of the Kremlin where he had first espied her and fallen in love. He hung his head in despair.

'Come James,' Ewen Putulo laid a hand on his shoulder and gently shook him, 'I will do my best for her.'

The chieftain looked up gratefully and determined to lift himself out of his self-pity. 'You are a good man,' he smiled wanly, 'and a true friend. I could not leave Katya but for knowing that she is in the kindest of hands with you and Sybil.'

The doctor smiled back. 'You must get some rest now; you have a long journey ahead tomorrow.'

They regarded each other in silence, each plagued with unspoken doubt. Suddenly the tall Highland chieftain stood up and clasped the doctor in a firm embrace.

'So be it,' he said hoarsely.

Behind them, through the wide Western-style windows, the blood-red sunset seeped into the uneasy mauve of the short summer's night.

***

Janet welcomes comments and feedback on her stories. If you would like to do so, you can contact her through her website: www.janetmacleodtrotter.com

276

Lightning Source UK Ltd.
Milton Keynes UK
UKOW02n0906150914

238549UK00002B/35/P

KM